NIGHT AFTER NIGHT

BY JULIAN FONT

DISCLAIMER

This novel is a work of fiction. Any mention of real people, places, companies, and historical events is used fictitiously. The contents of this book serve as a product of the author's imagination, and any resemblance to actual places, persons, or events is entirely coincidental.

Forever dedicated to my family.

"Love you more."

ONE | THE AMOR BROTHERS

CRACK!

My eyes opened abruptly. Silence. I stared at the ceiling. Was I dreaming? Was that loud sound *an actual* sound or something I dreamt? If I made the sound up in my mind, why would… I'm too tired to process this. I closed my eyes.

CRACK!

My eyes opened abruptly, but this time I was wide awake, and I knew this sound was real--the sound of shuffling boxes and maybe something being knocked over?

I quickly sat up and pressed my back against my headboard. My little brother, Josh, was still sound asleep in the bed next to mine--I could tell by the subtle rhythm of his breathing. I turned to check my alarm clock:

FRIDAY, 2:37A.M. - JANUARY 20TH, 2012

Where were the loud sounds coming from?? I heard more rustling coming from nearby, and I was almost sure it was coming from the garage. Our garage is detached from our house, but with my room being the closest, I could hear any time someone was in it. Still, this time, in particular, felt *different*.

It was 2:37a.m.… Now 2:38a.m. I knew it wasn't my father working on his Mustang. He works so hard that he's sound asleep before 10 o'clock and up just before the sun rises. It can't be Mom because I don't think she's ever even set foot in the garage. That means it's gotta be my older brother, Braden. I turned my body so that I was now sitting up facing Josh's bed. He moved silently under his covers and let out a sigh.

"I was hoping that wasn't a real sound," Josh whispered, rubbing his eyes, still half asleep.

"Go back to bed," I whispered back. "I'm gonna go see what it is."

"Can I go with you?" he asked.

"Shhh, no. It's probably nothing."

I proceeded quietly out of my room and down the hall, tiptoeing over the cold tile floor. I slowly opened Braden's bedroom door, praying it'd be empty so I could assume he was the one making the sounds in the garage. I peeked my head into his room, slowly--quietly. I could see the silhouette of his unconscious body, fast asleep, illuminated by the streetlight outside of his room.

Damn, I thought, quickly forced to assume the worst--an intruder is inside of our home--the garage... They're in the garage.

I silently shut Braden's door and crept down the narrow hall. My palms were beginning to sweat, and I could hear my father's words echoing throughout my head.

"*You'll figure it out*," he always says when I find myself in a predicament. "*Figure it out*."

Assuming someone's broken into the garage, it *had* to be with the intent to steal or mess with my dad's '67 Mustang. The whole neighborhood knows that car is his pride and joy. Plus, it's worth more than his three sons combined... So it was only a matter of time before someone came looking for it.

I took a deep, silent breath. This was *my* chance to protect my dad's pride and joy--to protect our home--to be the *hero*. Being the middle child of three boys didn't leave me with a lot of opportunities to make a name for myself, so I wasn't gonna pass this one up.

I made my way to the utility closet across from the backdoor of our home. It isn't a large home by any means and definitely not in the nicest part of Torrance--but it's *our* home. The sounds of shuffling from the garage grew louder, and I felt myself beginning to actually process what's happening.

What if the intruder came inside??
What if they were coming for us *next*??
A thief? Or worse... A murderer?

The hairs on the back of my neck stood, and I broke into a cold sweat.

Think, Jay, I thought.

There's an intruder in our home, potentially armed... *Most likely* armed in this part of Torrance. We were two blocks away from the sketchier side of town, which meant we had to deal with stragglers from time to time. Some were a part of L.A. County gangs or random drunks failing to make their way home. Either way, I wasn't about to confront this potential threat empty-handed.

Where are you? I thought, ruffling through the closet.

I ran my hands through the shelves of random junk my father

has hoarded since we moved here eight years ago. I was only 10 back then, but I remember those days like they were yesterday. I miss being a kid, but times like these make me realize I'm a man now.

Found you.

I reached for the dusty old dictionary on the top shelf, then peeked down the hall to make sure I was alone. I dropped to a knee and opened the book slowly, catching sight of the Astra 680, an 8-round cylinder revolver that was passed down to my father. Before I removed the gun from the book, I locked my eyes on it. The moonlight glistened off the polished steel--such a peaceful sight of a deadly weapon.

Was I really gonna kill someone tonight? Could I actually get myself to pull the trigger? Why me? I *could* call the police....

Nah fuck that, I thought. *This is my time to be the HERO.*

I held the revolver behind my bare back just below my waistline. This wasn't the first time I had held a gun, but it was the first time I'd take somebody's life with it. I crept out the backdoor.

I stepped outside with my knees bent, keeping as low as possible. It was colder than usual, but not freezing... Nothing out of the ordinary for winter in Southern California.

I moved slowly--silently--praying that I see the intruder before they see me. A large part of me was anxious, but I could easily mistake it for a sense of *excitement*--to be... *Heroic*. I envisioned myself as the main character of my own movie, which gave me a sort of rhythm that made me feel alive--that I'm playing the role God intends for me to play according to the script he wrote for my own life.

The door leading into the garage was slightly open, and I could see the fluorescent light was turned on. As I crept up to the door, I took one last deep breath, waiting for the rustling sounds to pick up again... That way I knew the intruder's mind was occupied.

This is how it happens, I thought. *The hero's origin story*.

I felt another cold sweat rush over me as I placed my hand on the doorknob, flung the door open, and raised the revolver.

"Don't *fucking* move," I whispered sternly.

The young man was digging around behind Braden's guitar amplifier. He paused immediately after hearing my voice.

"Put your hands up... Slowly," I warned. "I have a gun, but I'd rather not use it."

The young man was wearing a backwards hat, and his hair flowed down to his shoulders. He wore a black plaid button-up with black pants and some beat-up leather combat boots. I know those boots. The man laughed. I certainly know that laugh.

"What the hell are you *doing*, Braden? I could've *killed* you," I sighed, lowering the gun.

Braden slowly turned to me as he dropped his hands.

"What am I doing??" Braden snapped. "Jay, look at you. You're holding Dad's revolver to my fucking head. Are you insane?"

"I just saw you…! You were passed out in your room," I said, remembering seeing Braden's silhouette outline in his bed.

"They're pillows, Jay… I only stepped out for a bit. I wasn't gone for long."

He didn't seem too upset. His words slurred, and I could smell the liquor on his breath from across the garage. Braden was always good about playing it cool and not appearing as drunk around our parents, but I knew my older brother better than he knew himself.

"What are you doing?" I whispered as I set the revolver on the workbench beside me.

"Had to move some stuff around. It's my business, not yours."

I watched as he went back to moving boxes and bags behind his band equipment. He was avoiding looking me in the eyes.

"Look at me…" I raised my voice.

"Shhh, you'll wake up Mom and Dad," he whispered.

"Let me see your face," I said as I placed my hand on his shoulder.

Braden stumbled and readjusted himself. He was bent over, hair hanging over the sides of his face but maintained behind the hat. He turned to face me. I could see the big lively brown eyes that our family took pride in. However, tonight one of Braden's eyes was swollen and black, and it was swelling faster and faster as the conversation went on. I leaned back slightly as I examined the rest of his face.

"Who did this to you?" I asked.

"I fucked up an order," he replied while putting his hands on his knees. He let out a quick breath, realizing he had just said something he wasn't supposed to.

"YOU'RE STILL DEALING??" I asked, *really* struggling to keep my voice down.

"Shhhh!"

Braden put his hand out, drunkenly signalling for me to pause. He stood straight up and lifted his chin.

"I overheard Mom and Dad talking about money being tight a few days ago," he explained. "Once I sell the rest of this final round I picked up, I'll have enough cash to put you and Josh through school, buy Mom a new car, and maybe even start up that nightclub we've always talked about opening one day."

"You can't expect us to use your dirty drug money," I whispered while pointing at the boxes and bags behind the guitar amplifier.

It wasn't the *best* place for Braden to hide his drug stash, but he knew our father was so fixated on his Mustang, everything else in the garage was just background noise. So, no chance Dad would ever come across it.

"Listen," he slurred. "I'm repping this guy who's big time in Hollywood--just got involved in the game. He's *all* the way up there, and he doesn't mess around, so if I don't get this out, I'm a dead man, Jay… A fucking dead man."

Suddenly, we heard a sound come from the backdoor of the house. Braden's eyes instantly opened wide, and he frantically scanned the garage.

"THE GUN," he whispered, gesturing for me to pass him the revolver. I jolted a few steps toward the workbench, grabbed the revolver, and tossed it to Braden. He caught it and slipped it into the back of the guitar amplifier in one swift motion. He might've been drunk, but he was certainly still able to function.

The door slowly opened, and Josh stepped into the garage, rubbing his eyes. He was in his red plaid pajamas along with his favorite fur slippers. I suppose a 14-year-old boy like Josh should probably be sleeping in boxers by now, but his bony body frame wouldn't let him. He gets cold easily, so we never say anything about his matchy pajama outfits.

"What are you guys doing?" Josh asked, rubbing his eyes. He was still half asleep. Braden and I both looked at each other with no answer.

"We are…" Braden was about to trip over his words when he pulled it together and said, "... Putting Dad's tools back. I was using it to fix up my bike earlier today and thought I misplaced some stuff, but it's all there."

I turned back to Josh and nodded in agreement with Braden's statement.

"I saw you toss the gun," Josh said, looking directly at me. "Did you almost shoot Braden thinking he was robbing us?"

I looked back at Braden, who looked back at me and shrugged.

I said aloud, "I-... I was-... Just making sure Braden…" my shoulders lowered and I gave in. "I was making sure Braden wasn't anybody other than Braden."

Braden carefully lifted the revolver out of the back of the guitar amplifier.

He held it in his open palm and assured Josh, "Don't worry, Josh, it's not loaded. See? All good."

"Let's go," I demanded, turning my back to Braden and guiding Josh out of the garage. As I closed the door behind me, I watched Braden slip the revolver behind the guitar amplifier and go back to rearranging his bags and boxes.

When Josh was sound asleep once again, I went back to the utility closet to make sure the dictionary was put back where I found it. Within minutes of slipping back into bed, I was fast asleep.

"Jay…."

I felt my mind become conscious while I still lay half asleep.

"What?" I groaned without opening my eyes.

"Jay... Hi deny roaming highly sock door on to me?" my mother asked.

"What??" I groaned as I lifted my heavy head.

"I said… Why am I only finding your single socks in the laundry?" she asked again, then she mumbled something in Spanish.

It took me a second to process the question, and I couldn't bring myself to answer as I checked the time. 7a.m. 15 minutes before my alarm screams for me to get ready for school every morning.

Josh was already putting his clothes on, wide awake because God blessed him with the gift of being a morning person. Being the freshman he is, the kid is so excited for school that he lays his clothes out the night before. I'm *somewhat* of a morning person, but I'm certainly not too happy to start my mornings with a list of questions and complaints from my mother about my daily habits.

While there were times she nagged the three of us for the little things, my mother has the biggest heart in the world. She never left the room without saying, "I love you." My mother is a living saint, always laughing at our jokes, making sure we're *constantly* fed--sometimes overfed--and staying up every night in the living room until the three of us are in bed, sound asleep. She continued around my room with her list of questions and concerns.

"Your room is a mess, Jay."

"I'm going to the store today. What do you need, Jay?"

"Whose sweatshirt is this, and why do you keep coming home with clothes that don't belong to you, Jay?"

I opened my eyes and stared at the ceiling. I took a couple of long and deep breaths as I processed the fact that it's Friday. Thank you, God, for Fridays. It was my last semester of high school, and we basically did nothing on the daily, so I can't complain.

I felt myself become fully awake and went through my usual morning routine. There are few things I'm O.C.D. about, and my morning routine is undoubtedly one of them.

Wake up.
100 crunches.
Hot shower in the dark.
Brush my teeth.
Blow-dry and do my hair.

Throw on some face lotion and deodorant.

It was the same routine, just a different day. I spent the most time in the shower, where I indulged in my thoughts. In the 8th grade, I read a book where some kid would wake up really early and shower in the dark, tricking his mind into thinking he was still sleeping. It made it easier for him to wake up early and prepare for the day, and it does the same for me. Then it's pretty ridiculous how much time I spend blow-drying my hair. My mother always told me I have her side of the family's hair, which is thick and wavy.

Braden also has wavy hair that does its own thing on his head. It looks wild but still somewhat tamed. He's pretty skinny and doesn't work out much… Just genetically blessed with a fast metabolism… Or maybe it was all the drugs he did but claimed he didn't do. His clothes were typically black, white, or on the grayscale, which goes well with his dark and mysterious side the girls drool over. He's like that one guy in the movies--the misunderstood bad-boy who rides a motorcycle and is in a band. Every girl in our neighborhood is crazy about Braden, but I don't think there's a girl in this world who could handle the rollercoaster that makes up Braden's life.

Josh, on the other hand, is and always has been very well-groomed. He's got these dimples when he smiles, which is practically all the time. His hair is a darker brown, combed to the side, and he didn't have a single hair or zit on his face besides his naturally sculpted eyebrows. He was born with a growth hormone deficiency, which means his whole "growing situation" has him standing just about 5'3--sort of average for a freshman--but the way he carries himself makes him appear *much* smaller, especially when he wears his clothes a bit baggier. Our family doctor says he won't grow much more, but his perspective on life is real happy-go-lucky. He laughs at everything. It didn't take much to make him feel insecure, but it never mattered because nobody *ever* tried to put Josh down. They knew they'd be hearing from "The Amor Brothers" if Braden and I heard he was getting picked on. I never really get physical, but I would in a heartbeat to defend my family... Especially Josh.

Then there's me. I play the middle child role well, physically. I've always been a bit more on the muscular side. I played soccer growing up, which always kept me on a strict diet and workout routine, even now that I've stopped playing. I stay well-groomed like Josh, but I have a side of me that could let loose like Braden. I care a lot about my appearance, don't get me wrong… But it doesn't really matter, considering I had never really been interested in the girls at my school, and they had never really been interested in me. They were too busy pinching Josh's cheeks and drooling over Braden's bad-boy persona. The fact that Braden also works as a promoter for a nearby club contributed to his street cred, too… Gotta give him that. I had a girlfriend last year, and after she did me dirty, I never really looked back. I realized I wasn't ready for love, and with college coming up, I need to focus on myself, anyway.

"Anything interesting happening at school?" my mother asked as she slid Josh and me our breakfast.

"I think the Winter Formal dance is coming up," Josh said before taking his first bite.

"Enjoy it. It sure goes by quick," she replied. "College will go by even faster. Have you heard back from N.Y.U. yet, Jay?"

"Not yet," I said with a mouthful of eggs. I swallowed and continued. "I should be hearing back in less than a month… February 15th, I think."

"You should be fine… *Rriigghhtt*?" my mom smirked, then gave a playful wink.

She knows I've been stressing about getting into college, as would any sane second-semester high school senior. New York University is my dream school, and I need higher than a 3.7 G.P.A. to get into their business program. Then, I can hopefully minor in hospitality. I have a 4.2 G.P.A. and a ton of extracurricular activities under my belt, which I'm hoping gets me in with a scholarship. After all, my parents couldn't afford to send me there, otherwise.

A lot of kids my age have no idea what they want to study, but not me. I *know* what I want, and that's to own a nightclub with Braden, literally getting paid to throw parties. I've always been a social person. *I love* to read people--to engage, understand, and connect with strangers. Plus, I feel like getting into business would allow me to make decent money while living in Manhattan or L.A.

I've been to New York once in my life, but going once was all I needed to decide that that's the next step for me. I *love* dressing up, and it's the best place to people-watch. I've always found it so intriguing that so many people could function in such little space. Everyone has their different stories all overlapping and getting twisted in one another. Maybe that's why I love going to parties almost as much as I love throwing them.

It's also probably why I've had this internal urge to learn more about the nightlife business like Braden's been doing--learning more about restaurants, bars, and nightclubs. He's always tried to persuade me to help him eventually open up a nightclub, well-knowing I'd probably be putting in most of the work. He's not the smartest guy, but he's still one of my biggest role models--despite all the drinking and the drugs.

I drink, but nowhere near as much as Braden does. I'll *never* drink enough to lose control of myself because I feel like I don't have to. Socially, high school's been a breeze because of all the parties

Braden and I throw at the house while our parents travel on the weekends. My father *loves* his car shows, and my mother *loves* my father... So the two of them are always gone together. Braden and I, however, *love* having the open house they leave us with every weekend they're gone.

Braden knows how to hype up a party, and no girl is gonna pass up his charm when he invites them all to our house. I'm in charge of party operations and how they function throughout the night, and I take my role *very* seriously.

I created a formula for party throwing, and I follow it to the T. Each party consisting of me going through the protocol:

1. *Planning Process:*
    a. *How many people?*
    b. *Which parts of the house are activated/useable?*
    c. *Who's bouncing?*
    d. *Alcohol supply? Drug supply?*
    e. *Expected arrival time? (Note: People show up 30-45 minutes after... No good party ever starts at the exact arrival time.)*
    f. **Leave a note to all neighbors in a two-block radius, something like... "Hello! On _____(date) the Amor Residence will be hosting a celebration for __________(fake reason). We wanted to give you a 'heads up' in case we play the music a bit too loud. Give us a call if so, and we'll make sure to lower it!"**
2. *A Week Before the Party:*
    a. *Braden & Jay begin to promote the party.*
    b. *Braden confirms who our bouncer is.*
    c. *Braden contacts alcohol and drug plugs for appropriate supply*
3. *The Day of the Party:*
    a. *Tell a select group of friends to come straight from school, so we have guaranteed numbers as people begin to arrive that night.*
    b. *Alcohol and drug placement within the house.*
    c. *All valuables moved to our parents' bedroom.*
4. *The Party:*
    a. *Bouncer is in place.*
    b. *Music is ready to go for when Braden's band isn't performing.*
    c. *People show up and immediately go inside. (Never lingering out front because that's the*

quickest way to get the cops called.)

d. *Always more girls than guys.*

e. *No fights, and when the first person vomits, everyone's out… No exceptions.*

f. *Cops will typically come three times, and the third time means shutdown. (They communicate with Braden on a first-name basis because of all the trouble he's gotten himself into over the years. This is his department.)*

g. *Bouncer makes sure nobody drives home drunk.*

5. *Morning After the Party:*

   a. *Cleaning.*

As I finished my breakfast, I heard the backdoor open.

"Knock, knock," said a soothing female voice.

It was the same soothing female voice I heard every morning before school. It was a soft but animated voice--rich in character and full of life but could put you to sleep if she spoke soft enough. It was the voice of Valentina Moralis, but we just call her "Val."

She lives right next door and is basically family to us. I've known her since before I could walk because both of our parents grew up together. We're both 18, and I'd say she's the closest thing I have to a best friend besides the few guys I spent my time with at school. I can't deny the fact that she's beautiful, but I never felt a connection with her in an intimate way because she's like a sister to me… And mostly because I'm almost positive she's in love with Braden.

"What's for breakfast, Mrs. Love?" Val asked.

"Spinach and mushroom omelets! Here, there's extra," my mom cheerfully shoved a plate in front of Val.

"Aw, thanks so much, Mrs. Amor, but I'm stuffed."

Val leaned against me and threw her arm around my shoulder. She looked over at Josh, who was sitting by himself at the table across the kitchen.

"Who you asking to the dance, Joshy?" she asked while giving him a playful wink.

"Dances are dumb," replied Josh, straightening his posture and smugly lifting his chin.

"Oh, is that right?" Val responded. She squinted her eyes as if she wanted to squeeze Josh's cheeks then and there.

She smelled amazing, per usual--the type of girl to look her best without even putting on makeup. I didn't know a guy that was good enough for Val. She's got it all.

She has straight brown hair that goes down to her shoulders, parted in the middle. Her amber eyes, full of life and ambition at all times. Val is constantly looking for adventure, with a great head on her shoulders. She'd rather have a few genuine friends, as opposed to having a ton of shady acquaintances most high school girls would *consider friends*. Val is somebody who *gets* it, and not a lot of people our age *get* it.

Braden walked into the kitchen without a shirt, and Val's attention immediately shifted toward him. She eyed his scattered meaningless tattoos. He walked straight to the refrigerator, opened it, and began drinking directly from the orange juice carton. My mom slapped his shoulder, but it didn't phase him.

"It tastes better drinking from the carton, Ma," he said while putting the carton back in the refrigerator. Then, he turned to see Val.

"What's up, neighbor?" he greeted with a smirk.

"Hi, Braden," replied Val, immediately blushing.

Braden turned to look at Mom and gave her a big kiss on the forehead. She smiled, and you could tell she immediately put the orange juice carton situation behind her. Braden *always* knows how to work people.

After finishing our breakfast, Josh, Val, and I hopped in Val's car to head to school. We go to West Torrance High School, which is no more than a 15-minute drive from our house.

"Any parties tonight?" Val asked.

"I'm not really sure," I replied while scrolling through my phone. "Last weekend was *crazy*, though."

"Round two? I'd be down. That was honestly the craziest party I've been to in a quick minute," she replied.

"Can I come party with you guys?" asked Josh from the back seat.

I looked into the side-view mirror and saw Josh looking out at the houses we passed. He awaited our answer.

"Soon… But not yet," I said without looking up from my phone. "You *know* freshmen never go to the same parties we go to."

Full disclosure… West Torrance parties were some of the craziest in L.A. County. Somehow the houses were filled every time, and we partied until late. There wasn't much gang activity in the areas we went out in. Still, Braden's group always found a way to stir up trouble with other social groups they clashed with.

"So it's because I'm a freshman," Josh said in a discouraged tone. He looked down, twiddled his thumbs, and then looked up from over my left shoulder, saying, "Jay, *please* let me party with you guys. You don't understand the props I'd get from *literally everybody* I know if I was seen at one of the parties you guys get to go to… Just one."

I didn't answer… Instead, I kept scrolling through the various pictures of attractive girls I keep up with on social media. I heard him slump in his seat, and Val lifted her chin to get a view of a disappointed Josh through the rearview mirror.

"You can come with me to the next one, Joshy," Val said in an attempt to lift his spirit. "You can even be my date."

I could see Josh blushing through the side-view mirror as Val continued.

"You know it might even be time for the Amor brothers to throw one of their infamous parties. That might be the *perfect* party for you to go to, Josh... Right, Jay? What do you think?"

She nudged me with her elbow. I didn't respond. I've always seen Josh as my responsibility, and that meant keeping him out of trouble. I know Braden isn't responsible enough to look after him. My father is always too busy working, while my mother is juggling too many responsibilities as it is, raising all three of us while supporting my father's demanding work schedule. Val nudged me again.

"Yes, Josh," I sighed, finally giving in. "When we throw the next party, you can come."

I turned to look at Val, and she was giving me her signature smirk. She knew how to work me. She could work *anybody*, the same way Braden could. Beauty, wit, and self-awareness are an unmatched triple threat for any woman capable of possessing all three. Val was the only girl I knew capable of not using those traits for evil.

We pulled up to our high school and parked in our usual spot. As Josh went off to join his freshman friends, Val and I headed toward our lockers.

"When do you hear back from N.Y.U.?" Val asked while observing the other teenagers tending to their morning gossip.

"I hear back mid-February, I think. What about you? What's your next move?"

"It's sort of complicated," she replied, jamming her hands into the pockets of her baggy jeans.

I could never pin down Val's signature style because it constantly changes. From colorful dresses and rompers to crop tops and baggy pants, she reps *anything* she puts on. She just has that confidence to do anything she sets her mind to.

"Complicated in what way?" I asked as the school bell rang for us to head to class.

"I'll tell you about it later, Jay Love," Val replied. She flashed a friendly peace sign over her amber eyes as she strutted toward her class.

I didn't think much of it because I knew Val lived a great life next door. Her parents came to America from Spain and met my parents some time back in Miami. I remember my mother telling me some story about how they all decided to move to Torrance together. Then, they somehow landed a house right next to each other. Her parents are those "textbook" immigrant parents who really took on the

American dream... The ones who come to this country with *nothing* to create a life for their children that they, themselves, never had--in this case, their child is Val... The *only child* who grew up getting whatever she wanted without having siblings to share anything with.

I must say she's doing pretty well compared to a lot of other only children I know. Maybe growing up playing games and running through the streets with my brothers and me gave her that sibling perspective she wouldn't have had otherwise. Val is *definitely* a girl who can relate to the male perspective too, which is pretty rare.

The school day went by quicker than usual. I do my best to keep to myself and stay out of the drama as much as I can because school is school... And that's all it should be, in my opinion.

Braden taught me that it's best to be social *outside* of school, not that he had a choice because he basically ditched more school days than he showed up... But I understood why. Having friends from other schools allows me to bounce around and be in and out of social groups. When you invest in only one group of friends, and for whatever reason, shit hits the fan in that group, you're screwed. It also helps to be acquainted with different groups in case you ever need to call somebody up for a favor--it's just best to... Diversify.

I have friends from my school, don't get me wrong. I'd say the guys I spend most of my time with are Cole, Danny, and Nate.

Cole is brilliant. I can always count on him to help me with assignments I don't really understand, while I usually act as his wingman when we go out. Poor kid is a goof when it comes to girls but an A.1. guy.

Danny is a bit reckless but just for show because he will *never* open his mouth when he's in the same vicinity as Braden and his entourage. He'll play the "bad-boy" role when it's just us.

Then there's Nate, who I see a lot of myself in. He keeps quiet but is also really self-aware. He picks up on a lot of the same things I pick up on while others overlook them.

The four of us stood near Val's car after school, where we'd always stand to people-watch and talk about plans for the weekend. Teenagers always swarmed the senior parking lot on Fridays to sort out who was throwing the party and when. Some kids would even start *drinking* during this time, but not us.

"I'm tryna mack some chick from North High, but she's dubbing my texts," Danny said while looking down at his phone.

"How'd you meet her?" Nate asked. He exhaled smoke from his cigarette.

"We comment on each other's pictures on Instagram," Danny responded without looking up. "You should see the pictures she posts of her ass... It's crazy."

"So you haven't even met her yet?" I asked. "That's probably why she's not responding to your texts, dude."

"NATHAN!" an older man's voice shouted from a distance.

Nate's eyes widened in immediate shock as he dropped the cigarette and stepped on it. We looked up to see his geometry teacher standing with his hands on his hips.

"You should *not* be smoking on campus!" he shouted.

"It wasn't me, Mr. Walsh," Nate shrugged.

"No... Smoking," Mr. Walsh reiterated in a stern tone.

He continued on his way, and Nate turned to look back at us, saying, "He's got a point though, I should probably stop smoking... But until then...."

He lit another cigarette.

"There's our man," said Cole in the dorky tone that suits his personality so well.

Josh was making his way to the car with his head hanging low. He was holding a piece of paper that was heavily marked up in red ink.

"I failed," he murmured.

Danny grabbed the paper from Josh's grasp and looked over it.

"Holy shit," Danny laughed aloud. "Nate, you're taking the same class as Josh! You're both in geometry, and you're like five grades apart...."

"Freshman and senior are four years apart, dumbass," Nate snapped back as he snagged the paper from Danny and examined it.

"It's okay, Josh, I failed the test too," Nate continued. He handed Josh the paper and took another drag of his cigarette.

Josh took the paper and looked around as if he had been stuck in his own head this whole time. His gaze paused on a stunning blonde girl who stood three or four cars away from us. She was talking to two of her friends. Her bright blue eyes glistened as she turned to look at Josh, giving him a flirtatious wave. Josh smiled back at her, then blushed.

Nate, Cole, Danny, and I all exchanged glances and looked back at Josh.

"Easy there, guy!" Danny teased, playfully shoving Josh's shoulder.

Josh blushed even more and looked at the ground.

"Who *is* that??" I asked as I rubbed Josh's back. "Josh, is there something you're not telling us?"

"You best stay away from her, Joshy," Nate intervened, caressing his cigarette between his teeth. He took it out and continued. "I've heard stories about her... She's a wild one. She's *big-time* into hard drugs. She's also a slut."

"Wwwoooaaahhh," we all responded.

"What?" Nate snapped back in shock at our response. "It's true! Big coke chick."

I continued to pat Josh's back. He looked back at her with the new information he received from Nate.

"I'm sure she's a nice girl, Josh," I said. "You need a girl who's gonna treat you right and respect you over anything."

"Yeah," Cole agreed, clinging onto both of his backpack straps. "A girl like *her*."

He lifted his chin, signalling for us to look the same way he was facing. We turned to see Val walking with one of her friends.

"The one that we never had but still got away," said Cole, adjusting his backpack.

"Jay, when are you gonna wife up Val?" Danny asked.

"Shut up," I said as I lightly shoved Josh toward the car.

"What's up, boys?!" Val smiled as she walked around the guys.

"Hi, Val."

"Hey, Val."

"Hello, Val."

Josh, Val, and I got in the car and started out of the school parking lot. Josh and Val reflected on their days as I felt a vibration against my thigh. I looked down at my phone to see a text from Braden.

BRADEN: Mom and dad are outta town next weekend... SEND THE INVITES

TWO | THE MUSIC CONTINUED TO PLAY

HOME
TORRANCE, CALIFORNIA
FRIDAY, 7:01A.M. - JANUARY 27TH, 2012

I lay in bed, staring at the ceiling, waiting for my alarm clock to shout for me to get up. The last week *flew* by, considering there was much to do to prepare for the party we were supposedly throwing tonight. Things typically *did* go by quickly when I had something to look forward to, plus there was a lot I needed to take care of:

1. *Planning Process*
    a. *A party of 100-120 people.*
    b. *All rooms except our parents' and our rooms are activated.*
    c. *Big Tony is bouncing.*
    d. *Braden is on alcohol and drug supply.*
    e. *Expected arrival time is 9:00p.m. (Note: People to show up around 9:45p.m.-10:00p.m.)*
    f. **Left a note to all neighbors in a two-block radius, something that went a little something like… "Hello! This coming Friday, the Amor Residence will be hosting a celebration for Jay's acceptance into N.Y.U. We wanted to give you a 'heads up' in case we play the music a bit too loud. Give us a call if so, and we'll make sure to lower it!"**

The Planning Process was officially complete, and now it's time for us to start….

"Wake up," a voice said aloud.

I shifted my eyes to a half-naked Braden standing at the door with a cigarette in his mouth. His long hair frizzed to his shoulders, and he was in black sweatpants, which had me thinking he had just woken up, too.

"Are you *actually* smoking inside right now?" I asked.

"Yep," Braden responded before taking a drag and exhaling. "Get up. I need your help moving shit around for tonight."

"Bro, if Mom sees you smoking right now, she's gonna kill you," I snarled. "What time is it?"

"It's early, but it doesn't matter because Mom and Dad already left for that car show in Vegas. I called you out of school, now let's *go*...."

It didn't surprise me that Braden knew how to finesse getting me out of school the way he did. It's almost like everyone on this planet is a puppet in a show he directs, and he gets them to do anything he pleases at any time he pleases.

I opened my phone to more texts than I could view on the screen--texts from close friends, some girls I knew, and even from random numbers... *All* asking about the party tonight. I could feel myself waking up quicker than usual. The dopamine from all the attention I was getting was kicking in. You know, that one brain chemical they say gets you super hyped when something good happens. That's dopamine, right? Serotonin... Ah, whatever... Something like that. Regardless, it's kickin' in. I turned to see Josh's empty bed next to me.

"Where's Josh?" I asked as I stretched out my arms.

Braden responded by turning to look out of my window into the backyard where Josh was mowing the grass. The poor kid was using all the strength within him to push that heavy lawnmower from one side of the backyard to the other.

"I told him if he was gonna be allowed to party with us like you *supposedly* promised him, he was gonna have to earn the invitation," Braden laughed as he tossed me a white shirt. "Now vamo, Jay... Chop! Chop! Let's go!"

He turned to walk out of my room and down the hall. I followed him closely as I pulled over my shirt and rubbed my eyes. The house was *spotless*. We crossed the front door into the living room that also served as the kitchen. This was the largest room in the house, where all of the communal gatherings usually took place.

Braden exhaled a cloud of smoke as he casually signaled for me to help him move the coffee table.

"How long has it been? Since we threw the last one," he asked as we set the table down in the corner of the living room.

"I can't even remember," I itched the top of my head. "It looks like we're pretty much ready to go for tonight, though."

"I've gotta go grab some goodies, so we *for sure* have a good time tonight. If I were you, I'd start following up with people to make sure our numbers are solid. Be ready because some of my buddies are coming early to pre-game before people start showing up."

"Love it," I smiled, now feeling fully awake. "I'm gonna check on Josh and see how he's doing out there."

The inside of our house was lit by the morning light flooding through the large backyard windows. I walked across the living room and through the kitchen to look out into the backyard. Josh was wearing our dad's straw hat he'd always wear while landscaping. It was way too big on Josh, but it worked well with the large gardening gloves he was sporting as he continued mowing the grass. I opened up the screen door that led into the backyard.

"How you doin' out there, big guy?" I asked, crossing my arms.

"Good!"

He wiped the sweat off his forehead, gave me a quick thumbs-up, and then used his *full* body weight to continue pushing the lawn-mower. It was almost the size of Josh himself.

"I'm ready for tonight!" he exclaimed over the sound of the lawnmower. "I even laid my clothes out!"

"Whatever you say…!"

I stepped back into the house and shut the screen door. It had been a while since we had thrown a party, but I didn't think much of it. If Braden and all of his friends were there, *everyone* was going to make it out. My phone vibrated, and I looked down to see I was getting a call from my mom.

Nice try, I thought, letting it ring through to voicemail.

Calling me because she *knew* if I picked up, it meant I wasn't getting ready for school… Oldest trick in the book. I looked down to read the immediate text she sent after the call ended.

MOM: LOVE YOU

I smirked. It's funny how sometimes you can *feel* the emotion behind a text, even though the message is just words on a screen. I knew my mom didn't use her phone for anything except texting Josh, Braden, and myself. I waited a bit, then texted her back.

ME: Love you more!

She replied within seconds.

MOM: That's IMPOSSIBLE!:)

That's something we've been doing since before I could even remember. One of us says, "I love you," the other says, "love you more," and then we'd *both* say, "that's impossible!" I couldn't imagine walking out of a room without finishing the saying. It's one of those things that could probably go unaddressed if I didn't say it, but it just... It wouldn't feel right.

I turned on the shower and started responding to messages.

ME: Yessir.
ME: Yeah, they can come!
ME: Is she cute?
ME: No more guys, we've got too many heads already.
ME: Braden's picking up.
ME: Yes, Braden will be here.
ME: Yes, Braden will be here.
ME: No, Braden's not working tonight... he will be here.

I stumbled across a text from Val, and the dialogue began.

VAL: Jay Love, word on the street is it's going down tonight
ME: What do you think??;)
VAL: That's what I like to hear... you owe me a conversation.
ME: Done deal

I went through my morning routine the same way I do every morning....

100 crunches.
Hot shower in the dark.
Brush my teeth.
Blow-dry and do my hair.
Throw on some face lotion and deodorant.

I headed back to our room to find Josh's clothes laid out on his bed, from his shirt to his shoes. I laughed under my breath and went through it. It was a flannel shirt, beige pants, some colorful socks, and a nice pair of Vans sneakers he kept *real* clean. They were most likely saved for the first high school party he'd be attending.

I texted my group chat, consisting of Danny, Cole, and Nate. They responded within minutes, asking if they could come early to pre-game with Braden's friends. I said yes, even though I knew deep down that Braden's friends didn't care to hang out with my friends. We're around 18 years old and they're all between the ages of 21 and 30. It really doesn't matter when we all start drinking though, because that's when *everybody* gets along.

Braden's friends didn't start showing up until around 6:30p.m., but by the time it was 7p.m., the music was bumping. Three big guys were taking inventory of alcohol, weed, and all of the texts they received from the girls who responded to their invites. They were *all* coming. I walked into the kitchen, where Braden and his friends were all gathered.

"Well, well, well!" shouted a buzzed Braden holding up his red solo cup.

His three friends turned to greet me in an aggressively loving embrace. They've always treated me like I'm their little brother. For some reason, *everyone* seems to just gravitate toward our family.

"What's up, Little Jay?!" Tony's deep voice exclaimed as he picked me up and hoisted me over his shoulder.

"Big Tony!" I shouted playfully.

Tony works as a bouncer over at the nightclub Braden promotes at. He's *easily* 6'3 and over 250 pounds. He has this thick beard that defines his chin, accompanied by an intimidating shaved head. Nobody messes with Big Tony, but nobody also knows about his secret soft teddy bear-like personality. It only took one vague compliment to make him blush, and there was no way he could hide it, even if he tried.

"Congrats on getting into N.Y.U.! I always knew you were smarter than Braden, but N.Y.U.... That's *big-time*!"

"Hey, thanks, big man!" I shouted as he set me down and gave me a hug that somehow turned into a headlock. "But that's just what we told the neighbors... I find out in a month."

"He's book smart. I'll give him that," Braden intervened, shoving a red cup of vodka soda into my hand. "But I've got the street smarts on *lock*."

Vodka soda is my go-to drink. They have no sugar, which didn't have me too hungover the next morning, and I could pound them like water without getting too drunk too quickly. It's tequila I try to stay away from. That stuff *really* messes me up.

"I know, I know. I'm just playing around," clarified Tony, always feeling the need to make sure everyone knew when he was joking.

"Cheers, boys!" I shouted over the music as I lifted my cup.

The guys lifted their cups in response to my "cheers."

"Bottoms up..." one of them declared. That's when you knew the pre-game had begun. The first couple of cups go straight down without taking a breath.

After I downed another vodka soda, Nate, Cole, and Danny showed up with a couple racks of beer. They meshed well with Braden's friends, but only because of how quickly everybody was getting drunk.

Around 8p.m., the living room and kitchen were filled with our friends and a couple of girls Braden's friends invited. I could tell a couple of them were from Hollywood. That's where Braden spent most of his weekends when he wasn't working at the nightclub down here in Torrance. He would use his fake I.D. to get into the clubs up there as soon as he graduated from high school. That's when the dream of owning our own nightclub was first conceptualized. I will admit that it's a dream we share--getting paid to throw parties the way we want to when we want to.

"Where's Josh?" asked Nate, trying not to be overpowered by the music echoing throughout the house.

I scanned the room in an attempt to meet the gaze of Josh's big brown eyes. I couldn't find him. I'm also buzzed. Wow, am I buzzed.

Josh, I thought, *where the hell are you, little guy*?

I stood up from my seat on the couch and immediately felt the head rush from the vodka sodas. I carefully stepped around the guys and headed for my room. The door was closed, and I opened it slowly, peeking my head in to find Josh sitting at the foot of his bed. He looked up at me and raised his eyebrows in shock. He was wearing the outfit that had been laid out on his bed since the night before.

"Hey, Jay…" he said softly.

"What're you doing in here?" I asked, joining him on the floor.

"I'm gonna be honest with you," he looked down at his lap and twiddled his thumbs. "I'm kind of nervous."

"Nervous?!" I laughed. "Nervous about what??"

"Well…" he paused.

I could tell he was serious, so I shifted my posture to show him I was genuinely engaged.

"You and Braden have always been the *cool* brothers, and I don't wanna get in the way of that. I've never been to a party… I've never even drank before. I don't wanna do something stupid to embarrass you guys."

A loud uproar came from the living room. People cheered, which had me thinking they were well into playing drinking games by now. I felt the urge to get up and join them. I watched Josh's eyes dart up in the direction of the living room and then go right back down again.

"Look at me, dude," I said, lightly slapping his thigh with the back of my hand. "At one point or another, you're *gonna* drink. You're a social guy and a good-looking one, at that. You're an Amor brother, damnit."

I saw his face blush, and he looked up at me with a smirk.

"There's no better time or place for your first time partying than in your own home, and there's no better company than with Braden and myself," I continued. "I'll keep an eye on you, Josh. You know I've always got your back."

I stood up over him and lowered my hand to help him up. He grabbed it, and as I lifted him up, he embraced me tightly. I could feel his little heartbeat. It was beating quickly, and as he hugged tighter, I felt the beat slow back to normal. He was calm.

"Love you, Jay," he said.

"Love you more," I responded, playfully shoving him toward the door.

"That's impossible!" he smiled.

"Now, let's get you your *first drink*."

I kept my hand pressed against Josh's back as we headed down the short hall that opened up into the living room.

"JOSHY!!" screamed Nate, lifting his drink in the air from across the room.

People turned to face Josh and me as everyone cheered and invited him into the party that was quickly taking shape. Braden shouted for Josh to join him in the kitchen, where Josh's shot was waiting for him.

"Hey, Jay… Let me get a picture of you and your brothers," Cole awkwardly insisted while holding up his new polaroid camera.

I let out a laugh as Braden threw his arm around me and pulled Josh in for the picture. Cole snapped the picture, and within seconds, the polaroid was printed out the bottom of the camera and in his hand.

"You gonna whack off to that pic later or *what*, Cole??" Braden teased.

Cole chuckled as he shook the polaroid.

"I thought I'd take some photos to remember the night," he replied innocently.

He extended the photo toward me with a smile on his face.

"Here, Jay. It's a pretty cool pic, actually."

I looked at the polaroid that was now clear, showing Braden, Josh, and myself standing up against the kitchen counter.

"Thanks, Cole," I said softly. "I don't really know where to put it, though…."

"Just put it in your pocket!" he replied with a smile. "You never know when you might need to see it."

I slid the photo into my pocket and patted his shoulder in appreciation of his wholesome and innocent character. Josh hesitantly headed in Braden's direction, consumed by the height of the crowd. It seemed a bit overwhelming for his narrow body frame that barely stood over five feet tall.

Big Tony's face turned red with excitement as he hoisted Josh up on his shoulders. Braden handed him a drink after he took the shot. Josh laughed and greeted everyone from high up on Tony's shoulders with a big smile on his face. I went back to my small group of friends who turned their heads from Josh back to our inner circle.

"Jay… Just in time, my friend," Danny said, digging his hands through his backpack.

Nate rolled his eyes while Cole completely missed the statement, bobbing his head to the music he realistically *never* listens to.

Cole has always been one to listen to classic rock... *Never* hip-hop. I could see him looking around, doing his best to recognize and practice when to address social cues.

"Here it is, baby," Danny lifted a clear packet out of his backpack. "We're going on a trip tonight, bbooyyss."

"Here we go again," Cole rolled his eyes as he sipped his drink.

"Relax, they're just edibles," Danny said, tapping the packet against Cole's forehead.

"Last time I took those," Nate's eyes widened. "I ended up on my ass. I couldn't move for a solid hour, and my senses were all out of whack."

I was never big on drugs, but I drink. I'm just so in sync with my thoughts and mind, I fear that my bad trips could lead to the end of me. Braden has done every drug under the sun and could somehow still function. He's a tad slower than he used to be, but his friends are full-blown numbskulls now--walking around like they're high even when they're completely sober.

"Come on," Danny urged Nate. "I know Jay won't do it because he's got a party to throw, and Cole's a pussy."

Nate averted his eyes to the wall in deep thought. The front door opened as a large group of girls and some guys came pouring in, holding bottles and cases of beer. The living room suddenly got even louder. The girls complimented each other on their outfits and acted like they hadn't seen each other in months. The guys cracked open their beers and tried to get in on drinking games.

"Damnit, okay. Give me a small one," Nate shrugged as he realized the party had begun.

"YES!" Danny stuffed a gummy in Nate's hand, and they popped them in their mouths.

"Nate, if you start to feel like you can't manage, just go lay on the couch Jay's dad keeps in the garage. It should kick in around 45 minutes from now."

Nate nodded.

"Cheers, boys."

The night had just begun. Tony manned the front door, towering over the teenagers and young adults that funneled into the house. Naturally, the current of intoxicated teens made its way through the house and into the backyard. People cheered, laughed, shouted, and sang to the songs they knew the words to, although some certainly knew very little... But that still didn't stop them.

I greeted kids I know and made new friends within seconds of one another. Being the host of a party is always nice because it comes with instant respect, until:

1. You lose sight of the party or get too drunk.

2. You tolerate any form of disrespect.

I was willing to bet *anything* that everyone at the party knew Braden. Girls huddled around him, making faces at each other. I could hear them whisper amidst the blaring music as I walked through the crowd.

"That's him?"

"Yep, that's the guy."

"Braden Amor."

I always found it funny. Girls constantly threw themselves at Braden, but he never gave them the time of day. He was so focused on himself, and after having his heart broken by a girl he believed he was gonna marry a few years back, he never looked at girls the same.

"I'm gonna go out with a bang," he'd say. "I don't need a girl to hold me back. I'm out here building a man of myself. When they come lining up at the door of my nightclub, I know I'll meet her then and there."

Then he'd puff his cigarette and tuck his long hair behind his ears. He always fantasized about those Hollywood scene girls. I don't blame him... They're stunning. He never had any trouble pulling them either, given his confidence and reckless behavior. The tattoos also complemented his bad-boy charisma.

I did my usual sweep of the house, running through the list:

- *The Party:*
    a. *Our bouncer, Tony, is in place. Currently at the front door.*
    b. *Music is playing and most likely will continue playing because Braden never set up his band equipment.*
    c. *All people are in the house. Nobody's lingering out front.*
    d. *There's a whole lot of girls in comparison to guys.*
    e. *No fights or vomit yet.*

I sat up on the kitchen counter, where I always enjoyed people-watching from. A kid in a backwards trucker hat and a loose flannel made his way across the room to talk to a girl accompanied by her friend... Let's call him "David." He looks like a "David." David struggled to stand up straight, speaking his mind to this girl we'll call... "Jessica."

"I think you're beautiful and hot and if you wanna hook up then we should hook up. No B.S. or games shit you know okay-...?" David slurred.

Jessica laughed alongside her friend, who looked disgusted with both David's looks and manners. David's posture swayed as he tried to maintain eye contact. He most likely regretted having pregamed too hard upon showing up to our party. Jessica didn't break eye contact, though, which had me thinking she was somewhat interested. It was evident that he didn't have the approval of Jessica's friend, which might make it tough for David to close with Jessica. Let's see how this plays out.

"Did you just come up to me and ask if I want to hook up with you?" asked Jessica, staring at him skeptically. She was trying to hold back a smile.

"Yeah, if you're too then later is fiiine with me though," he said while fixing his hat and stutter-stepping away.

"You should leave," said Jessica's friend to poor David.

"Are you her bodyguard?" David asked. "A beautiful girl like her--can speak for herrrrselfff."

Jessica blushed. Her friend's jaw dropped.

Godspeed, David, I thought to myself as I turned to find a more amusing scenario.

I sipped my drink, looking across the living room in the opposite direction of David and Jessica. My eyes landed on a beautiful girl with long blonde hair. I recognized her instantly. She's the girl Josh was going crazy over last week. I had never seen him so captivated by anything in his life. Let's call her... "Rebecca."

I watched Rebecca chug whatever was in her cup and whisper into her friend's ear. Her friend slipped Rebecca a little clear baggy filled with a white powder I'm gonna assume is cocaine.

Nate was right, I thought. *She's a wild one*.

I sipped my drink and studied her movement. She made her way across the party, and I assumed she was looking for a bathroom. I watched as guys turned their heads to catch a glimpse of her, but she thought nothing of it. She was on a mission.

I swear, there's something about people who do coke that is so different from people who do any other drug. People who do coke are almost... More competent--more *determined*.

Rebecca found the bathroom as I assumed she would. As she approached the two guys in line, she tucked the baggy into her pants and gestured that she *really* needed to pee. The two guys, most likely buzzed and infatuated by her bright blue eyes, instantly allowed for her to cut them in line. They gave each other a look and then sized her up from behind. When it was her turn, she darted into the bathroom and shut the door behind her. The two guys continued talking.

I sipped my drink.

After a few minutes, she stepped out, politely thanking the two guys who let her cut them in line. The two guys went into the bathroom together, which I feel like I *should* analyze a bit more thoroughly but maybe later. I watched Rebecca.

Her smile toward the guys quickly transitioned into a look of satisfaction and relief. The crowd moved with her, almost in slow motion, as she carried a rhythm in her step that was synchronized with the music. She paused in the middle of the living room and continued dancing by herself. The people dancing around her didn't acknowledge her, as she was almost entirely one with the party. She lifted her chin toward the ceiling, opening her mouth with a smile and raising her hands.

She danced.
She laughed.

Rebecca was completely satisfied with her own state of being--of simply existing. To her, it seemed like nothing mattered except the moment itself. She swayed, and her head thumped to the beat of the music as if they were connected. Her eyes rolled back, and she began to dance more intimately. She had gotten her fix.

She started to get the attention of the people surrounding her, and they danced along. I could hear Nate's words echoing in my mind.

She's a wild one. She's a wild one. She's a wild one.

There was something about her that made me uneasy--one of those gut feelings that I didn't want to learn much more about....

She *knew* she was beautiful. She carried herself as if she were innocent, but a large number of people would probably argue otherwise. I received validation of that thought after watching her for just the past few minutes. Am I overanalyzing? I shifted myself and sipped my drink.

Maybe I'm just drunk... Probably just drunk.

I had always known I was good at reading people. It didn't take long for me to figure out people's intentions, regardless of how they tried to present themselves on the outside. My mother would tell me it was my God-given gift, and I exercised it regularly.

"Jay!" shouted a high-pitched voice to my right.

I turned my head, snapping out of my trance. I couldn't help but smile and laugh. Josh's tiny presence tried to maneuver its way through the crowd that could swallow him up whole if they didn't respect him the way they did.

"This is insane!" Josh yelled over the music as I hoisted him up to sit next to me on the kitchen counter. His face was red, and his pupils were massive as they darted left and right, taking everything in.

"I love you, Jay. You don't know how much this means to me... Being able to party with you and Braden. I'm like a celebrity... Everybody here knows me!"

"You are, dude," I laughed aloud and wrapped my arm around

his shoulder.

"Oh my..." his jaw dropped, "She's... Here."

His eyes grew bigger than I had ever seen, and he was fixated on Rebecca, who was now dancing with her friends.

"Rebecca??" I asked.

He looked at me, baffled.

"Is that her name??" he asked in excitement.

I caught myself and quickly took a sip of my drink.

"I, uh, I think I heard that's her name... I don't know. I'm drunk. It's probably not."

He puffed his chest out.

"I'm gonna talk to her," he said.

He hopped off of the kitchen counter, fixed his hair, then turned back to look up at me.

"Wish me luck," he winked, smiling from cheek to cheek.

"Be careful, man," I said softly.

He headed in her direction, disappearing into the large crowd that occupied our living room and kitchen. I finished my drink and did one last visual sweep of the space. Cole stood against the fireplace, head still bobbing to the music as he held the same cup he was "drinking" from hours before. Danny stood on the couch, headbanging to the music. His edible and a couple shots were in full effect.

I caught a glimpse of Nate sloppily making his way through the crowd toward the backdoor, and I assumed he was heading for the couch in our detached garage. Poor Nate. He never meshed well with edibles. I felt my phone vibrate against my thigh and looked down to see a text from Val.

VAL: Look up :)

My heart dropped. I looked up, and across the room, standing next to the fireplace, stood Val, with a big smile on her face. She was stunning--*is* stunning. Her brown hair fell straight down to her shoulders, and her tan made her amber eyes appear even lighter. She wore a tight black tank top with baggy cargo pants and some trendy shoes she probably bought at some thrift shop in L.A.

"*You owe me a conversation*," she had texted me this morning.

I thought about what she had told me last week--something about her college situation being *complicated*. I never followed up, which I should've. Maybe that's what she wanted to talk about tonight.

I signaled for her to come to where I was sitting on the kitchen counter. She squinted and signaled for me to go to her. I rolled my eyes and pointed toward the backyard, signalling for us to talk outside. She smiled and started making her way through the crowd toward the backdoor. I refilled my drink and did the same. I glanced at Josh one last time, who was dancing with Rebecca, happier than I had ever seen him. I smiled.

Acknowledging and greeting strangers and friends alike, I danced my way through the crowd. The key is to bounce to the rhythm of the music, each beat moving closer into the direction you want to head toward… That way, you don't have to shove your way through or give off confrontational vibes.

Every now and then, I'd bump into some guy who'd look back at me with a defensive snarl, but I was always quick to pat him on the back and apologize. Always best to keep the peace when people are under the influence. There's no telling what someone will do when they're intoxicated.

After all, *who* or *what* do we become when we *are* drunk--or even... Blacked out?

I know some people say we speak the truth with no filter when we're heavily intoxicated, but how could that work when somebody sobers up and genuinely has no idea why they said what they said or did what they did? Did they feel that way deep down before drinking?

God forbid somebody drunkenly jumps off of a balcony because they thought they could land in a pool that wasn't even there. If we're not in our right mind, then where are we? Who's occupying our right mind while we're not in it? Where does our consciousness go when we lose it? If somebody dies during the blackout, was their last moment at the exact point in time they died, or was it the last moment they spent sober and consciously aware?

"How the hell did you guys manage to pull this off?" Val asked, sitting down on a brick ledge in the corner of our backyard. "This party is insane."

"Where's your drink?" I asked, offering her mine.

She took a sip and nudged me as I sat down next to her.

"Right here," she lifted my cup and flashed a flirtatious smirk.

"Very smooth," I said. "I'm pretty sure I owe you a conversation."

"You do, you do," she said, looking down, processing what she was about to say.

She looked forward into the swarm of strangers filling our dimly-lit backyard. It wasn't tough to make out the somewhat sloppy conversations that were soon to be forgotten.

"So, I'm not going," Val said while avoiding eye contact. "... To college."

I watched as her posture slumped a bit. She sipped her drink that was once mine.

"What're you gonna do?" I asked.

"I've had a couple of agents reach out to me about some modeling stuff," she sighed as if disappointed in herself. "And... I figured I'd be saving some money. I'd be making a decent amount... Based on what I've been told."

"Are they big-name agencies?" I asked, grabbing the drink from her hand and sipping it.

"Yeah... IMG and Wilhelmina. I'd be able to travel and have a pretty flexible schedule... I think."

I rotated my body toward her and we met eyes.

"You don't sound too sure about this," I said in a stern tone.

"I'm not... Well, I am, but-..." Val straightened up and tied her hair back.

I could tell she was thinking intensely. She was perplexed. When Val adjusted something about her appearance, I *knew* something was bothering her. She's been doing it since we were kids and I was suddenly determined to find out what was on her mind. Before I could ask, she continued.

"You know how I feel about models. I'm not like them... Like, I *hate* relying on looks... I *hate* it. I like using my head, but I guess in a way, this is sort of like using my head. I can use the money I make to invest in something or to grow in some way. I don't know. I'm just not passionate enough about anything worth studying."

"I support it," I said, handing her the drink. "And I believe in you."

"My parents don't. They said if I'm gonna pursue modeling, they're gonna cut me off, financially. I'll be entirely on my own. If I get gigs quick, then *maybe* I could support myself living with some other girls. But still, it's a stretch."

"I say go for it," I leaned back against the wall. "You're hard-working. You're driven. You've got a good head on your shoulders, Val. There's no doubt you'll make ends meet."

She quietly stared at me, with her typical *Val smirk*. Even in the dimly-lit backyard could I see those eyes clear as day. I'm sure as hell buzzed. I'm also *really* starting to feel weird about her. Val is something straight out of a movie. I smirked back, and she turned to face the crowd. Her eyes suddenly grew large as Braden sloppily approached us, looking back over his shoulder a couple times. He stopped directly in front of us.

"You hear who decided to show up?" Braden asked over the sound of the crowd. He was fuming.

He ignored Val's presence and faced the rest of the party. Val and I looked at each other and then back up at Braden.

"No. Who?" I asked.

"Hold this," he said as he handed me his empty solo cup and

pulled out a cigarette. "Carter and his friends just fucking pulled up."

Two of Braden's friends walked up behind him with looks of mischief. They stood at Braden's right and left as he lit his cigarette with one hand and tucked his hair behind his ear with the other. He took a long drag, looked up at the night sky, and then down at me.

"Tony's keeping them out, but they threatened to roll the party if we don't let him and his boys in."

"They're outside??" I asked, standing abruptly.

Braden has the respect of *everyone* in Torrance, but whenever he and his friends went out in Hollywood, he'd find himself getting into scuffles with groups from nearby neighborhoods. He wasn't the best at meeting new people, considering he always utilized the first impression to make himself look tough. Other guys didn't take too kindly to a good-looking, reckless guy like Braden--hence the tension between his group and Carter's.

"Those *fucking* Palos Verdes kids have no reason to come all the way over here… I don't understand…" Braden sighed and took another drag of his cig.

"Who's outside?" Val asked.

Braden reached out for his empty cup and upon me handing it to him, he took a sip and finally realized it was empty. He was nowhere *near* sober, and I could feel the tension in the backyard begin to rise. He tossed the cup onto the ground.

"So a couple months ago, we went to Bootsies… Some club up in L.A. One of my boys got us all a table, and we invited these random girls in line to come sit with us. *Dimes*… Like, they were easily models."

One of Braden's friends let out a laugh under his breath, validating Braden's statement about how attractive the girls were.

"Turns out those girls were supposed to meet up with some guys from Palos Verdes… Carter and them," Braden continued. "So these guys show up to our table and start beefing with us. One of them ends up pulling a knife on Tony, a brawl breaks out, and all of us end up getting kicked out. Since then, they've been talking shit over social media, hiding behind screens. I wonder what made them want to pull up."

"Are you gonna confront them? What if they're calling the cops? Mom and Dad are gonna flip if they find out we threw a party," I said to the group.

"That's why I came to get you. I'm on shrooms right now, so I don't trust myself dealing with these guys responsibly. I gave one of my boys my gun before I lose any more of myself than I already have," Braden put his hand on my back and shoved me in the direction of the house. "Let's go."

Braden's two friends cleared a path through the crowd of boys and girls who didn't question us for a second once they saw who we were. I thought about my conversation with Val. Where was it going? Could something have happened between us? She *was* giving me a look before Braden came. Braden's always gotta find a way to take me on some sort of detour.

I stayed two or three feet behind Braden's two friends leading the way, and Braden's hands were on my shoulders. I couldn't tell if I was guiding him or if he was guiding me. Either way, we made our way past the garage and around the side of our house.

Suddenly, I noticed one of Braden's two friends pull out a gun he had tucked in the back of his pants. He cocked it back and then placed it back in his belt strap. I stutter-stepped, realizing what I might be getting myself into.

"He's not gonna use it, Jay," Braden whispered, still pushing me forward. "Plus, these P.V. boys are usually strapped too from what I hear around our club."

The music gradually became distant. I could hear our own footsteps in the darkness of the driveway that extended along the side of our house. The four of us turned the corner to the front yard where five surfer-looking guys stood on the grass in front of Tony, who was standing between them and the house.

"Well, it's about damn time," one of the surfer guys said to us while lifting his hands in disappointment.

He had long blonde hair that frizzed down to his shoulders from under his cuffed beanie. He was in all black, and his skinny pants were cuffed high, showing off his high socks and designer shoes. I looked at Big Tony, who stood firm with a straight face and his hands by his side--fists clenched.

"I told them no, Braden. Let me know if you want me to press 'em," Tony offered.

Braden let go of my shoulders and stepped past me and between his two friends.

"What's good, Carter?" Braden snarled.

"Is it cool if we come in?" Carter asked, putting his hands in his jacket pockets.

"Why the *fuck* would I let you into our house?" Braden shifted his glance to the guy standing to Carter's right. "This is the fucking dude who pulled a knife on us at Bootsies."

"Relax," Carter said without losing sight of Braden. "My girlfriend's in there... I just came to pick her up, and we'll bounce. She's not picking up her phone."

"Who? What does she look like?" Braden asked, drunkenly stutter-stepping toward Carter, who didn't react. The shrooms had kicked in.

"Hannah... She's brunette and she's got blue eyes. She went

to your high school."

"Wait, yeah, I saw her…." Braden's tone got softer as he inched closer to Carter's face. "She just gave me head in the side yard."

Carter shoved Braden back into my arms. One of Carter's friends pulled a gun from his waistband, struggling to not raise it at Braden. Braden's friend immediately pulled out his own gun, pointing it at Carter as both groups tensed up, preparing for the altercation.

"Woah! Woah!" I yelled, pulling Braden up and throwing my hands in the air. "You can come in. No guns. Put the guns away…."

Braden's friend kept his gun pointed at Carter while clenching his fist.

"Braden?" he asked, nervously shifting his weight from his right leg to his left and then right again.

"Just let 'em in," Braden said while fixing his jacket. "If you promise no *funny* shit once you're on my property, Carter."

"Don't disrespect my girl, and we're good then, yeah?" Carter snapped back, patting Braden's shoulder. He walked past us and through the side yard.

The tension eased a bit as the large group of us walked along the driveway and into the backyard. The sound of the music and various conversations grew louder and louder. We found ourselves swallowed by the mass of now intoxicated strangers and friends that flooded our home.

"Keep your eye on them," Braden said to his two friends as Carter's group trailed off. "They're lucky I didn't have my gun... Those stupid pricks."

Braden's friends obeyed and disappeared into the crowd. I watched Braden get even sloppier as he approached a group of girls. They excitedly embraced him, hugging him and complimenting him on his look and the party. I continued back to Val. She sat in the same spot I had left her, people-watching.

"Hi," I said softly.

I smirked.

She smiled.

I sat.

"Where's your drink?" she teased, repeating what I had asked earlier.

I looked around. "Uh oh… This might be an issue."

I leaned back against the wall next to her, making myself comfortable.

We talked and talked without a single second of silence. It's always been like this between Val and me, but I realized here and now that she wasn't the girl I had grown up with, but rather a woman--a *real* woman. Hopefully, it's not the alcohol making me feel this way, but I genuinely feel like there could be something here. We continued talking--laughing--and I felt nothing but comfortable sitting with her as the music continued to play in the background.

She's driven, smart, funny, stunning, self-aware... Most of all, she has respect for family. It's weird how she kind of reminds me of myself... Like I wouldn't want to *date* myself per se, but it's somewhat refreshing to relate. It was at this moment in time that I felt completely immersed in the present, and nothing else mattered.

I forgot about N.Y.U.
I forgot about the random school drama.
I forgot about the familial responsibilities.
I forgot about *everything,* and I was completely present.
I was in the *now.*
This could be love.
It might be love.
Is this love?
Am I drunk?
I don't know.
I don't care.

BANG!

A *gunshot*. The sound penetrated my mind and body with such force and intensity, I immediately became sober. Val quickly turned her head from me toward the crowd as people screamed and ran in all sorts of different directions.

I jumped to my feet in a panic, immediately processing where the gunshot could have come from. Was it one of Carter's friends that fired? Was it one of Braden's? Who shot? Who *got* shot? Where are Braden and Josh?

The music continued to play.

Teenagers hopped over the walls. They pushed. They shouted. They screamed. Through the frantic movements and chaotic reaction of the partygoers, I could see Braden's friend, who originally had the gun, standing still... Looking around to see who had fired. It wasn't him. He pulled out his gun, ready to find out where the sound came from. About 10 yards away, Carter's friend, who was also armed, looked around just as confused. It wasn't him, either.

The music continued to play.

"WHERE'S JOSH?" I screamed to Braden's friend. "WHERE'S BRADEN?"

I shoved my way closer to him.

"I DON'T KNOW!" he shouted back, keeping his gun down by his waist and scanning the perimeter of the backyard. "THE GUN-

SHOT CAME FROM THE SIDE YARD."

The music continued to play.

I jolted toward the side yard, getting knocked by drunk bodies and knocking drunk bodies myself. My heart was in my stomach, and all I wanted was to be eye to eye with both of my brothers.

"BRADEN'S PASSED OUT IN THE LIVING ROOM!" I heard one of Braden's friends scream from the backdoor.

I didn't turn back.

The music continued to play.

"JAY!" shouted Nate from the door of our garage. "IT'S JOSH!"

The adrenaline coursed through my body as I made way for the garage. I felt nothing, physically, but my heart weighed a trillion pounds within my chest.

Nate dropped to his knees in front of me as I made my way past him. He vomited and sprawled himself on the grass. I entered the garage and slowed myself to a halt.

The fluorescent light shone from the ceiling of the garage, revealing a scene straight out of a nightmare worse than any I have ever or could ever have dreamt. My body froze, and my breath left me as I began to choke for air I no longer wanted to breathe.

The music continued to play.

Josh sat with his legs straight and his back against the closed garage door. My father's '67 Mustang to his right, blood splattered across the tail light. To his left lay the revolver I had pulled on Braden last week, which we hid behind the guitar amplifier. The amplifier was tipped over in the corner of the garage, and bags of cocaine and other drugs were exposed--one of the bags had been cut open. I dropped to my knees, and tears fell from my face before I could even cry.

"No, no, no, no, no, no," I said, crawling toward Josh's lifeless body. "No, no, no, no, no. Josh, no. Josh… Josh?"

The music continued to play.

I leaned back against the garage door, now shoulder to shoulder with him--his eyes closed and head slouched over to his right. My hands shook. Everything shook.

"HELP!" I screamed, fighting for a steady breath. "SOMEBODY CALL SOMEBODY SOMEBODY HELP PLEASE CALL HELP SOMEBODY HELP."

I heard heavy footsteps reach the door, and Tony's face was lit by the fluorescent light as he stepped into the garage. He dropped to his knees, and the color was flushed from his face. He let out a sob I had never heard before and dropped down on all fours.

Tony began to pray, as the music continued to play.

Braden's friends entered the doorway behind Tony, analyzing the situation.

"Holy shit… Josh," one of them said.

"The police and ambulance are on their way!" shouted Cole from behind them.

"Bro, the *guns*," one of Braden's friends nudged the other. They reached for their waistbands, feeling for their guns.

"What about the coke??" another asked, signalling to the amplifier. "Fuck it... It's Braden's supply. Let's dip before the cops get here."

The music continued to play.

They left. Josh's head was now on my lap, blood staining my pants.

"No, no, no, no," I continued repeating, my fingers running through his still perfectly combed hair.

"JAY! Jay?" Val stepped in front of Cole. She covered her mouth in disbelief.

The sirens grew louder and louder as Cole pressed for the garage door to open. I felt it rise behind me, and the flashing blue and red lights flooded into the garage. As the garage door opened, my full weight fell back and my head hit the concrete driveway behind me.

I began to lose consciousness as the music continued to play.

THREE | SHE DANCED

TORRANCE MEMORIAL MEDICAL CENTER
TORRANCE, CALIFORNIA
SATURDAY, 9:29A.M. - JANUARY 28TH, 2012

I opened my eyes to find myself in a white room--all white. It was a small room. I looked right to see a monitor with some wires hanging from it. The lights were dimmed, giving the room a dull feel that made me feel colder than I already am. Even the curtains drawn into the corner of the room were gray, and I realized I was lying in a hospital bed.

Josh, I thought, suddenly remembering what had just happened. *Please be a dream*.

I closed my eyes. I wanted to go back to sleep.

I want to wake up at home in the morning and see Josh in his bed to my left.

I want to smell breakfast being made.

I want to do my morning routine.

I want to go to school.

I want to see my family.

I want to see my friends.

I want to see Val.

I DON'T want to be here.

I sat up slowly, and my head became heavy as if I had just been hit by a truck. I turned to my left to face the overcast sky. The room was a few floors high, and I could see people outside tending to their own business and lives. All of them with their own stories being written out as they continued to move. All of them completely unaware of my existence and what I had endured and will endure as a result of what happened last night. What exactly *happened* last night? I was still wearing the same clothes.

I looked up to find my father sitting in the corner of the room, directly in front of me. His chair faced the opposing wall, where his eyes were fixed. I could tell from his side profile that he was disappointed--distraught--ultimately... *Defeated*. His chin rested in his palm, and his elbow pressed against the arm of the uncomfortable-looking chair. He stared directly at the wall across the room, deep in thought. He said nothing.

He was in a collared shirt he was most likely wearing the night before at his car show out in Vegas. His hair was still slicked back and beard groomed as if he had driven straight here from Vegas upon getting the call from the hospital... *Or* the police.

I wanted to ask where Josh and Braden were. I wanted him to say they were in another room nearby... That Josh was still alive. I said nothing.

I played back what I remember in my head... Josh's tiny lifeless body on the floor of the garage, with his eyes closed. I remember seeing the revolver on the floor next to his open palm.

He didn't kill himself, I thought. *He was so happy... He wouldn't have. He would never.*

I remembered the last time I talked to Josh before he went off to dance with that girl... REBECCA. Could she have killed Josh? Was she *with* Josh in the garage? Are *they* the ones who found Braden's drugs and the gun behind the amplifier? My head began to throb. I was present in the moment, once again, staring at my father, who hadn't moved.

I reached into my pockets, looking for my phone, but instead, I felt a slim card-like object. I slowly pulled out the polaroid photo Cole took of Braden, Josh, and myself before the party began. My head throbbed even more as I shoved it back into my pocket.

"Where's Josh?" I asked.

My father slowly turned right to look at me. Without saying anything, his glasses fogged up, and I watched a tear fall from his eye onto the arm of the chair. He didn't answer. I've never seen my father cry before, and although he wasn't showing any emotion on his face, I could see the pain in his eyes. He remained silent and stared at me.

"You were supposed to keep us together," he said as another tear fell. "You were supposed to look after him... *Both* of them."

Tears began to fall from my eyes, but I didn't move. He didn't say anything more, nor did he have to. He was right. I *knew* my purpose and that it was my responsibility to look after both Braden and Josh. I was never told that this was my responsibility, but I didn't have to be told, given the way things had always been.

"Where's Braden?" I asked, voice shaking. "Where's Mom?"

He stood and picked up his jacket from the chair.

"The police station, where we're going. Vamo... Let's go."

I looked at the monitor and around the room, wondering what had happened to me and why I was in the hospital instead of the police station with Braden.

"They just wanted you to sleep here. You hit your head... But, no concussion," he continued. "They're investigating the house."

He tossed my shoes onto the bed and walked out the door without telling me to follow him. He didn't have to tell me for me to understand that I was supposed to.

We got into the car and drove to the police station. There was no music playing and no conversation between the two of us. I stared blankly at the scenery that passed, becoming a hollow vessel replaying last night over and over again. The day was gloomier than any other I had ever experienced, from the overcast sky to my raging migraine. I'm assuming it was from both being hungover and hitting my head on the driveway.

We arrived, and my father led the way. The sliding door opened, and he walked directly past the cop sitting at the front desk. The cop didn't question him, and I assumed it was because my father must have been here earlier. I followed his slow and steady pace down a long hallway with rooms on each side. The place was *equally* as dull as the hospital.

My mother sat in a chair toward the end of the hallway, her hands shaking uncontrollably as she stared at the floor and rocked back-and-forth. She looked nothing like my mother… This couldn't be my mother. This woman is *broken… Shattered.*

My father took the only seat next to her, and I stopped myself about three feet away. He stared directly forward as he did back at the hospital, and my mother continued to sway back-and-forth, praying under her breath. She didn't acknowledge me.

"Mom?" I whispered, holding back tears.

She continued praying and swaying as I took a knee in front of her.

"Mom…."

I placed my hand gently on her knee, and she just continued praying as if I wasn't even there. It was like I was the one dead, and my parents couldn't hear, see, or feel me.

Am I dead? I thought. *Did I hit my head hard enough to take myself out*?

The door next to my mother opened as the conversation inside of the room came to a close. Nate slowly walked out, and the bags under his eyes made him look worn and exhausted. His eyes lit up as he saw me, but the lady escorting him out of the room continued to guide him past me and toward the exit.

"Nate?" I stood up.

"I SAW HIM, JAY," he uttered--his eyes blood-red as he held back tears. "I saw it all… Josh and the girl. I'm sorry, Jay… I tried to stop them… I tried to stop them."

She kept him on his way as he tried to turn back to face me. Before I could stop them, I heard the stern voice of a man from inside of the room.

"Jay Amor?" the man asked, standing at the doorway with a clipboard in hand.

"That's me," I replied, looking up at him.

"I just need to ask you a few questions regarding last night."

I looked down at my parents, who didn't move, not even the slightest. As I slowly walked into the room, he shut the door behind me. We were in a room with concrete walls and a table in the center with two chairs on each side. There were no windows, and a fluorescent light shone from the ceiling--one similar to that of our garage. A cold sweat came over me as I sat down.

"I'm Detective Webber," he said as he laid out his notes on the table. He calmly pointed at his badge as if I'd question it in this setting. "My deepest condolences for your family's loss, Jay. I just want to ask you a few questions to confirm that this was a suicide and not a homicide of any sort. The sooner we finish, the sooner we can get you back with your family. Does that sound good to you?"

I shakily placed my hands on my lap, fingers laced in one another. I nodded.

"Did your parents give you consent to host a party while they were away in Vegas?"

"No," I answered nervously.

"Were you aware of the fact that an unregistered firearm was present in your garage?"

I suddenly flashed back to the week prior, when I thought Braden was somebody breaking into the garage.

I took the revolver out of the hollowed-out dictionary.

I pulled it on Braden in the garage.

I tossed it to Braden to keep Josh from seeing it.

I forgot to put it back after Braden hid it behind the guitar amplifier.

"*Don't worry, Josh, it's not loaded. See? All good*," Braden had said to Josh that night.

Did Josh think the revolver wasn't loaded when he pulled the trigger? If it was even him that pulled the trigger...??

"Were you aware of the fact that an unregistered firearm was present in your garage?" Webber asked once more.

"No," I answered, returning to the present moment.

"Were you aware of the narcotics and other illegal substances hidden behind the guitar amplifier?"

"No," I shook my head and paused. "Where's Braden?"

"Braden is currently remanded and will be brought in for

questioning some time after you. Are you aware of his involvement in selling drugs throughout L.A. County?"

"No."

Braden is being remanded? I thought to myself. *There's no way he doesn't get arrested for the bricks of cocaine he was keeping hidden in our garage. What's gonna happen to us? Josh's death, an unregistered gun, drugs, Braden being arrested… What else did they find*?

The detective wrote down the remainder of his notes and stared at me for a second. I couldn't see myself, but judging from the way his eyes were fixated on me, I most likely appeared to be a nervous wreck. I tried to keep my hands from shaking under the table. It was too easy for me to zone out of the conversation and picture seeing Josh last night. It already seemed like so long ago… And this room… It's too much like our garage. I need to leave. I need to leave now.

"Look, Jay…" Webber said, breaking the silence. "I have a witness account of the occurrence in the garage… From your friend, Nathan. I recorded everything he had to say about it. Claims to have been laying on the couch and watched the incident unravel. When we brought him in last night, he tested positive for a number of substances, which may result in his testimony losing its credibility, but... I have the recording here if you would like to hear it. Now you don't *have* to listen, but it may give you peace of mind, knowing your brother took his own life while under the influence and not as a result of actual suicidal ideation."

I remembered Nate talking about what happens to him when he takes the edibles Danny offered him--how the last time he took them, he wasn't able to move. I flashed back to seeing him make his way through the crowd to the couch in our garage, where he could lay low if the edible hit him too hard. This was just moments after I watched Josh go to talk to Rebecca. It was the happiest I had ever seen Josh, and I could have never imagined then and there… Those moments being his last. Nate really *must* have seen everything….

Webber calmly placed a small recording device on the table between the two of us.

"Play it," I said, leaning forward and firmly placing my elbows on the table. "I wanna hear…."

"I just want to warn you, Jay… Nathan was heavily under the influence when he gave us this statement last night. We tried bringing him in again this morning to clear things up further, but he was still shaken up a bit."

He pressed play, then skipped forward to a specific time, and I heard Nate's voice clear as day... As if he were standing in front of me... Although it was evident that he was still partially in shock.

"... And I couldn't find a jacket," Nate's voice recording began. *"I was freezing... But I found some blankets I buried myself in on the couch--so comfortable and quiet I--I just turned off all the lights and stared at the car. I couldn't move, bundled up in those blankets just staring at the car. It was so peaceful and nice and cozy.*

I must've been cuddled up there for hours--or minutes? Felt like HOURS... Me tucked away in the corner of the garage. My face felt fuzzy and my arms and legs got heavy so like, I just laid there enjoying the high.

After a few minutes or hours or whatever, that's when the lights turned on... And I saw the two of 'em--Josh and a blonde girl... Straight blonde hair. She had straight blonde hair and crazy eyes. She was stunning. She danced. They both danced together in the open space next to the car.

I didn't want them to know I was there, but I don't think it really even mattered cuz they didn't notice me. I was just like... Watching. I couldn't move, you know... Every 20 seconds her eyes were rolling back and she just kept dancing around the garage. It looked like Josh was trying to keep up cuz they were just on two different levels... I mean, like, she was definitely on some crazy drugs and Josh was definitely drunk but I don't know--something about her energy was off. I could see the colors around the garage, vibrant and full of life, but the colors that radiated around her were grim--gray.

I watched her twirl in circles with this crazy beautiful smile that was too beautiful to be entirely good and entirely real. That's when I realized what--no... WHO she was."

Pause

"She was Death. The Grim fucking Reaper. The devil. Temptation itself.

She laughed and twirled like luring him in, and Joshy followed. He was in a trance, lured by her beauty and laugh... That laugh. It was a giggle, but one of those giggles that echoed and didn't sound human to me. She wasn't human. It was like she was sent there to-to... Deceive... To ruin... To destroy. To take Josh away from us. She came to take him from us.

Her eyes rolled back again and she giggled and she lightly grazed Mr. Amor's car door with her fingers. She took Josh's hands and he twirled her, slowly and smoothly... You'd think they were in love and have been for a while or something.

Her forehead pressed against his and before he could kiss her, she gently pressed her finger on his lips and sat him back on the guitar amp. She sat on his lap and that's when the amp tipped over, and the bags and the gun fell out from under.

They both giggled, and then she looked down and realized she was lying on the bags of drugs… Her eyes lit up like a kid. Her jaw dropped and she picked up a bag.

That's when Josh tried to stop her... Leaning back against the garage door.

He couldn't keep his head up straight… He was too messed up from drinking probably. That's when she lifted a bag, bit her lip, and turned back to look at him.

She giggled and said something like, 'Do a little bit with me, Joshy.' She giggled and dragged her nail through the top of the bag, slicing it open. That's when she said… 'You've done coke before… I know you and your brothers have.'

Josh's head swayed, then he lifted his chin to stare at the ceiling and said Jay and Braden would kill him if he did any of that stuff… But she kept trying to persuade him--to tempt him. She did one line, then it was two, and then three. She started making these weird high-pitched moaning sounds… And she held up a powdered finger to Josh's nose.

She said... 'I want you…'
'To try it…'

Josh cracked. I watched him crack. I watched them do a couple lines, and she turned to look for more… I think. That's when she found it."

Pause

"*The gun…?*" I heard Webber's voice intervene in the recording.

Nate continued:

"*She picked it up with her pale, wiry fingers. Her eyes were black at that point… Jet-black. Like some sort of demon… Enticed at the sight of the gun. I watched her hold it with her open palms. It rested there in her hands, comfortably… That's when… That's when she turned to face Josh who was barely functioning at that point. He was shaking but trying to keep his cool in front of her... I could tell.*

She asked him… 'Are you a boy, Josh?' And then let out an eerie giggle--terrifying.

Josh asked what she meant, and she explained, turning to face him with the gun still in her open palms.

She said, 'Are you a sheltered boy…? Or are you a man?'

That's when Josh puffed out his chest and said he's a man...

Then she kept going... She said something like, 'Have you ever felt alive, sheltered boy?'

He said again... 'I told you, I'm a man.'

Josh was getting defensive.

She said, 'I don't think you've lived until you've flirted with death...'

I saw her look down at the gun and back up at Josh, then she said...

'Russian Roulette... Two shots. One for you and one for me.'

Josh then told her the revolver wasn't loaded, and she stood up and got real close to him.

That's when she said, 'I don't want to waste my time with a sheltered boy, Josh... I want to be with a man...' She wrapped her arms around him, the gun in her right hand, then said... 'If it's not loaded, then this shouldn't be a problem.'

Josh watched as she cocked the gun, pressed it to her own head, closed her eyes, and pulled the trigger. It just clicked and nothing came out....

I couldn't move, Officer Webber... I couldn't move and I couldn't look away."

Pause

"*That's when she handed Josh the gun and put each of her hands on the sides of his face.*

'Become a man,' she playfully whispered all seductively... She said, 'I'll be the first to greet you on the other side.'

Josh cocked the gun."

Pause

"*I watched him smile back at her...*
He pressed the gun to his head...
And he pulled the trigger....

I watched his body fall and hit the ground as she didn't even flinch. She didn't move--Josh's blood painted the side of her face. Her jaw dropped, and she let out a high-pitched squeal followed by a giggle. Then I watched her... Continue dancing.

She danced.
Josh's body hit the floor.

She still danced.

Josh shot himself point-blank in front of her.

She just danced.

Josh DIED.

And she fucking DANCED.

She grabbed the bag of cocaine she opened and danced her way out the door.

That's when I was so overcome with fear and adrenaline and shock and everything. I barely made it to my feet to get somebody to help.

She was no ordinary girl, Officer... She's a demon. She's a-...."

I quickly jammed my finger into the "stop" button on the recording device, cutting off Nate's sentence. Every part of me was shaking. I couldn't think properly, and I realized I was sweating but also shivering. I didn't know what to think, and I pictured Nate's description of the incident vividly as if I was there. That's when it hit me all at once.

I brought the gun to the garage.

Braden put the gun behind the amplifier with the drugs.

I let Josh get too drunk.

I let Josh leave my sight.

Josh found the drugs and the gun.

We killed Josh.

WE KILLED JOSH.

"The girl was there..." I said aloud as my vision remained fixated on the recording device. "I saw them dancing in the house. Ask anybody. She was *there*."

"Nathan is the only witness account we have that claims Josh was in the garage with somebody else," Webber flipped through his papers. "And based on the autopsy and what we found back at the house, everything points toward the wound being self-inflicted... His prints on the gun... On the bags... No witness accounts of any girl in there with him besides Nathan's, whose testimony is void due to his level of intoxication during the occurrence."

What he said instantly didn't sit right with me. Josh is--was--the purest and most innocent soul I had ever known. For his death to be forever documented as a suicide was not a testament to who he truly was. My stomach turned, and I suddenly felt sick. I felt terrible--as though everything that happened last night was being tattooed onto a massive portion of my body... To be forever a part of me.

The death of our beloved brother has tainted the very essence of who I am.

Irreversible.

Eternal.

Real.

I felt the thought set in and make itself at home.

I knew in my heart that Josh didn't take his own life. I knew that he was my responsibility, and I let his life slip between my fingers, whether the girl was actually there or not.

Was I to blame for moving the revolver into the garage where Josh found it? Was Braden to blame for bringing the drugs into our home that would fuel Josh's drive to pull the trigger?

A dark thought crossed my mind. If Josh was heavily under the influence when he took his own life, he wasn't in his right mind--he wasn't in *control*. What drove him to pull the trigger if he would have never done it while in his *right* mind? If Josh wasn't himself, who was he?

I remember seeing the girl dancing the way Nate had described in the recording.

A demon, the recording echoed in my mind. *She wasn't human. Was she even real?*

Josh's death wasn't self-inflicted--it wasn't suicide. I wanted to believe then and there that his death was caused by temptation itself--his body acting as a hollow vessel controlled by the devil--his mind consumed by substances that impaired his moral compass.

"*I only did it cuz I was drunk*," people say. "*I wasn't in my right mind.*"

If you aren't in your right mind, who is?

Webber's deep voice derailed my train of thought.

"I'll be speaking to your brother in a few minutes," he said as he looked up from his watch. "Thank you for taking the time, Jay."

"Braden's here??" I asked.

He stood and headed for the door. I slowly got up and followed.

"He should be walking up," he opened the door and peeked down the hall. "There he is now."

I stepped out of the room, and to my left, I saw Braden walking toward us from down the long narrow hallway. It was as if he was walking in slow motion, hands zip-tied behind his back as he was being escorted by two police officers. He was wearing the same outfit he had worn last night--his hair messily parted down the middle as it hung over the sides of his face. He walked slowly, staring at the floor. He looked *destroyed*... From the inside-out.

My parents, who still sat in the two chairs outside the room, slowly turned to look at Braden. My mother quickly looked back down at the floor. She continued to pray and shake her head, still in disbelief. My father rolled up one of his sleeves.

Braden gradually got closer and closer without lifting his head. My father slowly stood to his feet, rolling up the other sleeve now. He stood between Braden and me. Nobody said a word until Braden stopped about a foot away from my father, still not looking up from the floor. The two officers stopped in their tracks beside Braden, sensing the tension behind the father-son confrontation. The only sound echoing in the hallway was my mother's whispering of frantic prayers. The rest was silence.

I watched my father slowly and softly lift Braden's chin so that they were face to face. Braden's gaze was empty, full of sorrow and dismay. Never in my life had I seen him so defeated. He didn't shake. He didn't say anything. He just blankly stared into our father's eyes. A tear fell from Braden's eye without him moving a single muscle in his face.

As if in one swift motion, my father's right fist made its way straight into Braden's gut, bringing Braden's face forward into a second punch across his cheek. Braden fell into one of the officer's arms. Webber and the officers quickly pulled my father back as Braden fell to his knees, struggling to find the breath he lost. He gasped for air.

"YOU FAILURE. YOU PATHETIC FUCKING FAILURE," my father screamed as an officer and Webber struggled to pin him to the ground, pulling out handcuffs. Alternating from Spanish to English slurs, he continued... "YOU RUINED THIS FAMILY. YOU KILLED MY SON. YOU RUINED US."

I froze. My mother prayed louder and louder, continuing to shake her head faster and faster in an attempt to block out the noise. I couldn't get myself to move. I didn't know who to help or if this were even the time to help at all. Braden was on the floor facing the wall in a fetal position, bleeding from the mouth and still struggling to breathe.

It was at that exact moment, I realized my father was right.

We ruined this family.

We killed Josh.

We ruined "*us*."

It was at that exact moment, I realized life would *never* be the same.

FOUR | I LEFT MY HEART IN L.A.

7 YEARS LATER.

MY APARTMENT
UPPER EAST SIDE MANHATTAN, NEW YORK
SATURDAY, 7:41P.M. - APRIL 27TH, 2019

I stepped onto the marble bathroom floor--the steam from the shower coating me in warmth as I wrapped my waist in a white towel. Running my fingers back through my damp hair, I felt it rest just above my shoulders. Music echoed throughout my apartment--the sound bouncing off the marble floors and white walls, encompassing me from all angles. I slid the bathroom door open and made my way into the living room that extended into the kitchen. The lighting was dimmed, which is how I usually like it. It was my very own place, and every minor detail was adjusted specifically to my liking.

I walked across the living room to the glass windows that stretched from the ceiling to the floor, serving as my usual afternoon post-shower routine. I clenched the edges of the towel while looking over Central Park as the street lights began turning on. Sunset had officially turned to dusk. I have mixed feelings about this time of day. To me, dusk is the most beautiful, but it means the coming of night... And now the night makes me uneasy.

I let out a long sigh, stretched, and headed to my bedroom where my clothes were laid out for the night--all black... Always. I slipped my black slacks on over my black briefs, threw on a black designer shirt, grabbed my favorite black coat, and reached for my phone.

4 new emails, I read on the screen.

I slipped the phone into my pocket. It's Saturday night, and I don't care for business right now, though business has been treating me well since I graduated from N.Y.U. a little over a year ago. I love my work, don't get me wrong... I even like to think it saved my life.

My four years at N.Y.U. had flown by just as my mother warned me back in high school, but that's a given... As time flies when you're having fun, right? My concept of fun changed after Josh died--*a lot* had changed.

Braden faced a narcotics charge for the drugs found in the garage the night of Josh's death. After weeks of questioning and bringing in witnesses, it was evident that what they found in the garage was to be sold by him--leading to a *4-year state prison sentence*. That bad track record finally caught up.

My father was charged with second-degree murder and child cruelty, not to mention unlawfully possessing a firearm--the firearm that killed Josh. To word it in simpler terms, we couldn't afford a good lawyer.

Losing Josh, Braden, *and* my father all within six months left my mother a hysterical wreck, locking herself in our home back in Torrance. She slept in Josh's bed every night, right next to mine. I didn't recognize her after Josh died, with the numerous prescription pills she gradually became addicted to. Our roles flipped regarding who took care of who, as I picked up cooking and doing everything around the house while she just coasted through life on autopilot.

"Sure," she'd shrug in response to just about everything. "Okay."

It was just the two of us at that point, and I was thoroughly convinced that I would have to cut N.Y.U. out of the picture so I could take care of my mother full-time... Until one night, she completely lost it. I'll never forget this night... Considering it was the mental state one should never see their mother in. I remember it vividly--as if I'm still there.

~ *"TAKE ME," my mother screamed, breaking the silence of the night. "TAKE ME."*

My eyes opened abruptly as I immediately sat up, turning to see my mother rolling around in Josh's bed.

"TAKE ME INSTEAD. DON'T TAKE MY BABY, TAKE ME."

Her screams cracked and pierced through my eardrums, and she didn't stop, begging God-knows-what to take her.

"MOM!" I attempted to shout over her screaming. "MA, WAKE UP."

She fell off the bed and grabbed her knees, crying for Josh and gasping for air. I realized her eyes were open, and she was wide awake, or at least I thought she was. I reached for her, and she clawed at me, yelling for me to stay away.

"BACK. AWAY FROM HIM. STAY AWAY FROM HIM. DON'T TAKE MY BABY." ~

I couldn't help but cry back when it happened because I realized I had lost her--my own mother... Gone for good. The woman I looked up to. Every drop of sanity had evaporated, leaving her with a traumatized and shattered shell of a person. This was no way for her to live.

On the one occasion I caught her sober, she made me promise her I wouldn't pass up on N.Y.U. That's when we came to the agreement that I would attend N.Y.U. that fall if *she* got professional help… So off she went, as did I… And now, here I am seven years later in the Upper East Side of Manhattan.

I poured myself a glass of Patrón and downed it before I headed downstairs to call for a taxi. I slid into the back seat.

"To Ace, please," I instructed the driver.

We passed young men and women dressed to impress. They were catching cabs or anxiously waiting out in the cold to get into the restaurants, bars, and clubs that were filling up quickly. We were in the *heart* of nightlife.

"Are you meeting up with some friends at Ace?" the driver asked, breaking the silence. "I hear that spot is a great time."

"Yessir," I lied while continuing my fixation on the crowds that filled the busy sidewalk.

My wallet was warm as I pulled it out from my back pocket. Opening it slowly, I looked at the polaroid photo of Braden, Josh, and myself… The photo Cole had taken seven years ago on the night of the party. It went everywhere with me, considering it was the only piece of my past life I took with me as I created my new life here. I used to look at it every day, but as the years went on, I looked at it less and less.

I suddenly snapped out of my trance and realized we were passing Times Square. I swiftly moved from the right seat to the left, completely averting my eyes from the massive billboard that overwhelmed me every time I passed it.

It was a digital Louis Vuitton billboard that lit up half of Times Square--partially because of the lighting, but more so because of the eyes. I knew the eyes on that massive billboard--those *amber* eyes. They belonged to Val.

Whenever I passed through Times Square, I made sure to sit on the opposite side of her billboard. Each time I saw it, it took me back to a place I spent the last seven years struggling to bury.

She had done it. She became the renowned model she set out to be, and I'm happy for her… Truly. If anyone deserves the recognition, it's Val.

She knocked on our door every day for months after the night Josh passed. The knocks turned into phone calls... Then phone calls to texts. The texts went from 10 times per day to 5 times per day… Then 1 per day… 1 per week… 1 per month… Every effort she made I dismissed as if she didn't exist to me anymore.

I'm assuming things are going well for her, considering there are tons of men and women who move to L.A., and most of them will go their entire career without landing a billboard in Times Square. She managed to make it happen in a couple of years. I'm proud of her for it.

I'm sure she didn't take my withdrawal from her personally because I basically did it to everybody--deleting all digital traces of me on social media and all that. My teachers let me finish senior year online, and I didn't see Danny, Cole, Nate, or Val ever again. Just thinking about them or anything that had to do with that party made me sick to my stomach, so I settled for what I felt when I *wasn't* feeling sick... And that's *numb*.

I wanted nothing to do with the life I had on the West Coast or with the people in it. So I reinvented myself out here, and I did the best I could to convince myself that this was *it*.

I'm successful.
I graduated from a prestigious university.
I landed a great job making great money.
I moved into my own place in a nice part of Manhattan.
I'm out on my own in a city filled with opportunity.
I'm successful.
I'm successful.
I'm successful.

That's what I say when I feel myself slipping back into what once *was*.

And now here I am... By myself in the back of a cab heading to a club *just* to people-watch.

Over the past seven years, I've developed an obsession with nightlife, and I spend every night going to a different club or bar to people-watch. I watch how every club operates and the way people interact with one another. Each individual with their own unique story overlapping and intertwining with another--those stories unraveling, some for the better and some for the worse.

I didn't want to admit it, but diving into other people's stories seems to keep me going. I no longer wanted to be a part of my own story... Because I *hate* my story. I hate what it's come to, and to me, it's not one worth reading about. I can hardly live it.

I'm one in eight billion, and I like it that way.
Keep me in the background.

"Here we are... Enjoy your night, buddy," the driver said.

"You as well," I snapped back with an energetic flare as I paid and stepped out, only to never see the man ever again.

The line to get into Ace was just starting to fill up, but it meant nothing to me as I walked straight up to the bouncer, flashed a cunning smirk, and slipped him two hundred in cash. He opened the stanchion, letting me in as people crowded around the front of the venue looked over their shoulders to see if I was anybody worth paying attention to.

The sounds of traffic congestion and footsteps against the pavement transitioned into empty conversations--each conversation competing with the overwhelmingly loud hip-hop music that filled the venue. With every step I took, I became one with the music as the narrow hallway opened up into a large room with high ceilings. Lights flashed and danced over faces, walls, and everything they could reach--red, blue, green, purple. Women danced in drapes above the crowd, hanging from the ceiling.

"Double-shot of tequila on ice, please!" I shouted over the counter to the bartender.

He acknowledged me and reached for a glass. I tapped my card against the bar top, taking in the atmosphere around me.

Braden would love this place, I thought, turning to make eye contact with the girl next to me.

The sight of her surprised me, considering how beautiful she was. She was giving me an amount of attention I certainly didn't deserve. A girl like her doesn't come out alone, but she *was* alone for some reason.

"How's it goin'?" I asked with a subtle smirk.

"I'll be better after you buy me a drink."

She bit her lip and smiled. She could've easily been a model, actress, or *something* of the kind. I turned back to the bartender, who was just now putting my drink down.

"One more, please... A tequila soda with extra lime," I said while handing him my card. "You can keep the tab open."

I gripped my drink, turning back to the girl who was now signalling for her two friends to join us from a distance. From the corner of my eye, I watched the two girls ditch the guy they were with on the other side of the bar. I began to process the fact that these girls were most likely in pursuit of getting free drinks, considering they had moved from one single guy to another--now me--and I certainly wasn't drunk enough to get myself around to running up a tab. At least, not yet.

The bartender put the second drink on the table next to the first drink I had ordered.

"Can my friends get some, too?" the girl asked while caressing my shoulder.

I watched the guy across the bar turn back to see the two girls missing, who were now making their way over to me.

"Some of what?" I asked, sipping my drink. "Your delivery needs a bit more work."

"Delivery?" she tilted her head in confusion, so I continued.

"I guess there's nothing wrong with *wanting* somebody to buy you a drink, but typically the drink ties into a potential conversation, right? In this scenario, *you're* the one asking *me* to buy *you* the drink... And right away, you revealed what you're after... Leading me to believe that you only approached me because you saw that... *One*, I came alone, and *two*, I had just put my card down."

Her jaw dropped instantly, but she didn't move, so I continued with my analysis.

"You're extremely beautiful," I continued with a smile. "Breathtaking, really... But to me, it seems like... Your two friends who are making their way over here right now are on their way only because I made it look like I was gonna be the guy you mooch off of tonight. Trust me, I want to be wrong... I really do... But if they approach me right now and bring up me buying drinks without *any* desire to know my name or who I am, I'm just gonna assume that everything I said is right."

I felt a hand on my shoulder, and I turned to make eye contact with the two girls. I smiled.

"Hey!" I said with a cheeky grin.

"Are you buyin' shots?!" one of the girls cheerfully asked as the other sloppily felt up my arm.

"Oh...!" I exclaimed. "Shots?!"

I couldn't help but smile and look back at the original girl who approached me. She was now looking down at the floor, embarrassed. To my surprise, the bartender had been watching the entire situation unravel from just a few feet away. I felt bad.

"Alright, alright," I rolled my eyes, turning to face the bartender. "Four shots of Patrón, and I'll close out after that, please."

He nodded and poured the shots. The girl gave me a smile, but this time I could tell her smile was genuine and not some tactic used to get drinks bought for her.

"There she is," I laughed, distributing the shots to the three girls--two of them still not knowing what just happened. "Here's to new friends!"

We took the shots, I signed the bill, then turned to walk away, and that's when I felt a hand hold me back.

"Where are you going?" the girl asked with a snarky look I actually found rather cute.

"I'm gonna move to the other side of the club for a bit, but in exactly an hour, I'll be heading out of *that* front door," I lifted my glass in the direction of the club entrance. "If you *sincerely* want to get to know me, that's where I'll be in an hour."

She released me from her grip to check the time on her phone, which read *11:46PM,* and I used that as my cue to slip away into the crowd. Lights continued to dance with the swarm of people occupying the dance floor and pathways that security struggled to keep clear.

I swiftly navigated my way into the elevated V.I.P. section with a big group headed to their table. As the group reached their table, I introduced myself to a guy sitting on the booth next to ours, who was part of a completely separate group.

"What's up, man?" I greeted him sternly over the blaring music. "My group just got here... If you find yourselves running low on alcohol, feel free to join us and take some of ours."

"I appreciate that, brother!" he smiled and clinked his glass against mine sloppily. He was hammered, and it dawned on me that it was going to be much easier than I thought to join their party.

I turned back to the group I had followed into the V.I.P. section. I tapped on one of the guys' shoulders and held up my glass with one hand while respectfully placing the other over my heart.

"What's up, man?" I greeted him sternly over the blaring music. "My group has been here for a bit. If you find yourselves running low on alcohol, feel free to join us and take some of ours."

"My guy!" he patted my shoulder and nodded his head. "You're the homie."

Once I had my *ins* with the two groups, I leaned against the railing and looked over the sea of bouncing heads. It's pretty amazing--the things you can accomplish by keeping your chin up and portraying confidence through showing respect. I wouldn't say my ability to read people was the *God-given gift* my mother would refer to it as, but rather a resource to be tapped into and utilized.

I took a deep breath, taking in my surroundings. Lights hung at different heights just above us, giving the venue a sort of *depth* as the ceiling stretched high above our heads. It was cold but comforting, considering no one was indirectly threatening to sweat all over the clothes I set aside specifically for the night. And there was this... *Scent*... A fragrance that seemed oddly familiar, but I couldn't pinpoint where I recognized it from... Either way, it didn't get old. I *loved* it.

I sipped my drink and witnessed a young couple to my left... Let's call the man "Nick," and we'll call the woman "Jamie." Nick had his hands on Jamie's hips as they danced, overlooking the dance floor the same way I was. He was pressed against her back, moving to the rhythm--or at least *trying* to move to the rhythm.

I sipped my drink.

I studied his look--the gold $40,000 Rolex clashing with the sterling silver chain that hung over his black T-shirt. His blue jeans were *very* tight, and his shoes basically screamed, "GUCCI," with the red and green stripes along the sides. He's *definitely* got money, or at least he's pretending he's got money--most likely in his early or mid-thirties.

Jamie looked super young... At *most* 25 years old. She wore a skin-tight dress that was far too revealing for a cold winter night like tonight. She didn't seem too interested in Nick as her eyes hovered over the crowd. As they danced, Nick was engaged in conversation with his friend, who stood a few feet away, completely oblivious to Jamie staring down a guy just a couple rows into the crowd below. The guy returned the gaze with equal intensity.

The appearances of the two led me to believe that Nick pursued Jamie for her looks, and Jamie pursued Nick for money... But who am I to judge based on appearance?

If my thoughts right now were to be logged in some sort of journal or book for somebody to read, the reader would probably think I'm sort of an asshole for making my assumptions... But is it really that wrong if I'm just *thinking* this, though? We're all entitled to our own opinions and thoughts. Wow, I'm starting to feel burzz--I mean buzzed... Okay, alright, fine... I'll judge by action... Not looks.

I sipped my drink.

Jamie threw her hands up, swaying them to the rhythm of the music. Her gaze didn't break the gaze of the man on the dance floor. I watched as he was now essentially dancing with her from a distance. Her open palms closed as she pointed at the ceiling and then toward the outer part of the venue, still keeping her rhythm as if to keep Nick from becoming suspicious. The stranger's hands pointed in the same direction as he grinned and began maneuvering his way to the indicated spot.

I checked the time.
12:18AM.

Jamie turned to Nick and whispered something into his ear. He smiled and nodded. She kissed him on the cheek and made her way out of the V.I.P. section. Nick continued talking to his friend, completely oblivious that his girlfriend was meeting up with some other guy.

Should I tell him? I thought to myself.

I looked down at my drink, which was half-empty.

"You choose," I whispered to the drink as I finished what was left of it.

I paused.

I shrugged.

"Okay, okay… I'll tell him…."

I headed in the direction of his booth. As I got closer, I stood at a respectful distance to politely let them finish their conversation. Nick saw me in his peripheral view, and I could see him slowing his conversation to a stop.

"Hey, man," I said. "I think you should know-...."

"I'M HAVING A CONVERSATION," he snapped, then scanned me from head to toe. "Ah, perfect, actually. We'll do another bottle of Grey Goose. Bring that shit out faster than the last one… I'd hate to tell your manager you're a *shit* waiter."

He forced a dollar into my hand. My jaw dropped.

This guy thinks I'm his waiter?? I thought.

I bit my lip, squinted my eyes, took a deep breath, and relaxed my shoulders.

"You got it," I replied with hollow enthusiasm.

I continued on my way. The sign could not have been more evident that Nick was to be cheated on tonight and most likely any other night. Everything happens for a reason, right? Probably.

I clenched the dollar he had given me and... Upon looking down, I realized it was a *hundred*-dollar bill, not just a dollar bill. Thanks, Nick.

As I took my time walking through the remainder of the V.I.P. section, I noticed a staff member scrubbing a table that had just been abandoned by a group. The group had left a *huge* mess. I subtly patted him on the back as I passed and slipped the hundred-dollar bill onto the table in front of him. His eyes widened as he looked up.

"Thanks again!" I shouted as if I was a part of the previous group he was cleaning after.

I checked the time.

12:40AM.

If the girl by the bar was anyone worth spending the rest of the night with, she was going to be by the entrance where I told her I'd meet her. Usually, my one-night stands panned out similarly to how it's panning out now, so I wouldn't be surprised if she was *actually* waiting… But then again, I wouldn't really care if I didn't see her. Being as numb as I've become has taken away my ability to love or really even care at all. It's also blessed me with never feeling the weight of rejection or any other negative emotion.

I strutted out of the club entrance, and a cold breeze made me appreciate my coat as I tightened it around me. The honking horns and distant sirens replaced the mainstream hip-hop now muffled by the closed venue doors.

I looked right to see the line, which had died down a bit. I've always loved how people dress in New York. I find myself constantly making sure my fits are perfect and that each layer complements the next. It seemed like back in Southern California, I'd be judged for dressing up as nice as I do here in the city. I couldn't imagine what my parents or Braden would say about my appearance... Josh too... I could picture him making fun of the different suits I went out in all the time.

"Wow, for a second, I didn't think you were gonna show," a soothing female voice stated from behind me.

I turned to face the girl I had met an hour ago at the bar. The street lights reflected off of her diamond-studded earrings as she smiled. I smiled back.

"How could I not?" I replied. "You hungry?"

It was a stupid question. She seemed far too fit to indulge in late-night binging like I do... But considering how hungry I am, if the night is gonna keep moving with us still together, I need pizza.

"I'm still full from dinner!" she politely declined. "But I'll come with you...."

I smiled and extended my hand, which she grabbed almost instantly. I flagged down a taxi, and we were on our way back up Manhattan. With her lips pressed on my neck and her hands halfway down my pants, I kept an eye out for a decent pizzeria--one of those hole-in-the-wall pizzerias... The hole-in-the-walls are almost *always* the real deal.

"Stop here!" I shouted.

The driver pulled up beside the sidewalk, and I slipped him a 50 to wait and keep an eye on my new friend. Within five minutes, I was back in the taxi with an entire pizza, and her hand was right back in my pants.

We drove through Times Square, and this time it was a whole lot easier to dodge Val's billboard, thanks to my distraction. We sloppily made our way through the lobby, laughing and kissing as we rose above each floor until we were at mine, but even then... We couldn't make it to the room before the layers fell to the floor.

I tossed the box of pizza down against the marble and lifted my distraction onto the kitchen counter. Over an hour passed, which felt like less than half the time--and an amazing time it was.

When we were done, I lowered the music to match the mellow ambiance that followed the chaos which took place in my room and also a bit in the kitchen... *And* the living room.

Wearing nothing but my Calvins, I placed the box of pizza on the kitchen counter and continued eating. There's something about eating New York pizza past midnight that just hits *different*. I mean, there's something about eating New York pizza, period.

The sound of light footsteps came from the living room, and I turned back to see the girl I had just met in nothing but one of my button-ups.

"Hi," she greeted with a smile, wrapping her arms around my waist from behind.

She smelled amazing--looked amazing, too. Her dark wavy hair fell past her shoulders–her eyes a deep brown. She kissed the top of my back with her full lips, sending chills from my neck down to my feet. She *still* didn't ask for my name, and she didn't care that I didn't ask for hers--one of the perks of city life, I guess. Too many strangers for there to be drama.

This is how it's been. This is how it *is*. Out here, I was and am whoever I *want* to be. I make my money doing what I want and spend it the way I want. I'm in complete control of my own world, and people can come and go as they please… Given they don't move anything while they're passing through.

The days continued similarly, as I worked by day and people-watched by night, watching the way different clubs operate and how people adapted and responded to those operations. I was coasting through life, sleeping like a baby and enjoying drinks here and there… Enjoying being *me*… *Alone*.

Seven years of this, and I wasn't gonna get tired of it any time soon. I'm my own family now, and I have no desire to let anybody in or *back* in because I can't lose somebody I don't have. I'm kind of like a family of one… *A family of one*.

Some time had passed, and I heard nothing from the Ace girl--no numbers exchanged, no social media… Nothing. I didn't think too much of it, considering work had me busier than usual.

"Hey, Jay," called one of my co-workers from behind my cubicle. "Some of us are goin' out for drinks at Harry's. You want in??"

I rotated in my chair to face him.

"Sorry, man, I-... I've got plans…."

"You mean sittin' around Washington Square Park?"

My jaw dropped. "I… How did you--how did you know I go to...?"

"Someone from accounting said they've seen you around there a lot the past few months, by yourself. Come on, Jay… Come with us! They do this thing called the 'boob luge…' It's totally hot and gets you drunk *quick*."

"I appreciate the invite," I laughed. "Maybe later this week, I'd be down."

"Suit yourself," he said with a nod--then he was on his way.

I looked down at my lap, processing what had just happened. It made me feel a bit uneasy that people probably think I'm weird for spending my afternoons sitting around a park, people-watching... But I was over it in a few seconds. I finished a few emails and made my way to Washington Square Park.

There wasn't a cloud in the sky, but the chilling breeze made my eyes water as I found a seat in my usual spot. It was a cafe-style table with two chairs, and I claimed one, per usual. I set my laptop on the table, stuffed my earphones into my ears, and *watched.*

Families both big and small.

Couples flirting and couples fighting.

Homeless people shouting at pedestrians and at each other.

Thousands and thousands of stories playing out right in front of me.

I dissected each individual's scenario based on what I could see. I pieced together jewelry with hairstyles and clothing--mannerisms and conversations alike--just observing... Creating my own reality the way I wanted.

Not too far from me, I saw a young woman painting peacefully next to a tree. We'll call her "Sabrina." Sabrina's back was to me, and her sweatshirt was purple, leading me to believe that the front of it said N.Y.U. because purple is the school's primary color... Just a guess. She was in the art program, or art's a hobby for her... Just stating the obvious... But the complexity of the painting *screams* "art major." There's no way she does it just for fun.

About 30 yards to her left, a man stood with his three kids... All most likely under the age of nine. Let's call him "Francis." Francis had a camera wrapped around his neck, taking pictures of his kids in front of things most New York locals didn't find appealing at all. They had to be from out of town. I couldn't help but notice a date tattooed in roman numerals on his forearm. He also had a tattoo of a ring on his ring finger, but a family as happy as they were, traveling without the mother? I had a strong feeling the kids' mother might've passed, and Francis wasn't ready to let go... Hence the tattoos. He took a few pictures, then turned his head, most likely to find someone to take a photo of the four of them. I stood and quickly walked up to Francis and his three kids, offering to take the picture.

"I appreciate this more than you know," he replied with a genuine smile.

"My pleasure."

The four of them huddled together and smiled as I snapped a bunch of photos, so they had plenty to choose from.

"How're those?" I asked, handing Francis his camera.

"Amazing!" he said while scrolling through, then he took a deep breath. "My wife would've *loved* this place. God bless you, young man. Thank you."

I smiled, waved to his kids, and made my way back to my chair, assuming my position.

In the distance, I saw a man standing about six feet tall. We'll call him… Braden. The way he walked resembled Braden's walk, but this guy had short hair and a decent amount of scruff on his face. Still, he weirdly resembled Braden, from what I remember. It was obvious he wasn't from around here, given his eyes were squinted almost shut as he tried to keep them from watering. He wasn't used to the cold.

Braden wandered around the park, most likely looking for somebody in specific. He walked through the crowd, turning his head at each individual who could possibly be the person he seemed to be looking for. Something deep down had me inclined to believe there was something important he was going to share with this person… Judging from the focused look on his face and the urgency behind his search.

He shuffled through the crowd in my direction, getting closer and closer. The closer the man got, the more he began to *look* like Braden. He had similar eyes, but he was more muscular than Braden might ever be--I mean, I wouldn't know, considering the last I saw him, he was skinny, tatted, and had hair down to his shoulders.

We made eye contact, and I quickly looked away, playing it off like I wasn't completely dissecting this random individual. I scanned the park to find someone else to watch. I saw the man continue getting closer and closer in my peripherals until he was standing still, just ten yards away.

I didn't wanna look. The amount of times I've been caught staring and it's led to confrontations is just *too* many times at this point. Should I get up and leave? Maybe. What if he's armed? Did I *really* upset this guy *that* much by staring? Did I….

"Jay…" the man said, and immediately I became lightheaded at the familiarity of his voice.

"Jay."

I know that voice. I've heard that voice. I've grown up with that voice. My eyes began to water, but this time it wasn't from the cold. They were tears--none of sadness, but also none of joy--tears of shock? I can't explain it.

I looked up at the man, and to my surprise, it was actually him. It was *Braden*.

He lifted his hand and pointed at the empty chair across from me. I nodded. He sat. I didn't know whether to continue staring or say something, but then again, I didn't know *what* to even say. Should I even say anything at all?

You would've thought the scruffy and well-dressed Braden sitting before me would bear *no relation* to the nappy-haired, skinny Braden I last saw seven years ago--but I could see it.

He looked across the park as he reached deep into a pocket stitched into the inner layer of his peacoat. Pulling out two cigarettes, he offered one in my direction as he placed one between his lips.

"I had to stop a while ago," I declined softly.

He nodded, placing the cigarette back in the pack before lighting his.

"When'd you start?" he asked as he exhaled a cloud of smoke.

"When I first came out here," I replied. "I became a little too reliant on 'em."

Braden looked back out across the park as he took another drag.

"Eh, we've all got different ways of coping…" he exhaled.

"How'd you find me?" I asked with my hands jammed in my pockets.

"I'm out here for work and thought I'd stop by your office. All I had to do was google your name, and your company profile came up with the address, you know. I stopped by about an hour ago, and one of your colleagues told me I could probably find you here."

I lowered my head, then looked back out across the park. It was almost difficult for me to look at him, and I could tell he found it difficult to look at me, too. A lot can and *did* happen in seven years, and while I had my ups and downs, I could tell Braden had his fair share as well--I could hear it in his voice.

"It's cold as shit…" he uttered. "Can we talk somewhere warm?"

"Yeah, I know a spot right down the street."

We got up and made our way to a hole-in-the-wall cafe I passed from time to time but never went into until now. Just before entering, Braden flicked his cigarette, and once we were inside, he made himself comfortable by the window. Immediately making myself known to the barista, I held up the number two and then pointed back at the table.

"Two coffees, please," I mouthed politely.

I sat down to Braden taking off his coat, dethawing his fingers with a smile on his face. Now able to see him face to face, I noticed his pupils were extremely dilated and his eyes a bit red--the same way they looked when he'd come home from a late night out. Was he high? Now?? I mean, overall, he looked better--healthier--but how much healthier was he on the inside?

"I don't know how you do it," he laughed. "It gets even colder than *this*??"

"This is *warm* in New York," I replied with a grin. "You get used to it after a while...."

The waitress placed two coffee cups on the table between us and began to pour. I could see Braden staring at me between her torso and her arm, slowly nodding his head while smiling cheek to cheek. She finished her pour, and he leaned forward.

"You look good!" he stated playfully. "The long hair suits you better than it did me back in the day."

"Thanks," I replied. "I barely recognized you with the clean cut you've got goin' on. You filled in."

"Comes with the scene!" he sipped his coffee. "When it's sunny and 72 degrees year-round, you don't have a choice but to stay in shape."

"You're still in California?" I asked.

"Yeah, downtown L.A. It's a pretty nice spot," he nodded. "So you're in the nightlife business, too... Huh?"

Braden pressed his elbows against the top of the table. From just under his sleeve, I couldn't help but notice the diamond-studded Rolex on his wrist. He could tell I noticed, immediately sliding both arms under the table.

"Ssoorrtt of..." I practically mumbled. "I'm on the design side, so I'm not on the floor as much. More so designing nightlife venues from the office--you know... Nightclubs, bars, restaurants."

"Ah, floor plans and all that, yeah? I figured by the looks of your office that you're probably making good money but don't leave that cubicle too much," Braden said with a skeptical squint. He smirked.

"It's great pay," I confessed.

"But not your own nightclub..." he snapped playfully.

I nodded, looking down at the coffee between my fingertips. I could feel memories rising from the deep. The good and the bad... But I wasn't ready to reminisce about the dreams we shared that came with the detours and shortcomings. I'm no longer the same person I was when I saw him last--I didn't even *want* to be. As Braden read the disheartened look on my face, his smile faded.

"I'm in the business too," he added in an attempt to keep me present. "I've got a mentor... Jay, you've gotta meet this guy... He's got clubs *everywhere*... He's really good at reading people... Like *really* good... Gifted like you."

"What's his name?" I asked, assuming Braden was bluffing.

"Santi," he stated, well-knowing I knew the name.

"Santi?? Like the same Santi-...."

"Yep," he smirked. "I'm sure you've seen his name around the office."

"Yeah, no, *yeah*..." I stuttered in shock. "He's one of the biggest names in hospitality... He started *Lagneia-*...."

"*Lagneia Hospitality Group*," Braden emphasized. "He founded and owns it... He's got his hands tied in a bunch of ventures, but yeah, his nightlife venues are his claim to fame, for sure."

I couldn't help but smile at the thought of Braden working directly for one of the biggest names in the nightlife business. It was funny, considering his teenage track record dealing on the streets and partaking in all things "trouble." But here he is, far closer to reaching our dream than I ever fathomed between the two of us, combined. Sensing that he had gotten my attention, he placed his elbows back on the table, revealing his Rolex again, but with no shame this time.

"Jay, it's possible..." he whispered. "I'm doing it. I'm literally throwing parties for a living, and it's a pretty *decent* living."

I nodded, biting my lip as I took it all in.

"I'm happy for you," I professed.

"Don't be happy for me..." Braden leaned closer, and I could smell the liquor on his breath. "Come *work* with me."

"Work with you? In L.A.?" I asked, genuinely confused--was it an invitation or a job offer?

"Work with me... In L.A...." he repeated with his eyebrows raised. "'*The Amor Brothers'* back together throwing parties, but like... *Professional* parties--the real deal--what we've always wanted to do!"

His voice raised out of excitement, and I noticed heads starting to turn all around the cafe. His excitement radiated, and I couldn't help but smile at the thought... The thought of getting paid to host and throw parties in L.A. and the rest of the country. The thought of possibly being reunited with my family. I was immediately brought back to the last time I saw our parents.

"How're Mom and Dad?" I asked.

My question caught Braden off guard. His smile faded once again, and he stared at the table between us, then out the window, remaining silent. I asked again.

"How are they?"

He twiddled his fingers, looking everywhere but into my eyes, but I didn't break. Instead, I patiently waited for him to answer.

"They're, uh-..." his lip quivered, then he took a deep breath and exhaled. "There's no easy way to say this... There's--they...."

He paused, and my mind spun out into a million different directions as I processed what he was about to say. Whatever it is, it's anything but *good*. His eyes began to tear up as his fingertips tapped against the wooden table top. As much as I didn't want him to tell me something I didn't want to hear, I knew I needed to hear it.

"Jay, Dad had passed in prison... A couple years after you left. And Mom...."

His words struck my mind and heart as I prepared myself for the second blow.

"Then... Mom O.D.'d on her medication a few months after she found out Dad passed...."

I looked down at my lap--my vision now impaired by tears I refused to let fall. My facial expression remained the same, but my breaths shortened as I tried to keep my cool. With everything in me, I pushed it down--pushed it *all* down like I did the past seven years. I can take it. Better yet, it doesn't even *phase* me.

After a prolonged blink and exhale, I met eyes with Braden once again--his pupils still dilated as his fingers continued tapping against the table.

"Take a second," he suggested. "I'm gonna use the bathroom real quick."

He grabbed his coat and quickly made his way to the bathroom. I wanted to feel sad. I wanted to cry like a baby--to let it all out. To call everyone I knew and tell them the news and receive condolences from different angles, but... I just didn't have it in me. I have nothing in me but the physical things that keep me alive at this point.

I don't know what I did to deserve my family being stripped from me. I lived a fruitful childhood, doing the best I could to look after my brothers and be a kid all at the same time. Was it my decisions in a previous life that led to my current tragedy? Was it something I *will* do or may even *become* that's led to the destruction of my family? Is it worth even thinking about anymore?

"Sorry 'bout that..." Braden apologized as he sat down.

He was sitting still, much more still than before, yet his pupils were even more dilated. That's when I saw it. My eyes couldn't help but trail down to remnants of cocaine on his button-up. He quickly looked down and wiped his shirt with his open palm, then laughed under his breath.

"Why even bother, right?" he shrugged.

"Still? Seven years later? After everything that happened?" I asked.

"This isn't me, Jay..." he leaned forward, speaking with sincerity. "You wanna know who I am now? You wanna know what I do?"

Braden aggressively pressed his finger against the table top as he continued.

"I make *sure* that young people don't fall too far under the influence and do stupid shit. They come to *our* venues, and I can see it through that what happened to Josh will *never* happen to anybody else ever again--*ever*."

He took a deep breath, then kept going.

"Maybe you're happy out here… By yourself… Designing or whatever in this *shit* weather… But our paths crossed again for a reason, and this is our chance to not only do right by Josh... But to get *right* back on track to doing what we've always wanted to do… Own our own fucking nightclub."

I absorbed every word Braden said but couldn't help looking where the remnants of the coke were on his shirt. He made what he's doing sound like some form of redemption, and I was forced to think about what sort of redemption I was seeking out here. There truly was and *is* nothing out here for me.

The past seven years, I've been on autopilot--burying my past I see as the dark, and I did it, successfully. It didn't feel good, but it didn't matter because I no longer felt bad. Braden's act of pursuing redemption made me want the same for myself. As I looked into his bloodshot eyes, I smelled the liquor on his breath again. I realized a part of me wanted in--not only to keep our dream alive but to be there for the only family I have left… The one who needs me now more than ever.

"Okay," I said. "I'm in."

FIVE | SANTI

THE BEVERLY HILLS HOTEL
BEVERLY HILLS, CALIFORNIA
SUNDAY, 5:43P.M. - JUNE 30TH, 2019

"You're gonna love him," Braden assured me as he stepped out of his car.

"What's this place called, again?" I asked, shutting the car door behind me.

"The Beverly Hills Hotel. It's one of his favorite spots."

The valet attendant picked up Braden's key. I watched as Braden adjusted the collar of his loose-fitting shirt and took off his sunglasses. His arms were almost entirely covered in tattoos, and he had a decent tan he'd been working on since we ran into each other in New York. Since then, a lot had changed....

I cut off my lease.

I quit my job.

I dropped the life I spent seven years building to start fresh, once again.

But this time, it was different. This time, it's for family.

We were standing under a shaded structure with a ceiling painted in dark green and white stripes, making the hotel's entrance look elongated. Below me was a red carpet, seamlessly leading into the entryway that was painted a warm pastel pink color.

To the right and left of the entrance doors, tropical wildlife flourished and peeked over the railings, complementing the green ceiling stripes. We strolled past two parallel columns that read "The Beverly Hills" in elegant cursive calligraphy. It was evident that this hotel had history without them even having to say anything about it.

We made our way through the lobby that was home to elegant furniture and an impressionable chandelier that served as the centerpiece. I could smell a lavender scent that gave the vicinity a polished and historical feel--sort of like a rich grandmother's house.

Braden remained one step ahead of me, considering I had no idea where we were going. After spending the past seven years in New York, it felt odd not being surrounded by exceedingly large crowds, especially on a sunny Sunday afternoon like today. L.A. seemed so much slower than Manhattan, and I found it bothersome to try to maintain Braden's carefree pace.

The hallway we walked through was lit purely by the sun shining through the gaping windows. Our feet pressed silently upon the carpet as we passed through a doorway into a shaded terrace that overlooked the pool.

It was an afternoon more beautiful than any I had experienced in the longest time. From the clear sky to the laid-back social atmosphere, I felt at peace. I took a deep breath, smelling the culmination of meals and fragrances that filled the air. As if in slow motion, my eyes followed a white butterfly fluttering from the pool past the back of Braden's head. It didn't feel real--being back in L.A. with the only family I had left.

I became present in the moment as I watched Braden shake the hand of a man sitting alone at a table. The man stood to be the same height as Braden. He released Braden's hand and turned to acknowledge me with a smile.

He had light brown curly hair with hints of gold both on his head and in his well-maintained beard. He wore a silk black and white vertically striped long-sleeve. It fit him loosely, unbuttoned halfway down, revealing several diamond chains that danced in the reflection of the sun. His black pants were loosely-fitted, too, just barely covering his black designer loafers.

He extended his hand to meet mine, and his grip was firm and hands soft.

"Santi," he declared with a one-sided smirk, modestly showing off his white teeth.

"I'm Jay," I replied sternly, doing my best to maintain a professional posture. I couldn't help but notice how relaxed and approachable he is... Which made me immediately lower my guard.

His eyes popped in contrast with his tan. They were a light bluish-gray but full of life... And history--history like... *Wisdom* type of history, if that makes any sense. He didn't have a wrinkle on his face, but his eyes said otherwise. I felt like I could see everything Santi had seen in the gray--a man who had been to hell and back but had survived... And he's... *Alive*.

"Sit, boys," Santi politely insisted as he sat back in his chair.

I pulled out my chair and sat directly across from Santi, and Braden pulled out a chair between the two of us. It was a square table dressed in a lavish white table cloth with one chair on each side of it.

"Braden tells me the two of you grew up wanting to start up your own nightclub," Santi said in an engaging tone as he leaned back with his drink in hand.

He politely signaled for the waitress to bring two more of what he was drinking. Then, he nodded for me to begin with a gentle eyebrow lift accompanied by an encouraging smile.

"Absolutely," I said almost too formally. "We threw parties as teenagers, and they were probably some of the best in the area. We had this system that just seemed to work every time."

Santi let out a subtle laugh and sipped his drink. I noticed Braden smiling as he leaned back and chimed in.

"Really, though… They were next level."

"I don't doubt it. Braden has told me a lot about the two of you. He tells me you've got an eye," Santi said softly as he slightly leaned in and placed his elbows on the table. "He tells me you know how to *read* people."

Braden turned to me and tilted his head, which I assumed was my cue to own up to the statement.

"I wouldn't say I've got an *eye*, per se," I leaned back, making myself comfortable. "I'm probably just a decent judge of character, I guess."

Santi smiled, flashing his perfect teeth and gray eyes as he looked through me.

"Can you read *her*?" Santi lifted his drink to signal for me to look over my left shoulder. He leaned back and crossed one leg over the other, awaiting my response.

Braden and I turned to see our waitress talking to the bartender as he prepared the two drinks I assumed were for us. Let's call her... "Sarah."

Sarah is pretty--her somewhat ginger hair tied back into a loose ponytail. Her cheekbones popped, and her makeup was done up a little too intricately for a job as a waitress, most likely getting paid minimum wage. She didn't look old enough to be behind the bar but definitely old enough to live on her own in L.A. Sarah didn't seem rushed to get us the two drinks, as she took her time giggling at whatever the bartender was saying. This made me immediately assume that she's not as driven as she probably claims to be. She was bubbly in the way she carried herself, using plenty of hand gestures when she spoke. I could hear her animated voice that could easily be distinguished from a crowd.

I turned back to Santi to catch him observing me observe Sarah. His right elbow was placed on the chair's armrest, while his left hand groped his glass resting upon his crossed leg. He had a smile on his face, anxious to hear my response. His gray eyes studied me intently.

"She's an actress-..." I said, breaking the silence, but before I could continue, Santi cut me off.

"As is *every* waiter and waitress in this city," he laughed. "L.A. is basically actors serving food to other actors."

I continued, anyway. "She knows she has potential but doesn't have the drive to fully commit. Her makeup is done *perfectly*--much too perfect for this kinda gig--which got me thinking she gets ready every day in hopes of being *discovered* rather than taking the time to go out and get work herself. Now the only reason I chose an actress over a musician, model, or any other creative is because she's dynamic with her hands and voice… *Too* dynamic to pursue a career purely based on looks and image."

Santi squinted his eyes and slightly adjusted his position. He was engaged, so I kept going.

"She chose this job for the flexible schedule because she was probably told she can go to auditions when she's off the clock… But she needs to pay rent. I'm assuming she's from out of state. Her parents most likely didn't support her acting endeavor, which is why she had to pick up a job as a waitress. The only reason I bring her parents into the picture is because her makeup isn't fooling anybody… That girl is fresh out of high school and isn't a day older than 19. She doesn't plan to be working here long, considering she's lagging on our order which should be here by now… But it's okay because the restaurant manager is most likely an actor or actress, too. If you pretend you're a producer and tell her she has the image you're looking for regarding a specific role, she'll pounce on the opportunity and most likely give you a calling card... Or something even though I'm sure they're not allowed to do that here."

I took a deep breath and calmly ran my fingers through my hair, awaiting a response from Braden or Santi. Santi didn't break eye contact with me, smiling and now gently nodding his head. Braden looked down at his own hands in his lap, struggling to hold back a smile.

"I've got your two gin and tonics!" the waitress said in a bubbly tone as she set them down on the table. She put one hand on her hip and presented her palm with the other.

"Can I get anything else for you guys?"

Santi turned to her, and with a cunning smile, he said, "I apologize in advance if this is not the appropriate place to conduct business, *but*... You have a look about you that's just so-...."

He paused.

"Are you an actress?"

"Y-yes... I am!" she snapped back with enthusiasm.

Santi smiled.

"I'm actually a producer," he continued. "And we have a project in the works--an indie film… Nothing *too* crazy… I was wondering if-...."

"We aren't allowed to talk about acting work while on the clock," she whispered, lowering herself to Santi's eye level. "But...

Here's my card with my contact info… I'm interested… I'm *very* interested."

She reached into her bra and pulled out a card.

"Fantastic," Santi murmured, slipping the card into the chest pocket of his shirt. He looked back at me.

"I'll check on you boys in a bit!" she cheerfully turned and skipped back toward the bar.

The three of us let out a laugh, and Santi slammed his drink on the table.

"Damnit, okay! The actress was a given… That was easy…! *But* you called the calling card, which I'll give you props for…."

He scanned the terrace.

"What about *that* guy??"

He lifted his chin, signalling for me to look over my right shoulder this time. I rotated to see a middle-aged man in a khaki-colored suit with a bright red tie sitting at a table by himself. Let's call him... "Vince."

Vince adjusted his bright red tie, revealing his gold-plated Rolex. His keys were on the table. Though I couldn't see what car brand they represented, the key placement was ideal for whoever he was meeting to notice and potentially be impressed by the brand. If it wasn't a car worth flexing, he wouldn't have the keys on the table the way he did.

The bright red tie led me to believe it was a way for whoever Vince is meeting to know who he is without looking around too much. He wanted this encounter to be swift… Low-key. I wanted to assume it wasn't a prostitute, considering he wouldn't need to show off the car keys and Rolex if he was paying for whoever he's meeting... Maybe she's a more professional type of prostitute--an escort of some sort. He wanted this girl to stick around. She's young, considering materialism doesn't have as much of an effect on women his age, which is probably mid-to-late fifties.

He nervously tapped his right heel against the ground under the table. He was anxious. His left hand would lightly graze over his heart as if he was feeling for something in his chest pocket, and that's when I saw it… A tan line in the shape of a ring on his ring finger.

"He's a sugar daddy," I said as I shrugged and sipped my drink.

"Maybe he's here for work," Santi snapped back, crossing his arms.

"You could be right," I reasoned. "But there's no way that man is meeting a work colleague or client. He's been here since before we sat down. He's got two empty glasses on the table that have belonged solely to *him*. The man has been throwing down drinks because he needs that boost of courage to get him on board with what he's about to do."

"Maybe he's waiting for his wife," Santi suggested playfully.

"Or maybe he's *cheating* on his wife," I flashed a smirk and sipped my drink again. "Look at his leg shake. It's probably his first time, too. He's got his wedding ring in his chest pocket, and he feels for it every once in a while because he doesn't know if he's ready to fully commit to this just yet. The tan on his wedding ring finger is a dead giveaway, too... I don't think he even notices he has one."

"DAMNIT, JAY!" Santi slapped his two hands on the table and then threw them up in the air before locking his fingers behind his head. He looked up at the sky.

Braden and I were startled at his response, as were most of the people around us. Braden crossed his arms and shook his head with a smile that stretched from cheek to cheek.

"I told you he's got an eye," Braden said to Santi with a grin.

Santi leaned in once more and spoke in a soft tone.

"That guy is a regular at one of my restaurants. Opened up to me the other night about his wife having an affair, and he offered me *a lot* of money to set him up with one of the models that work for me."

Santi let out another laugh under his breath. He reached over the table, patting my shoulder firmly and then playfully nudging Braden before he leaned back once more.

"That's good shit, kid! Real deal... Now tell me... How much did Braden tell you about what I do?"

"Not too much," I shrugged nonchalantly. "He mentioned you being really involved in the nightlife industry."

"Well, that's a start," Santi laughed.

He ran his open palm over his curls as he readjusted his posture.

"Referring to it as nightlife doesn't really do the trick when explaining what I do in its entirety. I like calling it the *social* business."

I involuntarily nodded my head. I already liked where this was going, and I could see Braden lightly smirking because he *knew* I was gonna like what Santi had to say.

"I deal social currency," he continued--his eyes widening in unison with the dynamic rhythm of his voice. He began using lively hand gestures. "People carve time out of their lives to come to *my* restaurants, *my* clubs, *my* bars... To feel special... To be *served*--after all, that's what hospitality is about, right? With time being our most important asset--a *finite* asset at that--I need to make *sure* that my guests have the time of their lives while in my venues. You go out to be social--to *engage*. You go out to partake in moments that are shared with the people around you, and it's my job to elevate that experience."

"So you own more than just clubs?" I asked between sips of

my drink.

"Oh, I'm building an empire!" Santi practically shouted as he threw his hands up.

He smiled.

"Braden is my right-hand man," he continued. "He's done a lot for me the past couple of years, and he speaks very highly of you. I *could* give you some bull shit where I talk about everything happening for a reason and that our paths were meant to cross… But I want to shed light on another thought. I see a bit of myself in you and the way you can read people. We're not too different."

He smiled and squinted his eyes, fascinated by whatever he was making of my presence.

"Come work for me, and I'll teach you the business as I've already begun teaching Braden."

It was as if, at that moment, the hairs on the back of my neck stood up. I didn't know this man in the slightest, yet I innately wanted to make him… *Proud*… Like he was some sort of father figure I've been missing for years. For the past seven years, I was going through the motions without being able to *feel*, and suddenly here I am in the presence of family, once again… And a mentor who is promising me the *world*… A mentor who can make my dream a reality.

I saw Braden… My own flesh and blood to my left... And directly in front of me, I saw a man who I *knew* deep down was going to teach me more than I could ever fathom being taught.

"Yes," I gasped like a child being invited to Disneyland for the first time. "I-... I would love to be a part of this."

Braden clapped and let out a laugh that he must've held in throughout the entire conversation.

"I told you he'd be down!" he wagged his finger in Santi's direction and then downed his drink.

Santi smirked while looking down, shook his head, and looked back up at me… The blue and the gray in his eyes shimmered in the afternoon sun that was now setting.

"Here's to you joining the family," he lifted his drink and clinked it against mine. "Speaking of family… Let me introduce you to ours."

Santi stood, pulling two hundred-dollar bills out of his designer wallet. He placed them on the table under his empty glass.

"Tomorrow, we'll begin prepping for our function we host every Wednesday night at one of my main spots in North Hollywood… It's called *The Willow-*...."

"The Willow is *your* spot??" I blurted out in amusement.

I suddenly remembered all of the stories and articles I read about The Willow. Actors, professional athletes, billionaires, models… Anybody and everybody were trying to get into The Willow for as long as I could remember. Little did I know the venue belonged to the man now standing three feet in front of me.

"Yessir," Santi smirked, placing a cigarette in his mouth. He lit it before he looked back up at me. "Come by anytime tomorrow between noon and three, and I'll introduce you to the family, and we'll see where you fit in."

With the cigarette gently caressed between his lips, he slipped his sunglasses on, patted our shoulders, and walked between us back toward the hotel. Braden and I watched him leave and then turned to face each other.

"That went *much* better than you thought," Braden gave me a playful nudge.

"You think he liked me?" I asked excitedly while playfully deflecting his hand.

"Absolutely. But the question is… Do *you* like *him*?"

"Yeah, man. I got a really good read on him," I said as I relaxed my shoulders.

"He feels like family."

SIX | CIGARETTES

BRADEN'S APARTMENT
DOWNTOWN L.A.
MONDAY, 9:22A.M. - JULY 1ST, 2019

I opened my eyes and stared at the exposed pipes lining Braden's apartment ceiling. It was an industrial-style apartment composed of brick and cement. There's something about the industrial look that I find aesthetically pleasing. It's so interesting how something so imperfect can still be so attractive.

The bedroom Braden had me staying in was pretty small, but I suppose that's what you get when you live in downtown L.A. But still… Braden living in a two-bedroom was undoubtedly a step up from selling drugs out of our family's garage back in Torrance.

After rubbing my eyes, I stared at the large flat screen T.V. mounted on the wall in front of me. I pressed my back against the headboard. None of this felt real to me. I was lying in the spare bedroom of my brother's apartment. A few months ago, I lived in the middle of Manhattan surrounded by a world of different people and faces. Now, I've traded all that in for a new life here in L.A. that I know absolutely nothing about.

Seven years later… And now here I am. But why? How?

I yawned.

I couldn't help but think of Val. There was something inside of me that kept reminding me that she's there--here--that she's close.

Does that excite me? Maybe.
Am I gonna set out to see her? Nah.
If God's there and wants for it to happen… He'll make it happen.
I'll let fate run its course on this one.

I stood beside the bed and reached for the pile of clothes I laid on the ground, pulling out a pair of gray sweatpants. I headed for the window. I looked down toward the busy street where people tended to their errands and various routines--just another Monday.

It was almost 9:30a.m. I felt my stomach growl, despite having devoured two whole pizzas last night with Braden while binging random Netflix documentaries.

I opened the door leading into the communal space that the kitchen and living room shared. It was a wide-open space with a high ceiling.

Braden sat at the head of his modern dining table. His short hair was a little messy, and his five-o'clock shadow was prominent. His eyes were glued to his laptop screen, but he still acknowledged me.

"I got you a bagel," he said, pointing to the kitchen counter without averting his eyes from his screen. "It's from a bagel place a few blocks from here... So fire."

"You're the man for that," I said as I headed directly for the counter. "What's the plan for today? We're going to The Willow, right?"

I undid the bagel wrap and reached for the trash can.

"Yeah. Santi was stoked about meeting you," Braden sipped his orange juice. "We're gonna head over to The Willow in a couple hours so you can meet everybody."

I opened the trash can to find a small 50mml bottle of vodka half-buried on top of a crumbled bagel bag.

"Are you drinking?" I turned to Braden with my hand still holding the trash can open. "It's a Monday morning...."

"Some people drink coffee. I spike my orange juice."

He continued typing away.

"I mean, I *guess* that's the same thing," I murmured.

"Nevermind that!" Braden snapped. "Come here and check out the guest list for Wednesday night."

I took a bite out of my bagel and scanned the laptop from over Braden's shoulder.

"Wow," I gasped at the sight of the names.

From A-list celebrities to "Forbes 30 under 30's" top-ranked young entrepreneurs, The Willow was fully booked on a *Wednesday*....

"Crazy, right? Just look at some of these names," Braden chuckled. "You probably never thought you'd be in the same room as all of these people at the same time."

I took another bite of my bagel as I continued scanning the list.

"Are Willow Wednesdays really *that* fun?" I asked with a mouthful of bagel.

"Dude, yes, Jay... Willow Wednesday is the shit around here. Santi is a genius," Braden assured me. "You'll see when he's in his element. Go get ready. I wanna make sure we're there by noon, and traffic is a bitch."

I finished my bagel and headed for my room.

I did my 100 crunches.
I took my usual hot shower in the dark.
Brushed my teeth.
Blow-dried my hair.
Then threw on some face lotion and deodorant.

"Here," Braden tossed a black bottle of cologne onto my bed. "Spray it twice on your neck and once on each forearm. That's your scent. You'll thank me later."

Braden and I headed down through the lobby where his apartment's valet service had his Tesla already pulled up. Braden wore an oversized white T-shirt with black pants that drooped over his Dior sneakers. The sun reflected off of his white-gold chains that lightly hugged his neck and wrist.

I find it funny how people dress in L.A. The style screams "I try" but also screams "I'm not trying." That probably doesn't make sense… But in my defense, the style itself shouldn't make sense, but it somewhat *does*. It's almost like these people dress in baggy clothes that you'd wear alone around the house, but the brands and staple pieces portray a sense of luxury.

To the untrained eye, L.A. streetwear is just baggy oversized clothes... To the modern-day "cultured" individual, L.A. streetwear *is fashion*… But in my humble opinion, L.A. streetwear is a paradox complemented by a pretty face.

I wore a slightly oversized black button-up with some cropped black pants and Louis Vuitton high-top sneakers I found in Braden's closet. I haven't worn his clothes since we were kids, but according to Braden, my current wardrobe was far too "New York," and I needed to dress a little more laid-back… Or, as he's been saying, "more L.A."

There wasn't a cloud in the sky as we coasted through downtown, hitting every green light. Braden drove like he owned the street, zigzagging through the light traffic as his car moved silently along the aged asphalt. The windows were rolled down, and the music blared loud enough for all to hear. He didn't care what anyone else thought, and upon seeing that, neither did I.

The tall buildings we maneuvered under quickly opened up into the highway as we made our way to Hollywood. Braden carelessly zipped through traffic as people honked and flipped him off, but he didn't bat an eye.

"This place is like a playground," I shouted over the music.

"In this city, work is play if you do it right," Braden shouted back while smirking under his sunglasses.

He lowered the music.

"Jay, just wait till you see the people we're working with. They're *beautiful*... Like the women are unreal."

"Is Val out here?" I asked.

I couldn't help but ask... And I immediately regretted it. Braden put the car in autopilot, and after a pause with no response, he looked at me, lowered his shades, and grinned from cheek to cheek.

"How did I *know* you were gonna ask about Val?? It was only a matter of time...."

"Shuuttt uppp," I could feel myself blushing, turning to face the road ahead.

"You know it's actually funny you ask," he continued. "I've seen her at a few parties."

My blush flushed from my face.

"She's out here??"

"Yeah, she's modeling and pretty big in the scene, too. We don't talk much at all, really."

I was taken back to the night she told me about her plan to pursue modeling instead of college. The words I had spoken to her rang in my head as if the party was last night.

"*You're hardworking. You're driven*," I remember telling her. "*You've got a good head on your shoulders. There's no doubt you'll make ends meet*."

I remember her smirking back at me--the long pause that followed--I wonder what would have happened if Braden didn't pull me away at that moment. I wonder where it could have gone. That was the last I had seen Val... Before the mental fog set in... Before an entire seven years had passed.

What would she think of my response to what happened that night?

Would she hate me for cutting her out of my life? Would she understand?

What would she think of me now?

Would she even recognize me?

"You haven't talked to her, huh?" Braden broke the silence.

"Not at all," I sighed with a blank stare.

"The L.A. scene isn't *too* big," Braden continued. "But I don't think you need to worry about running into her. You'll be pretty distracted by the girls we keep around on a day-to-day basis."

"True," I said hollowly, hoping Braden would shift the conversation toward anything other than Val.

Not once in my life did I ever talk about my love life with Braden. He was always too drunk or high, getting into trouble, or out with his band. I never really thought he cared about anything I did... But I realized now that I didn't need to open up for him to see I had feelings for Val when we were teenagers. I guess it was pretty out there in the open.

We exited the congested freeway and were finally able to pick up some speed taking the streets. As we got off the next highway, I looked up to see a large building that read "NETFLIX" at the top in bright red letters, just as I'd see on my T.V. screen every night before bed. Across from the building was a massive movie poster decorating the side of a hotel. A colossal Mark Whalberg printed on the side of the building gave me a skeptical glare, and that's when it dawned on me where we are.

We're in Hollywood.

Braden silently maneuvered through traffic with ease, once again. We zoomed under the palm trees that bordered the road on both sides. From radio station and news channel buildings to small liquor stores and strip clubs, I took in my surroundings with a smile on my face.

The people and place itself weren't as pretty as they make them out to be in the movies, but I understood the vision. I didn't address the homeless people, considering seven years in New York had desensitized me to a pretty high degree.

I saw another large movie banner.

I saw another.

And another.

I saw billboards with massive faces--some I recognized and others I didn't.

I wondered what these celebrities made of being on billboards that big. I found it interesting how the entertainment industry could attach so much value to an individual and, in some instances... Merely just an individual's face. To me, it seemed that L.A. was the only place where you can get picked up off the streets and molded into an icon, then be thrown back onto the streets once your fans are no longer fans. Once your fans get a grip on reality and no longer need movie stars to help them escape it.

We took a sharp right and pulled into a spot on the side of the street.

"You ready??" Braden asked, patting me on the shoulder.

"I think so."

I got out of the car.

"Don't be nervous," Braden teased.

"I'm not nervous," I said as I nervously made my way around the car.

"Yeah, that's something a nervous person would say..." Braden threw his arm around my shoulder and playfully shoved me ahead of him. "Quit being such a hardass and smile, kid."

I couldn't help but smile at his command. I realized I *was* pretty nervous and a bit stuck in my head.

"I'm sorry," I sighed as he threw his arm around me once more.

"You're good, man," Braden laughed as he guided me across the street. I felt his grip on me tighten. "You're not alone anymore."

"*Not alone anymore*," his words echoed.

I felt a weight lifted off my shoulders. The fog that kept me from seeing and feeling for so long was finally beginning to clear. I had Braden to thank for that. I have no reason to self-sabotage the one life I have to live. Every decision I've made up to this point has brought me here, and I'm happy to *be* here.

Walking side by side, we turned the street corner. The sound of passing cars and our own footsteps filled the air as I felt the early afternoon sun on the back of my neck. I could smell the alcohol on Braden's breath but didn't care to think much of it anymore. He seemed to be doing just fine.

"Here it is," Braden signaled to a small dull-looking one-story building sandwiched between two taller buildings.

I would've never thought that it was The Willow, let alone one of the top-ranked Hollywood clubs... But I recognized the entrance despite there not being close to two hundred people outside trying to get in.

I remember the endless stories Braden told about this place when we were teenagers... Both stories he witnessed firsthand and also stories that circulated all throughout L.A. County. I'm pretty sure I've even heard The Willow mentioned in a bunch of hip-hop songs and seen it in magazines.

Braden typed in a code to unlock the front door, and I followed him through a narrow dim-lit hallway. One of the walls was decorated in abstract sketches of naked women that required a double-take for one to notice.

The sound of our footsteps echoed through the narrow hall, soon to be silenced by music coming from the end of the hallway. I studied the walls to both my right and left as the sketches became more and more vibrant with a floral design and texture as we approached the main room.

The music grew louder and louder as we neared an opening at the end of the hall. Braden took an energetic step through the opening. After taking a long deep breath to calm my nerves, I slowly turned the corner after him.

"Woah..." I couldn't help but gasp at the sight that unraveled as if in slow motion.

Braden excitedly opened his arms to embrace the people in the room who reciprocated his enthusiasm. People were scattered across the different levels of the club, all serving a different purpose in setting up.

I watched as two men stood on ladders above me, assembling a massive floral structure that would hang from an even *bigger* chandelier that lit up the venue. A large group of men twice my size lifted and rearranged rustic leather couches with ease. The floor was made of dark wood with a glossy finish that tied in with the dark green walls and floral decor.

I got chills as my gaze went from the high ceilings to the prestigious bar in the back of the club. There were about three or four women shuffling bottles and organizing glasses. Lush willow trees stood on each side of the bar, giving off the illusion that the bar was consumed by nature. Just above the bar on a second level were massive windows leading to what looked like a warm luxurious office space.

Golden railings separated elevated booths on each side of the main room. Men and women overlapped each other, taking care of the various preparations and requirements that needed to be met before Wednesday.

The songs being played skipped from one to the next, and I realized it was being controlled from an elevated platform to my left, where the D.J. was running a sound check.

"How's that?!" he shouted toward the back of the venue.

"Sounds great! Maybe even go a bit louder!" a voice shouted back.

Braden acknowledged a couple of guys who looked like they could be in their mid-twenties. They wore vibrant-colored designer clothes with diamond and silver chains that were similar to Braden's. I suddenly understood where he got his sense of style from. They were cool-looking guys, relaxing on one of the rustic couches looking up at Braden, who was making them laugh.

"Jay, get your ass over here!" Braden shouted back at me, suddenly pulling me out of my trance.

I approached the small group that was now looking at me.

"These are the Baker brothers... This is Kalani, and this is Kai...."

"I'm Jay," I extended my hand.

"What's up, Jay?" Kai smiled and gave me a firm handshake before lighting his cigarette.

"That's a cool name," Kalani said as he gave me a less professional handshake that turned into a fist bump.

I smiled. "Thanks, I appreciate that. Nice to meet you guys."

It suddenly dawned on me that Kai and Kalani were identical twins. Kai had a buzzed head, while Kalani's hair was slicked back on top and buzzed on the sides. They literally had the same face, and when they smiled, their perfect white teeth instantly caught my eye. What is it with these people and all of them having nice teeth?

"Braden tells us you're joining the family," Kalani said as he crossed one leg over the other and leaned back.

"I think it's ultimately up to Santi," I shrugged, trying not to come on too strong.

"What do you do?" Kai asked snarkily between drags of his cig.

"I was doing design back in New York… For some of Santi's venues, actually," I replied.

Kai didn't shift his position in the slightest. "Oh, so you were working corporate... You weren't cut out for corporate life?"

"Nah, it wasn't for me."

"What do you think Santi is gonna have Jay do?" Kalani asked Braden.

"Not sure," Braden shrugged. "I'd think promotion, but I've got no idea."

Kalani nodded and scanned me from head to toe. "If Santi sees something in you, then you've *really* gotta be special. Santi has an eye for reading people."

"So does Jay," Braden snapped back while patting my shoulder.

"Honestly, I'm just grateful for the opportunity," I chimed in.

The energy in the room shifted as people's eyes turned back toward the bar. A vibrant voice swept the venue, overpowering the other voices with its lively tone.

"BEAUTIFUL!" the voice shouted. "Have them here within the next two hours, and Michelle will brief them. I'm still waiting on the Grey Goose bottles. Eric, where are my Grey Goose bottles?? Where's Kai??"

The voice belonged to Santi, who was wearing a blue and white floral long sleeve with white pants. I recognized the shirt from a Dior advertisement I saw the other day, but it was tough to focus on the shirt that hid under an abundance of chains. He poured himself a drink behind the bar and scanned The Willow up and down, then left to right.

Two women approached him--one gesturing for him to sign something on a clipboard and the other simply waiting to greet him. He signed and dismissed both of the girls with a cunning grin. As they stepped out of his line of sight, his gaze caught mine.

"Jay Amor!!" he shouted in amusement, causing everyone's heads to turn from Santi to me.

I was beaming. It's not often that one of the biggest names in the nightlife scene is excited to see somebody, let alone a new guy like myself. Everyone was fixated on me, trying to figure out who I was… And I felt… *Special*.

Santi casually strolled over to our group as he pulled out a cigarette. Kai and Kalani fixed their posture as Santi approached us and gave me a handshake that turned into a hug.

"Have you met the boys?? Let me introduce you to the boys."

He lit his cigarette.

"I've met a few…" I uttered. "Just-…."

"Niall! Get down here!" Santi shouted toward the D.J.

The D.J. walked down one of the two staircases that bordered the elevated platform, then stood next to Braden.

"I'll give you a quick breakdown, Jay…" Santi took a quick drag of his cigarette. "Kai is our head bartender. He runs the balance sheets and makes sure our inventory is in proportion to the estimated guest count every night we're running. That goes for *all* of my venues. Then, Kalani is my *culinary king*, taking care of everything food-related. Before I took this kid in, he could barely make a bowl of cereal, but after setting him up with some of the top chefs in the industry, he's the reason I charge five times the standard amount for anything my guests swallow. This is Niall… I picked him up off the streets when he was probably... 18? Saw the kid making beats out of buckets and making more money than I did at the time… Huh, Niall?"

Niall smirked. His brown and golden wavy hair bounced against his shoulders as he nodded in agreement with what Santi was saying.

Santi continued. "Now Niall's in charge of booking talent when we decide to bring people in. Otherwise, he's D.J.'ing and he's damn good at it. You obviously know Braden… My right-hand man. One of my top promoters along with-…."

He paused and scanned the group once more.

"Where's Skylar?" Santi asked softly, raising his eyebrows. The cigarette rested between his lips as he lifted his hands and then dropped them back down to his side.

The boys looked around silently and then at the ground, unaware of how Santi would respond to Skylar's absence. Santi took a long drag of his cigarette and let out a laugh while looking up at the ceiling.

"Interesting..." he whispered. "You guys keep setting up. I'll catch up with Skylar when he gets in. I'm gonna give Jay a tour in the meantime."

Santi placed his hand on my back to guide me away. Before we were able to turn, he caught sight of Kai's cigarette.

"Hold up. Kai... What are you doing?"

Santi's gray eyes were now fixated on the cigarette Kai was caressing between his two fingers. It was as if when he smiled, everyone smiled... But when he appeared upset, the entire room grew silent out of fear and respect.

"That's a cigarette... That's a cigarette lit in my club... Correct?" Santi asked as he took another drag of his own cigarette.

Kai was flustered. His eyes scanned Santi's cigarette and then his own.

"I just... I thought-..." Kai stuttered nervously. "You s-smoke in here, and I just thought mayb-...."

"Do not be misled... For bad company corrupts good character," Santi said, cutting Kai off.

His words were spoken softly, but the tension was rising.

Santi continued. "You think it's okay to smoke in my club because I smoke in my club, is this correct?"

Kai reluctantly nodded. "Yes, sir."

"Do you think smoking is bad for you?"

"No... Well... Yeah, it is..." Kai's face went pale.

"So you're calling me a bad influence," Santi laughed as he exhaled a cloud of smoke.

"No, sir."

"You wanna smoke in my club?" Santi paused in thought, tapping the butt of his cigarette against his chin. "Very well, then. Where's your pack?"

Kai pulled a full pack of cigarettes out of his bag and set it on the table. Santi reached into his pocket and pulled out his own full pack.

"Damnit," Santi whispered as he tossed his pack on the table next to Kai's. "I *wanted* to smoke these, but I suppose the lesson is more important. Braden, I know you've got a pack... Toss it."

Braden tossed a half-full pack of cigarettes onto the table. Two and a half packs of cigarettes rested on the table between the group.

"You want me to throw them away?" Kai asked, hesitant to reach for the cigarettes.

"No," Santi checked his Rolex. "You wanna smoke in my club? You get to smoke in my club. You have an hour to smoke every last one of these cigarettes."

"All of them??" Kai panicked. "In an hour?? I'll get nicotine poisoning...."

Kalani, Niall, and Braden held back a laugh, and I could feel a sense of relief as the tension loosened.

"Smoke," Santi gave Kai a playful slap across the side of his head, grabbed two cigarettes for himself, and gestured for me to follow. "No smoking in my club without consulting me first. When on my payroll, you *think* before you speak and *ask* before you *do*."

As I walked alongside Santi, I replayed what just happened in my head over again. I had never seen a man go from being so cheerful to tyrannical, then go straight into being all loving and nurturing. He had the entire group in the palm of his hands... Controlling their emotions like a puppeteer. Right off the bat, I could tell how influential Santi is, but I didn't think he had *this* sort of effect on people. It's a relief he chooses to use his gift of influence for good, teaching lessons to the ones closest to him. I turned back to see Kai reluctantly grabbing his next cigarette with a look of disgust on his face. He had a long way to go.

"I'm excited to show you what we've got going on here, Jay," Santi said.

He had a strut that exuberated confidence and swagger. His charisma radiated and infected the staff members preparing the venue for Willow Wednesday. They made themselves available to him as he passed.

"It's amazing," I declared in genuine amusement. "The way you incorporate nature into an urban setting. The floral decor is unreal."

"I appreciate you for that," Santi replied as he exhaled a cloud of smoke.

The two of us were approaching the bar in the back of The Willow. The massive room wasn't even properly lit yet, but I could see the bottles and glasses glistening--calling my name. Santi leaned back against the bar counter and turned to face the entirety of The Willow's main room. He gestured for me to join him in doing the same. I leaned back against the bar top and faced the same direction as Santi.

We were on the lowest level, which made up most of the ground floor. Straight ahead was a line of large rustic couches sitting on dark-colored Moroccan rugs. I'm assuming this served as the area for general admission. Bordering the large open space to the right and left was an elevated level with plush booths angled in a way that suggested exclusivity--the V.I.P. section.

The V.I.P. section was only elevated three or four steps, but the difference between the two sections was prominent. Golden railings with a floral design lined the V.I.P. sections, separating the regulars from the social elites.

Directly ahead toward the front entrance was an elevated platform that stood about 10 feet tall. Standing even taller to the right and left of the platform were two large gazebo structures… Each with willow leaves and flowers hanging over the tops of them. The D.J. equipment and setup was just at the base of the two elevated gazebos, where Santi was running through his song setlist.

I slowly looked up to see the ceiling that was dressed in colorfully-lit willow leaves and flowers. Embedded in the hanging decor were speakers… *Tons* of speakers, but they seamlessly blended in with the decor. I was startled as I turned left to see Santi attentively watching me appreciate his work. I was so in awe, it was difficult for me to speak.

"The design--or… *Theme*… W-what inspired the design?"

"The design is a reflection of the experience," Santi grinned. "The experience drives the design, and the design drives the experience. Good hospitality is four-dimensional, Jay… The key is to engage *all* of the individual's senses in one experience the host provides, right?"

I nodded and watched as Santi reached over the bar top, grabbed a napkin, and ashed his cigarette.

"For example," he continued. "The willow tree is unlike any other, the way the leaves hang directly toward the ground. Standing below it gives off the illusion that you're being consumed by nature. With the club being located in an *urban* area while possessing a *natural* feel--the irony itself satisfies *sight*. Precisely two hours before the doors open, the temperature is set to 66 degrees. With occasional extra pumps of oxygen, I keep my guests and staff wide-awake, feeling good, and not sweating all over each other--this satisfies *touch*. Built into every other booth, each of the willow trees and lining the ceiling are speakers--all angled for you to hear optimal music levels from any spot within the venue--this satisfies *hearing*. We serve food to keep our guests from leaving, and our drink glasses are all chilled 24/7--this satisfies *taste*. And finally, within the lining of the walls and ceiling, a custom scent I had made will be released every 30 minutes while the venue is active. You'd be surprised how many people don't wear deodorant in Hollywood… It baffles me. Plus, I like for people to become familiar with an aroma that mentally takes them back to my locations no matter where they are in the world--this obviously satisfies *smell*. Those are the five senses for you... Just a brief little beginner lesson for *day one* on the job."

I couldn't help but laugh and cross my arms. My jaw dropped as I processed everything Santi had just said. Genius… All of it.

"AMAZING," I said in admiration. "I would never think to tailor an experience to each specific sense. That's *brilliant*."

"You haven't seen anything yet, Jay," Santi assured. "Wednesday will be just like any other night, but in this industry, every night presents you with something different. Let's keep moving."

Santi swiftly made his way past me and through a large swinging door. I followed him through the door into a large kitchen lit with bright fluorescent lights.

"I'm sure you've seen a kitchen before," Santi teased. "This is all Kalani's. Each and every appliance is placed strategically for maximum efficiency. I choose to let him run it the way he pleases. My boys are passionate about what they do. Thus, I let *passion* dictate their decisions here. Their *slack* is what typically drives me to intervene."

"Is there *usually* slack?" I asked as Santi turned toward the door.

"More often than not," Santi unwillingly uttered. "I have high expectations for my boys, and I'm always teaching them."

He pushed through the door. I followed as we passed the bar and headed down a dimly-lit hallway.

"You've got your restrooms," Santi raised his left arm, pointing at the restrooms on the left side of the hallway without stopping.

At the end of the hall, there was a double door Santi pushed through. The doors swung open, and suddenly we were on a wooden deck behind The Willow. Wooden booths lined the perimeter, and just behind the booths was a tall wooden wall coated in vines and flowers. Lights hung above us from one willow tree to the next.

"This is the smoke deck... No exit back here. The Willow has everything the guests need, and the placement of this deck is designed to make it difficult for people to get back through the venue to leave. The more time we spend together, you'll start to pick up on my venues and how they begin to overlap and share similar elements."

Santi lit a cigarette and extended another in my direction, offering for me to join him in smoking. I suddenly remembered the pattern of chain-smoking I picked up as a way of coping after Josh had passed. I was damn-near addicted, and it took months for me to break the habit. It had been years since my last cigarette… and I certainly wasn't ready to break my clean streak.

"No thanks," I said shakily.

Santi studied me with his gray eyes that looked illuminated by the early afternoon sun.

"You don't smoke?" Santi asked before blowing smoke over his shoulder. "Or you don't *wanna* smoke?"

I felt an urge within me to take the cigarette, but my mind said otherwise. Santi's gray eyes pierced through me as if he were speaking with them.

"*Take one*," the gray said. "*It's okay to not be okay--to be imperfect.*"

I reached for the cigarette, but before I could grab one, Santi pulled the pack toward his chest.

"Listen, Jay," he put his hand on my shoulder, then spoke

softly. “Over the years, I’ve learned a lot about the world I’ve created for myself and my involvement in it. I’ve become conscious of the fact that the people who come to work for me don’t come when everything in their life is working out. They come to me in a time of need, and I find ways to help them find purpose. I want you to know that whatever it is you need--whatever it is that’s weighing on you--I am here to provide what I can. This is *your* family if you choose to be a part of it.”

He lightly patted the cigarette over his heart twice and extended it in my direction, offering once more.

I felt sudden warmth--a feeling that had become so distant over the past seven years.

It felt as though for so long I was the victim.

It felt as though for so long I longed for forgiveness.

For so long, I longed for family.

For so long, I longed to be loved.

For so long, I longed for purpose.

Here was Santi, offering it all--the answer to my prayers--the family I *need*.

I took the cigarette.

SEVEN | WILLOW WEDNESDAY

THE WILLOW
NORTH HOLLYWOOD, CALIFORNIA
WEDNESDAY, 10:29P.M. - JULY 3RD, 2019

"You are to not leave my side unless I tell you to, Jay," Braden demanded as he fixed the collar of his silk button-up.

The Willow was fully prepped and ready for the doors to open in 31 minutes. Colored lights shone through the willow leaves hanging from the ceiling. Music echoed throughout the empty venue, soon to be filled with Hollywood's social elites. It was cold, just as Santi said it would be, leading me to feel alert and agile.

I could feel my heart flutter as I took in the scent along with my surroundings. I recognized the scent Santi claimed he had made, and it seemed all too familiar, but I couldn't pinpoint where it was from.

The willow trees bordering the front and back of the venue were majestically lit, casting colored lights off the bottles lining the back wall behind the bar. The wood floor seemed to have a fresh coat of gloss, illuminating the dancing lights that beamed from behind Niall's elevated D.J. platform.

I calmly ran my fingers back through my hair, tucking the curls behind my ears, trying to keep my cool. My all-black fit made my silver and diamond jewelry pop, catching the eyes of a few bottle girls who walked past us. I couldn't help but reciprocate the flirtatious stare as one of them didn't break eye contact. I felt a thump against the back of my head, then a tug in the opposite direction.

"FOCUS," Braden snapped. "I'm gonna quiz you...."

I straightened my posture as we kept walking toward the back of the main room.

"What time do doors open?"

"11," I confidently replied.

"What are the table prices?"

"Ground level tables are a $3,000 minimum, V.I.P. levels are a $7,000 minimum, and the two private villas are a $15,000 minimum."

"Where does Santi host his private guests?"

"The Eastern Villa."

I turned back to the front of the main room to see the two vil-las--one on each side of Niall. Each villa was made up of a luxurious gazebo structure with white drapes hanging from all four sides. Each villa had its own balcony that looked over the main room. It was quite a sight to see--the wooden stairs rising along both sides of Niall's 10-foot platform, then curving up another five steps where the gazebos were built halfway into the two willow trees. I turned to face the bar at the back of the main room.

"Which way is east?" Braden continued.

"The bar in the back is north, the villas and D.J. setup are south, which makes the wall to my right the east side, and the wall to my left the west."

"Do we let V.I.P.'s with tables in first or general admission?"

"V.I.P.'s."

"That was an easy one," he teased as we approached the bar.

He dug into his pocket and pulled out an earpiece and small circular device with a blue screen on it that read "Channel 3."

"This is a channel transmitter," he said as if I was a toddler.

I was busy looking back at the bottle girls. He gave me a light slap across my face. I looked directly at him with my eyes widened.

"This is a channel transmitter," he said once again, just as slow. "What is this?"

"A channel transmitter," I replied.

He continued. "The whole staff uses this transmitter and these earpieces to communicate from anywhere in the venue. The promoters--you, me, and Skylar--will use *Channel 3*. Kalani and the kitchen are *Channel 4*, security is *Channel 5*, Kai and the bar are *Channel 6*, and Santi is *Channel 7*. Don't worry about Kai tonight… He got nicotine poisoning on Monday and is still getting over it. Now it is *very* important that you know not to use Santi's channel unless it is an absolute emergency. You get that??"

My mind immediately jumped to the thought of Santi forcing Kai to smoke the two and a half packs of cigarettes in an hour back on Monday… Poor Kai. I'm sure he learned his lesson *real* quick.

"Yes, I get it!" I replied, rolling my eyes. "I get it, Braden. I understand how this works. I've been studying everything you've shown me the past 48 hours."

"Listen, man," Braden said sternly. "Santi has been chill with you because you're new… But you don't want to upset him. There are some *very* important people who come here on nights like these, and *a lot* of money moves through every service we provide... So just stick with me and do as I do unless I tell you otherwise."

"I get it, I get it," I shrugged as I tucked the earpiece into my right ear.

"Let's go."

Braden headed for the front entrance. Our loafers clicked against the ground of the narrow hallway as we opened the front doors to the warm summer night.

As we stepped outside, an overwhelming wave of conversations and laughter consumed me. The stories I had heard about The Willow couldn't compare to the real deal displayed before me. People flooded the sidewalk in both directions and even poured out onto the busy road. Beautiful women and good-looking guys talked and embraced one another as they waited to go inside.

Designer clothes.

Makeup.

Flashy jewelry.

Cologne and perfumes.

Everyone's eyes trailed from one individual to the next, yearning to lock eyes with at least *one* celebrity.

People slowly began turning to face Braden and me as we stood behind the ropes between two of the bouncers that must've been standing at *least* 6'5. Braden leaned over the rope to whisper to a young guy who had his back to us. The guy turned to whisper something to Braden, and I noticed his earpiece. He must've been Skylar, the only member of the group I hadn't met yet. I waited for the right moment to introduce myself, but before I could, he caught my eye over Braden's shoulder. His big brown eyes popped as he smiled from cheek to cheek with raised eyebrows. A diamond-studded tooth decorated the inside of his mouth, along with a tiny rose tattooed under his right eye. It was one of the *many* tattoos covering his entire torso and both arms.

"THE LONG-LOST AMOR BROTHER!" he shouted as he reached over the rope to shake my hand and give me a hug.

People turned their heads to see who I was. It was *quite* the intro. It was also the warmest and most genuine embrace I've felt since I moved to L.A.

"I'm Skylar," he greeted enthusiastically. "The *loud* one."

I laughed. It was as if the two of us clicked right away, and I felt my walls come crashing down--as if I had known Skylar for years. He reminded me of Danny a bit. For some reason, he reminded me of *home*.

"I'm Jay, the long-lost Amor brother," I jokingly replied.

"First night on the job... You nervous??" he teased.

"Honestly, a little bit."

Three women approached Skylar's back, poking and tickling him.

He turned abruptly. "WOAH, WHAT'RE Y-...."

"Hi, Skylar!" they all said in unison as if rehearsed on the way over.

They were stunning. The typical cookie-cutter Hollywood scene girls you've probably seen in the movies.

"What's up, ladies...? Damn, we look *good*!" he shouted as he eyed them from head to toe. "Is tonight the night or *what*??"

Two of them blushed, and the third locked eyes with Braden, who quickly turned away to avoid making eye contact. He pulled out a flask and took a long pull from it.

"Hi, Braden," she said. She had an accent that must've been Swedish.

"How you been, Annette?" Braden asked hollowly as he closed his flask.

I could sense the tension. This woman must have been a Victoria's Secret model, easily six feet tall with legs that went on for days under her black romper. She had a golden tan and bright green eyes. Her blonde hair was long and wavy, falling down to her lower back.

"Never better," she snapped back before sizing me up.

She made me feel like a piece of meat. I was also a little intimidated.

"We gonna start filling the tables?" Skylar asked Braden.

Braden checked his phone for the time.

"Yeah, let's do it."

Skylar opened up the walkway for the three women. Braden signaled for me to walk with him as we led them back through the entrance hall into The Willow.

"Santi likes for us to start the night by filling the V.I.P. tables," Braden said to me as we guided the group. "Then we let the rest of the crowd in, but we always keep them waiting in the front for a bit because the more people you keep out front, the more attention you get from street traffic. We increase demand that way."

I nodded.

"How do you know Annette?" I whispered. "She's stunning."

"We hooked up when I first moved up here," Braden said loud enough for her to hear, but they were too distracted by their phones to pick up what he said.

The sound of Skylar's voice flooded my right ear through my earpiece.

"*Yo Braden, I've got the rest of Annette's group here. I'm sending them through*," he said.

Braden stopped me, causing the girls to pause in their tracks right behind us.

"Go back to get the rest of the group and bring them to Table 2. No matter who it is, greet them as if you know them but be direct in your approach. You know where Table 2 is, right?"

"Yeah, I know," I replied.

"Break it down for me," he demanded in front of the girls.

I rolled my eyes.

"Table 1 through Table 12 make up the V.I.P.'s. Table 1 through Table 6 are elevated along the western wall, and Table 7 through Table 12 are along the eastern wall... Table 1 is closest to the front, Table 6 is closest to the back, then Table 7 is closest to the back, and Table 12 is closest to the front. The ground-level section is numerically laid out the same way, only it's Table 13 to Table 22."

He patted my shoulder.

"You're ready," he smiled.

I clenched my teeth, nodded, and headed back down the hall as Braden made his way to the table.

Coming through the front door was a group of around eight people--three men and five women. The three men *must* have been professional athletes, iced out in diamond chains from the waist up, standing over six and a half feet with athletic builds, but a little on the skinnier side. The women were dimes, and I actually recognized one of them. She was an Instagram model--super hot. My jaw dropped.

Be cool, I thought as my stride slowed down. *Just greet them like you know them.*

They approached me as their conversations continued among each other. I paused in place, ready to greet them.

"What's up? I'm J-...."

The group walked right around me, failing to acknowledge my existence. I turned back to watch their strides continue as if I was completely invisible. I looked down at my hands to make sure I wasn't. They had completely ignored me. I watched as their group entered the main room with my feet practically glued to the ground.

Be cool, I thought in an attempt to recover from being completely disrespected. *Don't overthink it.*

"*Jay, I see the group made their way in without you*," Braden's voice murmured through my earpiece. "*You alright up there? It's not too complicated of a job to walk people to a table*."

"I'm fine... I got this," I replied.

"*Jay? Answer, man. You good*?" Braden asked through the earpiece.

"I said, I'm fine!" I repeated out of frustration.

His voice came through again. "*Jay, if you're responding, I can't hear you... You've gotta press on the blue button while talking for the earpiece to work*."

I quickly felt for the device in my pocket, then held down the button.

"I'm fine," I said sternly. "I'll get the next group. I'm good."

"*Okay, sounds good*," his voice cut out.

I lied. I don't think I'm fine. I wasn't fine. I'm not fine. My hands began to shake. I felt a weight pressing down on me as I grew anxious. My head suddenly became hot, and I was uncomfortable in my own skin. I looked around at the abstract art pieces on the wall. The hallway around me seemed to stretch longer and longer. I can't do this. How did I get here? What am I doing here? Should I even be here? I felt alone.

This isn't me, I thought. *This isn't my scene. These people don't know me, nor do they care about me.*

I looked up at the ceiling, closed my eyes, and took a deep breath. As clear as day, I saw myself... In a distant memory that suddenly became so *vivid*.

~ I leaped out of the parked car and stood over Braden's unconscious body. I was in Torrance. I looked down and scanned my pale 11-year-old hands, not knowing what to do with them--not knowing how to help my brother, who was just severely beaten up by a local gang. They took everything he had on him. He was lying in the fetal position, and people continued to walk by us as if we didn't exist.

It was a Friday night, and we were in the parking lot of a shopping center.

"PLEASE help my brother!" I shouted for a lady, but she kept walking.

I reached for a man who was getting into his car. He ignored me and shut the door before driving away.

"SIR, please call 9-1-1, my brother... He's bleeding!"

I felt a cold sweat rush over me.

Braden was covering his stomach and chest that had been repeatedly bashed into--his face swelling so much I could hardly recognize him. Yet, the people around us acted as if we weren't even there.

The cold sweat quickly turned into a wave of frustration. I was angry at the fact that these people walked around us like we weren't human.

"God, please help us," I whispered under my breath. "God, please help my brother."

I shouted for help as the people kept walking, failing to acknowledge our existence.

I felt sick.
I felt helpless.

Then suddenly, I felt the urge to take control--to make myself relevant in this world--to manifest and bring forth the confidence God placed somewhere within me.

I stood. I turned to two men tattooed from head to toe, talking to each other on their parked motorcycles.

"HEY," I screamed at the top of my lungs.

They turned immediately.

I began walking over to the men, looking up at the one closest to me.

"I need a phone to call an ambulance right now. My brother was just beat up by some guys, and they took his phone. I need your help… Fast," I demanded while extending my open hand.

The words flowed out of my mouth so smoothly, and my voice was so stern I felt as though they were ready to do anything I asked. The projection of my voice and my ability to suddenly make the situation clear to others had them in the palm of my hands. It was as if my balls had finally dropped.

One of the men hopped off of his bike and made a dead sprint over to see if Braden was okay, while the other handed me his phone. I called, and within ten minutes, the ambulance was there to take Braden in. I was young but old enough to realize it was a drug deal gone wrong, which left my brother gasping for air on the pavement.

I remember looking at the sky, knowing in my heart that this one life I live cannot be lived from the background. I knew then and there that we fade into the background when we focus on life's conflicts rather than focusing on our response to the conflicts. It was at that moment I made the promise to myself to be confident in my ability to make myself known to those around me. ~

"*Braden, I've got another group coming in. Take 'em to Table 3,*" Skylar's voice snapped me out of my flashback, and suddenly, the sound of muffled music from the main room of The Willow flooded my ears. I held down the button of the transmitter in my pocket.

"I'll take them," I said abruptly into the earpiece. "What name is the table under? First and last…."

"*Blake Pettis. Tall guy wearing the backwards hat walking in front of the group,*" Skylar said before cutting out.

I watched Blake turn into the hallway with a man and about eight girls behind the two of them. The girls looked young, at most 22 or 23 years old. Judging from the rhythm of their footsteps, they had been drinking *a lot*.

I scanned Blake, looking for something to comment on--for something I could use to connect. I got nothing… Wait, no… Tattoos. I scanned his arms for his tats, and even in the dimmed lighting, I recognized a Portland Trail Blazers tattoo--the logo for the basketball team. Basketball, right? In Portland… That's in Oregon, *right*?? Here goes nothing….

"Blake? Whaddup, I'm Jay…" I casually shook his hand.

"Your name's *JAY?* That's a sick name," Blake slurred as he followed me from two steps behind.

"Thanks, man," I replied as I escorted them through the hallway. "It's not that common where I'm from…."

I walked beside Blake as the rest of his group followed.

"Where you from?" he asked.

"I was born in Portland but grew up in Torrance," I replied, waiting for the connection.

"NO…" he gasped. "I'm from Portland!!!"

"Lies..." I responded as if in shock.

"Scope it," he insisted as he flashed the Portland Trail Blazer forearm tattoo. "Born and raised!"

"Small world!" I laughed, and within seconds he threw an arm around me and turned to the back of the group.

"MY BOY JAY AND I ARE FROM RIP CITY…."

It worked. The connection was made.

As we turned the corner into the main room, Braden signaled to the group from Table 3.

"Braden over there is gonna take care of you guys," I said smoothly, patting Blake on the back. "I'll check in later."

Blake drunkenly rotated to give me a hug before following the group to Braden.

"Bro," he slurred. "I've never met you before, but you've gotta *good* vibe 'bout you… Jay. Come kick it with us whenever. My hometown homie, right here."

I felt the weight--both mentally *and* physically--lifted off of my shoulders as I watched Blake return to his group. I had spent the last few weeks stuck in my head… Dwelling on the unknown...

Could Braden and I really pick up where we left off after seven years?

Is the nightlife industry really for me?

Was Santi gonna like me?

Was I gonna get this job?

How am I gonna mesh with the people here in L.A.?

Will they like me? Will I like them?

I felt the pressure and tension relieve themselves as I fully took in the present moment. I'm here to contribute, and there is nothing else in this world that matters but The Willow... Until the night is over. I will no longer let the fog consume my mind and heart. I will no longer internalize what is around me and what I've endured. I'm here for my new *family*.

The night began. Left and right, I engaged with every person I came across, building a mental database of names and immediately attaching them to faces. I made one round around the club and then another as it filled up quickly.

"*I've got a group coming in*," Skylar would say, and within seconds, I was there to engage the group with The Willow experience.

I introduced one individual to another. They laughed. They smiled. I laughed. I smiled. People took selfie photos and videos with me, and I loved every part of the attention. I ate it up.

Bottle girls in revealing leather outfits shined their flashing lights and rang sirens as they presented bottle service to the various tables. People cheered, danced, and drank as the music blared and the lights flashed.

"Oh, no way! That doesn't sound right," I said in response to an actor who had just finished telling me about his show being canceled. "They canceled *your* show to keep one running about a talking dog??"

"Yeess, dude," the guy slurred, barely able to open his eyes. "Dogs don't even talk...."

He was barely able to stand. He swayed from left to right and then fell back onto the booth, spilling what was left of his drink on himself. The group laughed and pulled out their phones to take videos of him. Maybe it was a *good* thing he wasn't big in the industry yet, considering this would've made TMZ news before the night was over if he was already somewhat significant.

"Pretty embarrassing," I heard a voice say from my left.

"He'll be fine," I said without turning. "It happens... But if he throws up, we're gonna have to have him escorted out."

I felt a hand lightly graze my shoulder.

"Oh, so you work here," the voice said softly--her voice sounding like it was a few inches from my ear.

I turned, and her piercing blue eyes looked right through me. Her hair was slicked back, tied into a high ponytail. She wore a white tank top with blue-gray slacks. Her jewelry danced alongside the twinkle in her ocean eyes.

The rest of her large group was made up of women. Dancing between the group of women was Skylar sipping on a beer.

"I'm Jay," I said to the girl before even thinking about it.

"I know," she smirked. "My friends and I were talking about you earlier."

"I hope that's a good thing," I said directly to her lips.

I was instantly infatuated and content in the moment. I looked back up into her eyes that were now looking at *my* lips. She leaned in, just centimeters from my ear.

"Have a drink with me."

I thought I should, but I knew I probably shouldn't.

She reached for the table behind me and came up with a bottle of Grey Goose.

"I can't," I sighed, as it took everything within me to say no. "I'm working."

She laughed. "So is Skylar."

I looked up to see Skylar finishing his beer and reaching for another as he continued his conversation with one of the girls.

"Just one shot," she begged, thrusting the bottle into my chest.

She's breathtaking... Also short--too short to walk runway shows... But I had no doubt she was going places as a social influencer with a face like hers. She's direct, and given she made the first move, there's no doubt she works to get what she wants. Either way, if she wants me, I'll give me to her.

I looked over the crowd as heads bobbed under the dancing lights. From a distance, I saw Niall's long wavy hair bouncing to the rhythm of the song he played--his face lit by the laptop screen as he twisted knobs and adjusted volume levels. He was in his own world, and I admired it. This didn't feel like work. It really *wasn't* work at all.

I lifted a finger, signalling for her to give me a second as I held down the button of my transmitter. "Braden, you still out front?"

I waited.

"*Yeah, I'm out here... It's slowing down a bit. Come switch with me. I wanna run the floor and make rounds*."

"Alright, give me five minutes," I replied.

"*Sounds good. Just give me a heads up before you come out*."

I did one more quick scan of The Willow for Santi and saw him in one of the villas behind Niall. He was in deep conversation with a few older men who occupied one of the elevated gazebos.

My eyes met the girl's eyes again. She was looking up at me, bottle in hand. Biting her lip and squinting her eyes, she lifted the bottle toward my face. With my chin up, the chilled vodka fell right into my mouth, sending chills down the back of my neck all the way down to my fingertips. She slowly pulled the bottle back as the remainder of the stream spilled on my shirt. We both laughed as I wiped my lips.

"My turn," she giggled, handing me the bottle.

Her giggle was so full of life--a reflection of those lively blue eyes. She *knew* her eyes were like no other. I could tell by the way she used them. It was the perfect combination of flaunting them and also appearing engaged. Whether she genuinely was or wasn't, I was mesmerized.

She tilted her head back, lifting her chin. Her mouth slowly opened as I held up the bottle. I lightly poured as she maintained eye contact with me.

"Aye!! Thatta boy, Jay!!!" shouted Skylar from across the booth as he continued hyping up the group.

The whole group cheered, pulling out their phones, taking pictures and videos. I recognized Annette from earlier, standing among the group, although this wasn't her table. It didn't take a lot for me to realize that most--if not all--of these women know each other. L.A. is a big city with a small scene... And these women own it. They were locals, judging by the fact that our bottle girls didn't ask for a form of payment after they ordered their first bottle. I'm assuming Santi likes to keep the pretty faces around, so he cuts them a deal and sets them up with tables.

"You should give me your phone real quick," the girl playfully insisted as she reached into my pocket.

She pulled my phone out and typed in a phone number I hoped was hers. She called it, ended the call, and handed it back to me.

She stood on her tiptoes, pressing her lips to my ear once more. "You can work now, but play with me later."

She let go of my shoulder, gave me one last smile, then joined the rest of her friends for a dance. I subtly stumbled toward the stairs and grabbed the railing, processing what just happened--an instant connection. She drew me in and let me go, leaving me stunned.

I leaned over the railing, overlooking the crowd from the elevated V.I.P. section.

Alright, back to it then, I thought as I ran my fingers back through my hair.

I made my way through the massive crowd toward the entrance of The Willow. I suddenly remembered Santi referring to The Willow engaging all five of the senses at once.

I looked up to see the willow leaves reaching down toward me, ready to swallow me whole. I felt the cold air hug me as it kept me wired and alert. I heard the music being played from all angles, even below. I could still taste the chilled vodka in my mouth that went down smoother than ever before. I smelled the elegant aroma that was so foreign yet luring... The aroma... *Ace*! I finally recognized the scent. The last club I was at in Manhattan, along with many others, *must* have belonged to Santi. It had the same exact scent.

I inhaled and exhaled. I was *fully* immersed in The Willow.

Santi is an *artist*--an expert in his craft.

I entered the hallway that connected the main room to the

front entrance. I felt the warm air welcome me as I stepped past the two bouncers onto the sidewalk, looking for Braden. I noticed his silk shirt from behind as he peeked his head into the passenger's side of a souped-up B.M.W. parked along the curb.

Before I could acknowledge him, I watched as he reached into his pocket, pulled out a tiny round red bag, and slipped it through the window opening. My heart dropped. I recognized that red bag. It was similar to the bags he used to hide in his guitar amplifier back in Torrance. I turned back through the doors and peeked through the entrance. The bouncers didn't bat an eye.

Was Braden still dealing???
Did he not learn anything the past seven years???
Was losing Josh not enough???

I watched as he swiftly received a wad of cash and slipped it into his back pocket. My stomach tightened, and I felt myself getting sick, but before I could get sick, my mind was hijacked by the thought of the girl I had just met. Suddenly, I felt... *At ease*.

I reached for the transmitter in my pocket.

"I'm on my way," I warned Braden.

Still hiding behind the entrance, I watched Braden quickly say goodbye to the driver and dart back to the front doors, standing beside the bouncers. He lit a cigarette. I waited a few seconds and then stepped out onto the sidewalk.

"Hey."

"There he is. How's the first night going, rookie?" he asked as he exhaled smoke over his shoulder. He was buzzed.

"It's amazing," I sighed in genuine admiration.

In the moment, it just didn't make sense for me to call Braden out for what I saw. I wasn't in the mood or position to jeopardize offending the only family I had left after spending so many years apart. Braden was now his own man, and who was I to interfere with his life decisions? Without him, I wouldn't be here, and I didn't care to think about where I *would* be if I were anywhere but here.

It was 2a.m. when Niall's voice called for us to start wrapping up the night. Ubers, Lyfts, and designated drivers lined the sidewalk outside The Willow as people began to leave. Some stumbled while others approached cars asking if the ride belonged to them. Conversations consisted of after-party plans or who was going home with who. Some couples didn't even make it into the car without already having their hands in each other's pants.

"Let's go, move it, *move it*," Braden urged the leftover crowd.

"Bradennnn, you want to come-... Come to-over to my

place??" A drunk and sloppy Annette threw herself at Braden.

"Maybe. I'll call you when I'm done here."

She stutter-stepped and fell into the back seat of her Uber with the girls she came with. Braden took a few steps back and stood beside me. My hands were jammed into my pockets as I people-watched.

He lit another cigarette and exhaled.

"Can I get one?" I asked, extending my open palm.

He took a drag as he processed what I said. After giving me a skeptical stare, he shrugged.

"You're getting back into it?"

"Maybe," I shrugged back before lighting the cigarette. "When are you gonna tell me more about this Annette girl?"

We both let out a laugh.

"You'll hear about it eventually," he teased. "If not from me, it'll be from somebody else."

"Whatever you say," I murmured. "I met a girl tonight."

He faced me, and his eyes widened as he lowered his cigarette down to his waist.

"You met a girl!" he uttered. "First night on the job and Jay falls in love! What's her name??"

"I don't know," I shrugged. "I got her number, though. I'm gonna text her tomorrow."

"Don't get locked up too soon, Jay… You're officially in the nightlife business. This sort of stuff is gonna happen on the *daily*."

I took what Braden said lightly, but little did I know what I was *really* getting into and how right he was.

EIGHT | THEN ANOTHER… AND ANOTHER.

BRADEN'S APARTMENT
DOWNTOWN L.A.
THURSDAY, 11:47A.M. - JULY 4TH, 2019

I opened my eyes and stared directly at the ceiling of my room--well… The spare room Braden is letting me stay in. Realistically, I should probably start looking for my own place, but I have no desire to live alone after living alone for the past seven years. Plus, the sheets are *insanely* comfortable.

I could hear and smell fresh coffee being brewed in the kitchen from behind the closed door, and I realized how much I could go for a cup right now. I reached for my phone. A couple texts and notifications lit up the screen, but nothing important enough to get me to unlock it. I set my phone down and headed for the door expecting to see Braden making coffee. Upon opening the door, my jaw dropped at the sight of a woman making coffee instead. She was wearing Braden's button-up shirt… And *only* the button-up shirt.

I shut the door abruptly. I was in shock.

Good stuff, I thought as I sat on the bed.

I didn't recognize her from the club, but Braden definitely deserved some recognition later for what I just saw.

And just like that, I was suddenly wide awake and ready to start the day.

I did my 100 crunches.

I took my usual hot shower in the dark.

Brushed my teeth.

Blow-dried my hair.

Then threw on some face lotion, deodorant, and cologne.

I slowly and quietly opened the door, and the kitchen was empty this time. I peeked my head between the narrow opening I made for myself, scanning the kitchen and living room. No sight of a half-naked woman or Braden.

After starting up the espresso machine, I began scrolling through my phone. Braden's bedroom door was closed, and I assumed the woman was still in there, considering the two coffee cups she filled were nowhere in sight. I sat back on the couch and pulled up the number that belonged to the girl I met last night.

I *want* to text her.
I *should* text her.
Should I text her?
I'm gonna text her.
I texted her.

ME: Hey, it's Jay from The Willow last night

I'm not sure if it's obvious that I overthink things, but one thing's for sure… I almost *always* overthink texting. I wish it was as easy as just sending and receiving, but I've found myself reading into things since before I can remember. It'd be so much easier to just see things in black and white, but I live in the gray, and there's no escaping it at this point.

Braden's bedroom door opened. He walked out in his boxers, leading the woman toward the front door. She was wearing what I assume she wore last night. They didn't acknowledge me.

"It says he's here," Braden said while checking his phone and opening the door. "The Ubers usually pull up next to the valet."

"Thanks," she blushed. "I'll see you at Tiffany's?"

"Yeah, we'll probably head over there in a couple hours."

She leaned in to kiss Braden, and he reciprocated with very little enthusiasm. He shut the door behind her.

"Who was *that*?" I blurted out from the couch.

Braden leaped in shock at the sound of my voice. "JESUS, Jay! You don't scare people like that."

"Sorry," I laughed. "We've gotta come up with some sort of code for when we have girls over. I walked in on your girl half-naked in the kitchen."

"We're not in high school, Jay," he snapped back as he poured himself a mug of vodka and orange juice. "You can't handle a little bit of ass in the kitchen?"

I ignored the question I assumed was rhetorical.

"I texted the girl from last night."

Braden sipped his drink and sat next to me. "What'd she say?"

"Nothing yet," I sighed as I checked my phone. "But I mean, I just sent it, so I guess we'll see."

"You should invite her to Tiffany's."

"Who's that?"

"She's some model who's throwing a 4th of July pool party today up in Hollywood Hills. I'll text you the address right now."

"You think Tiffany would be fine with us inviting girls?" I asked.

"Yeah, trust. We hook these girls up every night at the club. You're fine."

"Okay... After she responds, I'll invite her."

I went back to scrolling through social media.

Braden and I got ready and walked down the street to get something to eat at one of the local cafes. There wasn't a single cloud in the sky, and the weather was so perfect, you couldn't even feel it.

"I don't think I have swim trunks," I said in-between bites of my avocado toast.

"You don't need any," Braden replied as he carelessly crossed the street between traffic. "People don't *actually* swim at these things... Just gives the girls a reason to wear bikinis while the pool is just kinda *there*."

"Woah, I would've never thought," I said, barely dodging a car as I hopped onto the sidewalk.

The sound of rushing cars zoomed past us as we turned the corner toward Braden's apartment. I took a large bite out of my toast and almost coughed it up at the sight of yet another billboard I could certainly live without seeing. I stopped in my tracks, appalled at the image that was propped up in the storefront.

Braden continued walking a few more feet before realizing I stopped. He turned to see me fixated on the massive image of Val hanging behind the glass. It was a side profile shot in black and white--only, her hair was cut short and dyed platinum blonde, accentuating her defined jawline.

"She's everywhere, man," Braden said from beside me.

"I know," I sighed. "I passed her billboard every day in Times Square on my way to work."

"Come on," Braden wrapped his arm around me and pulled me in the direction of the apartment.

As Braden showered and got ready, I sprawled myself on the couch and pulled out my phone. I took a deep breath and started typing into the Instagram search bar.

V.A.L.E.N.T....

Her full username popped up before I could even finish typing it out.

@ValentinaMoralis

I took another deep breath upon seeing her profile picture. It was the same image from the billboard in Times Square.

Before I could tap on her profile, a text notification from a random number popped up.

RANDOM NUMBER: Hii Jay :)

My heart dropped--or fluttered--I couldn't really tell which, but I opened the text before I was even able to decide. My mind was drawn to the memory of the girl's blue eyes looking up at me--the playful giggle replaying in my head as if it were happening here and now.

"*Hii Jay* :)"

I reread the text a couple times then sent her the address for the pool party.

Three or four hours later, I was clenching a bottle of Hennessy in my lap, listening to the bass of a hip-hop song fill Braden's Tesla. We sped up the hill. Houses passed us left and right, some modern and others rich in history or simply just worn and mismanaged. I looked down at the bottle of Hennessy. I don't even like Hennessy.

"*Just trust me*," Braden assured me back at the liquor store as he thrust the bottle into my chest. I took his word for it.

The G.P.S. warned us that we were approaching Tiffany's as guys and girls funneled through the street in the same direction as us. Designer brands, short shorts, flashy jewelry, and nice cars flooded the street as beautiful people embraced one another before entering Tiffany's house.

Braden suddenly whipped a sharp right turn into the driveway of a modern mansion as he downed what was left of his flask. The driveway had rectangle grass streaks that stretched from the street to the wooden garage door. It was wide enough to fit at *least* three cars. Two sports cars were parked carelessly on the driveway, and Skylar sat on the hood of one of them with a bottle of 1942.

"What's up, boys?!" he shouted in a high-pitched tone with a big smile on his face.

I stepped out of the car, and he gave me a tight hug before handing me the bottle of tequila.

"Take a swig, Baby Jay!"

Without thinking, I took a pull from the bottle, which went down smoother than I thought it would. My mouth burned but quickly smoothed over after I swallowed. The first shot is usually always the hardest, but that wasn't too bad.

People walked up from the street, already buzzing and introducing themselves to me. Skylar and Braden greeted most of them by first name, attaching inside jokes to the various faces that presented themselves. Skylar threw his arm around me and pulled me into a headlock as we walked up the driveway toward the front door.

"Is this your first time up here??" he asked before taking another pull of 1942.

"It is," I said without resisting the headlock.

"Love to hear it, Jay Money!" he laughed, throwing out yet another new nickname I hadn't heard until now. "I'll be the first to make sure it goes *smoothly*."

He tucked a tiny plastic bag into my hand with three flower-shaped pills in it that looked oddly familiar.

"Take 'em when you're tryna level up," he teased while squeezing my shoulder.

"Thanks," I said. I slipped them into my pocket and didn't think much of it as I took another pull of 1942.

Braden opened the massive glass door, and my jaw dropped at the sight of the interior. Two marble staircases lined the entryway walls. Below the exposed second floor above us, the vast hall extended directly to the infinity pool in the backyard.

Large abstract paintings hung on almost every wall, and everything just seemed... *Bigger*--all of it bigger than it should be. Bodies all moved at once but in different directions. People poured drinks, danced, played games, took pictures. It was as if Hollywood's youth was consolidated into almost 10,000 square feet.

The music blared throughout the house, engulfing Skylar, Braden, and myself as we walked in, holding our bottles up like we owned the place. Heads turned, and I must've made eye contact with almost every individual I passed.

I took another sip.

Then another... And another.

Something I couldn't wrap my head around was how this life was even *real*--to have a job that consisted of me inviting attractive people to clubs... Only to sleep in the next day and end up at a pool party in the hills. It felt *surreal*.

We made our way into the backyard that was partially made up of an infinity pool stretching straight into the horizon... And Braden was right... Not a single person was swimming, but they were scattered across large colorful bean bag chairs and daybeds on a deck surrounding the pool.

"Yo," I said in astonishment. I stopped walking.

Skylar and Braden stopped alongside me as I tapped their chests with the back of my hands to get their attention.

"That's Shawn Lane," I gasped. "We used to bump his music back in high school before our soccer games...."

Skylar laughed and nudged me as Braden shook his head, unamused.

"Don't worry, kid... You'll get used to seeing these kinds of people around..." Skylar teased. "Come on. I'll introduce you."

"I'm gonna get a drink," Braden declared as he headed toward the open bar.

Skylar and I zigzagged through the crowded yard, greeting both strangers and people I recognized from last night. We got closer and closer to Shawn Lane, who was all alone, rolling a blunt on the railing that separated the backyard from the cliff the house was built on. I took one last pull of tequila before Skylar spoke.

"Yo, Shawn, whaddup, brother?" Skylar greeted.

"Skylar, what's good??" Shawn Lane smiled as he embraced Skylar.

"This is Jay. Santi just brought him in."

Shawn Lane smiled and extended his hand. "What's up, Jay?"

"Nice to meet you," I greeted in awe. I shook his hand. Was that too formal? Is that a normal thing to do? A formal handshake at a house party?

"I'm 'boutta smoke one if you guys want in," Shawn Lane offered politely while he finished rolling the blunt.

"I appreciate you for that... I'm gonna get a drink, though, and probably come back in a few," Skylar said as he checked his phone.

"What about you, Jay?" Shawn Lane asked, pointing the blunt toward my chest.

Smoking a blunt with Shawn Lane?

"... Sure," I said hesitantly.

I smoked weed once in middle school and never again after that... But I wasn't gonna pass up a chance to connect with an artist I've idolized since I was 13.

"What brings you to L.A.?" Shawn Lane asked as he lit the blunt. "You a model or somethin'? You got a good head of hair."

"My brother is actually the reason I'm out here. I was in New York, and he got me set up in the nightclub scene here."

"How do you like it?" he took his first drag.

"It's *amazing*," I replied. "Everyone here is so laid back."

"No, I mean... How do you like the *scene*?" he reiterated before taking another hit.

"It's awesome, man. Doesn't really even feel like work."

He took off his glasses and intricately studied me. He wore a flashy Gucci outfit that matched from top to bottom. The sun reflected off of a series of rose gold chains that hung from his neck and wrapped his wrist.

"It's true," he said while nodding his head in agreement. "You just gotta be careful you don't get stuck in."

"What do you mean?" I asked.

He handed me the blunt and continued.

"I've heard stories about Santi, and that dude is somethin' else."

I took a drag of the blunt. "How so?"

"The dude is *mad* manipulative--*really* knows how to entertain and attract people into his clubs and shit. I just hear he's got a side of him you don't wanna discover... *Wild*."

I felt myself loosen up, and my attention started to deviate from the conversation as the tequila and weed kicked in. I hit the blunt again and handed it back to Shawn.

"Really? He's helped my brother out a lot since they started working together."

"Totally," he raised his palms, showing respect. "He's a genius. I just know that the business isn't the *cleanest* on the back end from what I hear... And Santi is *top dog* in the business, so I just assume...."

I didn't want to believe what he said, nor did I have the mental capacity to really grasp it at the moment. I was becoming less and less sober by the second. My phone vibrated, and as I pulled it out of my pocket, the clear baggy Skylar gave me fell to the floor, catching Shawn's eye.

"NO WAY," his eyes widened as he reached down to pick it up. "Can I bum one off of you?? I've been asking 'round for some E, but everyone's dry."

"Sure," I replied casually, acting as if I'm totally familiar with whatever "E" is.

I watched as Shawn chased the pill down with a shot of the 1942 bottle I had placed on the railing. I opened my phone to a text from a random number. It was a picture of me taken from across the party and then a text.

RANDOM NUMBER: I see you ;)

I looked up and scanned the backyard. Heads swayed to the music as people laughed and tripped over one another. It was progressively getting more crowded as teens and young adults poured out from the house.

My eyes trailed over the heads until I made *direct* eye contact with her, and my jaw dropped to the floor--it was the girl from last night. I couldn't help but smile as I weaved through the crowd in her direction. I maintained a rhythm, moving swiftly to the song that blasted from every angle of the yard. People leaned and rocked--some straight into me and others in different directions. I could've sworn somebody grabbed my ass, but I was on a mission and didn't care to find out who did.

I slid my hands back through my hair, feeling the afternoon sun on the back of my neck. I was more in tune with my senses, becoming one with the party. I remained fixated on her--the ice blue drawing me in like some sort of promising oasis in the middle of a desert. My infatuation with her eyes only grew more and more the closer I got.

Her hands swayed above her head from side to side as she danced alongside her friends. They were on the edge of an elevated deck, overlooking the crowd that stood on the grass. I was nearly under her when she stuck her hand out to hold mine.

Her baby blue bikini brought out the blue in her eyes against her tanned complexion. Her hair was dark brown and fell back behind her shoulders that bounced to the rhythm of the music.

"I *thought* I recognized you!" she said with a charming giggle. She pulled me up onto the deck.

"How long have you been here for??" I asked, competing with the blaring music.

"I just got here," she smiled. "You gotta drink??"

I looked around, immediately realizing I had left the bottle back with Shawn. I could feel the alcohol run its course as I became even looser, and I didn't mind the thought of letting go a bit more. I was officially in good company.

"I think I need one," I said while eye to eye with her, reciprocating her contagious smile.

"Come on, let's get one!" she playfully shouted as she grabbed my hand and stepped down from the deck.

"Wait!" I stood firm and stopped her from moving. "What's your name??"

"Sofia," she said softly before biting her lip and smiling once more. "But just call me 'Fia.'"

She pulled me toward the house again, and this time I let her. It's as if I was one with fate, letting it pull me in any direction it pleased. Everything around me was all molding together as one lively and colorful ambiance. To think that I had lived the last seven years in a fog was unfathomable at this very moment, and nothing could stop me from living life to the fullest. She led. I followed.

I felt... *Good.*

We weaved through groups at our left and right until we reached the long marble kitchen counter that was littered with bottles and food.

Fia poured both of us a shot of tequila.
Then another... And another.

We bounced from one part of the house to the next as she introduced me to her friends--some on their way to getting drunk and others already blacked-out drunk. Our drinks never hit the bottom, as people from all over offered to refill our cups before we could finish them.

"Jay!" shouted a voice I recognized immediately.

I turned to look over my left shoulder, where Kalani embraced me without trying to spill his drink.

"What's up?!" I shouted back, realizing how drunk I was upon saying it.

He must've been on a *couple* of different things because I could tell he was struggling to keep his eyes open while talking to me. I didn't care, though... I thought it was funny. We didn't know each other for very long, but it was almost like being intoxicated in the same place instantly made us *closer*.

"This is Fia!" I said.

"Whaadduup Fia??" Kalani slurred and then attempted to focus. "Hold up... You look *familiar*."

"Me? Really??" Fia giggled as she looked at me and then back at Kalani.

"Yeah," he squinted his eyes to get a better look at her. "I'm pretty sure I've seen you at The Willow before."

She tilted her head to the side while still smiling, trying to process where Kalani was going with this.

"I'm *always* there with my girls!" Fia said before sipping her drink.

"Nooo, like... I've seen you talking to Santi like during the day there--like you worked there or something."

"Nope... Wasn't me," Fia said before finishing her drink.

Kalani paused, staring directly into her eyes. After a few seconds of awkward silence, his head lightly bobbed to the music, and his attention was pulled away by the party.

"For sure," he said dismissively, altogether dropping the topic. He faced me once again. "You two should come hang with us up on Tiffany's balcony. I was just on my way back up."

Kalani turned and stumbled toward one of the staircases by the front door. Fia looked up at me and grabbed my hand.

"Up to you," she smiled.

We made our way through the living room and up the marble staircase. People were scattered across all parts of the house--downstairs, *on* the stairs, upstairs, and in almost every room we passed.

Fia and I followed Kalani into a spacious master bedroom

with a glass wall in the back that opened up into a wide balcony with furniture on it. Sprawled on the furniture and around the balcony were Braden, Kai, Niall, Kalani, Skylar, and a group of girls. Their faces lit up as we approached them.

"YES!" screamed Skylar as he gave me a big hug and then faced the girls. "Ladies, this is Jay! The *better* Amor brother."

Braden gave a lighthearted scoff as he sat up. The girl sitting next to him stood and leaped into my arms, giving me a hug so tight I could barely breathe for a second.

"I'm Tiffany!" she exclaimed as she pulled back and sized me up. "Braden's told me *so* much about you...."

She gave me another hug before catching sight of Fia. "Oh my God, Fia... Hi!!"

"Hey, cutie!" Fia shouted as they hugged.

I laid back on the couch next to Braden.

"How're you feelin'?" I asked Kai, suddenly remembering he had nicotine poisoning the other day.

"Better now," Kai replied. He reached for his drink on the table between us.

Kai wore a bucket hat and designer shades that covered most of his face. His button-up was unbuttoned all the way down as he sat holding a cigarette with one leg crossed over the other.

Niall sat motionless to his right, across the table from Braden and me. He was laying back with his chin up toward the sky and sunglasses on. His wavy locks were tied back into a bun, and he was shirtless, revealing random tattoos that looked like they had been stenciled on by an amateur artist... Or a *kid*. He had a subtle smile on his face, content with the world around him.

"I still can't believe Santi made me smoke all those cigs," Kai sighed, holding back a laugh as he took a drag of his cig.

"Does he *usually* do that kind of stuff?" I asked.

Braden handed me a cigarette, and I placed it between my lips before lighting it.

"Not really, because we rarely ever piss him off. I should've asked him before smoking it, though... He was right."

"Who was he talking to up in the villa the whole night?" I asked, remembering Santi up in the private gazebo with his guests.

"The less you know about what goes on behind the scenes, the better..." Niall chimed in sarcastically without moving a muscle. He was smirking, still staring straight into the sky. Kai and Braden both let out a laugh before sipping their drinks.

What did they mean by that? I thought to myself.

It seems like everybody's got something to say about Santi--whether it be positive or negative. Was Santi *really* as manipulative as Shawn made him out to be? Am I the one being manipulated without realizing it?

I know that Braden wouldn't willingly bring me into this business if he knew it was shady--or would he? Seven years had gone by without a single form of contact between the two of us. So, it would only be logical for me to not automatically judge our relationship based on where we left off, considering all that's happened since then until now....

I can't deny what I've seen and what I currently see.

I've seen what life is like alone, and I didn't like it.

I've seen what life is like having family back in it.

I've seen a glimpse of Santi's enthusiasm and passion for nightlife.

I see an opportunity to reinvent myself--to rewrite what went wrong.

I see an opportunity to learn.

I see an opportunity to live out our dream--Braden and me.

I snapped out of my trance as Fia squeezed her way between Braden and me on the couch.

"Is this seat taken??" she smirked.

"It is *now*," I replied softly, leaning back and immediately letting go of everything that was on my mind.

I smiled without even thinking about it. Fia did the same.

"HOLY SHIT!" shouted Skylar as he stared at his phone and bounced up and down.

We all looked up immediately, startled at his sudden burst of joy. Tiffany rolled her eyes after looking at his phone to see what it was about.

"BOYS..." Skylar stood with his hands raised. "I just got a text from Santi... And *we...* Are *hosting...* The 2019 SWIM WEEK after-party!"

"No way..." Braden gasped with his jaw dropped.

"YEP!" Skylar shouted with joy. "It's the Saturday night one, too... The most important night of Swim Week, bitches!"

Kalani raised his cup.

Niall grinned, still not moving a muscle.

"Jay... You joined at the right time, brotha," Kai slurred as he began pouring shots for the group. "You've only been with us for a couple days, and in a week, we'll be in Miami."

I reached for one of the shot glasses and lifted it as the group grabbed their own and did the same.

“I’ll drink to that.”

We took our shots.
Then another… And another.

NINE | WE LIVE TO SERVE

BRADEN'S APARTMENT
DOWNTOWN L.A.
THURSDAY, 3:21P.M. - JULY 11TH, 2019

"Do you have everything?" Fia asked as I squeezed my third pair of shoes into my Louis duffle bag.

"I think so," I sighed, trying to remember what I could be missing. I *hate* that feeling.

She was sitting at the foot of my bed wearing nothing but my T-shirt. I had just put a pair of sweatpants on after being in bed with Fia all morning and was finishing up packing for Miami. Sunlight seeped through my bedroom window, and chill music played off of the T.V. speakers. This was my life the past seven days when I wasn't at The Willow or some party in the hills. A week had passed since the pool party, and I spent every night with Fia since. I couldn't complain... The sex was amazing, and I just never got tired of looking at her.

Her body.
Her eyes.
Her lips.
Her smile.
Her *body*.

I know I said body twice... Only because I saw more of her body than I did the clothes she wore. She was everything I looked for in a girl... Physically. I can't deny that the past seven years have caused me to inherently build up these walls, keeping out any form of emotional connection... But it seemed like she didn't care to get to know more about me anyway... So it works out just fine.

"Text me when you touch down in Miami," I insisted as I zipped up the bag.

She tilted her head with a flirty grin. "Maybe...."

She slowly laid back on the bed, propping herself up with her elbows on my white sheets. She bit her lip, sizing me up. I checked my phone for the time and saw a text from Kalani--just some picture he thought was funny.

I looked back up at her and watched as she slowly spread her legs with a cheeky smirk.

"*Last* time," I said, trying to hold back a smile.

"We'll see," she whispered as she leaned forward and pulled me back into bed.

Within a couple hours, I was on my way to The Willow, zipping through traffic in my *own* Tesla--brand new. Every centimeter of it was matte white, including the decals--in perfect contrast with the black rims. Santi had given me a generous signing bonus, and I was officially on the payroll, making more than I ever thought I would in this business.

I shifted the car into autopilot mode and reached for the flask I poured myself back at the apartment. The tequila went down smoother than water, given how much I had been drinking while spending time with the boys the past week. The more time I spent with them, the more I found myself drinking. It seemed to be almost all they did, but I didn't mind it. We were living in the good times, and I knew more were on the way. I took a small pull from the flask and rolled down the windows to feel the summer breeze running through my hair. Life is good.

I pulled up to The Willow, duffle bag in hand. Kalani and Skylar were outside smoking a joint with their bags lying between them.

"What's up, boys?" I greeted as I embraced the two of them.

"Jizzle!" Skylar shouted.

"Jizzle??" Kalani blurted out, followed by a laugh that turned into a cough.

"I can't get *every* nickname down on the first try," Skylar rolled his eyes. "Man, Jay… You should've seen Kalani hit this new bong I came up on last night."

"Shut up," Kalani lowered his head in embarrassment as Skylar let out an obnoxious laugh.

"Dude, dude… Jay… He was sprawled out on his ass and wouldn't shut up about some pet guinea pig he had back in the 5th grade. I swear it's the weed we were smoking. I'm starting up a weed-gummy business with some buddies, and this shit *rips*."

"His name was Chester," Kalani snapped back, exhaling a cloud of smoke. "That weed strain got me in my feels."

"Hey, man," I comforted Kalani, rubbing his shoulder and trying not to laugh. "We've all been there. Where's the rest of the group?"

"They're inside tidying up the place before we head to the airport," Kalani explained as he handed me the joint. "Santi is already there, so we should leave soon."

"This trip is about to be *insane*," Skylar gasped, on the verge of drooling.

"How does Swim Week work?" I asked.

Skylar dropped the remainder of the joint and stepped on it with the sole purpose of explaining with both hands.

"You ready for this?" he lowered himself into a presenting stance. Kalani and I leaned forward, already intrigued.

"Every year, the world's *hottest* bikini brand ambassadors and models fly to Miami to create a hub for sun-kissed *booty*. For the next week, this event is gonna consist of bikini models walking the runway by day and raging face by night. When I say, 'bikini models,' I mean, 'BIKINI MODELS.' You understand? You don't understand... I don't think you understand."

Kalani and I looked at each other and then back at Skylar, nodding for him to continue.

"You've got three bikini tradeshows going on," he continued, numbering them off accordingly. "Swimshow, Hammock, and Cabana. But we don't have to worry about what *actually* goes on at that shit. Knowing Santi, he'll hook us up with V.I.P. passes and all that good stuff. Only *he* could pull off getting our hospitality group to host the hottest party of the week."

"Say no more," I raised my hands. "I'm sold."

The doors of The Willow swung open as Braden, Kai, and Niall walked out holding their bags.

"Let's run it, boys," insisted Braden as he walked between us and opened the back door of a blacked-out S.U.V. that was parked curbside. "Throw your bags in the back."

We packed the S.U.V. and were off to the airport. I sipped my flask, and I could feel Kai eyeing it from my left. I handed it to him, and he took a shot before handing it back and typing away on his phone.

"Are we supposed to have our tickets?" I asked.

Half of the guys let out a subtle laugh at the question before Niall chimed in while tying back his hair into a bun.

"We fly private," he said smugly. "We've got our jet, and then Santi's got his own."

"Two jets??" I uttered in shock.

"I know," Kai interjected without looking up from his phone. "You'd think we're blowing through funds... Which we are... But we manage to keep at a surplus with the business model Santi had me structure for him a few months ago."

He lightly leaned into my shoulder, showing me the spreadsheet of numbers he was looking at on his phone. My jaw dropped, seeing the unfathomable amount of income Santi was making monthly. It almost didn't even make sense.

"These are just his clubs, bars, and restaurants in L.A. Santi has venues on an *international* scale."

I looked forward, envisioning the empire Santi had built for himself and many others. Braden and I grew up with the dream of owning our own nightclub, and it was at this moment that I realized how fruitless a dream becomes if you don't execute in order to bring it to *fruition*. We had spent most of our lives gliding over the surface--even above the point of *skimming* it--only to now discover that Santi has built an empire in the depths, with the knowledge that we would need to one day do the same. I had Braden to thank for the position he put me in--the position to *learn* from a man I now idolize and *trust*.

"Yo, Jay, is this the girl you've been seeing?" Skylar asked while handing me his phone.

On the screen was a picture Fia had posted on Instagram. She was standing knee-deep in a pool, pulling her wet hair back. Her bikini was high-waisted, and the picture was evidently showing *much more* than her personality. I didn't seem to mind the guys and other people potentially objectifying her. In a way, it made me feel... *Proud*.

"Yeah, I've been seeing her but it's nothing serious," I replied calmly.

"I'm telling you, I've seen her around the club kicking it with Santi!" Kalani said while peeking over my right shoulder.

"Santi kicks it with *every* girl," murmured Niall as he inhaled a nicotine pen.

"I really wouldn't care," I assured them hollowly.

I felt a slight shift within me, and I didn't like the feeling. The fact of the matter was that I *am* starting to catch feels, and maybe these feelings were buried in the physical infatuation Fia and I expressed toward one another. I hadn't been in many relationships at all, but I know for sure that I've never been the jealous type. I don't intend on overthinking what I have with her because my main priority is The Willow and the guys--my new *family*.

We pulled up to the private jet terminal, passed through security, and before I knew it, we were back in another S.U.V. driving alongside the runways. The afternoon sun bounced off of large hangar windows and polished aluminum as we passed one private jet after another. The sun was preparing to set, casting a pink and orange shade over the clouds--the setting so surreal I felt as if I was the main character in a movie... But to the rest of the guys, it was just like any other trip as they remained fixated on their phones, unamused.

Our S.U.V. was now headed directly toward two jets that were relatively close to one another. A small group of three women and one man were engaged in conversation between the two jets, and as we got closer, I could see that the man was Santi. Our car caught his eye as we approached, and he spread his arms as a way of greeting us, smiling and raising his eyebrows above his sunglasses.

As we stopped, Santi walked toward us, and the women followed, remaining a few feet behind. He wore sunglasses with a shaded tint that grew lighter toward the bottom of the frames. His fitted black T-shirt was subtly tucked into black pants that fell over his loafers--diamond chains and bracelets illuminated, per usual.

"My boys!" he shouted with his arms still raised, competing with the roaring sound of the jet engines.

We piled out with our bags to greet Santi. Kai quickly made his way beside him, rambling on about some balance sheets he had been going over on the way to the airport, but Santi was quick to shut him out.

"Let's save it for the flight over," Santi insisted with a cunning grin.

The guys stood attentively, waiting to be directed. Santi adjusted his Rolex and studied us up and down, then left to right.

"Niall, Skylar, and Kalani… You guys are on *that* jet with my friends over here. Jay, Braden, and Kai... You ride with me," he said as he clapped his hands, and just like that... We were all headed toward our designated jets.

As we approached the jet, the engine's noise grew louder and louder, and I took one last look at the vast runway that seemed to stretch on forever. A five-step staircase led us up through the entrance of the small but agile-looking aircraft. Two female flight attendants stood inside to greet us with welcoming smiles. They were stunning, and I finally just accepted the fact that every woman Santi surrounds himself with is an absolute dime.

We passed a miniature bar stocked with bottles and elegantly shaped glasses as we made our way to the middle. The main cabin of the jet was designed to have two communal sections with plush cream-colored leather seats facing each other. Directly at the back of the cabin was a restroom and an open curtain that led to a bedroom.

I passed the first communal section before I felt a hand on my shoulder. I paused and saw the shiny rings that decorated the hand, immediately realizing it was Santi.

"Sit with me up here, Jay," he said with a smirk.

Kai and Braden paused awkwardly, waiting for Santi to ask them to do the same.

"You head to the back, boys," he insisted before gesturing for one of the flight attendants to escort them.

They nodded and did as they were told. I sat, and before I could even set my bag down, the flight attendant grabbed it with a smile. "Allow me!"

"Thanks," I smiled back.

"I'll be right back to fix you some drinks, gentlemen."

"Allow *me*," Santi said smoothly while gently caressing her shoulder in passing.

His back was to me, and I could hear the clinking of glasses and bottles as he prepared our drinks. I heard a few long pours before he turned, flashing his perfect teeth just below the sunglasses he was still wearing. He sat directly across from me and handed me one of the drinks. I thanked him as he crossed one leg over the other and looked out the window.

"You ever flown private?" he asked as he studied the runway, twirling the ice in his glass with his pinky. We were now picking up speed, and the jet was preparing to lift off the ground.

"Never," I sighed. "This still doesn't feel real."

He tapped his pinky ring against the rim of the glass. "Which part of it doesn't feel real?"

"Honestly, L.A., in general, doesn't."

"Well, that's because it *isn't* real!" he exclaimed, then laughed.

"Okay, okay... True," I nodded, raising my drink which he was quick to tap with his own.

We took our sips, and I instantly observed my glass with concern, blindsided by the familiar taste I hadn't come across in years--a vodka soda. I tensed up, and my heart dropped as I was immediately taken back to the last time I had the drink--the night of the party when Josh had passed. My stomach tightened, and I set the drink down.

"Too strong?" Santi asked, expressing concern.

"No," I replied softly. "It just took me back. This was my drink back in high school...."

"Ah, Braden told me this was your favorite drink. Is it not?"

"It was." I looked down at his glass.

"You should try gin and tonics," he replied. "It's been my drink for *years*."

I smiled, then relaxed my shoulders and took another sip of my drink, figuring the more I drank, the less I would *think*. The jet was now well into the air, and before I knew it, we were in the sky and onto our next round of drinks. I felt myself getting looser as Santi and I caught up on my getting used to the scene.

We talked about how quick I was able to pick up names of guests, remember drink orders, and basically learn everything from an operational standpoint quicker than any promoter he had hired at any of his venues. One night, there was this spur-of-the-moment decision I made to sprint to a nearby liquor store to pick up a bottle someone ordered that we didn't even have on the menu. I bought it for $40, and we charged them $1,600 for it without them even noticing the obscene markup. In all, I was quickly learning the ropes and loving every second of it.

"Listen," Santi said softly as he leaned forward. He rested his elbows on his knees. "I usually only have Braden and Kai fly with me. But, I wanted to use this flight to make sure that you're doing alright with everything. More importantly, I want for the two of us to reach a level of *transparency*."

"Absolutely," I agreed.

"So I want you to ask me whatever it is you're curious about and speak what's on your mind," he said as he leaned back in his seat and crossed one leg over the other.

Multiple thoughts crossed my mind. I thought about what Shawn Lane said about Santi being manipulative. I thought about Santi entertaining his private guests in his private villa and who those guests typically were. I thought about how he made the obscene amount of money he makes. And I was able to ask... *Anything*?

"How'd you start... All of this??"

A small burst of air came out of his nose as he held back his laugh. I suddenly realized I was sitting on the edge of my seat, awaiting his answer.

"I was in the real estate game for some time," Santi said while examining one of his rings. "My buddy and I used to flip houses, and then we got into commercial lots that we'd rent out to investors and companies... In the condition that they partner with us moving forward."

"Partner? Partner with you in what way?" I asked, feeling like a dimwitted schoolboy.

He took a sip and then leaned forward. "It was a business model we adopted... Where we'd rent out our land to the companies at a discount, in the condition that we get a small stake in the business that's conducted on it. If we *really* believed in the company's vision, we'd invest in their operations... *Just* enough to have some leverage when it came to how business is done."

"And one of the companies was a bar or restaurant..." I blurted out as if the light bulb in my head lit up the entire jet suite.

Santi snapped his fingers and nodded his head. "It was my ticket into the industry. It opened my eyes to *everything* I now see clear as day."

"So all of your restaurants, bars, and nightclubs..." I looked toward the ceiling of the jet, processing the conclusion I was about to make. "You own the land?"

"Yes, which I rent to the organizations or companies in the condition that they operate their venues *my* way," he interrupted sternly. "With *my* formula. I put in less work but maintain my control over what goes on. The only thing missing is *resorts*, for now... Which I've already deemed the next step for the business. I've got my mind set on the Caribbean."

"Genius," I whispered under my breath. "Why hospitality?"

Santi stared into the bottom of his near-empty glass, then looked up, tapping two fingers against his chin before answering.

"Service to others is the rent you pay for your room here on Earth. You know who said that?"

I shook my head.

"Muhammad Ali said it. I did nothing to deserve the life I was given. Therefore I found myself serving others in pursuit of earning my existence. Since the beginning of time, being hospitable has been instilled in the human mind... And I believe that's where we find our truest form of fulfillment. We hear about it in Catholicism, Christianity... Even in the *Paleolithic* era when hunters provided for their tribes."

Santi's words were piercing through my brain like daggers of wisdom, and I absorbed it all. I watched as his facial expressions and hand gestures contributed to the liveliness of his gray eyes.

"I'm a firm believer that we live to *serve*," he continued. "I serve by elevating the human experience. I provide space for memories to be created--for stories to overlap one another with the means to contribute to the overarching story of... *Us*...."

He stood up to pour himself another drink.

"... Stories are *fascinating*... The fact we've *all* got one that's brought us to this specific moment in time... And how this specific moment in time will serve to take us to another specific moment in time... And then *another*."

He sat down and sank into his chair, making direct eye contact with me.

"What's *your* story?"

"M-Mine?" I stuttered. "I was born back in Torrance in-...."

"No, Jay... Well, I guess--yes--but that's not what I mean. I mean... Why are you *here*?"

Santi's questions hit me like a truck... And I suddenly felt as though I was standing in a room with four walls. At my feet, I saw Josh, my family--my past--everything that made me so uneasy and ate at me for so long--the tragedy and conflict I've buried into the hollow depths of my memory now present in the form of darkness. It loomed at my feet. I watched the darkness rise, consuming my ankles, my knees, my hips, and there was no escaping it--or was there?

I looked up, and a hand extended down in my direction from an opening. The hand was dressed in rings, and I recognized this hand--it belonged to Santi. I felt the urge to confide in him, and I did not question it.

"Josh died," I said, fixated on his rings. "Our brother died seven years ago at a party we threw. He was on drugs Braden kept in the garage, then shot himself with the gun I forgot to put back in its hiding place."

I took a deep breath before continuing.

"My family split up after that, and before I came here, Braden told me our parents had passed. I was in New York for seven years redefining who I was… Trying to cover up having ruined my entire family--well… Everyone except Braden."

"You've taken responsibility for your family your whole life, haven't you?" he asked.

"I suppose."

Santi paused, then smiled.

"Seems like you internalize a lot of problems that belong to others. Seems to me like you want to be some sort of *hero*. You're looking for meaning--for a place to make your mark--a greater purpose to *serve*."

Santi took a long sip and leaned forward without breaking eye contact. I looked up from his chains toward his eyes as he squinted, studying me intently.

"So why are you *here*?" he asked in a tone as if he had already given me the answer prior to asking the question. The answer was in his eyes--lurking in the gray--and I knew without a doubt that it was *right*.

"To *serve*," the words poured out of my mouth directly from my subconscious mind.

"You clothe yourself in a troubled past," Santi sighed. "But it's your past that has no place here in the *now*. Your scars have brought you here to serve, Jay… To be hospitable."

I felt a sudden weight lifted off my shoulders. Whether it was because I had finally voiced what I've internalized for so long or because of Santi's acceptance of me despite my mistakes, I felt *good*. I felt… *Free*.

"We live to seek our purpose, Jay…" he looked directly through me. "And it warms my heart to know that you found yours here and now."

He clinked his drink against mine, then smirked. We both sipped.

"Now," he said with a smile. "Go grab Braden and Kai... And I'll show you how I'm able to afford flying our family across the country in two jets."

TEN | JAY LOVE

OUR PENTHOUSE SUITE
MIAMI BEACH, FLORIDA
FRIDAY, 9:38A.M. - JULY 12TH, 2019

I pushed the sliding door open, which connected our penthouse suite to our own private balcony. Our suite is big enough for 10 guests, but only the six of us were staying here. We have almost twice the amount of room we actually need, while Santi's own suite is right next door. Marble coated the floors and countertops, reflecting the morning sun that rose over the ocean in front of us. From the furniture to the walls, *everything* was white.

I stepped out onto the balcony and took a deep breath of fresh air, taking in the salty ocean breeze--it felt surreal. If you would've told me I'd be standing on a penthouse balcony in Miami preparing to throw one of the biggest parties for all of Swim Week, I would've thought you were insane.

Braden and Skylar were sitting across from each other at the dining table tucked in the corner of the balcony. Braden was in his boxers and wore a pair of sunglasses, while Skylar was in gray sweatshorts and white designer slides--the three of us running on only four or five hours of sleep after a night partying in South Beach. On the table between us were bottles of alcohol, a glass pitcher of orange juice, and some bagels and fruit someone brought up to us from downstairs.

I made myself comfortable at the head of the table between Skylar and Braden. After pouring myself a mimosa, I opened the weekend's schedule Santi texted us last night. It was a pretty straightforward document with the important gatherings and events listed in black:

FRIDAY
9:00PM - DINNER AT "TAISHO"
SATURDAY
4:00PM - "DAWN" CLUB VENUE SETUP
11:00PM - "DAWN" DOORS OPEN
SUNDAY
1:00PM - FLIGHT HOME

See you at these places at these times. Anything else you do is up to you.

Make good choices, please.

-S

"We can do *anything* outside of the stuff on this list?" I asked.

"Yep," Braden said, lighting a cigarette without looking up from his phone.

"What're you guys gonna do?"

"Scope the beach for some talent, obviously," Skylar said. He stood and looked over the balcony railing at the beach like a puppy outside of a dog park.

"Not until we get numbers for tomorrow night," Braden declared.

Skylar sighed and sat back down, pulling out his phone. Before we knew it, we were sending out invites left and right through social media.

Three to five days before any event hosted at one of our venues, it was vital for the three of us to find the *top* social influencers within a 20-mile radius--women, of course, with the exception of millionaire jet-setters or big spenders with cash to blow. It's important for the venue to make a profit, but even *more* important to create a social demand when it comes to getting in. These guys will put their cards down, but they're not spending a dime unless the women are present.

The process usually starts with us looking up the *geotag* or, in other words, the specific city or county our venue is located in. Instagram has an entire page dedicated to people posting or "checking in" at any given location. This makes it easier for us to scroll through and invite every hot girl or potential big spender we find.

I opened up a spreadsheet on my phone to keep track of the people who R.S.V.P.'d. This spreadsheet would eventually be considered the "*guest list*." Then, I opened up Instagram. I searched "Miami Beach" in the "Locations" tab, which brought me to a map of Miami Beach and all the top and most recent pictures people were posting. I opened one bikini girl pic after another, then copy-and-pasted my message into each of their inboxes. Something like...

"*Saw you were in town for Swim Week… I'm a promoter for DAWN here in Miami… If you and your friends pull up tomorrow night, we'll be more than happy to set you guys up with a free table and bottle service.*"

The message wasn't *entirely* true… I mean, we were setting

these girls up with tables and bottle service… They just didn't know the tables were already purchased by the rich dudes they were gonna be sharing the table *with*.

Santi insisted on our messages being personable, but not to the point where they knew we were essentially being virtual stalkers, only inviting them if we found them hot or influential. I found it funny, considering every misogynistic douchebag I scoffed at in the past would probably be drooling over me essentially getting *paid* to slide into an attractive girl's D.M.'s.

I started getting one response after another, per usual. It had only been just over a week of me being a part of the promotion game, but it really wasn't that hard to pick up with the help of Santi and the guys. It also felt good to have these girls constantly hitting me up days on end to either get into the club or even just to hang out. Also... Can't forget the social clout.

Was I being used by these girls? Probably. L.A. girls really are *something else*, but I didn't mind because I was having fun… And the attention I'm getting seemed to cement over the dark times I now buried ever so deep. I'm not ashamed to admit it... Let me *live*.

After about an hour or two of sending out the invites, we had compiled a list of about five or six hundred R.S.V.P.'s between the three of us, with 80% of tables assigned to names of purchasers.

"How big is DAWN?" I asked before finishing my third mimosa.

Skylar shrugged and looked at Braden for an answer.

"Probably around 30,000 square feet," Braden replied confidently. "It's downstairs in the lobby."

"It's in our resort??" I asked.

"Yessir. We got the best setup possible."

"Alright," Skylar hopped out of his seat. "Beach time. Braden, are you in or no?? Jay and I are gonna go down and scout."

"I'll meet you down there," Braden said as he stretched his arms. "I'm gonna take a nap."

"Let's hit it, JayPal!" Skylar shouted as he skipped into the penthouse. "Get it? Like *PayPal*, but your name… You get it."

We changed into swim trunks and made our way down to the lobby, through the pool, and onto the white sand. It was almost noon, and the beach was *packed* with some of the most beautiful people I've ever seen.

Maybe it's just a Miami thing, but I could literally feel my skin *absorbing* the U.V. rays. My feet glided through the white powder sand with ease. Skylar took off his shirt, and his chains reflected the sun tenfold. I slid my glasses on and took my shirt off, too. I probably should've done some push-ups for a quick pump before coming down, but whatever… My buzz has me feelin' pretty confident as it is.

"There's a group of girls from back in L.A. that hit me up," Skylar said while going through his texts. "They should be over here somewhere. It's Tiffany and them."

The water was almost lighter than the sky, somewhat clear but with a green tint that complemented the clear blue above us. We walked along the water, which was warm but still refreshing.

It suddenly dawned on me that Fia hadn't texted me, but I knew her flight was supposed to touch down this morning. Maybe I should text *her*… Nah, she probably has guys texting her from all over. It's probably best I make her chase at least a *little* bit. Plus, I was a bit preoccupied at the moment, anyway, and she was most likely preparing to walk her bikini runways or whatever.

I couldn't wrap my head around the fact that every single person we passed had a glowing tan and light eyes. I heard people speaking Spanish and various languages, and suddenly I wished my parents had taught me to speak Spanish so I could relate.

"There they are," Skylar pointed at a group of about eight girls lounging on and around a few daybeds.

Their servers had just left them with drinks, and they pounced on them quickly with their phones recording the moment. As the two of us got closer, I could hear the sound of their speaker playing the most mainstream music possible. It was obvious they were from L.A. I even recognized a couple of the girls who ran up to us with open arms.

"Hey you!" shouted Tiffany. She pulled me in for an unexpected kiss that I really didn't mind at all.

The rest of the group turned to see who we were. A few of them shouted for Skylar as he sprawled himself on one of the beds and immediately began running his mouth, making them laugh. I was a few steps behind him between Tiffany and another girl I had met at The Willow. We sat on a daybed, and within seconds, a tequila shot was in my hand.

"Cheers!!" Tiffany shouted as we all threw back the shots.

"Where are you guys staying??" I asked.

"We're at some boutique hotel our agent flew us out to," one of the girls said. "Come take a picture with us, Jay."

The girls and Skylar piled on and around me for what might be one of the sloppiest pictures ever taken. As the girls swarmed the girl taking the photo, asking for it to be sent to them, I noticed two girls walking toward us from the water--both breathtaking, even from afar.

It was as if the universe glued my eyes to them, and here I am with absolutely no desire to look away. The two of them talked among themselves as they got closer, dripping from having been in the water.

The girl on the left wore a high-waisted orange bikini--her dark wavy hair hanging down to her hips. The girl on the right wore a baby blue bikini that was high-waisted but more conservative than the girl on the left. The girl on the right… Woah. Her hair was platinum blonde, making her perfectly-done dark brown eyebrows pop just above her amber eyes--those eyes.

I took off my sunglasses to get a better look. I wanted to look away, but I couldn't… And it was for good reason. It was as if my entire existence was wrapped around this girl and her amber eyes--as if the only oxygen left for me to breathe was in her--as if there was nobody on this crowded beach but us… Just the *two of us.*

The surrounding conversations were muted by my trance as I watched her cross me with my jaw dropped. My head swiveled, following the two of them toward the daybed where Skylar was lying with a group of girls. They grabbed their towels and remained in deep conversation, somewhat ignoring our large group.

My heart was in my stomach, and my head was in the clouds. I became one with the moment as I waited for her to look my way--waited for our worlds to collide.

One of the girls next to Skylar shouted something to her, and I heard the voice I never knew I needed to hear until this very moment. The girl with the amber eyes responded. She smiled and gave a polite wave to Skylar as she dried herself off, and a second later, her amber eyes met mine.

VAL.

My jaw dropped to the fucking floor.

Almost immediately, she looked down, continuing to dry herself off as the girl she was with continued talking. She had dodged my glance.

Did she not recognize me?
Did she not want to see me?
Does she hate me? She HAS to hate me.

I looked down at the empty shot glass in my hand and then back at the empty tray I wish had a full bottle I could just chug right about now--anything to escape this moment. I was embarrassed--a bit confused--no, I was flustered. I wasn't ready for this… And now I honestly hope she *didn't* recognize me. Or did I? I don't know. I *do* know that I wanna say something. I *have* to say something.

Say something, I thought to myself.

"Do you know those two?" I asked the girl to my left, whose eyes were glued to her phone.

"Do I what?" she slurred back, looking up from her phone toward the water.

"The girl with the platinum hair in the blue bikini," I replied without looking away from Val. "Do you know her and her friend?"

She squinted her eyes, staring in the complete opposite direction, and I realized she was too drunk to comprehend what I was saying. I rolled my eyes and leaned across the daybed to tap Tiffany's shoulder. She politely excused herself from her conversation and turned to me.

"What's up, babes??" Tiffany smiled.

"Hey, sorry to interrupt--but... Do you know her?"

I subtly tilted my head toward Val and her friend, who were now making their way around our daybed to their own lounge chairs. Tiffany followed my eyes, and after a short pause, she flashed me a cheeky grin.

"That's Val and Marina," she whispered. "Do you think they're cute?? Let me put in a good word for you...."

"N-no... Wait!" I snapped back, but it was already too late.

"Val!! Marina!!" Tiffany shouted with her drink in the air.

I wanted to *disappear*.

Seven years of burying the existence of the one girl I respected the most in this world--cut her off without a word and moved across the country...

All the missed calls and texts.

Every ignored knock at our door.

Her existence was erased from my own, and while she fought and fought for me, I ran...

Only to be presented as a coward who can't even spark the conversation myself.

Val and Marina paused at the sound of Tiffany's voice. I nervously looked for a towel to cover my face with, but before I could, my eyes met Val's once again.

"I want to introduce you to my friend!" Tiffany shouted.

Val's eyes went from being locked onto mine to her lounge chair as if she didn't hear Tiffany at all. My heart dropped once more, realizing that this is how it's going to be... Completely ignored... As if my existence is null--zero. Safe to say, I deserved it for having done the same to her for seven years. I can take it.

Val grabbed Marina's hand, and the two of them continued making their way to their lounge chairs. I closed my eyes and let out a sigh of disappointment.

"That was weird..." Tiffany said.

"Yeah, weird..." I sighed.

I slid my sunglasses back on so that my defeated facial expression could be somewhat masked.

"She probably didn't hear me. Just go say hi!" Tiffany urged.

Everything within me wanted to say hi, but it was the fear of rejection that kept me from sprinting over to Val to see what was left of our friendship to salvage. I subtly turned my head in Val's direction to see her and Marina lying on their lounge chairs under their umbrella. Before I could consciously make the decision to stand up, my legs did it for me.

"You go get her, boy!" Tiffany giggled before turning back to the group.

I felt the heat from the white sand envelop my bare feet. I didn't want to move them... But it didn't matter because they moved anyway. After tossing my shot glass on the sand, my eyes were set on Val and Marina as I made my way over to them.

Right, left, right, left, I thought as I cautiously stepped toward the two of them.

I prayed that I appeared confident because on the inside... I certainly wasn't. As I stepped up to fill the gap between their lounge chairs and the ocean, there was nothing but silence. My hands were in my pockets, shaking like never before. Marina's eyes widened, and she tapped Val's thigh to get her attention. Val's head swiveled toward me, but she remained expressionless.

Say something, you idiot, I thought. *Or like... Do something, at least.*

"I... I...."

Val slowly stood to her feet and stepped out in front of the umbrella. There was so much to say, I didn't even know where to start. I stood in front of her, speechless, no longer trying to even speak at all.

As if saving me from looking like the baffled fool I am, she leaped into my arms and hugged me tightly. I looked around, and no one else seemed to pick up on the intensity of the moment, except Marina, who smiled from her lounge chair. I subtly pinched myself while in her arms, and yeah, this is happening--this is *real*.

She pulled back and looked up at me while holding my shoulders, studying every millimeter of my face.

"Your hair... It's... *Long*," Val stated.

"*Too* long?" I asked while looking up as if I could see it.

She continued to stare, and that's when I saw it--the infamous Val smirk. I couldn't help but smile back.

"Yeah..." she whispered softly. "Too long... Is what it's *been*. It's been too long...."

The intense mutual stare suddenly broke as I came back down to reality, looking around frantically as if we had just caused a scene. Val let go of my arms and did the same, but we both quickly noticed nobody was paying attention, considering they were all cheering for Skylar taking body shots off a row of models lying on the daybeds. We laughed and turned back to face each other.

"You wanna walk??" she asked as she slowly made her way toward the water, knowing I'd follow.

I caught up without even thinking.

"So tell me, jungle boy… Did you forget how to get a haircut?" she teased while still looking forward. She had a giddy pep in her step.

"Okayyy, your hair is *blonde*," I teased back. "What's up with that??"

"It was for a gig I recently had. They asked me to dye it."

"I've seen the billboards," I sighed as I jammed my hands into my pockets.

She looked up at me, shielding her eyes from the sun.

"You have?"

"Everywhere I go," I blushed. "You made it… Times Square… It's huge."

She looked forward as we continued walking along the shore.

"I wouldn't say I *made it*… But I mean I'm doing what I set out to do--what we talked about."

"I didn't forget," I smiled.

She fixed her hair and lightly kicked the water as we strolled through it. I felt myself fighting off my buzz so that I could be fully present in the moment. She was the one person I had been around who didn't reek of alcohol or cigarettes, and I felt embarrassed that she might group me with everyone that *did* reek of alcohol or cigarettes. Wait, no… I don't care. I *shouldn't* care. We're adults now, and I should have every right to do whatever I want.

"How long has it been?" she asked as she came to a halt. "Eight years?"

"Seven," I responded without making eye contact.

Her stance was squared up to mine, but she faced the water with her arms crossed. It was evident that there was a whole lot on her mind, and she was ready to let it all out. I braced myself.

"I reached out," she sighed. "In so many different ways…."

"I know," I replied. "I-…."

"Let me finish," she snapped, then she took a moment to think.

Her demand was stern but soft. It killed me inside to watch her process her emotions right in front of me--to watch her try to find the right combination of words that can communicate what weighed on her for so long.

"I texted, called, and made myself available to you before you left," Val looked up at me--her amber eyes reflecting the afternoon sun as she tucked a blonde strand of hair behind one of her ears. "You dropped me--no... You dropped *everyone.* You turned your back on the ones who were only there to *help*, and as if that wasn't enough, you didn't just remove us from your life... You removed *yourself* from *ours*. You left."

Her voice was shaky, and she turned to the horizon in an attempt to hide the tear that fell onto the sand between us. I lifted my chin and straightened my posture.

Don't cry, Jay, I thought. *Don't you fucking cry, Jay.*

Before I could, she continued.

"... But I understand why. You were coping. You *had* to do what you did to get over what happened. Losing Josh was difficult for all of us, and I know that for you, it must've been just... Unbearable. I get it. I *understand*... And I can't be mad at you for it. So, I don't know... I guess I just wanted to voice my frustration... But also... Just--like... Make it apparent that I still care for you, regardless."

She closed her eyes and let out a sigh, waiting for some sort of response. I looked out at the horizon... For an answer--for the right thing to say in such an emotionally heated moment.

I got *nothing*.

She could sense how difficult it was for me to process my emotions... To translate the light and the darkness within me into words. But the sad truth is, I don't even know how I feel after having gone seven years of not feeling at all.

Val smiled and used my silence as a cue to tease me light-heartedly.

"Well... It's nice to know you're *alive*, Jay Amor," she teased. "Tell me what you're doing hanging out with these L.A. kids."

Her tone was now light and pleasant, and I found myself somewhat excited to drop such a deep topic for something a little more... *Surface-level.*

"I'm at The Willow now," I said, breaking the silence.

"Ah, that's right... I saw you hangin' out with Skylar over there."

"You know him?" I asked.

"I do," she nodded. "Those boys don't seem like your type of crowd, though... Maybe Braden's crowd but not yours."

"They're practically my brothers now," I shrugged. "I've been learning a lot from them and Santi."

Val bit her lip and looked down at the water that flowed up and around our toes. She let out a deep breath.

"You should be careful with Santi, Jay."

"Why??" I snarled. "I don't understand what people have against the guy. He's *really* helping me out."

"I hear stories," she sighed. "About the business he's got going on. You're smarter than all that."

"Nah," I shook my head and scanned the beach. "Whatever you're hearing is a lie. The guys and Santi are the only family I have, and I don't intend on losing them the way I lost my parents and Josh."

"Your parents?" Val asked. "What do you mean you lost your parents?"

"Braden told me what happened," I said aloud, checking my empty pockets for a cigarette. My hands were shaking again, but I tried to keep my cool.

She covered her mouth with an open palm, and I noticed her hand was shaking, too.

"Braden told you *both* of your parents are... *Dead*??"

I froze. "He did."

She looked in all directions, then down at the sand between us. After a brief pause, she crossed her arms and let out a long exhale.

"Your mom isn't dead, Jay. Your dad passed while in prison, but your mom is alive. She's still here… Not... *Dead*…."

My eyes remained fixated on Val, but I no longer saw her. I saw a vulnerable Braden back in New York who still relied on drugs and alcohol to keep him going--telling me that he was the only family I have left. Little did I know he had lied and manipulated me into following him into God-knows-what I'm involved in now. In this moment, I questioned everything I held true, and I could feel my insides turning and twisting over one another. I took a deep breath and realized Val had no idea what to say, and neither did I.

I looked up.

I looked down.

I took another deep breath.

I thought very intensely about what I was going to say.

"We should go back," I insisted as I made my way back to the group.

"Jay... *Jay*!" Val shouted as she grabbed my arm.

I reluctantly turned to face her.

"Don't just go and confront Braden about it. I'm sure he has his reasons for lying to you… And I don't wanna risk losing you for another seven years because of something I shouldn't have said to you. It wasn't my place to say anything about it at all!" she said while tightening her grip.

The words left her lips smoothly, and I felt like God or the universe were speaking *through* her… Telling me not to withdraw again... To no longer play the role of the *victim*. I lost myself before, but now I'm in control, and I intend to keep it that way.

It turns out seven years of suppressing and burying my emotions wasn't a waste after all, considering I could literally feel myself letting go of what Val had just told me. I'm in a position of influence on a beautiful beach surrounded by beautiful people. This is no time for negativity--no time to dwell on the past.

I felt my shoulders loosen, and I smirked.

"You got plans the rest of the day?" I asked in a somewhat uplifting tone.

"I'm walking the runway for a few brands tomorrow, so I might head back to the hotel early, but that's about it."

"Perfect," I said. "I need a drink... Or 10."

"Me too," she let out a sigh of relief--relief that I had moved on from what would typically be a traumatic topic. Little did she know…

The trauma is there--it always had been and always will be--I had just become a professional at masking it with a sardonic half-smirk and a flirty gaze.

Val and I made ourselves comfortable among the group, joining in on the hollow laughs and never-ending gossip. It's amazing how much interest people express in each other's lives when a negative connotation is attached. Like, I don't understand how these people have the time to ask about and discuss their own and others' appearances as much as they do. A while back, these juvenile and unproductive conversations wouldn't interest me, but now that I was a part of this scene, I found it pretty funny… And I was *engaged*.

With every shot we took, it became easier to push down what Val had said. The mental image of my parents became more and more transparent until I was once again entirely in the present. Val and I talked about anything and everything--well, mostly about *her* anything and everything. I had no desire to share my own experiences, and though she may be the one girl who would call me out for it… She didn't.

She told me about her parents--how they weren't supportive of her becoming a model, and about how she *still* went back to pay off their debts and move them into a nicer house after she made a name for herself in the industry. She listed the various brands she's modeled for and how she was beginning to learn the business behind it all.

"You can't rely on looks forever," she said. "Some people do, and that's why their careers in the industry are so short."

It still baffles me how the modeling industry works. From my perspective, people will pay you to make you look pretty and make you more famous… Only to then pay you *more* to look *more* pretty and make you even *more* famous.

What a struggle it must be to be pretty.
What a struggle it must be.

I admire Val for being so involved in the scene without having been consumed by it. She knows she's beautiful, but she only relies on her looks professionally based on how she speaks and what she speaks about. It was the girls surrounding the both of us that did the opposite, flaunting their bodies to Skylar and me, asking when the next function is and who's gonna be there.

I ate it up, though, leveraging my ability to get these girls into the hottest parties and clubs we owned--well, *Santi* owned--but you get the point. In a way, I saw myself in a position of power. I had the authority to let people into the clubs and restaurants we promoted for. I voiced it the same way I continuously saw Skylar and Braden do, and I could feel the girls getting more and more handsy… But not Val. She kept her distance, unamused as if my behavior was *expected*. Whatever, I really don't care.

Hours had flown by, and the sun was beginning to set behind Val, who stood up and began gathering her things.

"Where you goin'?" I sighed in disappointment.

She smiled. "I've got a *big* day tomorrow, so I'm gonna head up early."

"*Laaame*," Skylar and I teased playfully.

"Here… Gimme your number and maybe we can meet up again at some point," I insisted.

Val smiled, put her number in my phone, then she gestured for me to get up and give her a hug. I stood and immediately realized how drunk I was as I stutter-stepped into her arms.

"You gonna be alright, Jay Love??" she teased.

I think so, I thought.

"I'm fine," I said.

I felt Skylar throw his arm around me. "He's with me, V!"

"Whatever you say. I'll see you guys later."

She waved goodbye to the group and began walking back toward the hotels. I might've been drunk, but I could see Skylar checking her out in my peripherals.

"The things I would do..." he sighed as he squeezed my shoulder, looking for validation.

I brushed off what he said and checked my phone for the first time since we had come down to the beach. The top of the screen read, *6:49PM*, and below the time were messages from Fia asking for my room number. Her texting was sloppy, which had me thinking she's just as drunk as I am... If not *drunker*. Is drunker a word? Drunker--*Drunker*.

"Is that the *Mrs.*?" Skylar teased as one of the girls crawled onto his lap, holding a bottle of 1942 to his lips.

"Yeah," I sighed. "I'm gonna invite her to the room."

"Love that for you," he replied after taking a shot. "I'll be up in a bit. Remember, we've got dinner at 9."

"Sounds good," I replied.

Somehow, I drunkenly made my way up to our empty suite. After several failed attempts at scanning my room key upside down, I finally flipped it over and made it in. A warm evening breeze swept the empty penthouse suite as I poured myself a drink and told Fia to come over.

Within seconds, she said she was on her way up, and within minutes, we were on top of each other in my room. There was something about being in a penthouse suite that had the sex hitting... Different... The *best kind* of different.

"What'd you do today?" she asked as she poured herself a glass of champagne by the bed.

She was looking out the window--her curves outlined by the sunset that seeped in through the wall of windows. Seeing both a naked Fia and the view of the Miami Beach skyline together was unreal. I *have* to be dreaming right now. I gave myself a courtesy pinch on the forearm to be sure I wasn't asleep.

"Skylar and I were down at the beach with Tiffany and some of her friends," I replied.

"I saw the pictures some of the girls posted," she said as she handed me a glass of champagne. "Where are the other guys right now?"

"No idea," I shrugged.

She sipped her glass, still standing naked beside the bed--her long brown hair falling elegantly past her shoulders. It was hard for me to comprehend how a girl so stunning could take time out of her day to isolate herself with me during an important trip for the both of us.

She crawled into the bed and pulled out her phone. Her screen was covered in texts from both guys and girls. I could tell she was trying to be discreet about responding and keeping me from seeing what was on the screen. As she typed away, texting whoever she was texting, I downed my glass and stared at the ceiling.

I couldn't help but think about Val and what she had said.

"Your mom isn't dead."

"Your mom isn't dead."

"Your mom isn't dead."

The phrase replayed in my mind over and over again like a broken record, bouncing off the walls of my now hollow head. There was so much to process, but emotionally, I felt so little--almost nothing at all. I don't *think* I feel the need to confront Braden at this point, but I can't deny I should think about it now… Fuck. I don't know.

"What're you thinking?" the smoothness of Fia's voice suddenly broke my sloppy train of thought, bringing me back to reality.

I turned my head to face her, not knowing how long I had been stuck in my head. She was gazing at me intently, eyes piercing and clear as day.

Do I tell her what I'm thinking? I don't think we've ever had a real conversation. We've always just hooked up.

"Nothing," I said with a cheeky smirk I hoped would charm her into kissing me then and there, but it didn't work.

"Tell me," she insisted as she ran her fingers through my hair.

We were now lying on the bed, facing each other, and I felt my chest begin to tighten, and my head felt lighter than air. I stared into her blue eyes, and without her even having to say it, I knew she wanted me to let out what was weighing on me.

Don't tell her… I thought. *Don't let her in. That's not you anymore… Don't go back… And DON'T take her back there with you.*

Before I could even lie, I felt a tear fall from my right eye onto the pillow. I knew that if I didn't distract myself now, who knows what sort of emotional wreck I'd turn into in front of her. My eyes trailed from her eyes down to her lips and then back up to her eyes.

As if on command, the two of us embraced each other, my lips caressing hers like never before. I felt her body mold to mine, every hint of warm physical touch suppressing the dark memories that were so close to coming to fruition. Our pulses became one, and our grips tightened as our breathing grew heavier with every kiss.

I could feel the alcohol taking over as I began to fade in and out of consciousness… Until I was *completely* out.

ELEVEN | RESPECT

OUR PENTHOUSE SUITE
MIAMI BEACH, FLORIDA
FRIDAY, 8:21P.M. - JULY 12TH, 2019

SPLASH!

The sudden splash of ice-cold water slapped me across the face, waking me up instantly. I shrieked as I leaped to my feet beside the bed, trying to process what was happening. I heard a familiar laugh as I rubbed my eyes to see Kalani cackling while recording me with his phone.

"FUCK, MAN," I screamed as I covered my naked body with a pillow. "WHY??"

He lowered his phone, still trying to catch his breath.

"Come on, dude. We've got dinner in like 30 minutes!"

"Alright, alright," I sighed.

I turned to see an empty bed, where I could've sworn Fia just was. It took me a second to realize how much time had passed. I was a bit groggy.

"Dress nice," Kalani said as he walked back into the living room. "Santi is introducing us to some pretty important people to-night."

I slicked my hair back and slid on a gray button-up with some cropped black slacks and my designer loafers. My head was throbbing from the champagne and tequila I spent all day drinking, and I could feel a minor buzz combatting the soon-to-be migraine. Since I didn't have enough time to shower, I practically drenched myself in cologne, and our group was headed to the elevators within minutes--everyone except for Braden.

"Where's Braden?" I asked the group as we walked.

"He's been with Santi all day," Kai replied. "Jay, you look tired as hell. Have some of this...."

Kai reached into his pocket and pulled out a tiny vial filled with a white powder--cocaine. I had never done coke before, but I see the guys do it pretty often. They seem fine... Why wouldn't I be? I grabbed the vial and took a bump off the base of my thumb without thinking. Almost instantaneously, a burst of energy made itself known in my body and mind. I became wired, ready to attack whatever the night threw my way. No more headache. No more grogginess.

"Thanks," I said, handing Kai the vial, though a part of me wanted to keep it.

Our footsteps tapped against the marble floor of the dim-lit hallway. We moved as one charismatic unit, fully fitted in designer from head to toe. There was a natural swagger that radiated as we overlapped one another, cracking jokes and hyping each other up for the weekend, which had just begun.

I could still feel the buzz and was almost itching for another drink… Or bump of coke. I felt loose, not thinking too much about everything that went down today with Val. The night is young, and I'm excited for what lies ahead.

After stepping out of the elevator, we made our way through the lobby and out the front entrance onto a grand terrace where cars pulled up to the valet. Kai flagged down a black S.U.V. and greeted the driver by his first name.

"What's up, Alberto?" Kai greeted as he shook the driver's hand. "Long time, no see."

Alberto acknowledged the group as he opened the doors for us, then popped the trunk and pulled out a large matte black box. He was an intimidating man, standing tall with a long beard and slicked-back hair. He wore all black, with a gold chain that complemented his gold Rolex. His tan made his bright green eyes pop.

"Santi told me to give you guys this," Alberto said as he handed Kai the box in the passenger seat.

As we funneled into the S.U.V., Kai placed the black box on the center console, unlocked it, and opened it slowly. As the box opened into an L-shape, a small white light shone from inside, illuminating three bottles of Dom Pérignon along with a note. Kai picked up the note and read it aloud.

"Boys… These three bottles, a table at PRIME, and plenty more await you after dinner, given you're on your best behavior. This is a very important dinner for the family… Santi."

Kai waved the note in front of us with a big smile on his face.

"You heard the man!" shouted Skylar from the back of the S.U.V., giving the group playful nudges. "LET'S GO!"

As we made our way down Ocean Drive, neon lights and crowds of people flooded the sidewalks and a good chunk of the street. The warm summer breeze filled the car as the music we blasted competed with the music blaring from the passing restaurants, bars, and clubs.

Beautiful women dressed in pastel colors traveled in packs,

and men hollered at them from all angles, as did Skylar from the back of our S.U.V. I felt a nudge against my right shoulder and looked to see Kalani gesturing for me to take a pull of his flask. Without hesitation, I took a nice big gulp and handed it back. At this point, I'm starting to realize that since I've met the boys, I've probably been drunk more often than I've been sober... But I'll worry about that later--perks of being young, I guess.

I couldn't help but think about how I was gonna confront Braden about what Val told me...

Should I catch him off guard?
Should I ease into the conversation?
Should I act like I know nothing and wait for the opportune time to catch him in a lie?
What if I lose my cool?
Is tonight even the night to bring up the fact that he lied about our own mother's death?

"*This is a very important dinner for the family,*" Santi's words from the letter echoed through my mind.

"Who do you think the dinner is with?" Kalani asked.

"Probably some celebrity," Niall snapped back in his typical smug tone.

"Some potential partners, I think," Kai replied, disregarding Niall's response. "I think it's about the deal he's trying to cut involving resorts in the Caribbean. He's been talking about wanting in on Caribbean hospitality for years."

Kalani laid his head back against his headrest.

"Damn... So it's business," Kalani sighed.

"Yeah," Kai replied. "This is big-time for him... *And* us. Just lay low for the dinner, and let's get out of there with him happy."

The S.U.V. made a sharp right turn onto a narrow cobblestone road, and despite the smooth ride, you could hear the rubber tires gripping the surface. Jungle stood tall on both sides of the vehicle as we pulled up under a large structure.

Groups of all sizes were being escorted from their cars into the restaurant. Before we even came to a complete stop, two men in black suits had already opened a door on each side, greeting us as if they already know who we are--and they *do*.

"Are they inside?" Kai asked one of the men.

The man nodded before saying something into his earpiece. The other man greeted Skylar with a big smile as Skylar crawled out of the back of the S.U.V. It was as if they were childhood friends who hadn't seen each other in years.

"Do we know these guys?" I whispered to Kalani.

"They work for Santi, too… Just out here running his Miami venues," Kalani whispered back.

The men gestured for us to follow them up the stairs and into the restaurant. As we followed, I noticed the guys were quieter than usual. They discretely fixed their hair and adjusted their shirts as we made our way through the entrance, and it made me question whether or not I should do the same.

As we passed through the massive tinted glass doors, the sound of laughter, music, and conversations filled the air. Instantly, I inhaled an attractive aroma that immediately made me think of The Willow. It was the same fragrance Santi used at our club, and his words played back in my mind as if on cue.

"*I like for people to become familiar with an aroma that takes them back to my venues*," I remember Santi saying at one point. "*Whether it be mentally, emotionally, or physically.*"

My shoulders loosened, and my mind cleared as I took in the aroma. I felt… Comfortable… As if *at home*.

Heads turned toward our group as we passed, cutting through the middle of the bustling restaurant with our two private escorts. The tables were made of a glossy dark wood that complemented the red velvet chairs and booths. Neon-colored floral designs decorated the walls, bringing out the shimmer of the bottles behind the bar top that stretched along the right side of the restaurant. Certain sections of the restaurant were elevated, radiating a sense of exclusivity for the parties occupying them. The setting was exactly what you would expect to see in Miami on a Friday night in the summertime… But on *steroids*.

The venue had Santi's signature style written all over it, and though I hadn't known him for very long, it wasn't hard for me to pick up on. Everything about this place reminded me of why this man is so well-respected.

We slowed to a stop in front of a modern glass elevator with a velvet stanchion blocking it off to the public. One of the men undid the stanchion and pressed the button while the other signaled for us to head in as it opened. The five of us swiftly entered, and the elevator rose above the restaurant.

The group was silent, not knowing what to expect besides having to be on our *best behavior*. As the elevator came to a silent halt, the door on the opposite side opened up into a long private room.

The walls were made up of a dark red color with exposed

vertical wood lining. The gloss of the wood reflected the light from the modern chandelier hanging over a long dinner table, prepared for guests but also untouched. An ambient soundtrack could be heard from all corners of the room, giving the setting an approachable and almost meditative feel. It was difficult to put the aroma into words... But let's just say that the room smelled... *Luxurious*--as if the furniture material was derived from the finest leather and velvet.

"Right this way."

A young woman with platinum-white hair wearing a black dress escorted us past the dining table. She then slid open what looked like a part of the wall, exposing a balcony terrace that overlooked an infinity pool. This place was straight out of a mafia movie... And never in a million years did I expect to find myself in a setting like this. But even in the face of luxury and beauty, a part of me suddenly felt... *Uneasy*.

We stepped onto the terrace, and our footsteps clacking against the wood turned the heads of a group standing on the other side of the balcony.

"There are my boys!" Santi shouted as he raised his hands.

He was in a tan double-breasted suit with a black tank top under that matched his black loafers. Lightheartedly signalling for us to join him, Braden, and the group of men to their left and right, we did so without hesitation.

"Boys, these are my good friends from overseas. The Ramos brothers," Santi said as he began introducing them, one by one.

The five men were almost all the same height. Each had a different look, but every look tied into a loose Caribbean flare--eyes blue and green against their dark leathery skin. They reminded me of my relatives from Spain--full heads of hair with thick beards or groomed facial hair. Each one of them embraced us with warmth and respect.

Our two groups intermixed with one another, making formal introductions. Their voices were deep, making their thick Spanish accents more pronounced and slightly intimidating.

I realized that something was different about Santi's look, and within seconds I noticed that he wasn't wearing his chains--no diamonds... No silver. I noticed none of the men were wearing jewelry or anything even remotely flashy, either. I was unaware of what these men do, specifically, but whatever it is, they like to maintain a low profile as they do it.

"Vamo!" one of the men insisted. "Shots."

As the platinum-haired woman brought out a wooden paddle lined with tequila shots, the men invited us to each take at *least* one. I could feel the conversation I needed to have with Braden lingering in the back of my mind, itching to make its way to the front, but it might have to wait.

"SALUD!" one of the men shouted as we all took our shots.

"CHEERS!"

I felt my sober thoughts fleeting as the tequila made its way down my throat, sending a chill through my chest. As Santi set his empty shot glass back on the paddle, he immediately made his presence known.

"Boys, my friends here are *very* influential men both on and off the shores of Miami… With a *BIG* footprint in hospitality. While there are hundreds and hundreds of resorts, restaurants, bars, and nightclubs in the Caribbean, you are looking at the sole founders and operators of nearly 90% of them."

The men pridefully nodded in agreement with Santi's statement. He continued.

"We've opened up the dialogue to *potentially* take part in the design and operations of their venues. As a trade-off, we'll be setting the Ramos family up with our distribution channels in our U.S. venues."

I wondered what Santi could have meant by "*distribution channels*." What were we distributing, and through what channels? Social currency? I scanned the group and saw nothing but subtle smiles and nods… So I did the same in an attempt to mask my curiosity.

Grabbing another shot glass off of a second wooden paddle, Santi held it up in the air, staring directly at me as the words left his lips, softly yet stern. "Here's to *family*…."

The Ramos brothers clinked their glasses against ours, smiling cheek to cheek and shouting, "TO FAMILIA," loud and proud. We did the same.

We spread ourselves across the lounge furniture that occupied the terrace, sharing stories and laughs that got more and more vibrant as the shots kept coming. From stories of the Ramos brothers fleeing Cuba as children to stories of Niall drinking ayahuasca in the jungles of Peru with village locals, there wasn't a *single* dull moment.

"A degree?? In hospitality??" one of the Ramos brothers snapped at me as I finished telling him about my experience in New York. "You can actually *study* how to serve people??"

His name is Mateo, and he was thoroughly engaged in everything I had to say.

"I guess it sounds pretty dumb," I laughed. "I just always knew I was going to college and that I wanted to get into the nightlife business after."

He nodded. "Okay, okay… I respect the discipline. Bueno. But how have you applied what you have learned?"

I opened up about what I learned and my views on the industry, then the conversation shifted to both of our families being rooted in Spain.

"Amor… Meaning *love*," Mateo said in admiration. "That is

quite the last name to live up to...."

I nodded back with a smile on my face, not really knowing whether or not to take the statement lightly. We saw eye to eye on values, morals, business, and more. I took him for somebody who lays it all out there with no hesitation because he claimed to have nothing to hide and spoke his mind without thinking twice, if even once.

"... And that's why it's easy for me to open up to strangers," he said while sophisticatedly stroking his beard. "Whether the talks I have with them are few words or many hours, I don't want to miss the chance to say something that may *impact* that person. I am, how you say... An open book. I am who I am."

Our conversation got deeper and deeper, and I found myself even giving him advice on things having to do with tech in nightlife--things my generation is becoming more fond of while traveling.

"There's an app for that," I'd say in response to most of the ideas Mateo shared with me.

He was fascinated with my youthful take on the ideas he and his brothers had, and I felt as though I was contributing toward the success of Santi's deal with Mateo and his brothers. Though I didn't know Mateo for long at all, the walls came down quickly, and it was evident that there was mutual respect and trust--it was *undeniable*.

Cigar smoke was in the air, and drinks were in rotation for about an hour before Santi announced that dinner was being served. Our large group made our way into the dining room. The seats filled in quickly, and as I was the last to step into the room, I noticed that the only seat left open was at the head of the table, directly opposite Santi's seat.

I reluctantly sat in the seat, hoping nobody would address the fact that the group's newest member was sitting in such a significant position. Maybe I'm just overthinking it. No one seemed to mind, as hands overlapped one another in pursuit of the dishes that were scattered across the table.

As I waited for the right time to reach for one of the plates, I felt eyes burning a hole in me. Just as I had anticipated, I looked up to see Santi staring at me with a hollow half-smirk. The rest of the group chatted among each other, and though I tried to play it off like we didn't just make eye contact, I could feel he was still staring.

"... We're always looking for ways to switch things up," one of the Ramos brothers said just before stuffing his face with some seared ahi tuna. "You young guys probably have a good understanding of what is hot right now in the party scene, no?"

The boys were silent, and even I didn't know whether or not it was my place to step in and say something.

"Usually, we see trends starting in America and a little bit in Europe," one of the other brothers chimed in. "We try to be proactive instead of... How you say... Reactive--to keep the resorts packed... But it's tough for us to set trends by ourselves, considering our venues are isolated out in the Caribbean."

I thought about bringing up some of the customer service apps and tech I had used back in New York... The ones I had briefly discussed with Mateo--how the tech could be used to pick up on the trends and how I didn't understand why more venues weren't using them. I felt the idea itching at me--begging to be brought to the forefront of the conversation, but I didn't know if I was in a position to just throw out an idea. Would I be overstepping?

Fuck it...

"A virtual concierge could help with that," I blurted out confidently.

Every head at the table immediately turned to face me. I continued before I could over-analyze what I was about to say.

"Amazon, Google, Facebook, and basically all of the most powerful companies out there all have one thing that they value more than anything... Their customers' *data*. With the data they collect through user behavior and the decisions an individual makes, the algorithms can pick up on what the customer is likely to do next or whenever they come back."

At this point, jaws were nearly dropped to the floor, and the Ramos brothers eagerly nodded for me to continue. Santi studied me intently... With his drink hovering near his chin. I felt as though he didn't want for me to continue. I obeyed, and in the silence that filled the room, the Ramos brothers whispered to each other in Spanish before turning back to me.

"Keep going, mang!" Mateo shouted with his fork pointed toward me.

I looked at Santi, who didn't move a single muscle in his face, not even to blink.

"So if you have a virtual concierge..." I continued hesitantly. "Then, during your guests' entire stay, you can track what they do, when they do it, and how often they do it. Then you can have that data translated into heat maps, graphs, and other ways to compare and contrast the behaviors. You might even be able to access more than that type of data if you word your terms and conditions right."

One of the Ramos brothers dropped his utensils and threw his hands up.

"One large program that oversees the resorts... VAMO!! GENIUS! Do we use this?? Why do we not use this??"

"I like this *guy*, mang," another Ramos brother said as he stood up to pat me on the shoulders with his massive, rugged hands.

I scanned the table to see the Ramos brothers excitedly talking to each other in Spanish while the boys expressed looks of both respect and shock. Santi's face, however, stayed the *same*. I took a big bite out of my salmon, feeling on top of the world. I guess having somewhat paid attention in class and in meetings at work wasn't a waste of time after all.

"Good shit, Jay," whispered Braden from the seat to my left.

Despite having been in my head the entire day after talking to Val, the sincerity behind Braden's statement brought me a sense of peace. While I knew the conversation was to be had about our mother, the thought of it being a conversation rather than an altercation made me feel more at ease.

After all, I *did* somewhat owe it to Val to not say anything, having told her I wouldn't just blatantly confront Braden about lying. The thought of Val back in my life was almost instantly bringing me more clarity. I set my drink down. I was no longer feeling the urge to sip.

The conversation picked up again, but this time, revolving around a heated debate about whether L.A. or Miami women are more attractive. I noticed Santi shot me an occasional look as if studying my involvement in the conversation.

Had I spoken out when I wasn't supposed to earlier?
Was the idea I pitched a bad one?
Was it not even my place to pitch something at all?

I grabbed my drink and looked at it, swishing it in a circular motion. I contemplated taking a sip but decided against it, setting it back down. The dinner continued as one course came out after another, and around 11:30p.m., we were saying our goodbyes.

Reeking of cigars, good pork, and fish, the Ramos brothers gave us a warm embrace before we headed down the elevator.

"Mr. Jay," Mateo called for me before I turned away. "Come with Santi tomorrow on our yacht to talk more of what we're doing. We need a young guy like you to give input."

He handed me his business card, and I subtly slipped it into my pocket, making light of our interaction, so Santi didn't get suspicious.

"I appreciate that," I replied cautiously. "I'll see if I can make it."

Mateo responded with an aggressive hug that consumed me with an aroma of Cuban cigars and expensive rum.

The six of us made our way into the elevator, buzzing about the night lying ahead at PRIME. I couldn't help but wonder what Santi thought of my interaction with the Ramos brothers. While it seemed like I helped in a way, I felt like Santi didn't care whether what I said did or didn't help secure the deal he yearned for. Something told me he was more concerned about my having overstepped.

We filled the same black S.U.V. that brought us to the restaurant, and immediately the champagne bottles were in full rotation as the music shook the car.

With my mind still fixated on the dinner conversation, I texted Fia.

ME: I'm kinda trippin … can you talk?

After sending the text, a calming thought presented itself… The thought of texting Val. I pulled up Val's number and texted her.

ME: Hey it's Jay.. I'm kinda trippin … can you talk?

I instantly felt butterflies at the thought of confiding in Val like I use to.

CLINK!

A champagne bottle was shoved against my chest as the boys shouted for me to drink. I gave in, and before I knew it, it was time to get rowdy. The windows were rolled down, and Ocean Drive was littered with beautiful people getting sloppy in and around the bars and clubs that stood side by side.

I held Skylar's legs to keep him from falling out of the car as he flagged down models with his half-empty bottle of Dom. In his defense, the women were *actually* reciprocating his enthusiasm. On the opposite side of the car, Niall pulled out a colorful pill and downed it with another bottle of champagne. Snorting sounds came from the back of the car as Kai and Kalani took their bumps of coke while Braden lit a joint in the front. It was absolute mayhem on wheels, but I had never seen the boys happier.

Was it true happiness? Probably not.
Were they, in fact, happy? I guess you could say so.
I wondered if the higher they got, the happier they'd look.
At what point would they reach the highest level of happiness?
Does that highest level come with the price of not remembering how happy they are when they hit it?

I took a sip.

Our car pulled over in front of a massive crowd of people that took up half of the street, and we sloppily spilled out. Girls came running up as if on cue, and I recognized some of them from the beach and back in L.A. They stayed close as we skipped the line, two of them half-wrapped around my torso--one under each arm. Everyone in line stared as we approached the front entrance, but no one questioned why we were able to cut.

The sidewalk was lit by a neon fixture that extended over the tinted glass doors. In blue and pink, the sign read, "PRIME," and photos were being taken of and by everyone around it.

"AMOR," one of the bouncers said in a deep voice as he embraced Braden.

"What's good, my guy?" Braden replied. He made room for Kai to squeeze through our group with the note Santi gave us.

The bouncer scanned the note quickly and handed it back to Kai with a smile as he turned to Braden.

"Santi said you brought us some gifts," he said in a low voice.

"It's in the S.U.V.," Braden signaled back to Alberto, who was still parked curbside.

"Have him bring it around the back," the bouncer commanded as he gestured for Alberto to drive around the back of the building.

The S.U.V. slowly passed through the crowd, disappearing around the corner, and the bouncer opened the stanchion for our group to pass. As we entered the venue, I felt the girls' grips loosen on me, and it was apparent they had used me to get into the club. I was used to it at this point, so I didn't mind. I let go and made my way up to Braden, who was right behind the hostess showing us to our table.

"What was in the car??" I asked, competing with the music that was getting louder the deeper we got into the club.

"Don't worry about it," Braden replied dryly.

"You're dealing again, aren't you??" I lashed out, inches away from his ear.

"It's complicated, Jay... Just have a good time tonight, and we'll talk about it later."

Our group arrived at what I thought would be a booth, but instead, it was an entire section to ourselves. The section included four booths, and an entire mezzanine, overlooking a sea of people talking, dancing, and drinking. I checked my phone to see that Val had responded, but before I could read the text, Skylar handed me a glass he had poured. I slid my phone back into my pocket as he gave a toast.

"Here's to the fucking *family*!" Skylar held up his glass.

I felt an arm wrap around me, and the first rotation of shots began... Then another round... And another round after that. Women were walking up and down the stairs to our section, making themselves at home, ordering drinks, and recording the exclusivity behind where they were. We weren't just dealing social currency... We were swimming in an ocean of it, totally fine with all the pretty faces doing the same.

I felt a good buzz coming on as the next round of shots came up, and I remembered the text I forgot to read from Val. I stealthily turned away from the herd of people reaching for shots from Skylar so I could check my phone. I leaned against the mezzanine railing and read her response.

VAL: Did something bad happen? We can meet up if you wanna talk

As I began typing my response, I felt the urge to see if Fia had responded. I opened our conversation and saw that she read my text but didn't respond. It stung a bit, considering even though Fia and I weren't serious, I still wanted to somewhat confide in her. I looked up into the sea of people below me and took a deep breath.

I had the dinner conversation, Fia's unreliability, my mother still being alive, and Braden still dealing drugs *all* swirling about in my mind. For the first time, I had no desire to suppress these thoughts with drinks like I had become so comfortable doing. I need…

No… I thought. *There's no way.*

Among the bobbing heads below me, I saw Fia walking through the crowd with her friends--her hair slicked back in a high ponytail as she wore the *same* outfit she wore when I met her. My heart sank.

They weaved through the crowd, joining a group of guys by the bar across the dance floor. Without thinking, I headed for the stairs. My gaze was fixed on their group as I reached the bottom level.

I subtly bounced to the B.P.M. of the music, making it easier to slip through groups of people doing the same. I clenched my fists out of frustration, seeing her giggle and get handsy with another guy the same way she did with me.

I felt betrayed.
I felt stupid.
I felt *jealous.*

I was too angry to even process a level-headed opening line before I was going to get to her, so I figured I'd let my emotions do it for me. People around me tended to their business as they drunkenly laughed, cheered, and hooked up with each other. Suddenly, I felt my phone vibrate.

Val, I thought, suddenly remembering I didn't send a response to her last text. I slowed to a stop, pulling out my phone and opening a text she had sent as a follow-up to her previous message.

VAL: Are you okay?

I stared at the text, no longer moving at all as people bumped into me from all angles. I tuned the music out and processed what exactly was going on--that this isn't *me*.

How could I feel betrayed when I willingly let a girl like Fia into my life? That might have been a stupid decision, but it didn't make me a stupid *person*. I don't get *jealous*, and I most definitely don't go out of my way to confront people I didn't expect much out of in the first place. I was pursuing Fia, knowing it wasn't really bound to go anywhere. At this point, I suddenly realized she was no longer worth the time… And I felt good about it.

So now here I am, staring at words on a screen that served as so much more than just words on a screen. It wasn't so much *what* the words were, but rather *who* the words came from. It's what finally opened my eyes to the fact that the past couple of weeks, I'd been slipping--prioritizing in a way that benefitted me in the short-term, but not the long. I replied.

ME: Let's meet up.. I'm leaving prime now

As the text was sent, I made my way back to the mezzanine to tell the guys I was leaving. I dodged the drunks left and right, sobering myself up enough to be able to fully remember the night I was about to have with Val.

I reached the top of the stairs to see that the large group had been split up into smaller groups. I rushed to Skylar and Kai, who were both standing over a girl lying half asleep on the booth. She was fading in and out, but she looked too impaired to just be… *Drunk*.

"Why should *you* get her??" Skylar scolded Kai. "I sneaked her…."

"Yeah, but I brought her up," Kai barked back.

"Bull shit!" shouted Skylar. "The bag goes to the sneak, bitch."

The two of them abruptly turned as I approached the booth.

"What's up, Jay-Dawg?" Skylar slurred.

"I'm 'bout to head out," I said. "What're you fighting about?"

Kai tried to hold himself up straight as he explained.

"Skylar thinks *he* should be able to take this chick home cuz he slipped her the roofie, but I'm the one who brought her up to the booth in the first place."

"Why don't you just tell the whole fucking world, Kai??" Skylar snapped.

"You *drugged* her??" I snarled with my face just inches away from theirs.

"You don't tell a fucking *soul*, Jay," Kai said sternly. "You're new to this, so you don't know half the shit that goes on but just know that what we're doing... We do for a reason... And we do it for Santi... For *us*."

The clarity I had reached while on the dance floor was suddenly replaced by confusion. Here Kai and Skylar were, fighting over who would be taking home a girl they had both set out to roofie. Why was it that I was finally starting to see the true colors being shown *now*? At what point will I know the *truth* behind what's really going on here, and at what cost?

I wish I hadn't come across this situation, and since I couldn't just erase it from my memory, I settled for the next best thing--to simply walk away. Just before turning back to the stairs, Kai grabbed my arm.

"You keep this kinda shit within the family, Jay... It stays between us."

I nodded as he let go of my arm and patted my shoulder as a form of dismissal. I swiftly turned, subtly shaking my head as I darted down the stairs, thinking that would help me forget what I had just witnessed. I dodged familiar faces and strangers alike, struggling to text Val as I squeezed through the crowd.

The location she sent me was just across the street from where I was. As I picked up the pace toward the exit, the music got quieter, and the sound of moving cars got louder. I slipped between a group of people walking in and felt the warm midnight breeze as I stumbled onto the busy sidewalk. I checked Val's location to see that we were even closer than before.

I looked up, and there she was--her platinum hair reflecting the neon lights from the clubs and bars on my side of the street. Behind her was a series of palm trees joined by hanging lights that separated Ocean Drive from the shore. She stood alone, patiently waiting, peacefully studying the ambiance surrounding her. The closer I got to her, the more I felt at ease.

"Hi..." I greeted her warmly, standing just below the curb as if I was a complete stranger.

"Hello, Jay Love," she replied with a cheeky smirk.

I stepped up onto the curb, now standing over Val. I must've grown since high school because I easily had about four or five inches of height on her.

"Don't you have to be up early?" I asked as we started walking along the sidewalk.

"I do, I do... But I mean, how can I experience Miami while sleeping, Jay?"

"True, true," I nodded, trying to keep myself from blushing. "I guess we're both in for an experience then."

My state of mind changed like night and day, from instability and confusion to a genuine sense of clarity. We bounced from one venue to the next, and whether it was dancing, talking, eating--everything we did, we did while completely engaged in each other. Our conversations were all over the place, but we spoke only of things we were happy to indulge in.

I told her about New York.

She told me about L.A.

I told her about how I spent my time people-watching.

She told me about how she can't *stand* the scene drama.

I told her all about college life.

She told me all about her obsession with vintage clothing.

"You haven't talked to *anybody* at all from our high school??" Val questioned in-between bites of her street taco.

"Not a single person," I shrugged.

For the first time in seven years, I didn't cringe at the thought of something having to do with life before Josh passed. Val had made me feel comfortable again, and I found myself warming up to the thought of revisiting the *good* times rather than immediately falling subject to the bad.

"Tell me about them," I playfully urged.

"Okay, okay," she sighed as she balanced on the curb we walked along. "After high school, Nate started working at a bike shop in Torrance, where he's been since. Last I heard about Cole, he was preparing for med school... And then I'm almost positive Danny is working in a bakery somewhere in Europe."

I couldn't help but laugh after hearing about Danny.

"A bakery??" I laughed. "Danny??"

Val giggled while lowering her head, attempting to swallow the last bite of her street taco.

"No, yeah, I'm being completely serious!"

Her eyes lit up. She knew I would get a kick out of hearing this.

"Danny ended up going to school at Berkeley, somehow... And Nate told me that he spent a weekend tripping on shrooms in a nearby forest and hasn't been the same *since*."

"No way," I laughed as I stopped walking and shook my head. "That's insane."

"You've been missing out, Jay Love," she teased with her arms out, still balancing on the edge of the curb.

"I know," I sighed, standing just beside her to be there in case she fell.

I watched her look up at the sky, mid-twirl. She was in a lace bandeau covered by a cropped flannel, trimmed to just above her waist. Her baggy jeans flowed down her long legs until they scrunched over her high-top sneakers. Her outfit was modest but not enough to go without recognizing that she was *fit*.

The amber eyes that I thought once followed me were now in front of me, and I felt as though nothing else in the world mattered. I had buried everything that had to do with Val's existence along with my entire childhood, but now I could feel myself gradually coming to peace with everything that once was as I looked at her.

"You got somethin' to say?" Val teased as she hopped off the curb, landing a foot away from my face.

I stood--staring--speechless. Was I *really* speechless? Or did I have too much to say? I wanted to just keep talking and talking… But in the moment, I felt the urge to kiss her. Was it too soon? Was it even an option? Did it matter that we had spent seven years apart? It didn't feel like it mattered. It all just feels… *Good.*

I felt a sudden vibration in my pocket, bringing me out of this rom-com movie moment. I pulled out my phone to see three texts from Santi, spaced out over the past hour I had been with Val. My heart dropped into my stomach, and I felt a cold sweat come over me as I read the texts.

SANTI: Meet me back at the hotel. Suite 1500
SANTI: Jay- Where are you
SANTI: This isn't a good look for you

The guys would've deemed the first text a death sentence… Let alone the following two. I instantly felt something was *off*.

"What's wrong?" Val asked, processing my panicked facial expression.

"It's Santi… Fuck… Val, I'm *so* sorry, I-...."

"Don't worry!" she smiled. "I understand!"

The tone of her voice was uppity and genuine, but I could tell she was disappointed I was leaving at what could have been such a crucial moment.

"I can call you an Uber to your hotel," I offered, feeling guilty I had no choice but to pick Santi over Val.

"It's fine," she put her hand on my shoulder. "Go! My hotel is literally down the block… I can walk!"

"I'm sorry," I apologized once again.

I flagged down a taxi that immediately stopped, and before getting in, I looked back to see that Val was still watching me. Fighting the urge to stay with everything in me, I slid into the back seat of the taxi, stating the name of our hotel. Off we went, and I looked back to see Val slowly turning away toward her own hotel.

As the cab pulled up in front of the massive glass doors of the resort entrance, I tossed a wad of cash onto the passenger's seat and leaped out. While hitting a dead sprint up the stairs and through the lobby, I couldn't help but notice how packed it was in front of DAWN, the nightclub we were hosting tomorrow night. I recognized celebrities, models, and influencers... All waiting to get into the venue that was already overflowing with people. I darted through the crowd, seizing gaps between people as I made my way to the elevator.

"Wait!" I shouted as I stopped an elevator door from closing.

There wasn't enough room for me, but I squeezed in anyway.

"What floor?" one of the guys asked.

"Penthouse, please," I nervously snapped back, realizing how pretentious my response might have sounded.

I didn't care. All I knew was that from the very beginning, I feared being on Santi's bad side... And tonight may potentially be the fruition of that fear. The elevator was silent, packed with people, stopping at almost every floor imaginable until it was just me. My legs felt light, and my hands were shaking. I wanted to take a shot... Or two... Or 10.

The elevator doors slid open, and I sprinted down the hall. My shoes tapped against the floor as I zoomed past the suite doors and hallway lights. My head rotated left and right, processing the suite numbers. I was approaching the end of the hall where the wall was made of glass, overlooking the Atlantic Ocean. After reaching our own suite, I found Santi's, which was the last door on the right side of the hall.

"1500," I confirmed under my breath before knocking three times.

I could hear music playing from inside the room, and within 30 seconds, the door slowly opened. I saw Santi wearing the same outfit he was wearing at dinner. His gray eyes were lit by the hallway lights as he smiled and gestured for me to come in. I hesitantly did so.

"You're alive," Santi said in a way that could be interpreted in a variety of different ways.

He was grinning, and his tone was warm, but I felt like the matter wasn't something worth celebrating, whatever the matter may be.

"Yeah, I'm sorry I spaced on your texts. I was barely on my phone, and I had no idea you'd be reaching out. I was just with the guys and then left for a bit because I-...."

"Jay, it's all good," he grinned as he shut the door behind us. "It's better to be a man of few words... Otherwise, you sound guilty."

He headed past the open kitchen toward the living room, which was more spacious than most apartments I've seen. The suite was so clean it looked like it was sanitary enough to lick the floor. While everything in our suite was marble and white with a more chilling feel, Santi's suite was warm and dimly lit. Just past the kitchen, the ceiling rose high enough to expose a second floor of the suite, taking you up to the master bedroom and eventually to a private rooftop deck.

"You smoke cigars?" he asked as he stepped up a modern staircase that lined the massive windows.

"Only a few times... With my dad," I responded, following him from a few steps behind.

Massive art pieces hung on the walls of the master bedroom, and I could smell the same scent Santi used in his venues. He passed through sliding glass doors that separated his bedroom from the rooftop deck, where a cigar box and two glasses of rum were placed between two plush seats. He sat and extended his hand as a way of inviting me to sit in the other chair. I did so, sinking in further than I anticipated. We were overlooking the ocean with the moon directly above us.

"This suite is incredible," I said, panning from the ocean to the Miami shoreline lined with hotels and vibrant lights.

"Thank you," he replied. "I stay in the same suite every time I come visit."

I watched as he pulled out two cigars and punched a small hole into the end of each with a tiny diamond-studded tool.

"What's that?" I asked, hoping the more answers I received, the easier it may be to pick up on Santi's mood.

"It's a punch cutter… Better for the cigar drag you inhale as opposed to using a regular cutter."

I nodded in admiration as he handed me my cigar and lit his own before passing me the lighter. I held the silver lighter that was more of a torch than anything, emitting a piercing blue flame I held at the edge of my cigar. It lit slowly, and I puffed lightly, trying not to cough and make a mockery of myself.

Santi stared directly ahead, into the Atlantic horizon lit by the full moon. He had a half-smirk on his face, and I was still struggling to get a read on him. Music played through surround sound speakers, and an overwhelming smell of cigar smoke swept the deck. It was warm, and if I wasn't so terrified of what was to be discussed, I think I would've really been enjoying this moment. Santi broke the silence.

"The Ramos brothers took a liking to you at dinner," he smiled between puffs. "I saw one of them talking to you on the way out."

I felt a sense of relief, assuming this conversation had to do with the Ramos brothers liking me. Given the fact I was scared I might've overstepped by speaking out at dinner, it felt good to know I was about to be recognized for my contribution.

"Yeah, one of them invited me to join you guys on the yacht

tomorrow," I replied, taking a nice long puff of my cigar and making myself comfortable.

"That's good to hear!" Santi exclaimed before turning to face me. "Do you think you should go?"

I exhaled a cloud of smoke and carefully processed his question. I *want* to go, but do I think I *should* go? Santi had asked the question in a tone that made me think he didn't want me to say yes. Was I overthinking this? Why *wouldn't* he want one of his own to join him for a potential business venture? He wanted us to learn, didn't he?

Say no, I thought.

"Yes," I said.

He skeptically narrowed his eyes, and the gray read me from the inside out. If I were to over-analyze the situation, he might have wanted me to say no, but in my heart, I felt he wanted me to say *yes*. That's what a good mentor would want, right?

"Amazing," Santi smirked as he lifted his glass. "Here's to *opportunity....*"

I felt my self-esteem shoot through the roof as I tapped my glass against his and pridefully downed half of it.

"Now..." he let out a deep breath. "Why do you *think* that you should go?"

"Well, they like me," I replied. "They invited me...."

"I see..." he said before letting out a sigh as he ran his hand through the curls in his hair. "It's a damn shame...."

Before I could ask what he meant by that, the cigar fell from my hand as if in slow motion. I watched the ash and embers land in my lap. The cigar rolled onto the floor in front of me. Within seconds, my arms and head became too heavy to lift, and I sank back into my seat, looking straight into the darkness of the night--sinking deeper... And deeper. My eyelids closed shut, and before I could process what was happening...

I blacked out.

TWELVE | HERO

OUR PENTHOUSE SUITE
MIAMI BEACH, FLORIDA
SATURDAY, 11:58A.M. - JULY 13TH, 2019

I opened my eyes. The side of my face was buried halfway into my pillow as I stared out the window at buildings lining Ocean Drive. My head was heavy as I felt my pockets for my phone. I was fully clothed in what I was wearing the night before, shoes and all. Upon pulling out my phone, I unlocked the screen to a missed text from Santi among other notifications and texts. I wiped the drool from my face as I read Santi's message.

SANTI: Heard you weren't feeling too well. We'll miss you on the yacht - rest up for tonight. Be down at DAWN Nightclub just before 4PM

I sat up slowly and was struck with a migraine like never before. I tried to process what happened last night.

I remember being at the dinner.
I remember going to the club.
I remember Skylar and Kai drugging that girl… Fighting over who gets her.
I remember seeing Val.
I remember the Ramos brothers liking me… Inviting me onto the yacht today.
I remember celebrating with Santi.

Shit, I thought as I reread Santi's text. *I fucked up.*

Did I drink too much? I suddenly remembered being on Santi's rooftop deck, smoking a cigar, which just so happened to be my last memory before waking up moments ago. I pictured Val last night, balancing on the curb, telling me about her life and her being so intrigued to hear about mine. The last thing I wanted was for her to be mad at me for having to leave, but I knew she'd understand why.

I pictured myself drinking too much while with Santi last night, looking like a fool for not being able to handle a cigar and some rum while celebrating a successful dinner.

"How you feelin'?" Braden asked from the bedroom doorway.

"I feel... *Heavy*," I said while laying back against the headboard.

"Santi said you drank a lot last night. I remember seeing you at the club, but then you were gone."

"I left to see Val," I confessed, not caring about the tough time he was about to give me.

He crossed his arms with a grin, just as I had anticipated.

"Who would've thought...? Seven years later, and you're still crushin' on our next-door neighbor...."

"Shut up," I sighed while rubbing my eyes.

I watched as Braden's posture softened and he leaned against the door frame.

"Kai said you saw what went down with him and Skylar at the club," Braden said sternly. "I told him that there was nothing to worry about and that it wouldn't be brought up again."

"They roofied some girl, Braden," I whispered. "They were fighting over who was gonna basically *date-rape* her."

He closed his eyes and nodded. "Jay, where we're at in this industry, you're gonna see some fucked up stuff, but you've gotta stay focused on the job. Santi is running a tight ship, and he's been running it for a while. You're protected... So don't trip."

"Look, I obviously won't say anything," I assured him. "I just don't want any part in that."

"You need to understand me when I say... The less you know about what goes on behind the scenes, the better. Just learn everything you can about the nightlife *business*, and we'll have our own spot in no time... Without all the shady shit that goes on in the background."

I nodded, processing everything Braden had said. He had never come across this poised before. Despite his justifying Skylar and Kai's actions, he was right about me focusing more on the business side of things. I lost my way, getting wrapped up in the drinking and messing around... And tonight was my chance to prove that I was an asset to the business.

DAWN NIGHTCLUB
MIAMI BEACH, FLORIDA
SATURDAY, 11:34P.M. - JULY 13TH, 2019

The night was a night different from any other I had ever experienced--an entirely packed venue--more packed than I had ever *seen* a venue. Maximum capacity was quickly reached, and we were still letting people in through the lobby. After all, we *are* hosting the entirety of Swim Week--agents, models, groupies, influencers, celebrities, athletes--there was no other place in the country they'd rather be.

I moved through the crowd with the mindless bodies that swayed as if they were one with the music--almost in one massive wave. I felt the music played at the perfect B.P.M. to let intoxication run its course and dictate each and every movement the body made, good or bad. The beauty of being this intoxicated was that there wasn't a single bad move you *could* make besides choosing to be sober on a night like this.

I made my way to the edge of the crowd, and the bouncer opened up the walkway for me. This was the first night in weeks I was completely sober while on the job, and as a result, I felt sharper than usual.

I noticed four young girls dressed to the nines... Saint Laurent bags and dresses so tight they might as well be targets exposed to every professional athlete, artist, and jet-set entrepreneur hovering over V.I.P. tables. They were making their way past me. I turned to the bouncer and held up my hand as if I were holding an invisible card.

"Were they I.D.'d?" I mouthed.

He shrugged as he watched the girls continue to walk with confidence. Before he could take two steps in their direction, I placed my hand sternly on his chest.

"I'm on it. Keep on the entrance," I said.

He obeyed.

It's nights like these that could ruin a professional's career.
It's nights like these that could ruin the perception of...
An organization.
A club.
Santi.
Even me. But I won't let that happen.

I proceeded forward slowly, watching the girls' movements, well-knowing they weren't 21. They maintained their beauty and elegance with a decent posture. The fact was that they were stunning, and that fact was validated by the men who turned their heads to face the strides of the four girls. They were being scoped out by basically *everyone* in the V.I.P. section, as they most likely knew they were going to be. Why else would they have gone through the trouble of putting on layers of makeup, tight dresses, and intolerable heels? Was it not to arouse these young millionaires and threaten the women these young millionaires were currently sharing their time with?

Ahhh, there he is, I thought. Darian O'Reilly, second-string quarterback for the Tampa Bay Knights--easily one of the best positions on the team because he doesn't bear the leadership responsibilities of the first-string quarterback, but *he is* still a quarterback... And he *does* still suit up every game in case the first-string quarterback goes down. I wish I could take credit for that analysis, but I heard it on some T.V. show.

I watched as O'Reilly hugged the first girl out of the four. She kissed him on the cheek. It was a shaky and unsettling embrace on her part. She's most likely nervous, which led me to believe she's sober. As she finished hugging O'Reilly, she eyed the bottles in the ice chest on the table.

Too young to buy alcohol to pre-game with, I thought.
Save yourself... Don't pour a glass.
This isn't your scene. You know you shouldn't be here.

That's when I recognized her. Yesterday morning, when we were on the balcony going through invites, I came across her Instagram profile. After doing some digging, I saw that not only was she *not* 21, but she wasn't even 18... I remember seeing the birthday post celebrating her *17th birthday*. I didn't send the invite, but after Skylar's actions last night, I wouldn't put it past him to send it, regardless of her being a minor.

I watched as O'Reilly embraced the other girls with a warm introduction as he towered above them. I held down the button on my transmitter.

"Skylar, I've got four girls over at Table 6 in V.I.P. with some Knights football players. Came in together--pastel dresses. Wanted to confirm that you I.D.'d them all."

I stood in place, leaning against a column to the side of the walkway.

"*They're with O'Reilly's party*," Skylar's voice responded.

"Did you I.D. them?"

"*No, they're with the fucking group, Jay... They're fine.*"

"I know at least one of them is 17, Skylar. I found her on Insta...."

I heard a static sound and looked at the transmitter to see that he had switched to a different channel.

I rolled my eyes and looked back at the table. O'Reilly was between two of the girls, and the other two were dancing on the booth above him. I began to walk toward the table. Darian took out a packet of what looked like four colorful pills--the *exact* same pills I've been seeing exchanged between Skylar, Niall, and the rest of the guys the past few weeks. He offered some to the girls, which they reluctantly accepted.

Don't, I thought. *Don't take the....*

The girls took the pills.

I was only two tables away when the siren began. Purple and white flashing lights lit up the section as Table 6's bottle arrived. O'Reilly and his group pulled out their phones to record the bottle girls bringing them their third bottle of the night. I noticed the girl O'Reilly was with didn't pull out her phone. She *knows* better than to be posting about a place she shouldn't be in illegally, and I assume that's undoubtedly the case.

It was at that moment, I heard Santi's voice in my head echo... "*One of the biggest mistakes you can make in nightlife is threatening to degrade the guest's social stature. We're not a liquor store. We don't sell bottles. We're dealing social currency.*"

I knew that meant letting these guys receive their bottle service without being disturbed, but I watched as the girls began to slowly lose control of themselves below the flashing lights. It was time for me to intervene. I wasn't gonna let another incoherent girl end up in the hands of a potential scumbag or even a Skylar and Kai for that matter--not again....

I took a step forward but was immediately pulled back by the arm. The music blared as I heard each word Skylar said as clear as day.

"Leave them."

I turned to face him as I freed myself from his grasp.

"They're underage, man," I said. "They're a liability."

"It doesn't matter, Jay. These guys are dropping more money than you're *worth*. O'Reilly asked specifically for these girls, and they're paying us a shit ton for it. Santi wants us off their case... So let 'em drink."

"Paying us??" I snapped. "What do you mean he asked *specifically* for *these girls*, and they're paying us for it?? What's *it* that they're paying for? The girls?? What the fuck's going on??"

I turned to face O'Reilly's table once again, standing still. You know those moments in life when you have complete control over something that will significantly impact the lives of others while leaving yourself untouched? Those moments where you have the opportunity to act as a guardian angel would, making the person turn right instead of left to save them from a catastrophic incident. The guardian angel vs. a proposed fate most likely stemming from karma.

I don't know what wrong O'Reilly must have done to be here in this moment--a moment that could potentially lead to jail time and becoming another professional athlete-gone-sex offender... But maybe O'Reilly *isn't* in the wrong... Maybe it's the *girls* who are in the wrong.

What have *they* done to deserve being taken advantage of? Do they *know* that they're about to be taken advantage of? Do they care? Is it considered being taken advantage of if their primary pursuit was for sloppy drunk sex with a professional athlete in the first place? I know little of either party's intentions, yet I *still* felt the urge to intervene.

I turned back to face Skylar.

"Fuck that," I said.

Before I could look back at O'Reilly's party, I caught the gaze of Braden amid the flashing lights from the entrance of the V.I.P. section. He knew what I was about to do. It was in that gaze I recognized a sense of familiarity, but it was not warm. It was not comfortable.

~ I stood at the doorway of the garage. I was back in Torrance. I silently poked my 8-year-old nose between the narrow opening and adjusted my head so I could see what was happening inside with one eye. It must have been 2a.m., and I was still half asleep--my body led by curiosity to sounds from the garage I had heard from the quiet of my bedroom.

"Go ahead, laugh. Laugh, Braden," my father said.

Braden laughed uncontrollably from the chair he sat in. My father's back was to the door I peeked through, and I could see Braden's face lit by the faint fluorescent lighting attached to the ceiling. He was high, and he continued to laugh with no capability of stopping.

"This is funny, yeah?" My father stood slowly, looking over Braden. Braden laughed, and he laughed, and he laughed.

SMACK!

My father slapped Braden with his right hand across the left side of Braden's face, which could have sent him flying across the garage floor if he wasn't held against the chair by my father's other hand. Braden's laugh turned into a sharp squeal, similar to that of a hopeless puppy. He quickly expressed a look of panic. I had never seen a facial expression shift so quickly from one extreme to its exact opposite.

I felt the sudden urge to intervene as my father pulled Braden back to his straightened position, upright in the chair. I couldn't watch my brother take another blow to the head like this. I knew very little of how my father would react to me stepping in, but I didn't care. I remember this being my first opportunity to be the... Hero.

As Braden was firmly guided to an upright position in the chair, my father stood tall over him once more.

"Where's the backpack?" my father asked in a stern tone.

Braden's face began to swell, and he lifted his hand shakily to the corner of the garage where the backpack was lying. I slowly opened the door as my father walked toward the backpack. Braden turned to face me, and his eyes enlarged almost immediately. Fixated on me in the disillusioned mental state he was in, he tilted his head.

As I silently prepared myself for my heroic moment, I stared back into Braden's eyes. I paused. He shook his head, signalling for me to leave before our father finished searching his backpack.

"Don't," he mouthed.

I didn't want to do what he asked for me to do, but the look in his eyes demanded that I not intervene. I obeyed, silently stepping back outside and continuing to peek through the door's narrow opening.

Maybe I wasn't supposed to intervene.
Maybe Braden calling me off while out of his right mind was God communicating that Braden was to learn his lesson here and now.

It was this look he gave me that served in exchange for a thousand words--a painted picture, even. I understood my role, and it was to not intervene. This moment led me to understand that I was to look over my brothers so that they may never be harmed by those who love or hate them. It was this look that I never forgot, as it made me who I am. ~

I now stood here in the V.I.P. section, my eyes fixated on the exact look Braden gave me from the night our father first laid hands on him in front of me. He shook his head.

"Don't," he mouthed.

"I'm sorry," I mouthed back as I turned toward the V.I.P. table.

I had always been a firm believer that memories of specific occurrences serve to warn and guide us from potential dangers. Otherwise, what *other good* do memories serve? To be unalterable mental clips we reminisce about in order to either be sad the good times are over or relive the bad? Nah. I proceeded to O'Reilly's party.

I watched as O'Reilly started to dance with the girl more aggressively. I remained focused on their group as I maneuvered my way through the crowd that occupied the walkway of the V.I.P. section. Drunk women leaned against me, and sweaty men refused to move but quickly decided to move upon seeing my earpiece and determined facial expression. One of the young girls with O'Reilly became sloppy immediately, throwing herself onto one of his teammates. I could tell they were already far from being in their right minds, and I wasn't gonna let another girl get taken advantage of… Not while I was able to do something about it.

WAM!

In an instant, I received a major blow to the stomach. An involuntary sound came from the depth of my body as I slumped forward. I covered my torso in self-defense. It was already too late. The music continued blaring, and no one heard or realized I had completely lost my breath. I stared at the ground as my stance staggered, then I found my balance but still not my breath. I straightened my posture to find myself at eye level with Santi. He had my arm in his grasp within seconds.

"Join me, Jay," he said softly, almost touching my ear with the warmth of his breath, which reeked of alcohol.

The low frequencies and sternness of his voice had me immediately following him out of the V.I.P. section without question. I gathered my breath and wiped my head of the cold sweat that came over me after Santi's lethal punch--a literal *low blow.*

We walked through the crowd of dancing people who didn't react much to us passing through the main bar lining the wall of the club. I looked up at the elevated platform to see Niall vibing to the song he played, controlling the crowd. He studied his laptop but looked down for a split second to make eye contact with me. It was a look that led me to immediately believe that he had summoned Santi to stop me. Niall could see the entire venue from up there.

Santi shoved the door of the kitchen open without looking back as if he *knew* I was only a few steps behind him.

"Get the FUCK out! All of you… Get out, please!" Santi screamed at the chefs.

They filed out without question, one after the other. I put my hands on my hips, looking at the ground, feeling within me that I had more from Santi coming my way… And it was *not* going to be good. Santi leaned his back against the wall, and I could feel his glare of frustration burning a hole in the side of my face as I refused to make eye contact. I watched the light footsteps of the chefs funnel out of the kitchen, and the last pair of feet came to a halt as Santi stopped them in their tracks.

"You stay," Santi said to the owner of the footsteps. It was Kalani.

Kalani paused and slowly turned to face me. I looked up at

him, and he had no expression on his face. I knew by now that it probably wasn't best to portray emotion in front of Santi. I was beginning to feel like he could *weaponize* emotions. It was evident that Kalani's experience working for Santi made him an expert on this subject. We both stood, silent, and emotionless.

Santi grabbed a large metal spoon with a charcoal grip on it, turned on the stove, and placed the head of the spoon on the open flame. He then pulled out a cigarette, lit it using the open flame, and turned back to look at me with a stern look on his face.

"Jay," he said softly, putting the cigarette between his lips.

He took a drag as he looked at the ceiling then back down to me.

"I've been nothing but good to you since you came around, and lately, I've noticed that you've been *overstepping*," he examined me. "What're you chasing here? Do you think you're some sort of *hero* when you undermine my work?"

I didn't respond. Instead, I continued staring at the ground.

"Are you the *hero*?" Santi asked again, but louder.

I looked up and thought carefully about the words that were about to come out of my mouth. Without moving his head, Kalani's eyes studied me, Santi, and then me once more.

"Hero?" I asked, still processing what he had asked.

Santi took another long drag of his cigarette. He took a couple of pondering steps toward the space between Kalani and myself. I could see Kalani now attempting to avoid eye contact with me from over Santi's shoulder.

"Yeah, the hero. Are you the fucking *hero*?" Santi questioned me while laughing unsteadily. He placed his open palms on the sides of my head and continued with the cigarette lightly clenched between his teeth.

"Everyone's got a story. Every story has a *hero*. So, I feel as though it would make sense for you to think that you're the hero of your own story, no?"

I could smell the liquor on his breath. His face was so close to mine, I began to feel a minor head rush coming on from the smoke that trailed from his cig. I didn't know where this conversation was going, nor did I understand where it even was at this very moment. I stared into his gray eyes--now eyes of recklessness and instability. They twitched. Santi has to be on *heavy* drugs, and there's no telling what he's going to do or say next. He continued.

"How does it work if two stories overlap? Do you think there can be two stories... *Coexisting*? With *two* heroes that don't believe in the same greater good?" he laughed again, let go of my face, and tilted his head to look at the ceiling in thought.

"You've obviously got some sort of agenda you're pushing. I

can see it in the way you *overstep*… And I'll tell you, your agenda is not working with *mine*. Therefore I say, Jay… I'm the hero of *my* story. I know that. But tell me... If I disagree with you and what *you* believe should happen in and around my life and business--my *story*… Does that make me the villain of *your story* while I remain the hero of my own?"

I watched him take another drag and blow it toward the ceiling. He turned to face Kalani with his back to me.

"Kalani, who's the hero of *your* story?" Santi asked, putting a firm hand on Kalani's shoulder.

Kalani stood expressionless--his apron in hand.

"You are," Kalani said softly without thinking much about it.

Without letting go of Kalani's shoulder, Santi turned back to me, smiled, then turned back to Kalani.

"Why would you say that?" Santi asked.

"You took me in when I had nothing," Kalani said. "You gave me a home… And a purpose."

Santi released Kalani and turned back to face me.

"Braden talked me into giving you a shot, Jay. You've got an eye--I'll give you that. You know how to *read* people. You understand the rhythm of connection among individuals. Now, I took you in because I see myself in you. You're different from Braden, and I can feel that you have a lot to offer to this family and business," he said while slowly making his way back to stand face to face with me. "Why are you sabotaging your own purpose--your own story?"

"Why would I sabotage my own story?" I asked, genuinely confused.

"Your job here is to learn… To *listen*. You have absolutely no place to make executive orders or be on your own out there on *my* fucking floor. This is *my* venue--*my* space. You're breathing *my* air," his voice began to rise.

His eyes were just inches from mine as he read my mind, heart, and soul. He owned and was able to control me at this very moment, and he was aware of it as I did my best to hide my shaking hands.

Say something, I thought. *Do something AT LEAST. Defend yourself.*

Instead, I stood, speechless.

"Braden respects me like a father, and I love Braden like a son," Santi said softly. "I love *all* of my boys. I will earn your respect, Jay, and you *will* learn to fucking listen before I'll have to earn your respect through fear."

He placed the cigarette back in his mouth and grabbed the large spoon lying over the open flame.

"Kalani," he said with his back to the both of us. "Give me your hand."

Kalani's eyes widened in fear of the unexpected. He obediently lifted his right palm toward Santi, fully extending his arm with a concerned look on his face.

Santi slowly turned and walked over to Kalani while wielding the spoon. He firmly grabbed Kalani's hand and pressed the scorching metal spoon into his forearm.

"AHH!" Kalani shrieked and slowly dropped to his knees as Santi pressed the spoon deeper into his skin.

The music continued to play in the club just outside of the kitchen, where the crowd continued to sway and dance, unaware of the havoc currently taking shape in the kitchen.

"DON'T-..." I gasped, jolting forward.

Santi quickly turned his head halfway to face me with just one of his twitching eyes.

"You stay the fuck back, hero," he demanded, pressing the spoon against Kalani's arm. Kalani's shriek became a helpless scream.

"Santi, I'm sorry!" I shouted, stopping myself from moving forward anymore.

He pressed the scorching hot metal spoon against Kalani's arm with more force, and Kalani let out a scream I had never heard come from any man I had ever known or even heard in a movie I've seen.

"Get on your fucking *knees*, HERO!" Santi shouted back at me as he pressed harder.

"Santi, I'll *listen*!" I screamed aloud, dropping to my knees. "Let him go! I won't overstep! I'll listen to you!"

Santi released Kalani and Kalani rolled onto his side, holding his severely burned arm up with his other arm. He was shaking, and his breathing was unsteady as he rolled in agonizing pain.

He wasn't able to touch the burn. The pain seemed to be unbearable. Santi calmly walked to the kitchen freezer while still wielding the large spoon. He opened the freezer door, tossed the spoon inside, and grabbed a handful of ice.

I slowly crawled toward Kalani, reaching out as if he were a distressed animal that had just been wounded by a predator. He held back tears, unable to touch his burned forearm. It was a horrific burn as it blistered and swelled immediately. Santi cut me off, kneeled before Kalani, and handed him the ice.

"As a family, we ride as one, or we die as one," Santi said in a soothing tone. He leaned in and placed his palm on Kalani's shoulder, then stood above the both of us, now looking down. I looked up at his slim figure, standing above me in black.

"Stop speaking without having been spoken to and stop making calls without my direction, Jay. I thought you were going to be a contributor to this family... Not a *nuisance*," he said calmly while adjusting his chains and diamond-studded Rolex. "Now go get the chefs back in here. We're running a fucking *business*."

Santi calmly walked out of the kitchen and back into the club, leaving Kalani and me on the floor, both in complete shock. My hand was still extended toward Kalani as I slowly stood to my feet. He tapped his arm with the ice while hyperventilating and groaning in pain. His forearm continued to swell, and tears trickled down his face.

"Kalani, I-...."

"Don't..." he blurted out, signalling for me to not get any closer. "It's fine. I'm fine. We're fine."

"He *burned* you, Kalani. You need to see somebody... To get help because this... *Isn't* okay."

"It's a lesson," he whispered in a faint tone--hands shaking as he struggled to ice his burn. "We had to learn the lesson, and we know now. He won't hurt us if we learn from our mistakes."

Kalani's shaking hands, his whimpering, and the words he spoke portrayed a disturbingly clear image I had failed to see since my arrival in L.A.

Kalani said, "*WE learned the lesson. WE know now. He won't hurt US. OUR mistakes*."

He had taken responsibility for something I had done wrong... And what I was doing wasn't even wrong in the first place. Santi remained respected by Kalani, despite this absurd act of abuse Kalani had just endured. It was evident that this "family act" Santi had been using on the guys served as a manipulation tactic that had worked all along.

"*Family this and purpose that.*"

How did I manage to completely *misread* Santi?

My moral compass had been buried in the glitz and glamour of a nightlife scene that was truly tainted on the inside... Tainted by Santi. My original goal coming here was to protect my brother from losing his way, but little did I know that my brother could very well be the victim of something much greater than merely losing his way. He had sold his soul to a man he sought guidance from.

Has Santi manipulated Braden the same way he's manipulated Kalani and potentially the others?

What does Santi have on the guys if they're willing to remain loyal to him after being abused like this?

Braden and I have a lot to talk about... And I now realize we need to address it all before Santi finds out I finally got a read on him.

THIRTEEN | A WEEPING WILLOW

BRADEN'S APARTMENT
DOWNTOWN L.A.
MONDAY, 9:40A.M. - JULY 15TH, 2019

"We gotta talk," I said sternly, watching Braden shove the rest of a bagel down his throat.

I just woke up after an entire Sunday of traveling and sleeping. The past weekend had taken such an emotional toll on me, I couldn't help but sleep almost 16 hours. From the roofie situation to my confrontation with Santi and Kalani--reconnecting with Val and hearing the news about my mother still being alive--I was emotionally exhausted... And *dreading* this conversation, but I knew we needed to have it.

"Can't," Braden murmured before downing a cup of his spiked orange juice. "I need to be at The Willow in 20 to interview the new bottle girls."

"It's important, man," I insisted. I hoped the sternness of my tone would penetrate his thick skull.

"Jay, I can't right now."

"Braden, it's serious. I don't wanna drag this out."

I watched as he scooped his wallet off the kitchen counter and finally caught on to my sincerity. He paused.

"Just meet me at The Willow around lunchtime," he said as he turned for the door. "Bring food. There's this place called Joe & The Juice that has bomb sandwiches. I'll text you my order."

The door shut behind him, and he was out on his way. I jammed my hands into the pockets of my sweatpants and looked around the silent kitchen. I had no plans for the day, which was a first. Skylar had laid off talking to me since Friday night, and I didn't blame him. Maybe it was because he didn't trust me after I saw what happened--regardless, I didn't care.

I sank into the couch and stared at the exposed piping that lined the ceiling. I wanted to see Val, but I didn't want to risk her dropping another bombshell on me before I talked to Braden. I'm one revived relative away from having some sort of mental breakdown.

I looked around the apartment and couldn't help but wonder how the hell I got to this point. Just a few months ago, I was in New York, denying the existence of Braden, Val, and everything out here, promising myself that I'd never end up exactly where I am now... Which is *back*.

I came to L.A. to face my demons without even realizing it, only to find out I was literally partying and sleeping with my demons--befriending them--*trusting* them. I set out to watch over my brother with the capabilities of a queen chess piece. Yet, Santi had molded me into a pawn, only able to move in one direction before being knocked out of the game. He made it apparent that I was on thin ice... And that I'm playing on *his* chessboard.

I didn't have to know Kalani that well to believe that he had been manipulated into thinking Santi is some sort of "god." I'm sure all the guys think it too, and even after taking the verbal and physical abuse, they *still* ride or die for Santi.

My father would tell me all the time, "*Ask good questions, get good answers*."

My questions were horrendously hollow since I got here, and my current situation was the manifestation of those questions. I really hadn't gone anywhere with my life since I touched down in L.A., living a life that seemed so perfect on the outside, but was actually so empty on the inside--a true testament to the city itself.

I let Santi get in my head--I was doing anything and everything he said without question.

I began drinking more than ever before. Smoking, too.

The people I've met don't genuinely care about me.

What Fia and I had was toxic. Purely physical.

Braden is *still* an alcoholic and *still* deals drugs. He might even be worse than before.

And overall... I had become desensitized to such terrible things.

I was in a rare mood with so much going on in my head, I didn't care to think about anything at all. I decided to throw on an oversized T-shirt, hat, and some slippers, then head for the door with nothing but the apartment keys.

It wasn't even 11a.m., and I felt like I had already taken on an entire day. My steps felt heavy against the sidewalk as I watched the people pass me by, tending to their usual business. For the first time, I looked at Val's storefront billboard without cringing at the thought of running into her for once. Instead, I couldn't help but smile, feeling at peace somewhat having her back in my life.

As I approached a homeless man, I checked my pockets for some cash but realized I left my wallet back at the apartment. He smiled while petting his dog, who was obediently looking across the street.

"May God bless ya," the man said softly while looking up at the building over my shoulder.

I smiled back. "You too."

He wasn't wearing any shoes, and his dog's bowl was nearly empty. I felt bad for the two, but there was nothing I could do, having left the apartment empty-handed.

Suddenly, the sound of a roaring muffler filled the street behind me. I don't know cars at all, but this sound in specific was a sound that was all too familiar. The sound of the car was chilling--an intimidating growl.

The hairs on the back of my neck stood. I watched the car pass in the reflection of the window the homeless man sat under. It was a black, two-door '67 Mustang. The rims glistened off the reflection of the store window. I turned slowly to face the beautiful car as I reached peak nostalgia.

It's Dad's, I thought. *It has to be*.

I began walking alongside the street, attempting to see the driver of the car. The Mustang slowly started up again as the light turned green, and I picked up my pace to a fast walk... Then a jog. The Mustang's exhaust roared over my shouting for the driver to stop. I was now running alongside the moving traffic, the sound of my slippers slapping against the pavement. I reached full speed.

"Wait!" I shouted, running with a hand raised.

Tripping over one of my slippers, I left it behind as I hit a dead sprint on the sidewalk. Within about five steps, the second slipper was gone. I reached full stride with everything I had in me. I was now running *faster* than I ever thought I could.

"Stop!!" I yelled again as my hat was next to fall off.

The Mustang hooked an abrupt right turn, then zoomed down an empty side street. Within seconds, I could no longer see it. I threw my hands back over my head, struggling to catch my breath.

"Damnit."

Maybe it was absurd for me to think that it was actually my dad's car or that he'd be the one driving it. There must've been hundreds of them in Southern California, alone. Regardless, I considered it a sign--a sign that it was time for me to find out what's *actually* left of my family. It was time to talk to Braden... *Now*.

As I collected everything I dropped, I stopped by the homeless man again on the way back to the apartment.

"May God bless ya," the man said the same exact way he did before.

He was staring past me, over my left shoulder.

"What size shoe are you?" I asked him.

I looked down at his filthy and bruised feet. It was obvious he had gone days, if not months, without shoes. He simply shrugged.

"I-uh… I'm not sure… I can't see my feet."

I kicked off my slippers, taking a knee in front of him. As I picked up the slippers, I looked up, and to my surprise, a tear trickled down his left cheek. His messy hair took away from his glossy bright blue eyes, and it suddenly dawned on me that he was blind.

"Try these on," I said as I gently slid the slippers onto his feet--a perfect fit.

"You're an angel, aren't you?" his voice cracked as another tear fell below his smile. "I prayed God send an angel to gimme shoes… I can't walk on my bare feet no more."

My heart dropped into my stomach as I realized how grateful he was for some slippers I rarely ever wore in the first place. While still on a knee, I took off my hat and put it on his head. He didn't flinch. He just... *Smiled*.

"I don't have any cash on me, but take my hat too," I said as I stood, running my hands back through my hair.

"God bless you, sir," the man said, holding out his hand.

I held it without hesitation.

"You too," I replied, fighting back tears of my own.

I made my way back to the apartment, my bare feet pressed against the cold concrete sidewalk. People I passed looked down at my feet and then back up at me, whispering to one another their thoughts and opinions as if I couldn't hear.

I smiled as the sun peeked over the high-rises above me. I felt lighter than ever before… Mentally, spiritually, and at this point, I guess you could say physically, too. I let out a long exhale, preparing myself to confront the demons I've let dwell within for so long.

THE WILLOW
NORTH HOLLYWOOD, CALIFORNIA
MONDAY, 12:04P.M. - JULY 15TH, 2019

BEEP! BEEP!

The Willow entrance doors unlocked as I scanned my key card. I walked up the narrow hallway, hearing the sound of my footsteps echo within the silent venue. The lights were on, exposing drink stains and other visual imperfections I noticed as I turned into the main room.

Fluorescent lighting filled the entire venue, and it reminded me of our garage back in Torrance. Braden was tucked in the corner of the V.I.P. section, taking notes as a girl rambled on about her successful career as an exotic dancer and bottle girl. Her valley girl accent echoed throughout the room as she flexed how far her fake tits got her here in L.A.

I sat down at the bar in the back of the venue and scanned the main room, realizing this was the emptiest I had ever seen The Willow. No bustling cleaning staff. No blasting music. No flashing lights. No half-naked Instagram models. Not even the guys were anywhere to be found.

I leaned back against the bar top. I remembered that Santi had flown up to New York straight from Miami, where he was opening up a new venue. So, I made myself comfortable without worrying about him coming in to lecture or threaten me.

Under the fluorescent lighting, even the willow leaves that hung from the ceiling looked fake and cheap. I noticed stains on the wood floor and leather booths. I wondered what Santi would think if he saw one of his venues looking this way--if he ever worried about the wrong person coming in and seeing it like this. Did it even matter what it looked like when it wasn't being used?

Braden walked the girl out toward the entrance, and the second she left, he tossed his clipboard on a booth and stretched out his arms.

"I'm DONE!" he shouted. "Who would've thought interviewing hot girls could be this exhausting??"

He poured himself a drink and leaned back against the bar top next to me.

"No lunch?" he asked with a genuine look of disappointment.

"Sorry, I just wanted to get here the soonest I could."

"All good, we can go after we talk about whatever it is you wanted to talk about," Braden said while making himself comfortable in the seat next to me. "What's on your mind, mang?"

I took a deep breath and twiddled my fingers like a kid sitting outside of the principal's office. I didn't know where to start, and I had absolutely no idea how Braden would respond to any of it. I could see him studying me in my peripherals. He tilted his head, most likely realizing what I was about to say had truly been weighing on me. I took a deep breath.

"When I came here, it wasn't just to pursue the whole nightclub dream we shared when we were kids," my voice trembled slightly, but the more I spoke, the easier it got. "I came here because I thought you were the only family I had left… I was worried about you and thought that being a part of this would be good for the two of us… But to be honest, I don't think it's good for *either* of us."

Braden silently listened as I continued.

"When Josh died, I was so quick to start a new life in New York. I wanted to leave everyone and everything behind, thinking it was best for me but also thinking I had no choice... Because, I took full responsibility for ruining our family. I still do today."

"Don't, Jay..." Braden intervened as he looked down. "You

shouldn't."

I could feel myself holding back tears and I had no intent on letting them fall in front of Braden.

"But I do," I continued, nodding my head while fixated on the front of the club. "I *do* take the blame. I took the revolver out that night and left it in the garage. Josh would still be alive if he didn't find it the night of the party… Then, I thought I could redeem myself by coming to L.A. to help keep you out of trouble. But this place is *fucked*, Braden. Santi isn't the father figure or mentor you think he is…."

Braden pulled out his pack of cigarettes, hands shaking as he struggled to light one. A tear fell on the pack just before he set it on the bar top. I watched and now listened.

"I fucked up, Jay," Braden sighed before taking a calming drag of his cig. "You didn't do anything. I have and *always will* take the full blame for what happened to Josh. I relive what happened, night after night. Not so much *that* night, but what led to it. It was the last deal I was gonna sling, Jay… I really *was* done dealing, and I swear I was doing it for the right reasons. I forgot to take the gun out from behind the amplifier, and it was the coke I hid back there that led to Josh pulling the trigger while not in his right mind…."

My eyes were fixated on Braden's quivering hands, one wiping his tears while the other lifted the cigarette back up to his mouth. This was truly the most vulnerable I had ever felt. It was also the most vulnerable I had ever seen Braden. I watched as the darkness rose while the tears fell--tainting his designer shirt.

"I met Santi once I finished doing time, and he saw the good in me--Dad *never* did. After a few years, I found out where you were at in New York and staged running into you. Then we talked about Mom and Dad. I didn't wanna lie, Jay… I didn't wanna-...."

It was evident that Braden was so repulsed by his own actions, having lied to me about our mother being dead… He couldn't even get himself to say it out loud.

"I know she's alive," I said softly, avoiding eye contact.

He sat straight up in his seat, took a drag, and let out a long exhale.

"Jay, they blamed me for *everything*, rightfully so. I tried seeing Dad, but he refused to see me before he had the heart attack… And Mom isn't even Mom anymore… Jay, I didn't think you would've come out here if you knew she was alive, let alone want to even see *me*. I wanted my only brother back, and if that meant having to lie to convince you that I was the only family you had left--that I needed you to look after me… I'd do it again and again… Because I wasn't gonna live another day without my brother. I can't go on alone much longer, man… I'm on the edge."

At this point, Braden and I were both crying but still avoiding eye contact. Having been raised in a house with two brothers and a tough father, tears were a sign of weakness… But it felt good to finally let it all out.

It finally, truly felt okay to not be okay.

I slowly stood up, standing over Braden's lowered head and slumped shoulders. I patted his back, and for the first time since we were kids, I hugged him. Tears continued to fall, and I could feel our demons and the darkness--all the doubt, all the blame, all the insecurities--being let go of once and for all as we wept under the willow leaves.

"I *know* this isn't a good place, Jay," Braden confessed. "You're right about Santi… And about the guys… And about everything."

He wiped his final tears and fixed his shirt before taking another drag of his cigarette.

"You told me to focus on the business side," I reminded him. "What's going on in the back end of everything?"

With the cigarette in his mouth, Braden scanned the venue for any potential ears or cameras, then leaned toward me while keeping his voice low.

"It's all a front," he whispered. "He's got it set up where the promoters and the bartenders work together to drug these girls so the V.I.P.'s can take 'em home and take advantage. They pay him big money to coordinate all that kinda shit, but there's more…."

He ashed his cigarette and scanned the room again before continuing.

"These rich guys and celebrities end up taking these girls back to Santi's guest house. Then Santi ends up fucking these dudes over by recording them and using the clips to blackmail them into doing favors for him--investing in his real estate deals and funding his endeavors--even blackmailing them into taking advantage of *more* girls. Back in Miami, when you asked about the whole *dealing* situation… It's because the clubs, bars, and restaurants are also distribution channels for some of the biggest names in narcotics and other fucked up things he's pushing…."

I attentively listened to Braden's words, struggling to comprehend everything but not finding it all that difficult to believe. Santi is manipulative, smart, and business-savvy... Utilizing his charisma and charming personality. He was a people person who sought out the destruction of the people he surrounded himself with. I felt sick to my stomach, having not seen this coming--having not been able to read Santi accurately enough.

He earned the trust of important people and then used their mishaps, lust, and greed against them… But he justified it so well with this talk of him teaching lessons for *good*--quoting scripture and philosophy only to warp the false narrative he lived himself.

"We can quit," I whispered. "We've learned enough to start our own deal. We can go somewhere else and open up our own club now... Making sure none of this shit happens... Under *our* control."

"I can't quit, Jay," Braden sighed. "He's got me pinned."

"What do you mean??"

"A couple years back, we went out as a group... Santi, the guys, and me. We were at some club downtown, and I blacked out after having a drink with him."

Braden clenched his teeth shut and leaned back against the bar top, looking up at the ceiling. He was frustrated.

"What happened??" I asked.

"I woke up in Santi's guest house...."

I leaned forward, waiting for him to continue, but he didn't.

"And...?" I urged.

"He showed me the video," Braden continued while staring at the ceiling. "I don't remember *any* of it... But it's all on video... And he's holding it against me... Like the *rest* of the sick fucks he scams. I'm just like them."

He reached for another cigarette and refilled his drink. It started to frustrate me, seeing him refill glass after glass without realizing he was even doing it. It had become part of his nature.

"That's why you stuck around," I whispered.

"He claimed that it was for my own good," Braden leaned forward and grabbed my arm, raising his voice. "I didn't mean to, Jay... I didn't mean to take advantage of her! You know I'd never do something like that. I wasn't in my right mind... I've done my time, and I can't go back."

I nodded, processing everything he was saying.

"Does he have anything on any of the other guys?" I asked.

"Yeah," he snapped back with a subtle laugh. "I'm pretty sure that's how he keeps us stuck in. That's why we're stuck here... If we threaten to leave, he'll ruin us."

I immediately thought about the last time I saw Santi, smoking a cigar on his rooftop deck back in Miami. My mind ran through all of the worst-case scenarios that could've happened.

Did Santi know I was out spending time with Val that night in Miami?

Did Skylar tell him I talked to her all day at the beach?

How loyal are the guys to Santi?

Would they turn on each other to keep Santi happy?

Would they turn on me?

I'm the newest. It only made sense for me to be considered the weakest link.

I instantly pulled out my phone and texted Val, asking what she was doing. I wanted a response... *Any* response--anything to know that she's okay and that Santi wasn't doing anything to jeopardize her or her career. This is one of those moments where I truly didn't care that I overthought... I just wanted to know that she was okay, and I can address my thought process later. She responded.

VAL: just eating .. What about you Jay Love ?

I took a deep breath and exhaled. Braden looked at me, confused.

"What are you doing?" he asked before sipping his drink.

"Nothing," I replied, setting my phone facedown. "What're we gonna do?"

"We kill him..." Braden whispered just loud enough for me to understand what he said but not take him seriously.

I laughed under my breath, then turned to see Braden's head tilted toward the floor as he glanced around the room. I waited for him to continue. He didn't.

"Are you serious??" I uttered, genuinely confused. "This isn't a fucking mafia movie, Braden. We can't *kill* him...."

He stood from his seat and paced from side to side, itching the top of his head, thinking.

"We've gotta keep doing what we're doing," I said sternly. "Otherwise, Santi is gonna think we're planning an out."

Braden downed what was left of his drink and reached for the bottle behind the bar. I stood to my feet and shoved his arm away from the bottle, *instantly* triggered by his attempt to drink more as if it were a solution to our problems.

"STOP DRINKING!" I shouted, shoving him back away from the bar. He tripped over himself and fell to the floor. "STOP DRINKING... STOP SMOKING... STOP BEING-... JUST STOP...!"

He looked up at me from the ground in utter dismay. His jaw dropped as I continued with my rant.

"YOU chose to come work for Santi... YOU got yourself stuck in this mess... YOU then dragged *me* into *your* mess... You told me Mom was DEAD... I-... You-... How could you...??"

I was standing over a vulnerable and defenseless Braden, but this wasn't the new adult version of Braden I stood over. I saw the skinny, tatted, long-haired troublemaker I spent my entire childhood looking after. The kid who took years off of our mother's life with all the trouble he got into. The kid who worked as a promoter at the only nightclub in our hometown. The kid whose recklessness and irresponsible nature led to me being exactly the way I am today. The Braden I stood over was now a bit more clean-cut with a deeper voice and broader shoulders, but on the inside, he's still my liability of a brother, and I could currently see it in his petrified eyes--in a way, he looked like Josh.

I slowly dropped down to a knee, then the other, letting out a heavy exhale as I sprawled myself face-up on the floor next to him. We were both facing the ceiling, completely silent. I had just gone off on him like never before, and I had no idea how to follow-up.

"That was buried pretty deep, huh?" Braden asked without moving a muscle.

"I'm sorry," I sighed, fixated on the willow leaves hanging from above.

I let out a deep breath. I felt like shit, and the silence really didn't help.

"I saw Dad's Mustang… Outside of your apartment…" I said in hopes of changing the subject.

Braden didn't respond as we continued staring at the ceiling.

"You wanna see her?" he asked, breaking the silence.

"See who?"

"Mom."

I paused, suddenly realizing this was possible.

"Yeah," I replied. "I do."

Braden turned away and stood to his feet, fixing his shirt and chains as he stood over me. I waited for him to snap at me or kick me--something to get even for my having shoved him to the ground and basically calling him a screw-up. Instead, he held out his hand to help me up. I accepted his offer, and he pulled me up to my feet.

"You drive," he insisted. "Because supposedly I have a *drinking* problem."

He couldn't help but smirk, knowing it was true, and I could tell he was messing with me as he playfully tossed me his wallet with the key in it.

"Bro… You put alcohol in your *orange juice*!" I shouted, holding back a laugh as we walked toward the entrance. "I mean, you can drink all you want, but at least *try* to do it in moderation."

"I'll cut back on the drinking when you admit you're in love with Val," he teased as he playfully shoved my shoulder.

"Then keep *drinking*," I blushed as we pushed through the front door together.

We zipped through the usual L.A. traffic, making our way down to Torrance. Heading back to our old neighborhood was a bittersweet feeling, and I couldn't help but mentally run through our hometown restaurants and faces of friends I hadn't seen in so long. I wondered who still lived in Torrance, what restaurants were still in business, and whether the neighborhood was cleaner or dirtier than it was seven years ago.

I pictured my mom seeing me for the first time after all these years--how quick she'd jump to her feet to wrap her arms around me. I pictured her crying tears of joy, rambling on in both Spanish and English about how her sons were back in her life. I could smell her scent--the perfume she wore, giving her a distinct aroma that I had been familiar with since I was a baby. I looked to my right to see that Braden was quietly looking out the window.

"Why are you so quiet?" I asked, breaking the silence. "You can play music if you want."

He remained silent. Before I could ask my question again, he crossed his arms and cleared his throat.

"You deserve to know… Mom is different now…."

"What do you mean?" I asked.

"Seven years on heavy meds can take a toll on you," he sighed. "She's like… A robot…."

Braden's voice was shaky, and I could tell he was holding back tears again, so I refrained from responding to give him a chance to push his emotions back down. When I first found out that Braden lied about our mom being dead, I was infuriated, but now I got the feeling that he was subconsciously trying to protect me from seeing something I might not want to see.

It was a weird time… After Josh's passing and before I left for New York. I was living life on cruise control, which included numbing myself to my own mother trying to numb *herself*… Just in a different way. Running away from my problems to cope was no better or worse than her relying on medication and constantly being sedated--they were just… *Different* ways of coping.

The traffic began to loosen up, and we picked up speed as I watched downtown fade in the rearview mirror. Regardless of the way it is on the inside, Los Angeles was beautiful from the outside--from a distance.

The 35-minute drive wasn't too bad when there was little traffic on the 110-Freeway. The drive was a straight shot down the highway, and before we knew it, we were passing our old high school.

I smiled like a fool as I slowed down to get a good look from the front entrance. The grass was in terrible condition, but come to think of it… I don't think it was ever in *good* condition to begin with. It was early afternoon, and teenagers were tending to their summer sports, playing and talking about whatever was taking up these kids' minds nowadays.

"They look… Tiny," Braden uttered.

"Were we really *that* small?" I asked.

"Nah… Kids are smaller now compared to back when we were kids."

"You're probably not wrong…."

It's crazy to think that these kids are in high school now… Most of them without a care in the world other than what other kids thought of them. Here we are, two guys in their mid-twenties, reminiscing on the good ol' days in front of kids who were currently living in the good ol' days.

"Do you wanna see the old house before we see Mom?" Braden asked.

"Let's do it…" I replied hesitantly, not knowing if I was truly ready.

Given the conversation Braden and I had a few hours ago, driving through our hometown, and coming to peace with everything I pushed away for so long… I thought I might as well face it all.

I instinctively took the same route I'd take coming home from school every day with Val and Josh. My hands were shaking as vivid memories slipped to the forefront of my mind.

I saw Val next to me, laughing about some stupid picture she found on her phone.

I heard Josh from the back seat, begging for me to play a song he knew the words to.

I felt my arms making the proper turns purely out of sheer muscle memory, until we reached our old street. The car was silent, moving smoothly over the rugged asphalt. One small house passed after another. I could see ours approaching, closer and closer, until we were directly in front of it.

I heard Braden adjust his posture to look through my window at the house. The yard looked as if it wasn't trimmed in weeks, if not months. The shutters were closed and the driveway was empty, giving our once lively home a chilling and abandoned feel.

"Does anyone live here?" I asked.

"Doesn't look like it…" Braden replied. "It's kinda eerie, huh?"

"Yeah…."

While I feared seeing the house would trigger some form of crippling anxiety or make me feel sick to my stomach, it was almost as if it wasn't the same house we grew up in at all. I felt… Nothing. Braden and I sat silently, staring at what looked like an empty house rather than the childhood home we shared countless memories in.

While I felt as though visiting our old neighborhood would give me some type of closure, I began to think my closure wasn't in something tangible at all, but rather in a person or moment.

I took a deep breath.

"Let's see her," I said softly, staring directly ahead with both hands on the wheel.

"Make a left at the second stop sign," Braden directed while nervously itching the scruff on his face.

We continued our drive outside of our neighborhood toward a part of Torrance I wasn't familiar with at all. The two of us were quiet as I ran through scenarios where I knocked on the door, and she opened it.

In one scenario, she's ecstatic.

In another scenario, she hugs me so tight I can barely breathe.

In another, she's upset with me for never calling or making an effort to connect.

She's angry, she's confused, she cries, she screams of joy...

I had run through every scenario imaginable, then I heard Braden.

"Pull in here," he pointed toward a half-empty parking lot.

At the end of the parking lot, there was a large one-story building that struck me as one of those buildings you drive by but never *actually* expect to go inside of. As we parked, Braden pulled out a cigarette and reached for his lighter.

"Are you not coming in?" I asked.

"You should go in without me," he insisted before putting the cig in his mouth. "She doesn't wanna see me...."

He flinched as I snatched the cigarette from his mouth before he could light it.

"We're seeing Mom, together," I demanded.

I stepped out of the car and flicked the cigarette onto the floor in front of Braden. He reluctantly stepped out of the car behind me.

"What is this place?" I asked, scanning the building for a sign. "Mom lives here??"

"It's a rehab clinic. She's been in and out of it over the years."

Without answering, I made my way toward the large sliding glass doors. As the doors slid open, I read a statement engraved into the concrete that read...

"*EXPECT A MIRACLE.*"

The concrete turned to a glossy beige tile as we stepped into the cold and quiet lobby of the rehab center. Natural lighting filled the room through the large glass windows behind us, and it smelled like some sort of luxurious doctor's office.

"This place is nice," I whispered to Braden, who was a few

steps behind me.

"Nicest I could find," he whispered back. "I'm paying for it, so it better be nice."

Braden's statement hit me like a truck. My own mother, living in a facility and not a home--living without her husband and her sons, being visited by friends if even *that*. I began to feel sick, thinking about what I could have done to help her--to at least keep her sane. Her late-night panic attacks and episodes were a cry for help, and I chose to run--to bury it all and act like none of this existed or ever happened. Even though she and our father wanted nothing to do with Braden after Josh died, he *still* paid for her to be here... He *still* decided to help while I *ran*.

"Good afternoon!" an older lady calmly greeted us from behind the front desk.

She stood beside another lady who had an equally calming presence. Braden stayed a step behind me as I nervously tapped the edge of the desk before clearing my throat to speak.

"H-hi... I'm... Jay...."

My fingers continued tapping the desk as I fought to get the words out.

I shouldn't be here, I thought. *Mom doesn't want to see us*.

"I'm... We're..." I struggled some more.

The ladies smiled, patiently waiting for me to speak like a normal human being. It suddenly dawned on me that working in a place like this, they *must* be used to witnessing someone process their emotional trauma in front of them. Before I could get the words out, I felt a warm and gentle hand on my shoulder.

"We're here to see Carmen Amor," Braden said from behind me.

I lowered my head and let out a sigh, accepting defeat.

"You got it," one of the ladies replied as she typed away on her keyboard. "May I ask for your names? So we can get you some guest passes."

"Braden and Jay Amor," Braden said. "We're Carmen's sons."

"Oh," she sighed as she suddenly stopped typing. "You're back."

"This time is different..." Braden responded while he lightly squeezed my shoulder.

"I understand, Mr. Amor, but you see, your mother doesn't r-...."

"He's paying for her to be here, and we need to see our mother *together*," I sternly interjected. "This time is different...."

"I see..." the lady whispered, staring at the computer screen.

In my peripherals, I noticed the second lady standing beside her, setting down the paperwork she was filing.

"Right this way," the second lady smiled as she stepped around the front desk and waved for us to follow her.

Without hesitating, we followed her down a hall that seemed to stretch on forever. Ambient music played through speakers built into the ceiling, as we silently walked behind the woman.

"Can't guarantee she's gonna want to see you," the lady said without turning back to face us. "But from time to time, she mentions your brother, Jay, so maybe you're right about this time being different."

Braden didn't really react to the statement. The lady came to a stop and knocked on the door before scanning her key to unlock it.

"Ms. Amor? You have some visitors," the lady said in an uppity tone.

There was no response, but the lady held the door open, gesturing for us to enter the room anyway. I entered first, with Braden a few steps behind. The door shut softly behind us, leaving us with nowhere to go but deeper into the room.

I was instantly brought back to our home in Torrance, as the room's aroma was nothing but that of my mom's perfume. While the room itself looked like a spacious and pretty luxurious hotel room, it was… Bland. The only photos hanging on the walls were of the ocean or mountaintops. Only a few pieces of jewelry and perfume were neatly displayed on the dresser like Mom used to lay them out back when we were kids.

The back wall of the room was made up of a large window with white curtains hanging from each side. Sitting just a few feet from the window in a plush chair, staring peacefully out into the courtyard, was the silhouette of our mother--skinnier than ever before… Sitting motionless.

Braden quietly tapped my shoulder and pointed at a photo that sat on the nightstand by her bed. The photo was of Josh and *only* Josh. I turned back toward Mom, who hadn't moved a muscle.

"Mom?"

There was brief silence, then she let out a sniffle, and her head turned slightly toward us and then back toward the window.

"Mom…" I said once more, getting closer. "It's Jay... And Braden…."

I placed my hand on her shoulder as she sniffled again. Her shoulder was skin and bone, and she felt frail. Seven years had stripped my mother of her warmth and left her with this cold vessel of a corpse I could hardly recognize.

Her sniffles continued, and as I stood over her shoulder, I could see tears falling down the side of her face, dropping onto her floral blouse. Her earrings sparkled, and her makeup was done as if she lived her life as she normally would, but she couldn't cover the pain and betrayal endured from both her past *and* her sons.

As I made my way around the chair to look her in the eyes, she suddenly turned away. I instantly felt *gutted*--like every ounce of my being was dumped onto the floor, and there was nothing left of me but a body. My own mother--the one who brought me into this world... Removed me from her *own* world. I stepped back toward the bed in shock.

My lip quivered, and my vision slipped behind tears that fell onto the chair she sat on. I silently sat on the edge of the bed a few feet behind her, trying to come up with something to say. Never in my entire life would I have expected my own mother to refrain from embracing me.

She was the mother who loved her family before herself.

The mother who woke up early to make sure we were ready for the day.

The mother who stayed up late at night until she knew we were sound asleep.

The mother who cried when we cried.

The mother who found the good, even in the bad.

The mother who loved, unconditionally.

She was my mother, but like the house that was once our home, I didn't recognize this woman sitting with her back to us.

"Say something, Ma," my voice cracked as another tear fell. "We're your sons."

Braden stood behind me with his back against the wall and his arms crossed. His face held no emotion. He had no tears left to cry--not *here*, anyway… And I now understood why.

"Sons?" she finally answered without moving. "I have no sons…."

The statement sent chills down my spine.

"I lost my three sons after that night, seven years ago…" she continued. "One will *never* come back, one decided to *leave*, and one *destroyed* our family with the life he chose to live."

I clenched my jaw tight, refusing to let it drop after hearing the words leave my mother's mouth. I recognized her voice, but not what she said. I could never fathom my mother refusing to accept her own children… At least, not until now.

With over a million combinations of words in the English language that I could put together right now to salvage whatever relationship we had left, I chose the only combination I felt with every ounce of my being--a simple combination of words that could mean both so much and so little… So many words to choose from, and I settled for the two I chose to speak aloud.

"I'm sorry."

I watched my mother's head lower as she rocked back-and-forth in her chair. She shook her head as tears fell, and she began to pray under her breath. She swayed, and my heart dropped as I suddenly saw her as the same lady sitting in the hallway of the police station after the night of Josh's death.

I leaned forward and placed my hand gently on her knee, and she just continued praying... As if I wasn't even there. It was like I was the one who was dead, and she couldn't hear, see, or feel me. She began to pray louder.

Braden had mentioned that she was in and out of this facility for years, and now I understood why. There were times where I replayed my returning moment in my head. I saw her embracing me and telling me everything was okay, when in reality, she needed to hear that everything was okay more than I did. But, not even *that* was enough anymore. There was nothing in the world I could do to save my own mother, and it killed me inside to come to that realization.

To her, *I am dead*.

Her prayer got louder and louder as she began to repeat words and sway in her chair more aggressively. My hand was still placed on her knee as I turned to Braden for help. He shook his head and gestured for us to leave. Braden knew this would happen, and I had no doubt that it shattered him before the same way it shattered me now. I now knew he was trying to protect me by telling me she was dead. He didn't want me to see her like this. I let go of her knee and stood up, looking down at the back of her head as my tears trickled down the sides of my face.

"Love you more," I said softly.

It was the phrase we never left the room without saying to one another. For once in my life, I knew that this one time I said it, it was true. I *do* love her more than she loves me, and now I need to let her go. Braden quietly opened the door for the two of us, and I heard our mom's prayer get quieter and quieter until the door shut behind us both.

"Was it any different this time?" a voice asked.

The lady who escorted us was still standing in front of the room. Braden shook his head as the two of us began walking down the hall toward the exit, emotionless.

I couldn't tell whether I was better off before or after seeing our mom. A part of me was glad I at least *tried* to reconnect with her, but another part of me wishes I never saw her like this--so fragile and distraught.

Josh's death took an overwhelming toll on our entire family, and it pained me to see that I wasn't the only one who suffered. I chose to bury that night and everything that had to do with it deep within the confines of my mind and heart, while my mother never escaped it. She prayed the same prayer the same way she did that morning at the police station.

While I feel as though visiting our old house and our mother didn't have the emotional impact I thought it would, it made me realize that Braden was right when he basically told me that he's the only family I have left. I now know I need to make things right once and for all.

"So, *now* do you understand why I do the things I do?" Braden asked as he picked up and lit the cigarette I flicked in front of the car earlier.

"I do," I replied, wiping my remaining tears. "You still got your flask?"

The two of us leaned back against the car, sipping and passing the flask to each other.

"What do we do now?" he asked between puffs.

I stared up into the afternoon sky, taking in the past week and struggling to come up with a logical answer--the *right* answer. *Is* there a right answer to his question?

What do we do now?

Here we are… The Amor brothers… Seeking some kind of redemption for killing their brother and destroying their family, leading them to chase a hollow and superficial dream, only to find themselves at the mercy of a deranged and evil nightclub owner.

What do we do now? I thought, still staring into the sky.

I shoved my hands into my pockets and suddenly felt a rectangular card I didn't remember feeling before. I slowly pulled it out and flipped it to see one word printed in gold letters, with a phone number written out under it. The word read…

"*RAMOS*."

I was immediately brought back to the night of the dinner with the Ramos brothers. I remembered one of the brothers sitting closest to me had slipped me the card before inviting me onto the yacht the next day. Mateo… I think that was his name.

Santi was in rare form that night which led me to believe that these men were not only influential but could potentially even be a threat to the hospitality empire that Santi has built. With Braden stuck in the grasp of Santi and on the cusp of finding himself back in prison, maybe this is the out we need. Maybe *they* are the out we need. I turned to face Braden, who was watching me study the business card.

"I think I know what we need to do…."

FOURTEEN | FAMILY TIES

OMNI CAFE
WEST HOLLYWOOD, CALIFORNIA
MONDAY, 4:42P.M. - JULY 15TH, 2019

"She should be here soon," I said between sips of my cocktail.

I didn't think we'd be drinking right now, but Braden and I had no choice after the heavy emotional toll we took on earlier today. I felt like somebody just cut me open, removed all the toxins from my body, and then sewed me up again, but not properly.

I was so used to burying conflict under bad habits that felt good, and it felt bizarre to have shared that with the person sitting directly across from me. I watched Braden take a large sip of his third cocktail.

"You think she'll be on board with everything we talked about?" he asked as his eyes trailed a tall brunette walking past our table.

"Yeah," I confidently replied. "If there's anybody we can trust around here, it's Val."

We sat in the courtyard of a small cafe tucked between two large buildings. Being one of the higher-end cafes in West Hollywood, we recognized random celebrities who recognized *us* from The Willow. The courtyard had plant decor hanging at different elevations and in all directions, which might've appeared messy to the untrained eye, but I found it pretty aesthetically pleasing. The setting was nothing short of peaceful.

I took another sip of my cocktail that actually had some plants in it for some reason, but I didn't question it. Some things you just don't question when they're trendy... Because they're just... Trendy, I guess.

"Hello there, Amor brothers," greeted a familiar voice.

I looked over my shoulder to see Val approaching the table. She wore a black long-sleeve that hugged her body frame, while her baggy black pants drooped down over her black shoes. Her platinum hair was slicked and tied up into a top bun that made her facial features pop. She wasn't wearing any makeup, and still, she was the most beautiful girl in the vicinity.

"Hey," I replied as I stood up for a hug.

I didn't plan on giving her the hug... But the thought of what I was about to do had me acting on my best behavior. Braden stood to his feet and did the same, in a manner that was far less smooth, and she was instantly onto us.

"You both hugged me…" Val teased as she sat down with a cheeky grin. "You're up to something, aren't you?"

Braden looked at me for a response, and Val let out a laugh.

"Okay, before we get into it… I need a drink."

"Here, take mine."

I slid my drink in front of her. She shrugged and sipped.

"Mmmm, that's good!" Val studied the glass, then set it down. "You said it was urgent… What's on your mind, Jay Love?"

Val and Braden were both looking at me at this point, awaiting my response, which in reality was more of a pitch… So I cleared my throat.

"We need your help," I sighed. "You were right about Santi… You were right about *everything*."

I continued, and I watched her smile then bite her lip as she took in every word that followed.

I told her about Santi's business model.

I told her about the mind games played behind the way he designed his venues.

About the women being pawned off to wealthy men and celebrities in exchange for pay.

About Santi blackmailing the wealthy men and celebrities to get them to invest in him.

About the women drugged so Santi could have a hold on Braden and the guys.

About the physical abuse and manipulation behind his "family" talk.

About the pending Caribbean deal with the Ramos brothers.

With every point I made, her jaw dropped lower and her eyes opened wider. Braden remained silent, nodding his head in agreement with every word I said. When I finished speaking, she sat back and looked across the cafe, processing every word.

"Jay, I told you he wasn't a good guy," Val said. "I heard stories from girls I know, and the guys who know Santi well never really touched on anything involving him…."

She quickly turned to face Braden, causing him to flinch.

"Santi got *you*, too??"

"Shhhhh!" Braden and I shushed her.

"Sorry, sorry," she whispered before taking a deep breath.

"I mean… yeah," Braden said. "Santi showed me the video and I don't remember *any* of what I watched myself do to the girl. I didn't ask him any questions after he told me it was for my own good. I left it, and when I considered quitting at one point, he brought up that he has the video. He told me to never bring up quitting again if I knew what was good for me… Then he went on to tell me that working for him is what's good for me and it always will be."

Val had both elbows on the table and looked down while deep in thought. I knew she had no idea this conversation was going to be as deep as it is, but I had to let her in, and she was handling it well. I watched as she sat back in her chair and crossed her arms, looking in a different direction.

"So what are you guys gonna do about it?" she asked, making direct eye contact with me.

I quietly slid the business card Mateo Ramos gave me onto the table in front of Val. The sun glistened off the gold lettering that made up most of the card.

"We think Santi is gonna set them up next," I said quietly. "I'm gonna call them before he can do it and tip them off. Then, hopefully, they'll deal with him in some way that'll get us off the hook."

Val leaned forward and lightly slapped my knee under the table.

"And what if these Ramos guys expose you?? And Santi finds out you crossed him?" she asked.

"What *else* are we supposed to do??" I snapped. "If we turn him in to the police, they'll take us all with him. We're basically accomplices at this point. We also can't just quit. Who *knows* what Santi would do to us then…? Given who he knows and what he's got on Braden."

Val relaxed her shoulders and looked up at the sky for a response. I let out a sigh and leaned toward her.

"So what do you need me to do?" she asked, tilting her head and crossing her arms.

"You're the only girl we trust that doesn't know Santi directly. We might need someone like you to help us set him up."

"Call these Ramos guys…" she said. "Find out what you need and what's gonna happen, and then I'll help… But there *has* to be a plan."

"There *is* a plan," I assured her.

I felt a weight lifted off my shoulders. Val bit her lip once more and looked around the cafe, nervously tapping her foot against the tile floor. It was the same way she'd react to me asking for favors back in high school that could get her into trouble… Only this time, much more was at stake, and I could tell she was genuinely nervous. For seven years, I cut Val out of my life, and here I was, asking for her help. I felt bad, but another part of me felt… *Grateful*.

"Thank you," I said with a cheeky grin I knew would make her blush.

Braden's chair scraped against the floor as he stood up and gave Val a hug.

"Thank you, little sister!" he shouted.

"Anything for my Amor brothers," she rolled her eyes, then smiled.

After finishing our drinks and ordering a couple rounds of appetizers, the three of us headed back to the apartment, where we sat scattered around the living room. The sun had just set, and the room was dimly lit, creating a calming atmosphere for a tense conversation to be had over the phone.

I sat back on the couch, staring at the business card in my hands. I was running through every potential outcome in my head--every possibility--good and bad. My mind began to play tricks on me as I thought about the good that came from working for Santi.

The clubs, parties, jets, women, good pay… Life is *good*…

… Or is it?

I liked running the club and the social stature that came with it, don't get me wrong. I have my brother in my life once again, and it felt good knowing we were on the path of owning our own nightclub at some point in the future.

I took a deep breath, coming to the realization that I was holding the solution in my fingertips while trying to reconstruct the problem into something unproblematic at all. I never understood why it's so easy to only remember the *good* when it comes down to making a life-altering decision--to stay or to leave--to change.

"Are you gonna call?"

Braden's voice derailed my train of thought, suddenly bringing me back to the present moment.

I ran through the possible scenarios, again and again, knowing it really didn't do much for me. I don't know... Nine times out of ten, I overthink situations and outcomes that never actually happen… But I refuse to stop because the one time the outcome I overthink comes true, I'll be ready for it.

Best-case scenario, I call the Ramos brothers, tell them everything, they believe me, and they get Santi off our backs while also saving themselves from getting wrapped up in this shady business.

Worst-case scenario, I call the Ramos brothers, tell them everything, they *don't* believe me, and they tell Santi what we told them, leading Santi to deal with us however he'd plan to--not good.

In an alternate scenario, I *don't* call the Ramos brothers, they get wrapped up in Santi's business the same way we have, and life continues the way it's been… At the mercy of a manipulative and twisted individual who claims to be the opposite of what he is.

"Jay…."

Braden's voice derailed my second train of thought, and I turned my head to face him.

"Yeah?" I hollowly replied.

"Are you gonna call?" he asked again.

Val studied the two of us from the table across the living room--her eyes darting from me to Braden, then back to me. Without responding to him, I pulled out my phone and dialed the number written on the card.

I pressed the phone to my ear, waiting for any sound to break the consistency of the ringing. I ran my fingers through my hair, fighting off a cold sweat. Three rings passed, then four, then five… Then s-....

"Dalé," said a deep voice.

The voice was crystal clear and a bit hoarse--it was the intimidating voice of danger, and I immediately pictured the face behind it. I remember Mateo being engaged in our conversation, listening to every word I said that night at the dinner table in Miami. He was buzzed that night and most likely sober at the moment, which had me immediately thinking calling him may be a mistake.

"This is... Jay," I said nervously. "From Los Angeles… I-I… I was with Santi and the group when we got dinner the other night back in Miami…."

There was no response, just silence. Braden was leaning forward with a look of concern while Val was anxiously tapping her nails against the top of the table. Before I could say another word, the deep voice broke the silence.

"Amor! The eh-smart guy!!" Mateo shouted. "You partied too hard for us, Jay. We missed you on the yacht the next day!"

Braden's eyes widened, and he leaned over the coffee table to get a better listen. I couldn't help but smirk as I put the phone on speaker and set it between us.

"I almost thought you wouldn't remember!" I replied with a laugh. "I'm sorry I missed you guys. Sometimes I don't know my own limits."

"It's okay, mang. Don't worry about it! To what do I owe this pleasure? Speak your mind!"

I made eye contact with Braden and took a deep breath, preparing for what I was about to say… Allowing for any lingering thoughts to suddenly convince me not to say anything at all. I thought nothing, and instead… I spoke.

"It's actually pretty serious, Mateo. If you have some time to *really* talk...."

There was a ruffling sound, and I assumed he was moving. I heard what sounded like a sliding door close and then a loud thump. Then once again, silence.

"Vamo," he said sternly. "What's the matter?"

I took one more deep breath with my eyes closed, fingers laced over my knees as I leaned over the phone lying on the coffee table. Braden and Val both watched.

"Santi's hospitality group is a front," I sighed. "In more ways than you may already know. The distribution channels for what you want to sell are a part of it, but there's a whole 'nother side of things you may be getting tied into, without wanting to be...."

I waited for some sort of acknowledgment, but instead, I heard nothing, so I continued.

"The guys Santi partners with invest in his business because they don't have a choice. He uses his venues to get potential business partners to take advantage of women he invites to the clubs. The women don't know any better. They think they're getting some sort of V.I.P. treatment until they end up roofied and taken to his guest house... Along with you and any other person he wants something from. He'll then use the footage from the cameras in the guest house to blackmail you into investing in his venues and other deals. In this case, I think he wants your resort chain. He talks about wanting his company to run Caribbean hospitality... And he's gonna set you up when he hosts you at The Willow, whenever that is."

I braced myself for a response but heard nothing--silence. Braden's hands were laced behind his head as he nervously tapped his foot against the cement floor. Val's facial expression was vacant as she awaited Mateo's response.

"All of this..." Mateo said. "This is all true? You know this to be *true*?"

"I have no ulterior motive other than doing what's right," I uttered, fixing my posture. "In this case, it's to prevent your family from making a mistake."

"I see," he said before letting out a deep breath.

I ran my now sweaty hands through my hair, preparing for my overall *ask*.

"But Mateo, I have something to ask of you. My brother and I, having worked for Santi for some time, found ourselves wrapped up in a similar way to his partners. He has things on us as well, and we don't see a way for us to get out anytime soon. All I ask is that if you decide to confront Santi about what I tipped you off on, you do it in a way that will allow for my brother and me to get out of his business without making a mess. If you decide *not* to confront Santi, I ask that you please don't mention what I just told you, and I promise you will never hear from us again."

My shoulders relaxed and sank into the couch. I had delivered, and everything that was on my mind was officially out in the open, to be interpreted by Mateo however he decided. I didn't question the silence that followed my spiel, considering it was a lot to address and comprehend. I scanned the room for some sort of validation for what I said, but instead, Val and Braden simply stared at the phone.

"I'm listening to you, Jay… And I hear you," Mateo said. "I know it took a lot for you to turn your back on the ones you work for, and while I would *hate* to have somebody turn their back on me, you did it for family--for you and your brother--and I respect that. I respect you for choosing to do what's right. Santi plans on hosting us at The Willow and then at his home this coming Saturday. We were supposed to fly in Saturday morning to meet with Santi, but instead, why don't we come on Friday to talk more about this? We will arrange a stay for Friday night. Bring your brother Friday afternoon, and we will talk then about how we plan to deal with Santi."

Braden and I both leaned forward, trying to decipher whether Mateo's response was what we wanted to hear or not. There was no verbal agreement for them to help us, but there seemed to be another pending discussion, which meant Mateo wasn't necessarily saying "no."

"Y-yes, we'll be there," I said nervously.

"Jay…" Mateo continued. "Do not speak to Santi about us coming early, nor talking--at all. I will call when we land and tell you where to go then."

"Sounds good," I replied.

"Vamo. Ciao, Jay."

He hung up, and immediately the three of us let out a loud sigh followed by Braden's groan.

"Jesus," Braden blurted out. "That's good? Is that good?? What just happened?"

"I *think* that's good," I responded while staring at the blank T.V. screen across from me.

"That man sounds *terrifying*," Val whispered from behind us.

"What do we do now?" Braden asked.

"Nothing," I said, still staring straight ahead. "Nothing until Friday… Till then we do everything we've been doing the same, so Santi suspects nothing."

"So we go back to work?" Braden asked.

"Yep…" I answered. "We go back to work."

Judging from Mateo's tone over the call, I had a good feeling about what was to come. The past few days had me emotionally, mentally, and spiritually drained, but the call gave me the morale boost I didn't realize I *needed*. I felt my mind being cleared of everything weighing me down.

I felt… *Hopeful*.

For the first time in seven years, I felt like things were changing, but this time, for *the better*. This time I knew I wasn't buying into lies or looking for a temporary fix to keep me from drowning in the darkness I suppressed. This time, there was nothing I fought to bury. I let the darkness rise--no, I *invited* it to rise--I'm ready to make peace with it.

This time, I wasn't choosing what felt good... This time, I was choosing what felt *right*.

FIFTEEN | NO REMORSE

CASA RAMOS
HOLLYWOOD HILLS
FRIDAY, 3:10P.M. - JULY 19TH, 2019

Tropical plants of lush green reached over the Spanish tile flooring of the pathway leading up to Mateo's house. My shoes tapped against the driveway as I stepped out of Braden's car. It was supposed to be a 30-minute drive from Braden's apartment, but the L.A. traffic made it an hour.

Braden and Val closed their car doors and waited for me to lead the way. I faced the stone staircase leading up through the courtyard I assumed served as some sort of entrance. The Spanish-style house took on the shape of a compound or fortress... The way its massive ledges and balconies overlooked the driveway we stood on. This house seemed like it was straight out of a cartel movie.

It had been a couple hours since Mateo called me. He told me to come to the address he made me write down *twice* to make sure I had it right. I checked my phone. We were 20 minutes early with no idea what to expect.

"Ready?" Val asked as I stepped up beside them, looking up the intimidating staircase.

"I think so," I replied honestly.

Without saying another word, I made my way up the stairs. As we approached the top, the sound of a fountain carried through the courtyard, stretching from where we stood to the house entrance. We walked under an archway into the lush green courtyard, lit by the sunlight flooding in from above.

The fountain had a modern feel that contrasted with the traditional Spanish architecture. Water trickled down the sides, and I watched Val run her finger along it. Her posture mirrored confidence, but I could tell she was nervous from the lack of pep in her step. She was nervous--we all were--and I knew she was here for me, which made me appreciate her all the more.

The wall dividing the inside of the home from the courtyard was an accordion glass door spread wide open, and you could see all the way into the backyard from where we stood.

"How do we knock?" Braden asked, studying the inside of the

home we were practically inside of at this point.

"I'll try calling," I said, lifting my phone to my ear.

The call went to voicemail, asking for me to leave a name and number. I lowered the phone and felt a hand lightly urge me to move forward.

"Looks like we're goin' in," Val whispered.

The Spanish tile turned into a rich dark wood flooring as I stepped into the house. The ceilings were high, with exposed wood rafters that contrasted with the egg-shell colored ceiling and walls. Light funneled in through both the courtyard and the large windows that separated the inside of the house from the backyard.

To the left was a spacious kitchen with large bowls of exotic fruit--some I've never even seen before. To the right was a dining room with a luxurious-looking fireplace made of stone. As the sound of the trickling water from the fountain faded behind us with every step we took into the house, the sound of salsa music played in the distance.

"Is that coming from the backyard?" Braden asked, cautiously keeping two or three feet behind me.

"I think so," I replied quietly. I didn't know if we were technically trespassing at this point.

I made my way through the common area toward the window. My jaw dropped at the sight of the backyard that overlooked all of L.A. Most of the yard was made up of perfectly mowed grass, and stone steps led down to a lower level with a pool surrounded by hanging vines and fountains... Then below *that* was a vineyard that extended further than I was able to see.

A loud familiar laugh came from the corner of the top level of the backyard. Just to the right of the perfectly maintained grass was a gazebo providing shade for Mateo and one of his brothers. Cigar smoke trailed off into the afternoon sky as they cracked jokes--switching from Spanish to English, then back to Spanish.

"I found them," I blurted out with a laugh. "Over there, in the backyard."

Here were these two brothers, visiting L.A. without a worry in the world, blasting salsa music in the backyard of a house in Hollywood Hills while smoking cigars. A part of me was intimidated at the sight of them, but another part of me felt comfortable, hearing Mateo's animated voice tell a story I know nothing about.

I headed for the large glass door that was slid half-open and slipped through with a smile on my face. Braden and Val trailed behind me, once again keeping a respectful distance as I approached the gazebo Mateo and his brother sat under.

Mateo and his brother laughed and joked, puffing their cigars with their feet up as the salsa music brought life to the conversation.

Mateo's back was to me--his long hair falling past his shoulders. He leaned forward to ash his cigar on the marble ashtray between them. His brother caught sight of us and smiled with the cigar between his teeth.

His teeth shined brighter than the Patek Philippe watch on his wrist, and I noticed a diamond-studded tooth that seamlessly reflected the sun. I smiled back, respectfully raising a hand to acknowledge that we might've been interrupting. Mateo quickly shot a look at us over his right shoulder and flashed a smile equally as bright as his brother's.

"THE AMORS!" Mateo shouted as the two of them stood to greet us.

"Sorry for not knocking," I said while shaking his heavy hand. "We didn't really know *how* to knock in a place like this."

"Aye, Jay… No problemo! Mi casa es su casa! And you must be the brother! Que pasa?? How're you doing, mang?"

"Doin' good… I'm Braden," Braden replied as Mateo brought him in for an unanticipated hug.

"Mucho gusto, Braden! And who is this beautiful woman??!" Mateo shouted before taking a drag of his cigar. "A girlfriend to one of you? If you're lucky!"

Val stepped forward between Braden and me, extending her hand to shake Mateo's.

"I'm Val," she said with a genuine smile.

Mateo held her hand and lifted it lightly.

"A woman of class! Welcome, Val. Vamo... All of you sit down and let's talk. This is my brother, Rodrigo. You met in Miami."

Rodrigo leaned over the table to shake our hands, with a smile so contagious we couldn't help but return our own.

"Very nice to see you again," Rodrigo greeted warmly. "And a pleasure to meet you, Ms. Val."

We stepped around the white sofas surrounding the stone coffee table, filling in so that the group sat in a half-circle around the cigars and bottle of rum.

Mateo wore a white dress shirt with his sleeves casually rolled up. His shirt was tucked into fine black pants that were cropped above his bare feet. Rodrigo wore a similar fit--his navy blue silk shirt tucked into a slim-fit pair of black slacks. Both brothers were dressed to impress but effortlessly as if the elegant swagger came natural to them. Their jewelry consisted of gold and *only* gold, resembling that of the business card I had spent the past week nervously twiddling in my fingertips... Anxiously awaiting this exact moment.

"So, kids…" Mateo teased as he ashed his cigar. "You found yourselves caught up in our bad business or what?"

"Sort of," I sighed, awaiting some sort of response from Braden and Val, who said nothing.

"When we spoke on the phone… You said Santi plans to set us up… Why do you say this?"

Rodrigo passed a box of cigars toward the three of us, which Braden and I grabbed as Val politely declined.

"He's been doing it for years," Braden chimed in by surprise. "I work directly with him on the day-to-day. I'm in his house, his venues, his cars--almost everywhere he goes when he's in L.A. Santi uses his venues' reputation and stature to attract people from all over. He'll link with these guys and offer to hook them up with girls who come to the clubs… And these girls have no idea they're about to be drugged and pawned off to these sick fucks. Then these guys are blackmailed by Santi into keeping their mouths shut and investing in his endeavors."

"Blackmail, how?" Mateo asked without looking up from his cigar.

Rodrigo tilted his head... Almost as a way of communicating that he, too, wondered how Santi intended on blackmailing them. Mateo looked up from his cigar. The mood suddenly shifted like night and day as the looks on their faces became intimidatingly hostile.

"He talks about dealing social currency… And it makes sense," Braden continued, unphased by the mood shift. "These girls want a piece of the exclusivity he has to offer at his venues--being a V.I.P. and all that--so they never say no when he has us offer them tables and bottles being covered by the guys who take advantage of them later on."

"You didn't answer my question," Mateo said. "Blackmail, how? It sounds like the girls are the only ones being put in a situation here, which doesn't sound like a problem that affects *us*."

Val and I looked at Braden for the answer, which he delivered immediately.

"The girls aren't the only ones being put in these situations," Braden explained. "You're gonna be put in one too if you get involved in this deal you're making with him."

Braden puffed his cigar, well-knowing he had just dropped a bomb on the Ramos brothers. Rodrigo and Mateo waited for him to continue.

"I guess, yeah… Santi *could* stop at that… Taking the money these guys give him to sleep with these girls. But, he doesn't," Braden continued. "He's got a guest house he has these guys use when it goes down. It's wired and got cameras and all that. He'll save the footage of the men taking advantage of the girls and hold it against them… Then they're basically his puppets."

Suddenly, Mateo raised his hand for Braden to stop and turned to Rodrigo, saying something in Spanish. Rodrigo nodded, set his cigar on the ashtray, and clenched one of his hands into a fist as he briefly wiped his mouth with the other.

"The fucking *nerve*. The fucking... *balls*--... This man has..." Rodrigo blurted aloud as he clenched his fist tighter, exposing the veins on his forearm.

I could feel Val's posture nervously shifting at the sight of their frustration until Mateo whispered something in Spanish to Rodrigo. It calmed him down a bit. Mateo turned back to the three of us.

"This is some shit, mang," Mateo said before taking a deep breath. "So what you're saying is he plans to do the same to us... Tomorrow?"

"We think so," Braden said. "It's lined up like this multiple times before. Some of the guys he partners with come back to the venues to do it again and again, and others we never really see again. But I mean... Either way, I've seen the balance sheets, and he's come up on the better end of the deals, and it's *not* from negotiating. These deals are almost entirely one-sided, always in favor of Santi."

Rodrigo spoke to Mateo in Spanish, and I couldn't help but want to understand what they were saying. Mateo nodded his head in agreement with what Rodrigo said, then leaned forward, resting his elbows against the top of his knees.

"I don't imagine you came here to warn us, only to go right back to living life the way you did before. With Santi being the man you know him to be, you have a lot at risk by betraying him the way you are doing...."

"It's because he has something on us, too," I replied.

"Not on us," Braden intervened. "On *me*."

I turned to Braden, shocked by his ability to take ownership. My entire life, it had always been about *us*... As I always took ownership for the wrongdoings committed by my brothers... And for the first time, Braden fought me on it.

"I began working for Santi a few years ago, without Jay," Braden continued. "The guys who also work for him brought me in, and I picked up on everything Santi was and is still doing. As time went on, Santi had me working closely with him compared to the other guys we work with. I came back into contact with Jay a couple months ago, and I got him sucked into all of this shit--it's my fault. I re-sold him on our dream of owning our own nightclub... And how Santi could help us get there. Now, Santi is using what he has on me to keep me working for him, and I'm stuck... And Jay reached out to you because you have something Santi wants, and you might be able to help me cut ties with him. Jay is just looking out for me because he's a good brother that way--and he always has been. I'm the fuck-up here...."

Braden's words sent chills through my entire body. I felt Val nudge me under the table, picking up on my appreciation for what Braden said about me. I was holding back tears.

"Eso fue hermoso, Braden. That was beautiful," Mateo said

with a grin. "Trust me. I know what it's like for my brothers to fall short, but also to fall short myself. It's one thing to fuck things up. It's another to *be* a fuck-up. Now for what it's worth, your heart's in the right place… And we'll help you. I mean, I've got a brother, too--a few of them--so I understand. But Santi… Set out to wrong us, and *that* is our--... How you say… Main *motive*."

Rodrigo nodded at Mateo's statement. Braden let out a deep breath, and his shoulders relaxed, as did mine.

"How do you expect us to help you?" Rodrigo asked. "I don't picture you coming to us to ask for something like this without a plan."

"We have an idea," I said, somewhat nervous. "We worked through it this week."

Mateo and Rodrigo smirked at each other. They made me feel like a kid, and I still couldn't believe that they were *actually* considering helping us... Let alone even giving us the time of day. Then it clicked. I could see Braden and myself in Mateo and Rodrigo, and something was telling me that Mateo and Rodrigo could see a bit of us in them, too. I continued.

"Tomorrow night, Santi is gonna be hosting the two of you at The Willow," I said. "Chances are he's gonna have you guys up in the private villa, where he usually takes his partners and other people he personally hosts. At some point, he'll ask you which girl you might take an interest in--any girl at The Willow--he'll promise you her… One if not *more*. That's when you tell him you want Val, who we'll have posted up at a table nearby."

Val's eyes widened at the sound of her name, considering it was the first she was hearing of our plan in detail. Braden, Mateo, and Rodrigo remained completely engaged in everything I was saying so far, so I continued.

"If this happens the way it usually does, he'll send Braden or me to get Val and talk her into coming up to the villa where you guys will be. He's gonna ask what Val wants to drink, and she'll say she wants a gin and tonic, which is what Santi is also gonna order… Only... Hers is gonna be drugged. The drugged drink usually has a marker on it… Whether it be a lime or mint leaves or something like that. He'll order the drinks with one of the bottle girls, and I'll intercept the drinks after Kai makes them at the bar, swapping the marker for Val's drink with Santi's. You following so far?"

The group nodded.

"So once the drinks are delivered to you guys, it'll take around 30 minutes for the roofie to start kicking in. Braden said the types of drugs he uses on drinks in his venues are slow-hitting. Val will have to start pretending to get sloppy, but we'll all have to keep an eye out for Santi, who will *actually* begin blacking out from the drugged gin and tonic. There's a Mercedes Benz sprinter van parked behind The Willow that takes Santi and his guests back to his house from the venue for the nightcaps. So, we'll need to get in the van and take Santi back to his place where we can take care of the laptop he keeps all of the videos he uses to blackmail on. Then you can deal with Santi however you guys decide to...."

I paused for a second, trying to read the faces of everyone around me and see whether or not they liked what I was saying. The group was giving me looks of skepticism, but I didn't think they were ruling out what I was saying completely. I waited for a response.

"Wow," Val said aloud. "That actually sounds like it might work."

"I mean, I'm open to any other suggestions," I shrugged.

"Do you know where this laptop is?" Rodrigo asked.

"I do," Braden replied. "Santi keeps the laptop hidden in a large humidor in his bedroom closet. I see it from time to time, and I know the laptop's there, along with a few other things he keeps close in a nearby safe. I have access to the safe where he keeps his gun and a few other important documents. It's just the humidor and laptop passwords I don't have."

"So let me understand..." Mateo said as he set down his cigar. "Rodrigo and I will be going about our business with Santi. All you need is for us to pick Val out of the crowd. Then, we deal with Santi the way we decide to when we get to his house, as you get into his laptop to delete whatever he has on you...."

"That's right," I replied before turning to Val. "Then, Val... All *you* need to do is drink your drink and start acting like you've been roofied about 30 minutes later--start gettin' super sloppy and all that. Once Santi starts *actually* slipping, we can convince him to take us back to his house where hopefully he'll be out for the count, and we can go through the laptop."

Mateo turned to Rodrigo, speaking in Spanish. Rodrigo smirked as he took a drag of his cigar before leaning back in his seat.

"How will you find the humidor and laptop passwords?" asked Rodrigo.

After taking a long drag of his own cigar, Braden confidently replied.

"Kai has a document on his phone with the humidor password. Santi disperses the passwords among the six of us who work for him. I've also worked with Santi long enough to know that his password selection isn't very diverse--that's just the way he works. So, chances are, whatever's *inside* the humidor that requires a password will have the same password as the humidor itself. He's got a humidor at The Willow and a humidor in his house. I highly doubt the passwords will be different between the two humidors."

"This all sounds crazy... But all this shit sounds crazy enough to *work*," Mateo said.

This was the first time I heard the plan out loud, and it actually didn't sound as absurd as it did in my head. Worst-case scenario, Santi is roofied, and we can't get into the laptop, drawing the conclusion later on that it was simply a common mix-up between the glasses at the club.

"After this night," Mateo continued. "We will *never* speak of this again."

He and Rodrigo both intently scanned the three of us. Their smiles were now stern looks that shifted their aura from approachable to dangerous once again.

"We trust that the three of you aren't messing around--that this is all true, and this plan will be followed. We respect that you not only warned us but also what you are risking for your *family*. It'd be easier for us to not get involved at all, but for Santi to come after everything we built for our own family... Esta muerto--he's finished."

"Finished??" I asked. "Look... We don't wanna kill the man. We just wanna erase what he has on Braden and everyone else he's blackmailing. It's the laptop we want."

Mateo and Rodrigo laughed at my remark, instantly making me feel like a kid again.

"You've seen too many movies, Jay," Mateo teased. "We won't kill the man for wronging us... But if it's willed that he gets what he deserves, así es. Then that is how it is written."

"We'll be fine," I assured him. "We know Santi well enough now to be sure that this will work."

I puffed my cigar immediately after speaking as a way of expressing my confidence. It seemed to work, as I saw the group somewhat relax as a result. I had no choice but to act confident because, deep down, I truly believed this was our only way out. Deep down, I believed our plan was the answer. But also, deep down, I believed there was a chance that Santi would find a way to somehow *win*--that he'd catch on.

"Jay, we've gotta head out," Braden said, breaking the silence. "Doors open soon."

THE WILLOW
NORTH HOLLYWOOD, CALIFORNIA
FRIDAY, 11:37P.M. - JULY 19TH, 2019

"Jay, man... You've gotta deal with this prick. He won't get off my back, and he's annoying as fuck!" Braden shouted over the blaring music.

I approached the entrance of The Willow from the hallway and pushed the door open, feeling a cool breeze as I stepped out onto the crowded sidewalk. The bouncers were almost shoulder to shoulder, straight-faced and ready to snap on the belligerent guy who was demanding they let him in.

"What's goin' on??" I asked as I tapped on the bouncers' shoulders. They let me step up between them.

"He says his friend is inside, but he doesn't remember the name," Braden said from behind me.

"Who's your friend?" I asked the guy.

"He's inside, bro," the guy snapped while raising his hand toward the door. "I don't remember his *fucking* n-name--just let me in bro pleasse dudxe cmonnn."

The guy reeked of alcohol, and he was barely able to stand still. He swayed left, then swayed right. He was fully dressed, heavily intoxicated, and all alone. This led me to believe that he was left behind at the pre-game, or this guy was simply just off his rocker. A part of me wanted to slap him sober before one of the bouncers threw him in the middle of the street, and another part of me felt sorry for him. I stepped forward and put my hand on his shoulder.

"Listen, man," I whispered. "I wanna help you. You just gotta give me a name, and we'll see if it's on the list."

"I'm *Rob*," he slurred.

"I mean the name the table is under. Not yours," I replied.

Rob scrunched his face, trying to focus with everything in him. I turned back to the bouncers giving them a nod to acknowledge the next group, as I would take care of the situation. He pulled out his phone and stutter-stepped as he struggled to hold it up straight. I placed my hand sternly on his back, and he finally stood still. There was a pause, and then he lifted his phone toward me, realizing he was too drunk to open it. I let out a laugh and couldn't help but respect him for acknowledging his incapability to do such a simple task.

I looked at the screen and on it was a series of texts asking where Rob was. The contact name was Kevin, and he seemed to be very concerned about where Rob was and if he'd be there soon.

"Your friend is Kevin?" I asked, looking up at the guy while my hand was still pressed against his back.

"YES!" Rob shouted, leaning forward to hug me. "You got it, bro… *Yes*."

"Table 7…" Braden said sternly. "God blessed you with patience, Jay. If you didn't come, I would have dealt with this guy differently."

"If you throw up, you leave," I stated clearly enough for Rob to comprehend.

He nodded as I opened the door for him to enter. We made our way up the hallway and into the club, immediately consumed by the crowd. Lights flashed, and people danced, enjoying the night like any other night at The Willow. I kept Rob in my peripherals as he stayed close, obediently following me to the table.

He was wasted, but I really didn't care at this point. My days working here were now limited. So I mean, if this guy made a mess, he made a mess. If he threw up, he threw up. If he started a fight, he started a fight. In a matter of days, what happened within the walls of The Willow would no longer be my issue. I had faith in my plan, and it comforted me to know I was on the way out once and for all... My brother and I both. As we maneuvered through the crowd, Skylar's voice spoke into my earpiece.

"*Braden, there's a guy dancing on the booth at 20. Call him down. I've got a couple Laker guys coming inside in 5*," he said.

"*That's on you, Sky… Jay's inside somewhere, and I'm on the door.*"

"*Fuck. Aight, fine.*"

"I got him," I said into the earpiece.

Almost directly in my line of sight and slightly to the left, I saw a man standing on the table, obnoxiously waving a bottle around. His shirt was unbuttoned all the way down, and the dancing lights reflected off of his chest sweat. Half of his party laughed and pointed their phones toward him, while the other half didn't acknowledge the nuisance he was quickly becoming.

I heard Santi's words echo in my head... "*The only thing worth elevating in a venue is women. They're the true bait for big spending.*"

It was one of Santi's more simple lessons, and I'm sure anybody would agree that this was an indirect way of saying "sex sells." I mean, it makes sense. If only Santi used his social knowledge and self-awareness for good… Then he'd be successful for the *right* reasons and not the *wrong*.

In one swift motion, still guiding Rob behind me, I leaned toward the bouncer who was manning the V.I.P. section.

"We need him off of 20," I demanded sternly without stopping.

The bouncer obediently nodded and waited for the two of us to pass him before pulling the man off the table.

"Here you are," I said as another bouncer undid the section's stanchion so we could walk up the steps.

"You're a lifesaver, man, forreal," Rob slurred, stumbling up the stairs.

"No worries."

I watched as his friends embraced him with open arms, making remarks about how they thought he'd never make it there. Crazy how some "friends" treat one another--in this case, leaving your wasted "friend" outside of the venue you're at. I couldn't help but envision Braden beating the shit out of this guy for simply being so belligerent in public. For some reason, I felt like helping h-....

My heart dropped into my stomach. I broke into a cold sweat. Before I turned away from the table, my eyes became fixated--fixated on a sight that served as the incarnation of my worst nightmare--a nightmare about a specific moment in time that ruined my family and everything I love--a moment that stripped me of not only my youth but my livelihood.

My eyes landed on a beautiful girl with long blonde hair. I recognized her instantly. She's the girl Josh was going crazy over before his final moments that night. I had never seen him so captivated by anything or anybody in his life. That night, I called her Rebecca, and tonight Rebecca is *here*.

I watched Rebecca chug whatever was left in her glass and whisper into her friend's ear with a wicked yet cunning smile on her face. Her friend slipped Rebecca a colorful pill I'm gonna assume is ecstasy.

Nate was right, I thought. *She was a wild one, and seven years later… Still is.*

I stood frozen at the bottom of the stairs and studied her movement. I watched as men surrounding their table turned to catch a glimpse of her beauty, and though it appeared like she thought nothing of it, I could sense she used it as fuel.

I swear, there's something about people who innocently wrong you that is so different from any other type of people who exist. People who innocently wrong you are typically unaware of the wrong they've committed, making them more likely to wrong another since they never faced the consequences for their actions in the first place. She got away with what happened to Josh... Who's next?

Rebecca pressed her lips against the ear of one of the guys near her, flirtatiously mouthing something. He dug into his pocket and pulled out his keys and a tiny clear bag of cocaine. The other guys, most likely drunk and captivated by her presence, instantly allowed for her to do as she pleased. I watched her have at it. The guys gave each other a look and then lustfully sized her up from behind as she did a key bump of coke.

Her eyes rolled back as she did another bump, and then another. I watched her close her eyes, open her mouth, and smile charmingly toward the willow leaves hanging from above. She became one with The Willow itself.

She lifted her hands.
She danced.
She laughed.

Rebecca was wholly satisfied with her own state of being--of simply existing--though her current state was heavily dependent on substances impairing her mind. To her, it seemed like nothing mattered except the moment itself. She swayed, and her head thumped to the beat of the music Niall played as if they were connected. Her eyes rolled back, and she began to dance more intimately with herself. She was getting her fix.

My heart began to race, and my head felt light. I could see her dancing the way she did with Josh in our home. My breath became irregular, and I tried to find my rhythm--I couldn't.

Breathe, I thought... But I can't.

"Jay??" called the bouncer from behind me. "Jay, you good??"

My eyes watered, and within seconds, tears fell as I pictured Josh's final moments, while staring at the girl who took him from me--who took Josh, my family, and everything I *am*. My legs began shaking. I no longer felt the will to stand. The lights danced around me with the people--now complete strangers--utterly unaware of my suffering. They don't care. They never did. They never will. Why would they?

I could hear my heartbeat in my head as it attempted to beat out of my own chest. The lights bounced off the walls, mocking me. The music, conversations, and every sound in the present moment blended into one ambient noise I felt detached from. I was trapped in my own head.

Rebecca laughed and danced by herself, surrounded by the group she was with, and I could see her taking on the form of who she was the night of the party. I dug into my pocket while still trying to regulate my breath, pressing an array of buttons on the channel transmitter. I finally heard the beep, urging me to speak.

"Braden," I desperately called into the earpiece. "She's here--the girl from the night with Josh--I need you man I'm struggling to breathe I need your help I think I'm having a heart at--a heart attack where are you?"

I turned quickly into the bouncer, shocking both him and myself as we collided.

"Jay, you good??" you asked. I mean, he asked. He asked me if I'm good.

I frantically stumbled around him, looking for an exit. I was in my garage. I was with Josh. She's holding the gun.

"DON'T," I shouted as I watched Rebecca hand it to him and cock it back with a malicious grin. "DON'T DO IT JOSH DON'T SHOOT PLEASE DON'T SHOOT DON'T...."

I bumped into people dancing around me as the colorful lights painted my reality into a bad dream. I grasped the channel transmitter and pressed again.

"BRADEN!" I shouted. "I NEED YOU, MAN... PLEASE."

I was turning in circles, reliving Josh's final moments and what could now very well be my own. I turned and turned, overwhelmed with anxiety. I felt sick to my stomach, head pounding with my heart still beating out of my chest. I watched Rebecca smile, tending to her daily life as if she had no part in Josh's death.

I was gonna pass out. I needed to... No... I *need* to. NOW. This was no way to live--to exist. As I drowned in the sea of people, two hands firmly grabbed me by the shoulders. They pulled me into a firm grasp, guiding me through the crowd.

I surrendered myself to the hands. I had nowhere else to turn. They guided me, and the scene unraveled in front of me in slow motion as people respected the owner of these hands while we moved toward the backdoor of The Willow. With one arm now around me, the other shoved the backdoor open, and a gust of cool air embraced me as I inhaled and caught my breath once again. The arm was still around me, and a hand was now patting my chest.

"It's okay, Jay," a familiar voice comforted me. "You're okay. It's all good--you're fine."

I had no control over the tears running down my cheeks as I steadied my breathing, seeing vivid thoughts of Josh's final moments fade. My arms were now extended, holding myself up by the wood railing that lined the outdoor deck of The Willow. The same hands that saved me were on my shoulders. They were warm and softly patting me, reminding me that it's okay to not be okay.

"You alright?" the familiar voice asked, and within seconds I knew who the voice belonged to. "You were on my channel by accident. I heard you calling for Braden."

I turned to see who it was, and of course... My savior was the man I spent the past week conspiring against--Santi. I watched him pull out and light a cigarette as I turned and leaned back against the wood railing, finally able to breathe again.

I couldn't believe it. Of all the people in the entire venue that could come to my rescue, it was the one person I wanted to hate with everything in me--and now, deep down, I couldn't help but feel somewhat grateful for his presence. The last thing I wanted was to feel like I owed him something, and now I couldn't help but feel that way. I lowered my head in disappointment.

Santi extended an unlit cigarette in my direction, gesturing for me to join him. I accepted without thinking, and he lit it for me as I clenched it gently between my lips. Exhaling a cloud of smoke in the opposite direction, I avoided eye contact. Just a minute ago, I was having an episode-panic-attack thing, only to be saved by the one leading me to my potential downfall. I was in no mood for his shady antics.

"You said you saw a girl--from the night with Josh...?" Santi said as he exhaled a cloud of smoke. "She's the one, huh? The one who got him to pull the trigger?"

I took a long drag, keeping my head down. I didn't want to answer--I couldn't afford to get sucked in the night before I'd get out of Santi's grasp once and for all. Yet, even without a response, he continued.

"It's a terrible thing, reliving traumas. It's like the war that wages within. One battle after another, but the war never ends whether you win the battles or not."

He spoke softly, just loud enough for me to hear over the music playing from inside the club. I kept my head down, still teary-eyed, and in my peripherals, I could see Santi's stance squared up to mine with his hands in his pockets. Staring at me, he awaited my response. I wanted to thank him, but I didn't want to risk sympathizing with a cruel man I plotted to cross within the next 24 hours. And still, he went on.

"Something I still can't wrap my head around is the fact that everyone's got *something*--whether it be a past trauma, a current struggle, or even getting sick over the unknown--everyone struggles with something, mentally."

"Excuse us, Santi!" a girl shouted as they slipped back through the club doors behind him.

I felt him move from in front of me to my right, leaning against the railing next to me. I looked at the closed door ahead of me, wanting to just go back into The Willow and keep working--anything to get me out of this conversation. I *could*, but something within kept me from moving.

"I feel like we can't escape our past because it's a part of us... Others say forget about the past as if it's something we can just drop--but I think it's pretty relative," Santi continued calmly. "I think you and I are the same in the way we see the world. We've both dealt with trauma. I've got years on you, though, and I'm telling you that it gets *easier* to suppress the trauma--to bury it--you just need to be patient."

I caressed the cigarette between my lips, refusing to let his words penetrate my perception of him. I didn't want to think for a second that he was trying to help me. I wanted to believe that he was in the process of manipulating me.

"We're not the same," I finally snapped. "You hurt. You manipulate. You're only out for your own gain--you live for yourself, and *only yourself*, and I don't do any of that... So don't tell me we're the *same.*"

I suddenly realized I was pointing at him while making my accusations, as we were now eye to eye, and my finger was just inches from his chest. I trembled deep down, and was somewhat shaking, struggling to hide it.

Santi stared directly back at me without moving. The gray in his eyes remained true as he read me--I could sense it. His still facial expression remained the same as he raised his cigarette to his mouth. I wanted him to punch me--to punish me in some outrageous way I'd never expect, like he did to everyone else--so that I could go about backstabbing him tomorrow with no remorse.

Just hit me, I thought. *Cuss me out and lecture me on how disrespectful I'm being*.

It suddenly frightened me to actually believe that I was different from the others he brought into his business. It frightened me that I could potentially come to believe that everything Santi did, he did with *good intent*, and therefore it wasn't his fault. It frightened me to think that I was in the wrong for plotting against him and that I was voluntarily ruining the opportunity of a lifetime--to learn and to be a part of his family.

He didn't cuss me out.
He didn't hit me.
He didn't lecture me on how disrespectful I am.
Instead, he shed a tear.

The man Hollywood loved. The man Hollywood feared. The man men respected. The man women threw themselves at. The man who dealt an abundance of social currency. The man who could *make* and also *break* anybody who walked his way with the connections he has. The man who has it all… Shed a tear in front of me.

Santi lowered his head and pressed his back against the railing, taking a final drag of his cigarette before dropping and lightly stomping it out. He slid one hand into his pocket and wiped his tear with the other as he looked from down at the ground to the night sky above us.

"I think most things in this world are subjective…" Santi's lip quivered. "But an objective truth I stand by is that trauma felt is a lot more tolerable than trauma caused. I've wronged people far more than I've been wronged--caused traumas for most beyond belief, but after a while, the level of guilt you feel hits a ceiling--no matter how much more wrong you commit, you feel the same."

He reached into his pocket for his now-empty cigarette pack. I offered him *my* cigarette, and he let out a laugh as he reluctantly accepted it. Santi was in rare form, and I felt myself beginning to let my guard down because of it.

"I've numbed myself over the years--didn't just dive into the life I made here, but instead I let it consume me… Entirely," he continued before taking a drag of the cig. "I brought all of you boys in because I want the best for you, and that's *still* my intent."

I leaned against the railing next to him, processing his words and the fact that this was the first time Santi was being genuinely vulnerable. It made me think that I was truly different from any of the other names on his guest lists or even on his payroll--different from the others... But similar to Santi.

Seeing Rebecca tonight made me realize that I wasn't entirely over losing Josh, and I may never be. A part of me wants Santi's ability to numb himself with the simple pleasures life has to offer--to occupy my mind and keep it from derailing itself like it did tonight. For the past seven years, I had numbed myself the way Santi had for most of his life. It seemed like he *perfected* the art of coping, and in a way, I envy him.

"Why do you blackmail the people you work with? And Braden? And Skylar and the other guys?" I asked with a much less aggressive tone than the tone I used before.

He took another drag of the cigarette, which was practically nearing the filter at this point. He wanted every last bit of it as if he relied on it to get through expressing his emotion.

"They don't get it, Jay. They don't see the opportunity. They don't see what I can give them... Or teach them. They lack *self-awareness*, which you and I have been blessed with. If I didn't have something on them, they wouldn't stick around long enough to understand the *bigger picture*."

My heart suddenly dropped at the thought of Santi justifying the wrong he has committed and continues to commit. He truly believes with everything in him that he is doing these people a favor--that he's saving them from the lives they thought they wanted to escape, rather than helping them actually face whatever it is that brought them here. He didn't care that it was out of force because he believed there was good intent behind his actions. Was it good? To him, maybe, but to me, that doesn't necessarily make it right.

"Do you have anything on me?" I asked, not expecting an honest answer.

He dropped the cigarette and stomped it out with a smirk, then played with one of his curls.

"I don't *need* anything on you, Jay," he sighed. "You know what's good for you. That's why you're still here after having figured me out. This is where you wanna be. This is where you *need* to be after having been through what you've been through."

He was right, and I hated him for it. I could leave and move on to something better for myself. All-day, I could convince myself that Braden was in the perfect place, doing what he wanted. By staying on this path, Braden could one day start the nightclub he's always dreamed of starting while drinking all the alcohol he wants and doing all the drugs he wants. I wouldn't be there to constantly slap his wrist and tell him no. That's when it hit me.

Santi has nothing on me--nothing besides... *Braden*.

It clicked. It suddenly *clicked*. Santi was pulling everything he could on me right now--the tears, the vulnerability, the honesty--he sensed that I'm on my way out of his grasp. He said he didn't need anything on me, *well-knowing* that he's had something on me since I met him. Santi has a *two-for-one* by pinning Braden, knowing I wouldn't go anywhere without my brother... And here he is trying to convince me otherwise... He truly *is* a master manipulator.

This realization was all I needed to completely detach myself from Santi.

This was all I needed to betray him with no remorse.

SIXTEEN | VAMO

BRADEN'S APARTMENT
DOWNTOWN L.A.
SATURDAY, 8:59A.M. - JULY 20TH, 2019

I felt myself become fully awake, almost instantly, staring at the ceiling in my room. It didn't matter what day it was. It didn't matter how I felt. It didn't matter that tonight could potentially change our lives forever. There are few things I'm O.C.D. about to this day, and my morning routine is still undoubtedly one of them.

Wake up.
100 crunches.
Hot shower in the dark.
Brush my teeth.
Blow-dry and do my hair.
Throw on some face lotion, deodorant, and cologne.

Once done, I stepped out into the living room to see Braden approaching the day in a much different way.

"Finally..." Braden groaned from the kitchen counter.

He was sitting on the countertop, wearing nothing but his sweatpants. His hair was messy, and he hadn't shaved all week--he looked rugged, holding a mug in his lap, which subtly shook, despite his tight grip. I checked my phone for the time.

"What do you mean, 'finally?' It's only 9."

"How could you even sleep?"

Braden had a point, considering everything that was at stake. We have a plan that's soon to be executed, stemming from a decision made in the same week. We were outnumbered and potentially setting ourselves up to be outsmarted by a veteran in the art of deception. We were out to betray the betrayer himself, yet I slept like a baby.

"I honestly don't know how I was able to sleep," I sighed as I sat at the counter across from him. "Have you heard from Val?"

"I haven't talked to *anybody*. You're the one calling the shots here, Jay. Shouldn't *you* know where everyone's at??"

"Relax, man. Relax," I said while calmly running my hands back through my hair.

"I know, I know... I'm sorry," he sighed. "I'm nervous."

"I know," I replied. "Don't be. It's just another night. If everything goes to plan, you won't even have to do anything. You just gotta act normal."

He took another sip of his mug and let out a long sigh. There was truth to his statement about me calling the shots, but I felt that if I came on too strong with the shot-calling, everyone would get nervous and begin to overthink their roles. I couldn't afford Santi catching on to anything, so I think it makes sense for everyone to go about their day as normal as possible.

"You think those Ramos guys will hurt him?" asked Braden.

"I don't know," I replied. "Ideally, we just delete everything in Santi's laptop files and move on, leaving him with nothing on us anymore. Do you know if the files are backed up on some other hard drive?"

"It's not," Braden assured me. "It's all on the laptop. I've been around his prized possessions for years now, and I've never seen any hard drives. He's not the most tech-savvy when it comes to this stuff."

I nodded. There was plenty of room for error, but I didn't want to think about the plan not working out perfectly… Not even for a second.

I opened the freezer and pulled out the half-full bottle of Grey Goose Braden only used for his *breakfast* cocktails. I emphasize breakfast because he just got the bottle two days ago, and half of it was already gone. I pulled the cork off, gesturing for his approval to pour it in his mug like he always does.

"One step ahead of you," he admitted while swirling what was already in his mug. "It's not doing much for me, though."

"You'll be fine," I assured him. "We'll all be fine. I'm gonna go check on Val to make sure she's ready one last time."

I grabbed my wallet and headed out the door. I knew I was stuck in my head, considering before I knew it, I was in the lobby and then suddenly in the car. My palms were sweaty as I ran through the plan over and over again, and every time it was different.

In one run-through, Santi caught me switching the markers on the drinks.

In another, Santi didn't go about his usual routine at all, and we had completely missed the mark.

In *another*, Santi had no intention of scamming the Ramos brothers in the first place.

In each and every run-through of the situation, something didn't happen according to plan… And there Braden and I were the next day, with no way out. There wasn't a single run-through I could process where it worked out just fine--exactly the way I had conceptualized the plan in the first place… No way. I couldn't help but hate a specific run-through above all… The one where I somehow lost Val. I couldn't help but fear having-....

KNOCK! KNOCK!

A loud knock against my car window brought me back to the present moment, sending me into a sudden panic. I gasped and instantly relaxed at the sight of Val, laughing at having startled me. I rolled down the window to catch the end of her giggle.

"WOW," she laughed. "I'm sorry, Jay Love. You were just so deep in thought. I couldn't help myself."

"You're no bueno," I said between heavy breaths I was struggling to catch.

I rested my head against the seat and closed my eyes, realizing I was so deep in thought, I had no idea I already made it to Val's apartment. It was 20 minutes behind the wheel, stuck in my own head running through the scenarios, one at a time.

I can't deny that Val had a calming aura about her that made me smile. I lifted my chin and opened my eyes to see her elbows pressed against my door. She was leaning against the car, with her chin resting on her palms as she looked at me with her typical cheeky grin. Even on a day as stressful as this, she still managed to make me smile.

"Don't tell me you're nervous," she teased. "Aren't you supposed to be the man with the plan?"

"I'm not nervous," I lied. "I just wanted to check on you."

"What... To make sure I wasn't bailing on tonight?" Val teased again.

"More so to make sure you're okay with doing this," I said as calmly as I could.

She maintained eye contact as her grin turned somewhat into a look of admiration. I studied her, confirming that this is the same Val I've known my entire life--the same Val that shouted "Knock! Knock!" every morning before school. The same Val my mom constantly nagged me to marry one day… And now, I was quickly beginning to learn that it was all for good reason.

"I'm okay with doing this. Of course I am," Val said as she straightened her posture. "You and Braden are my family."

"I understand," I sighed. "And I'm grateful, really. I just had to make sure you know that even though we've got a plan… Anything can happen… And I just don't want to see y-...."

She suddenly pressed her finger against my lips, stopping me from speaking. Her eyes were fixated on mine, and her perfect white teeth appeared between her full lips as she smiled once more. Her perfume filled the car as her shoulders were now halfway through the window.

"You and Braden are my family," she repeated. "I'm okay with doing this. We're *doing* this."

She lightly nudged my shoulder as she bit her lip.

"The real question is... What are you and Braden gonna do once you're actually able to quit and do whatever you want?"

"I don't know," I answered. "Maybe disappear somewhere in New York for seven years."

Val slapped my chest as I let out a laugh.

"Don't even joke like that," she giggled, struggling to hold back her own laugh. "Too soon, Jay Love... Too soon."

"What time are you coming to The Willow tonight?" I asked while starting my car.

"Just past 11. Is that okay?"

"Yeah," I replied. "The Ramos brothers shouldn't be there till 11:30."

Val stepped back from the curb, standing with her hands in the pocket of her oversized hoodie. The sun was just breaking through the clouds, bringing out the amber in her eyes. She smiled. I smiled.

"I'll see you then," she said.

Everything within me wanted for tonight to be like any regular night--to look forward to seeing Val without any worry. But instead, it felt like we were going to war, and this was the last we could see each other, not knowing if we were going to make it out the other side.

"Thank you, Val," I replied softly, and though I found it difficult... I turned the car around and left.

I drove back to Braden's in silence. No song could distract me from the thought of tonight. I know it's not wise to overthink potential situations because, at this point, I'm just wasting energy on the unknown, but the closer we got to tonight, the more I found myself *thinking*.

Maybe it was because I was unsure--unsure of what was going to happen... Of whether or not Santi truly deserved to be crossed. He blurred the line between good and evil. He believed his actions were justified as long as he based the actions on the *intent* behind the actions. This made me think that maybe... All the wrong he's committed in his life... He believed was actually *right*. So, who was I to interfere? If Santi believes what's right and wrong is subjective, does that mean *my* perception of right and wrong is *also* subjective?

I had no urge to weave through the traffic like I usually do. Instead, I took in my surroundings. It was 72 degrees out, and the sun shone through these puffy clouds that looked like explosions in the sky. My windows were rolled down, and I listened to the cars moving around me at the same speed. We'd stop and go at different times... Yet, we all moved in the same direction. Cars would exit and hop onto the freeway, yet we kept moving in one fluid motion.

Was I about to compare life to L.A. traffic? That I simply merged onto the same freeway Santi and Braden were on, and Braden and I were ready to exit? Or did I merge onto the freeway, invite the Ramos brothers to do the same, and together we forced *Santi* to exit? My head hurts. Why am I even going there with this?

I checked the time. It was almost noon, and I was already emotionally exhausted. I had all these faces in my mind--Santi, Braden, Mateo, Rodrigo, Val, Mom, plus the guys back at The Willow. Even Fia managed to slip in there.

The traffic began to disperse, and I was finally picking up speed again. I weaved through the cars, never looking once in the rear or side-view mirrors. Only forward. There was no lag while driving the Tesla, which I was occasionally reminded of, zooming left and right with the windows rolled down and a smirk on my face. It was almost as if I was meditating, just zooming my way through moving hunks of metal on wheels scattered throughout the highway.

I saw the faces in my mind begin to fade as I drove faster and faster...

Goodbye, Braden.
Goodbye, Santi.
Goodbye, Val.
Goodbye, *responsibility*.

I felt free. I *am* free--free to go left and free to go right... To hit the brakes or to floor it... To simply keep driving and never look back--and that's when it happened.

A loud metal thump came from a few cars ahead.

SKRRRRRTTTT!

A massive S.U.V. clipped the front of a small car, sending the S.U.V. spinning in my direction. Before I could even think to slam the brakes, the vehicle quickly made its way from the far right lane, across mine, and directly into a truck to the left. The car to my right came to an abrupt halt, causing a car to ram into it from behind. I swerved right, allowing for me to *just* make it out of the way of the massive S.U.V. before it made contact with me.

Drivers to my right and left adjusted themselves, as did I, making my way to the shoulder of the road where I could calm myself down. I had both hands on the wheel, taking deep breaths through my mouth and nose, looking directly ahead. My heart was beating through my chest. I laid my head back against the headrest, looking through the glass ceiling of the car at the sky above. I couldn't hear anything over my heavy breathing. I knew I was in shock--no I *am* in shock. I couldn't… Can't think. After pausing a few seconds, with both hands still cemented to the wheel, I closed my eyes and did what I haven't done in years…

I wept.

My shoulders shook up and down as tears ran down my face… Onto my shirt, my pants, my seat belt, the seat itself. Everything I had kept within me for years up until this moment, buried in the confines of my mind, heart, and soul, poured out of me like a flowing river. Hands still on the wheel, I looked at the sky.

"I can't," I whispered with a quivering voice-crack. "God, I can't."

I stared aimlessly into the sky, waiting for an answer... As if God was gonna pat me on the back or I was gonna hear a voice in my head tell me it's okay or that it's *not*. My hair was hanging down on both sides of my face, and I tightened my grip on the steering wheel in an attempt to stop shaking. I lowered my head and took deep breaths, watching the tears fall onto my denim.

Since I could remember, I took on my family's responsibilities. I blamed myself for every wrong--for any form of dysfunction or bad decision made. I had always blamed myself--blamed myself for Braden's bad behavior, for my dad working too hard, for my mother's stress, for Josh's death.

Every little thing… *Buried*… So deep… For so long… Only to be brought back up to the surface now… On the side of a freeway in L.A. I took a deep breath and let it out, looking in the side-view mirror. Other cars were lined up behind me, checking in on the cars halted in the middle of the highway. I took another deep breath and let it out.

Clothes I had piled up in the back seat were flung all around the car, including the things I had in my center console. Pens, loose change, a cologne bottle, my phone, and pieces of paper littered the passenger's seat and the floor in front of it.

Between the random junk scattered on the floor, facing upward, was the polaroid photo of Braden, Josh, and myself from the night of the party. The hairs on the back of my neck stood as the tears kept falling. My death grip on the wheel loosened, and I lunged toward the picture, only to be pulled back by my seat belt.

I unbuckled it and lunged over the center console, grabbing the photo and lifting it just inches from my face. The shaking slowly subsided, and I studied the image. Josh was leaning against the kitchen counter alongside Braden and myself... All of us smiling… All *happy*… Without a worry in the world… When life was simple. I took one last deep breath as a tear fell onto the photograph.

With tears still welled up in my eyes, I smiled and let out a laugh. Family is *why* I came to L.A. Family is *why* I decided to join Braden. Family is *why* I will make sure tonight goes according to plan. There was no more room for doubt. There was no other option, and coming to terms with that brought me hope that after tonight, Braden and I will be free once and for all.

THE WILLOW
NORTH HOLLYWOOD, CALIFORNIA
SATURDAY, 7:56P.M. - JULY 20TH, 2019

"It's good, right??" Skylar asked as Kai handed him back a pack of gummies.

"I feel like it's not supposed to taste like weed," Kai replied while still chewing on the gummy. "And all I taste is weed."

Skylar intensely observed the pack of gummies as Kai walked over to the bar.

"They taste like weed?? I taste cherry," Skylar retorted, still observing the bag for the ingredients. "Jay, come try these."

"I'm not hungry," I replied without looking up from the guest list on my laptop.

Skylar rolled his eyes, well-knowing I knew that weed gummies were meant to get you high and not to satisfy your hunger.

I intently studied the guest list, scrolling through the different reservations and individuals that were locked in for tonight--some professional athletes, a few actors, other names I recognized from Forbes and other publications--nothing out of the ordinary, except two names under Santi's villa's section… Mateo and Rodrigo Ramos. Their names were italicized, just as all of Santi's potential partners typically are. That's how we knew to keep our distance. They were Santi's deal, not ours.

Staff members overlapped one another and made their way from one side of The Willow to the next as they prepared for the evening. Niall ran his sound check, skipping through songs that echoed throughout the fully-lit venue. Skylar rambled on and on about his new weed gummies while Kai and Braden experimented with new cocktail ingredients behind the bar counter.

I checked my phone for the time… *8:06PM.*
No texts from Val. No texts from Mateo.

"Where's Santi?" I asked the guys as they made themselves comfortable along the booths.

"I haven't heard from him all day," Kalani replied while scrolling through his phone. "I think he's setting up his place for his guests tonight. It's the dudes from Miami."

"Oh, no way," I replied calmly. "The guys we went to dinner with?"

"Yeah… The Caribbean guys."

I nodded and went back to staring at the guest list. I scrolled up and found Val's name and couldn't help but think about seeing her this morning. It felt like a lifetime ago since we were all in Miami, and I felt nostalgia creeping in, only to be interrupted by the kitchen doors swinging open.

The energy shifted as Santi entered the room, walking with a strut like I had never seen. He had a cheeky grin on his face as he greeted the bottle girls he crossed paths with, gently patting their shoulders. He was chewing a piece of white gum in a way that showed off his pearly white veneers. His beard was thicker than usual but freshly lined up below his curly hair.

"Where are my boys at??" Santi shouted over the staff, then made eye contact with us on the opposite side of The Willow. "Ah, *there* they are. Waking up from their naps??"

There was no denying we looked like we had just taken a nap, considering we were sprawled along the booths in one of the V.I.P. sections. Skylar tucked the pack of gummies in his back pocket as Santi approached us. Braden, Niall, and Kai stepped up from behind Santi, and naturally, our group made somewhat of a circle. Santi's gaze panned around the circle as he chewed his gum with a one-sided smile on his face. His gaze stopped at Skylar.

"How's the gummy business, Sky??" he asked, almost sarcastically.

"Business is booming, Santi! You know the deal," Skylar yapped back with a smile, flashing his diamond-studded teeth.

Santi's eyes panned left from Skylar to Kai, who he stood shoulder to shoulder with.

"We got a new drink in the mix??" Santi asked, maintaining the same intensity he came at Skylar with.

"Yessir," nodded Kai, lifting a sampler glass up to Santi.

Santi took the glass and downed it in a single gulp. He tilted his head and nodded in admiration.

"Wow," Santi gasped before returning the glass. "That's damn good. The citrusy syrup pairs well with the… Is that grapefruit juice?"

"Yessir," Kai nodded. "Garnished with a fresh tarragon sprig."

"I love it!" Santi shouted as he clapped his hands. "Add half an ounce of Aperol and make it a 'special' for tonight. That's a fucking *drink*."

Santi nodded and scanned the group once more, this time from left to right. His gray eyes met mine.

"Jay, how you feelin'?"

"I'm good," I replied with a nod, hoping he'd just move on.

"You sure?" he asked with a pleasant smile that slowly turned into a skeptical stare.

"Yeah, I'm good," I replied confidently this time around.

He studied me for about 10 more seconds, lifting his chin slowly. Just before the pause was considered awkward for the group, he continued.

"Big night, tonight," Santi declared, taking his eyes off of me. "Our guests I introduced you to in Miami are coming. It's the usual situation, but I want to remind you guys to keep your distance... Just because I know you'll recognize them... I don't want them to get *distracted*."

We nodded, some maintaining eye contact and the others not so much. Santi was more serious than usual, and we all knew it without it having to be addressed. He wore a loose black button-up shirt with black jeans and Dior loafers. The blue and gray in his eyes were piercing in contrast to his solid black fit, making it even tougher to maintain eye contact.

Santi casually dismissed us and went on to talk to the bottle girls. Our group went right back to lounging around, and I reopened my laptop to look over the guest list once more. I triple-checked Val, Mateo, and Rodrigo's names. Skylar threw himself back onto the booth within inches of me.

"Yo, Jay, add Tiffany and a 'plus-ten' by her name. Braden said they're coming through," Skylar said without looking up from his phone. "How's the V.I.P. table situation? We got any open tables that they can get in on?"

I opened up tonight's floor plan. We were completely booked--not a single table available.

"Fuuuck," Skylar sighed. "Aight. I'll have them hitch onto one of the other tables. Who's dropping the most money?"

I scanned the floor plan, hovering over each name.

"Tables 9 and 10 are under one name," I said. "The last name is in the system already, and they drop 10 to 12 grand on average."

"Tables 9 and 10? Perfect."

He walked off, still not looking up from his phone.

I checked my phone for the time... *8:37PM.*

No texts from Val. No texts from Mateo.

Time was passing by much slower than I wanted it to, and I

was starting to get anxious. I wondered how Braden was feeling about everything. I looked across the venue to see him taking a shot of tequila alongside Kai. I quickly stood to my feet and made my way to the bar. As Braden bit into his lime slice, Kai turned to grab a different bottle off the shelf.

"What're you *doing*??" I whispered in a stern tone.

He took his lips off the lime.

"Jay, I'm losing my *shit* over here."

"You can't get drunk, Braden. We've got too much going on tonight."

"It's just to *relax*, Jay. It's fine."

I glared at him with my teeth clenched. We were in a similar situation before… Seven years ago… Where he got too drunk to see an important night all the way through. And as a result, we lost Josh. I preferred we didn't lose *anything* this time.

Kai refilled the shot glasses and swiftly sliced through a few more limes with ease.

"You want one, Jay?" Kai asked, casually pointing the knife in my direction.

"I'm good, man. Thanks though," I politely replied.

"Take one!" Kai shouted as he slapped a third glass down on the table and filled all three.

"Jay's good," Braden uttered as he took my glass and downed the shot.

I pressed my lips together, well-knowing Braden was already buzzed, and it was too late to stop him without making a scene.

I checked my phone for the time… *8:47PM.*

No texts from Val. A text from Mateo.

A TEXT FROM MATEO!

MATEO: Santi is sending a car to pick us up at 11

ME: Sounds good

"Jay!" shouted Santi from up in his private villa.

I looked up, startled at the sound of his voice. I slid my phone back into my pocket. He was standing next to two bottle girls making decorative arrangements to one of the villas.

"Grab Braden and Kai. I need the three of you real quick!"

I relayed the message from where I stood. Without question, Braden and Kai followed me up the stairs behind Niall's D.J. setup and into Santi's villa. White linen drapes hung from the rooftop of a gazebo, which was laced in vines and floral decorations. Santi lit a cigarette before being handed an iPad from one of the girls. Between exhales of smoke, he kept the cigarette in his mouth as he scrolled through the guest list.

"Kai, come here," he demanded.

Kai stepped forward while Braden and I obediently stayed put. Santi gestured for Kai to look at the iPad.

"That's the new password for the humidor in my office upstairs," Santi said between drags. "At exactly midnight, I want you to send one of the bottle girls with everything I have on the top shelf."

Kai nodded and was about to step away when Santi abruptly grabbed his arm.

"Put it in your phone," Santi insisted. "So I know you won't forget it. Also, go test it now to make sure you got it right."

"Got it," Kai replied as he typed it out.

Santi let go of his arm, and Kai headed down the stairs.

"The Amor brothers," Santi teased as he handed off the iPad. "I'm gonna have Skylar on the door all night, and I want them open at 9:30 to get this place packed for when my guests show up. I want you two inside, making sure no funny shit happens on the ground level. I've got extra security blocking off the private villas, so don't worry about anything going on up here."

We nodded as Santi took a few steps toward us, gently placing his palms along the sides of our faces.

"You guys came to me with a dream," he said softly. "I haven't forgotten about what you want, and if tonight goes smoothly, you'll be a whole 'lot closer than you would've ever thought."

Braden and I nodded again, this time with hollow grins that masked our intent to betray the man who promised us the world. Santi smiled and then turned his back to us as an act of dismissal.

"Braden, stay for a bit," he ordered before stepping back behind the white drapes.

I reluctantly made my way back down the stairs onto the ground level, wanting with everything in me to hear what Santi was telling Braden. Was he onto us? Did he know what was going on? After a few minutes, Braden came down the steps onto the ground level. He avoided eye contact.

"What'd he say?" I asked.

"Just that..." Braden struggled to find an answer. "We just talked about the extra security...."

"Are you *sure* that's all you talked about?" I asked. I wasn't convinced that his answer was entirely truthful.

"Yeah!" he snapped back. "How're you gonna switch the drinks with all the extra security? And what are we gonna do about the changed password??"

I overlooked his odd behavior in an attempt to come up with a solution.

"I probably won't get up there unless Mateo and Rodrigo personally ask for me," I replied. "Otherwise, there's no way I'll make it up."

I looked upward toward the back of the venue, where Kai was *just* walking out of Santi's office. I thought about the password Santi handed off to him and what else Kai knew. The humidor password was our best bet at getting into the laptop tonight, which means Kai's phone is what we need to get into first.

"Santi said there's a new password. You think the humidor passwords are the same between the one here and the one at his house??" I asked Braden.

"Yeah... And like I've said... There's a high chance the new password is the same for the laptop. Either way, Kai's got it in that document on his phone," Braden answered. "I know what you're getting at. But how're we supposed to get into the phone? He uses the face I.D. to unlock it."

"Damn," I sighed.

My eyes circled around the back of The Willow, aimlessly looking for an answer.

From the leaves hanging from the ceiling to the back mezzanine. No answer.

From the booths on the left to the booths on the right. No answer.

From Niall elevated just over my shoulder to Kalani by the...

Kalani.

My eyes lit up, and Braden slightly leaned forward to find out why.

"Kai and Kalani have the same face... Like, they're twins..." I whispered as I grabbed Braden's shoulder. "If we can get Kai's phone, I'll come up with a way to get it in front of Kalani."

"Wow... Not bad," Braden whispered back.

I checked my phone for the time... *9:03PM.*

No texts from Val. I texted Mateo.

ME: Make sure to ask for me to be up there with u guys - otherwise security's not gonna let me up

After an hour of last-second rearrangements and convincing Skylar that I still had no desire to try one of his weed gummies, the venue was already *packed.*

Music echoed throughout the main room, which was now filled with colorful flashing lights. Niall's hair bounced, and his face was lit by the computer screen 10 feet above the ground level where heads bobbed. I adjusted my earpiece while making my way from the back of The Willow to the front.

I passed unfamiliar faces left and right, leading me to believe that Skylar had already started letting the general admission in. I greeted the ones I knew by first name and introduced myself to the rest. Regardless, they all made their way to the bar, which filled up quickly.

Security was in place... One man in front of each booth and two on each side of the staircases leading up to the private villas. I held down on the channel transmitter.

"Either of you know where Santi is?" I asked.

A couple moments passed before Skylar responded.

"*Check the mezzanine… Otherwise, maybe the deck, smoking.*"

"Thanks."

I looked over my shoulder up at the mezzanine above the bar, where Santi was speaking to a group. Santi's eyes hovered over the sea of swaying people as he and the others leaned against the railing, talking to each other.

I felt a slight shove, and I stutter-stepped as a guy and a girl walked past me.

"Oops! Sorry, Jay," the guy said.

I smiled and nodded, letting the two of them pass. I didn't know him, but he knew me… Which is honestly something I don't think I'll *ever* get over--being recognized is a feeling that just never gets old.

"*Jay, I got a party of 8 coming your way. Table 6*," Braden said through my earpiece.

I turned right to see Braden pointing in my direction from the opposite side of The Willow, signalling for the group to make their way to me. I lifted my hand to flag them down with an inviting smile on my face. I held down on the transmitter in my pocket with the other hand.

"What's the full name?" I asked Braden with my hand still up.

"*Arya Azadi. Blue shirt.*"

I released the transmitter and extended my hand to meet Arya's.

"What's up, Arya? I'm J-...."

"You're Jay!" Arya shouted while giving me a half-hug. "What's good, bro? I follow you on Insta. You're the fucking man, bro."

I let out a laugh as he threw his arm around me, and we walked toward their table.

"I'll follow you back," I insisted, but he was already shouting something to the rest of the group.

The night proceeded as planned. Braden passed on one group after another, and after each sloppy introduction, I'd show them to their tables. After showing each group to a table, I'd quickly scan The

Willow for Kai, Santi, Val, and the Ramos brothers.

Santi made his rounds as any decent nightclub owner would, but the villa remained untouched and barricaded by bouncers and security. Kai was working the bar. Still no sight of Val or the Ramos brothers.

I checked my phone for the time... *11:07PM.*
No texts from Val. A text from Mateo.

MATEO: On our way - We will make sure to ask for you

I scrolled down to the last text I sent Val. Seeing her outside of her apartment this morning felt like a decade ago, and I can't deny there's a part of me that doesn't want her to show up at all. Deep down, I knew that tonight she'd be putting herself at risk. Deeper down, I knew that tonight... *I'm* the one putting her at risk.

And as the colorful flashing lights danced to the beat of the song that played, I saw Val standing among the rest of the crowd. Her sparkling silver dress wrapped her body frame almost skin-tight, accentuating her hourglass figure. Her platinum hair fell straight down to her shoulders. She was a dream--something straight out of a movie--*anything* but real.

Heads turned from all around as both men and women sized her up from head to toe. She took a few aimless steps through the entrance as she wandered into the venue, tapping her tiny black purse against her hip. Her chin was up, portraying a sense of confidence, per usual. I've known Val long enough to know that this posture was her way of indicating that she didn't want to be bothered... And it worked *every time*, on everybody but me. She continued to look around, and I had a feeling I knew what for.

I stepped down from the V.I.P. section while keeping her in my sight. Braden was standing behind her, just over her shoulder, scanning The Willow the same way she was. I maneuvered my way through the crowd, slipping between various groups and conversations. I didn't lose sight of Val.

She was looking up over her right shoulder toward the nearest V.I.P. booth--her side profile illuminated by the colorful lights beaming down from the hanging willow leaves. A man was standing on the booth with a drink in his hand, attempting to get her attention. She gracefully smiled and turned back toward the center of The Willow, where her gaze met mine. Her eyes lit up, and mine did the same. We smiled. We had *both* found what we were looking for.

"Jay Love," she mouthed under the thumping of the blaring music.

She extended her arms, and I fit so perfectly, I could feel her heartbeat against my chest... Or was it mine? Either way, it was beating faster than usual.

I really wish you didn't show up, I thought.
"I'm glad you showed up," I whispered.

I pulled back, and my right hand slid down from her shoulder to her hand. I gave it a slight tug toward the back of the venue. She smoothly began walking with my hand pressing gently on her lower back. Braden and I nodded at each other, acknowledging what we had both realized at the same exact time...The night has officially begun.

People continued to stare at Val, then at me, then back at Val, as we made our way along the V.I.P. section to the bar.

"I can't spend a lot of time talking to you," I said sternly from over Val's shoulder. "Nobody can know we already know each other, or Santi will catch on."

"I figured," she replied while looking forward. We kept walking.

Her fragrance brought a calming sense of familiarity. It was her signature scent, and I preferred *her* scent over The Willow's any night. She was calm--collected. Her lipstick was a nude color that was just a hint darker than her tanned complexion. Though she rarely ever wore makeup, the minor amount of mascara she wore brought out the amber in her eyes more than ever. There was no doubt in my mind Mateo would've chosen Val, even if it *weren't* a part of the plan. I would do the same.

"Listen," I said with my lips almost pressed against her ear. "I need the bartender's phone. It's in one of his pockets, so I'm gonna need you to spill your drink over his pants, and I'm *hoping* he takes it out and leaves it on the counter."

"You think that's gonna work??" Val replied with a look of skepticism.

"How else am I gonna get the phone?"

"Whatever you say," she sighed nervously.

As we reached the bar, I made room for Val and me. Kai darted from one side to the next, with two women assisting almost every move he made. He mixed and poured multiple drinks in one motion, and I had forgotten how *good* he is at what he does. A clink here and a clink there, followed by pours, slicing of fruit, and piercing of olives--it almost looked like Kai had four arms... That's how *fast* he was moving. He slid drinks across the counter to people as they slapped their cash and cards down. The women working alongside Kai struggled to keep up but still managed.

"What can I get her??" Kai shouted to me without taking his eyes off of the drink he was making.

"Gin and tonic!" I shouted back.

Before I even finished saying the order, he was going straight for the gin.

"You ready?" I whispered to Val. "Get it under your purse as quickly as possible."

She nodded. I turned back to see Kai finishing up the drink. Taking a swift step back, I let a man in front of me. Val leaned over the bar top, extending her arm across the man that was now between us, waiting for his turn to order. Kai carefully lifted the full drink toward her open palm, and just as she grabbed it, I shoved the man from behind.

His heavy elbow flung forward, abruptly knocking Val's hand. The full glass of gin and tonic splashed directly onto Kai's lower body. Val let out a gasp as the glass fell and broke against the floor under Kai. Kai threw up his arms out of frustration.

"What the *FUCK,* man?!" Kai shouted at the man standing between us.

"I didn't mean t-... That wasn't me, I-..." the man stuttered in shock.

I placed my hand on the man's shoulder, making room for me next to Val once again. Kai pulled his soaking phone out of his pocket, wiping it with his shirt.

"Phone," I nudged Val.

Val and I watched as Kai set his phone next to the cash register a few feet to the right of us.

"Everything good, Kai??" I asked with my hand still on the confused man.

"Yeah," Kai sighed.

"I'm so sorry," the man apologized. "Someone shoved me. I didn't mean to knock over the drink, I…."

Kai ignored him, making his way to the towel on the opposite side of the bar. Without looking, Val smoothly placed her purse on Kai's phone and dragged it across the bar top in front of me.

"It's all good," I assured him. "We'll get it cleaned up."

Val slowly lifted the purse, and I grabbed the phone and slid it into my pocket. I patted the man's back and then Val's.

"I *do* think you owe her a new drink, though," I insisted, taking a step back. "This is Valentina."

Val smiled at the man, picking up on exactly what I was putting down. I took a step back as their small talk began, making my way straight to the kitchen. As I approached the swinging doors, a waitress pushed through, almost running into me.

"Oops, sorry, Jay!" the waitress shouted.

"All good," I replied as I quickly stepped around her and through the kitchen doors.

The kitchen was thoroughly lit, showcasing the white walls,

tables, and deep red tile floor. A thousand smells overwhelmed me as I dodged one food runner after another. Smoke rose in one corner of the kitchen, while water boiled in pots in another corner. Chefs shouted at each other, passing one dish to the next while doing taste tests. I had to act quickly, with no room for overthinking a single move.

I stuck out like a sore thumb, being the only one not wearing all white, but no one batted an eye considering how focused they were on the meals.

"More salt!!" Kalani shouted from behind a long table. "*Much* more. This shit tastes like cardboard!"

I followed his voice, slipping between chefs who completely ignored my existence. At the end of the long table, final dishes were spread across trays, ready to be grabbed by food runners. I discreetly placed the phone face-up between two dishes at the edge of a tray, awaiting the food runner. The plates were main entrees, a few of them being large bowls of what looked like our tagliolini pasta. I did a subtle lean over the tray to read the order.

"*TABLE 22: 4 tagliolini pastas. 1 with no black truffles.*"

Knowing I'll need Kalani to get as close to the phone as possible, I'll need to give him a reason to look closer into the dish itself.

The truffles, I thought.

I looked up to see Kalani, who was slowly making his way across the long table, thoroughly analyzing the finished dishes spread across the trays. With my fingertips, I gently took one of the black truffles and buried it in the only dish without any truffles at all. Kalani got closer... And closer... And *just* before he got too close, I moved the phone so that it was peeking out from *just* under the now-ruined dish.

"Jay?? What're you doing back here??" Kalani asked.

"Table 22... The guy sent me over to make sure there were no black truffles in his dish," I explained. "Is this tray for Table 22?"

"Yeah," Kalani replied as he took a look over the tray.

His face slowly panned over the tray, from right to left, then top to bottom. He thankfully didn't notice the phone... But the phone also didn't notice *him*--it didn't unlock. I broke into a cold sweat.

"Good to go," Kalani declared to the food runner standing to my left.

"Wait," I blurted out. "Is that a truffle...? Buried in there...?"

I subtly tapped the phone screen.

Kalani paused.

"Fuck," he sighed. "Is it?"

He leaned closer so that his face was almost touching the dish. The phone unlocked, recognizing Kalani's face as if it were Kai's.

"God damnit, it *is* a truffle. Good catch, Jay. Damn."

Kalani reached in, grabbed it, and placed it on the dish I grabbed it from.

"Whose phone is that??" Kalani asked.

My eyes widened at the remark.

"Ah, shit. Sorry, that's mine," I said as I quickly grabbed it from the tray. "So it's good for Table 22??"

"Yeah, it's good to go. Send it out," Kalani told the food runner.

She nodded, picked up the tray, and was on her way. I turned to follow her out with the now-unlocked phone I covered against my thigh.

"Yo, Jay," Kalani's voice called from behind.

I slowly turned.

"What's up?"

Please don't bring up the phone, I thought. *Don't bring up the phone. PLEASE don't.*

"Good catch," he smiled. "Santi would've tore me a new one if I screwed up our signature dish."

"No worries," I nodded, then turned and slipped out the door behind the food runner back into the madness.

Mainstream songs blasted throughout the Willow as the venue was packed in far more than I ever thought it could be. Santi wanted to give the Ramos brothers the *full* experience, and he was most certainly delivering--maybe even *over*-delivering.

I snuck into the corner just outside the kitchen doors, looking to make sure Kai's phone was still unlocked. It was. I let out a sigh of relief as I grabbed my phone and held the two phones in front of me. I opened the "search bar" on Kai's phone, and with my thumb, typed out:

P.A.S.W.
BACKSPACE.
S.W.O.R.D.

The "password" document suddenly popped up, prompting me to open the notes app. I quickly looked around the venue, only to see bobbing heads engaging in conversations with one another. The bar was overflowing with strangers, and I could see Kai continuing to serve drinks, *completely* unaware of his phone being stolen. Val was still talking to the man I shoved. I leaned my shoulder against the wall, keeping a low profile, and tapped the notes app so that the "password" document filled the phone screen.

Gotcha, I thought while scrolling through the document.

Spotify password? No.
Bank account password? Nah.

Instagram password? No.

I couldn't help but think about how dumb it was for someone to keep all of their passwords in one document, but then again, Braden and I do the same thing.

"*Jay, I'm sending another group your way. Table 21,*" Skylar said through my earpiece.

My hands began to shake. I wasn't able to respond. With one hand, I scrolled through usernames, passwords, and passcodes, while in the other hand, the phone's camera was open and ready to take a picture of the humidor password once I found it.

"*Jay?*" Skylar asked.

I broke into a cold sweat. *So* many passwords...

Desktop password.
Dating app password.
Another dating app password.
Willow entrance passcode.
Humidor passw-...
HUMIDOR PASSWORD!

"*Jay, what's good? Where are you??*"

I quickly lifted my phone to take a picture of the password on Kai's screen and then slipped my phone back into my pocket. After closing out the document on Kai's phone, I made sure there was no trace of anyone going through it, then I made my way back to the bar.

"I'm here," I replied into the earpiece. "I'm on my way."

I squeezed through people who leaned as close to the counter as possible, watching Kai continue pouring and mixing drinks in my peripherals. In my direct line of sight, Val was getting a mouthful from the stranger I basically forced her to talk to. She gave me the "save me" look, and I swept in just in time.

"There you are!" Val shouted, grabbing the side of my arm, which turned into a pinch.

"Ah-...!" I attempted not to flinch. "Sorry. I was checking on th-the... Table...."

I stood between them now, and I could tell the guy was figuring out it was time for him to bring the conversation to a close.

"It was, uhh... Great meeting you," he sighed--his eyes bouncing from Val to me and then back to Val. He turned and disappeared back into the crowd as I took his spot against the bar top.

"Here," I said softly, gently placing the phone near her purse.

Val nonchalantly pressed her purse against the phone, then slid it across the counter and into the original spot she took it from about 10 minutes prior. Kai remained on the other side of the bar, still oblivious to what had just happened. We had done it.

"What's next??" Val asked after sipping her gin and tonic.

"I need to help Braden and Skylar," I said while looking over my shoulder toward the front of The Willow. "Tiffany should be here sometime soon. You think you can finesse being a part of her table till we call you up?"

"Yeah, easy," she agreed. "We were texting earlier. I think she'll be here soon."

Val checked her phone then looked into the crowd as she fixed her hair.

"Perfect," I replied. "Are you okay?"

It was a stupid question, but also an important one. I could tell by the way she fixed her hair… She was nervous.

"I'm good," she smiled, turning to face me. I wasn't convinced.

"We're gonna be fine," I assured her, whether it was true or not.

I smiled and offered her my hand. She took it, lightly squeezed, gave me one last smile, and then I turned back into the crowd.

The night proceeded as any other night would, with the exception of the extra security that stood just before the vacant private villas above Niall. I escorted one group after the next, making brief introductions, mixed in with giving and also receiving hollow compliments.

"Jay! Grab one!!" a random woman shouted while shoving a tequila shot into my chest.

Her group sloppily grabbed shot glasses off of the massive tray held by one of the bottle girls. They laughed, joked, and shouted, raising their glasses. I couldn't say no at this point. With the shot in my hand, I downed it alongside everyone else. The smoky serum made its way down my throat, sending chills from my chest down to my legs.

"I appreciate it!" I said with a genuine smile. Lord *knows* I needed a shot. "You guys have a good night!"

Just as I stepped down the stairs, I heard Skylar's voice through my earpiece.

"*Santi's guests just pulled up*," he said. "*I'm on the door. Jay… Braden… Where are you*?"

The hairs on the back of my neck stood, and chills ran down my arms. It was time--to act and not to think. The pieces were in place, and now it's time to put them into play. I took a deep breath, then held my finger down on the transmitter.

"Just stepped down from Table 3," I replied.

Suddenly, a hand tightly gripped my left shoulder. I turned left to see Braden, who pulled me close.

His mouth inches from my ear, he said... "They're gonna be

surrounded by security all the way up to the villa. You need to make sure they see you so that they can invite you up."

He shoved me in the direction of the club entrance, and I continued without question. I straightened my posture, subtly nodding to the music as I calmly made my way through the crowd.

To my left, I noticed Val dancing on one of the booths with Tiffany and the large group they joined. Even from across the entire venue, her dress caught my eye. There's no chance Mateo could miss it. I kept moving.

A flashing white light illuminated the entrance hallway, bouncing from side to side. It came from a flashlight that belonged to a massive bald bouncer wearing a black suit. People moved out of his way as he entered the ground level of The Willow, just below Niall's elevated setup. He kept a straight face, holding up his hand, which he used to shake the flashlight.

Heads turned to see the procession walking on the path this cyclops-of-a-man created. Nonetheless, the path was being paved for Santi--his diamond chains, bracelets, and rings dancing in the light. The diamonds danced as he laughed and engaged with Mateo and Rodrigo… One Ramos brother on each side of him.

The brothers were each in loose-fitted shirts--Mateo in lighter earth-tone linens, while Rodrigo wore darker shades of gray. The three of them, alone, shifted the mood of the entire venue as they made their way from the entrance of the main room toward the stairs leading up to the private villa. *Everyone* turned to see who they were.

I had a feeling the security was tipped off that I may try to intrude on the private gathering, given my having overstepped back in Miami. Otherwise, *no one* gets up to the villa while Santi's guests are there... Unless he allowed it.

"*Not a single person gets up here while my guests are here*," I could picture Santi saying to security. "*Not even my boys. Especially not Jay.*"

I couldn't help but remember the conversation he and I had on the rooftop of his suite back in Miami. While I remember the conversation only in bits and pieces, my suspicion was that I overstepped, and I remember Santi confirming that by feeling the need to roofie me that night.

I kept making my way through the crowd, now picking up speed. I needed for them to see me, and I needed to make it look like it was by accident. Otherwise, Santi would make sure I don't come anywhere near the villa tonight.

I know Santi would *hate* for me to overstep again.

I got closer--now 10 feet away.

I know Santi would *hate* for me to join their private party.

I got even closer--now 5 feet away.

I know Santi would *hate* it if I just…

I stepped into the path of the massive man leading the group, and with little effort, he knocked me into a group of people. My stumble quickly turned into a fall directly in front of the stairs.

"Bud, you can't see the light??" the large man shouted while standing over me, flashing the light directly at my face.

Perfect.

"Yeah, well, I can now!" I retorted in an attempt to make a scene so that I was noticed.

He rolled his eyes and reluctantly offered to help me up.

"Jay??" Mateo shouted, peeking his head around the side of the cyclops who knocked me over. "Jay!! The smart guy. Qué pasó, mang?! Why are you on the ground??"

I took the man's hand and was pulled up in less than a second. Seeing that I was acknowledged by Santi's guests, the man opened up his stance to let me respond.

"Hey...!" I shouted with semi-open arms.

Santi's vibrant smile transitioned into a skeptical smirk. Such a small distance between the entrance of The Willow and his private villa, yet somehow he manages to come across the only potential threat to him being in *complete* control. Just his luck.

Mateo lunged forward and gave me a warm hug, then turned back to Santi and Rodrigo.

"From the dinner back in Miami!" Mateo shouted, tightening his grip on my shoulder.

I have to hand it to him… He was playing it off better than I thought he would. I smiled and offered my hand to Rodrigo, who smiled back as if he *just* remembered who I was.

"Good to see you again, Jay," Rodrigo smiled as his big hand shook mine.

I gave a respectful nod. With one of Mateo's arms still wrapped around my shoulder, he wrapped his other arm around Santi.

"Where are we going??" Mateo asked Santi before turning back to me. "Jay, you must join us!! Vamo. Come on."

Santi tilted his head and bit his lip. With no verbal response, his gray eyes looked directly into mine.

"*Say no*," his eyes demanded. "*You will respect*."

Mateo and Rodrigo's eyes bounced between the two of us.

"I mean… I'm working at the moment," I replied while pointing at my earpiece.

"No, NO!!" Mateo shouted. "We are *all* working. We are *always* working, even while we *play* in this business. It's all the same. Vamo, Jay…."

Santi lowered his head, smiled, and let out a laugh.

"Let's do it!" Santi shouted with a raised palm lifted toward the villa above us.

The massive bald man, now standing outside of our social circle, flashed his light once again, leading us up the stairs.

"This place, Santi... All of it... *Fucking beautiful*!!" shouted Mateo as he danced up the stairs.

Pausing just halfway, Mateo placed his hand on the railing, taking it all in. From overlooking the sea of people below him to the willow leaves hanging just above our heads. From the V.I.P. booths lining the left wall to the booths lining the right. From the mezzanine in the back of the main room to the fully-lit bar below it. It was all truly a sight to see from where we stood, and both Mateo and Rodrigo made sure to give credit where credit was due.

"The Willow..." Rodrigo said as he, Santi, and Mateo spread themselves across the three white booths under the gazebo. "This is incredible, Santi. How did you manage to take a vision and turn it into something real, yet still so... How do you say... Like a dream...?"

Santi laid back on his own booth between the other two booths. Pulling out a cigarette, he smirked and lit it with ease as it burned between his lips.

"I appreciate that," Santi said while exhaling a cloud of smoke. "To answer your question, I think there's no fine line between tangible space and how you perceive the purpose of it. I mean, that's all it is, really. It's a *space*... A place for people to simply exist and make memories. I just have to provide the space and the resources for people to use in order for them to elevate their *own reality*, really. The *people* bring quality to the venues in this industry... Not me."

Rodrigo and Mateo nodded in both agreement and admiration as Santi continued.

"The beauty of creating a space for the public is that you can design it any way you like. People will all come together with different perspectives to share while experiencing a similar experience... Both good and bad... Preferably *good*, but the liquor ultimately has a say in the end, right?"

They laughed and continued nodding.

"Come, Jay... Sit with us!" Santi patronizingly shouted from across the villa.

It took me by surprise. I hadn't realized I was still standing at the entrance of the gazebo between the white drapes, separating us from the back of Niall's D.J. setup. Santi signaled for me to sit next to him, and I obediently smiled and made my way around the small table and onto the booth. We were practically touching elbows.

"Before we continue, let's get drinks going!" Santi shouted loud enough for a hostess to hear and step up in-between the drapes.

She immediately caught our eyes, making her presence known--her skin-tight leather dress accentuating her figure. She held a glossy wooden tray of tequila shots. Rodrigo sized her up at *least* once or twice before she even opened her mouth to speak.

"I heard… Drinks?" she asked with a cheeky grin, reaching over to set the tray down on the table between us.

She had an accent, and I assumed she was Spanish. I wouldn't put it past Santi to fly in a hostess from Miami or the Caribbean *just* to appeal to the Ramos brothers. Her dark red lipstick was the perfect shade against her tanned skin and light eyes. Her hair was wavy, flowing down past her lower back. Mateo and Rodrigo's eyes lit up immediately as she reached over the table with her chest practically being held back by a thread--literally--the leather was ready to give out any second… And I couldn't tell if Mateo and Rodrigo's amusement was a result of the woman or the talk of drinks. The temptations and distractions had made their way into the villa, and it worried me knowing I wasn't the only one that needed to remain focused on the overall objective.

"¿Tú hablas?" Mateo asked as he leaned forward.

"Sí," she replied flirtatiously. She stood straight up and adjusted her top. "¿Qué te trae por aquí?"

"¡Busco amor!" Mateo teased. "Y creo que lo encontré…."

She smiled back, and once again, I found myself wishing I took the time to actually learn Spanish as a kid. Whatever Mateo said, it was evident that there was a connection. She turned and majestically disappeared behind the white drapes--Mateo and Rodrigo both staring... Sizing her up one last time before she was no longer visible.

"*Fuuuck*, man. I thought Miami had the women, but L.A.... L.A. is a different beast, mang!" Mateo shouted, leaning back in his booth. He gently placed his hands on the top of his hair which was pulled back into a slicked bun. "How do you stay focused on the game??"

Santi picked up a shot glass and gestured for us to do the same.

"She's a part of the game," Santi replied. "They *all* are…."

He lifted his glass.

"Then viva el juego," Mateo said as he clinked his glass against Santi and Rodrigo's glasses. "Long live the game."

Mateo and Rodrigo inhaled their shots like a breath of fresh air while Santi turned to address me and my empty hand.

"Go on, hero..." Santi said softly with a cunning half-smirk.

Without breaking eye contact, I reached for the shot glass nearest to me, quickly lifted it to my mouth, and downed it. I set it back on the table without looking away.

"Back to what I was saying…" Santi continued as he leaned forward. "Every single one of my venues engages all five senses--

touch, taste, smell, sound, and sight. If I can't uniquely engage each of them, the potential of the space will never be reached."

Mateo and Rodrigo leaned forward, actively engaged in the wise words pouring out of Santi's mouth like it was some sort of divine wisdom. To them, it *is* divine wisdom.

"And here we are only focusing on the alcohol…!" Rodrigo laughed.

"... Which is a *big* part, no??" Mateo snapped back with a chuckle.

"Oh, it's one of the biggest!" Santi shouted. "But by no means is it the end goal… Having top-shelf liquor is necessary, but the focus is to keep your guests *engaged*… Keeping them *entertained*… It's not about providing a good time, but rather providing the *platform* for a good time to be had. Give them the resources and the tools. They'll do the rest."

Mateo and Rodrigo nodded their heads in agreement, as did I. Santi sold the bigger picture with ease, and the Ramos brothers had dollar signs in their eyes as they absorbed every word like a sponge. I didn't want to agree with Santi, but his natural ability to persuade and engage was undeniably… Brilliant. He grabbed another shot glass from the tray and held it above the table, but this time, he was standing.

"Enough talking about the experience!" he shouted with his glass raised. "You experience for *yourselves*!"

The brothers stood with glasses in their hands, and I reluctantly did the same. I couldn't afford to keep drinking--to lose my edge. I was beginning to feel loose, and it was in my best interest *not* to fall victim to the ignorance and sloppiness alcohol wraps the mind with. I need to remain focused… I need to-....

"*Take the shot*," Santi demanded with his eyes.

I shouldn't, but I feared if I didn't, Santi might begin to think something is up. At this point, however, I knew that the more I lost *my* edge, the more he may be willing to lose *his*. We downed the shots, and as if on cue, another bottle girl came in with another round of shots.

"Jay! Take our guests to the villa overlook to show 'em the view. I'll get some food in rotation," Santi said.

"Sounds good," I nodded, then gestured for Mateo and Rodrigo to follow.

I separated the two drapes on the northern side of the gazebo, exposing the small balcony that entirely overlooked The Willow. Mateo and Rodrigo stepped onto the balcony, placing their hands on the railing to fully take in the ambiance. I stepped up between them as Rodrigo looked back over our shoulders for Santi, I assumed.

"Which one is she?" Mateo asked as he puffed out his chest

and fixed his collar.

"Silver dress... Along the right wall on the booth," I replied.

"Una reina," Mateo gasped. "She's stunning."

"I know."

I looked left to see Niall standing over his D.J. booth. He had been staring at me with a straight face. He played it off as if he wasn't, but it was already too late. Did he suspect something? Or was he maybe just jealous that I finessed my way up to the villa to hang out with Santi and the other V.I.P.'s? Did he care? I'm being paranoid.

My eyes trailed from Niall's setup to the crowd below, where I saw Braden showing a group to their table. It was just another night at The Willow, though the energy was much higher than usual. I continued looking right, and my eyes locked onto Val dancing on the booth--her platinum hair and silver dress making her a sight to see, though her charisma did the most. She carried herself as though she was above each and every other soul in the vicinity, but she did it humbly--she did it with grace--with ease.

"Chances are he's gonna ask you about the *women situation* soon or at some point," I said, breaking the silence.

"We're ready," Rodrigo said, placing his hand on my shoulder. "Cálmate, Jay... Relax. You look tense."

"He's a smart guy," I snapped back in a whisper while looking over my shoulder. "I was just making sure you're not getting distracted with the drinking."

"Believe me. We're fine. *You're* fine."

I couldn't help but think that maybe Rodrigo was right. We needed to act natural for the night to go as planned, and that was exactly what they were doing. But in my defense, they were acting a little *too* natural. I took a deep breath, followed by a long exhale.

"Coño, Rodrigo... Our clubs need *work*," Mateo sighed as he scanned The Willow, appreciating every detail.

A hand gently grabbed my shoulder.

"I've got something for you guys," Santi said from behind. "I hope you're hungry."

The brothers' eyes lit up as they stumbled back into the gazebo and onto the booths. Santi kept his hand on my shoulder as we approached the table now littered with an array of food, filling the air with an exquisite aroma that made my mouth water. I'm *hungry*.

We took our original seats, and in front of each seat, another tequila shot was placed, *waiting* for us. Each shot glass had a thick gold trim along the bottom, and from the bottom stemmed a tiny mint leaf that stood straight up in the center of the tequila that filled the glass to the brim. Santi lifted his glass.

"To nights we may struggle to remember with family we will never forget," Santi said smoothly while raising his glass.

"Familia," Mateo and Rodrigo said in unison before drinking.

I raised my glass, and before I knew it, the shot was on its way down my throat. The shot was saltier than before, which caught me by surprise. I observed the glass in the palm of my hand as I pressed my tongue to the roof of my mouth.

"Too strong?" Santi asked me as he set his empty glass on the table. "I would've thought the third might go down easier than the first two."

"N-no," I replied, shaking my head. "Maybe it's the mint leaf... That gave it a weird aftertaste."

"The food will help with that," he smiled. "Kalani! Come break it down for us!"

Kalani stepped forward between the drapes, in apron and all. After respectfully acknowledging Mateo and Rodrigo, he caught sight of me. He did a double-take as if he didn't believe I was actually sitting up here with the V.I.P.'s of the V.I.P.'s. I bit my lip and gave an awkward smile, not really knowing what to say.

"So in case you didn't remember from Miami," Santi stood. "This is Kalani... Our head chef... Youngest and *best* in the hospitality game. Kalani, you wanna tell our guests what you've made for us?"

Kalani's stare toward me gradually turned into a glare--a telling glare of envy.

"Yeah, sure..." Kalani replied dryly. He looked at the table, and with one hand, pointed out each dish, breaking down the assortments, ingredients, and origins.

"Beautiful," Santi said aloud. "Thank you, Kalani. Looks amazing."

"My pleasure," Kalani nodded with a hollow smile.

He slowly turned, maintaining eye contact with me. It was evident he didn't know why or how I made it up here, and it most certainly didn't sit right with him. He left, and the white drapes closed behind him.

"Please... Eat!" Santi said as he passed plates around.

Mateo and Rodrigo began filling their plates without hesitation. I had lost my appetite and couldn't tell whether it was because of the last shot I took or the extremely awkward interaction with my now disgruntled co-worker. I placed a couple items on my plate and set it down. The hostess presented an array of cocktails, introducing them as tonight's specials. She then placed Santi's gin and tonic in front of him as he rambled on about his desire to run venues across the Caribbean.

He referred to his Greek and Russian descent...

His passion for the tropics...

How resorts were the most pristine form of hospitality...

His admiration for the Ramos brothers and their stamp on international hospitality...

He showed his respect. He gave credit where credit was due...

He showcased his charisma. He charmed the group.

I listened to every word he said, attentively...

I nodded in agreement with every impactful point made, respectfully...

I laughed at every punchline.

I asked the occasional question.

I *learned*.

If it weren't for the herd of unaddressed elephants in the room--the fact that I shouldn't have been up here, that I was overstepping, that a betrayal was in order, and that I was sharing a lighthearted laugh with very dangerous men--it was safe to say that we were having a good time. There wasn't a single moment where awkward silence was able to creep in, and for a second, nothing outside of the villa mattered.

"I think it's time to add to the party," Santi insisted as he set down his now-empty plate. "Follow me."

He stood and made his way to the overlook. Rodrigo and Mateo followed closely from behind. I stood and almost immediately felt the alcohol hit me like a sudden smack to the head. I let out a quick exhale and struggled to not stutter-step in the opposite direction of the group. After swiftly managing to keep my balance, I stepped through the drapes and onto the overlook where I was just a step or two behind Santi and the Ramos brothers.

The three were now leaning against the railing, talking and pointing toward random spots throughout the venue. A minor thumping made its way to the forefront of my head, but I shook it off in an attempt to make out what they were saying.

Before I was able to pick up on the conversation, Santi turned back to me and grabbed my shoulder as he said... "Silver dress at Table 9. Platinum hair. Get her and her friends up here and do it with Braden if you think it'll take the two of you to persuade 'em."

"Sounds good," I replied with a nod.

I stepped back between the drapes separating the overlook from the gazebo, squeezed through the booths, and headed out between the drapes that served as the entrance. Niall looked up over his right shoulder at me, half of his face lit by his laptop screen as he nodded his head to the music. I acknowledged him, but he remained emotionless, just watching me pass him by as I headed down the stairs to the ground level. I suddenly stumbled down the bottom three steps, keeping myself up by clinging to the back of a bouncer who I caught by surprise.

"Do could??" he asked, helping me stand straight.

"What??" I snapped back.

"I said... You good??" he asked louder this time.

"Yeah..." I replied as I shook my head and stepped into the crowd.

My arms and legs suddenly got heavy as I was bumped from both my left and right, receiving snarls and scoffs from strangers. I could feel myself getting sloppy faster than ever before, and almost instantly, I could only focus on what was directly in front of me--tunnel vision.

Why is this happening? I thought.

The music and conversations blended together to form one ambient sound that enveloped my conscience.

What is happening? I thought.

Tree. Shot. Shot? I had 3--3 shots. My tolerance was... No... *Is* better than this... I'm not shouldn't be am I for drunk that bad?

The SHOT, I managed to think. *He fucking did it. He roofied me. I need to throw up NOW*.

My walk became an aggressive haul, as I used my heavy hands to shove people out of my way. I made out random words and phrases here and there as I picked up my pace. My tunnel vision became more and more narrow.

"Woah, woah!"

"Watch it!"

"Fuck off!"

"Chillll...!"

"The fuck??"

I ignored the responses from people I shoved aside. I kept moving. I didn't look back. I heard talking through my earpiece but couldn't make out who it was. Stumbling out of the crowd into a walkway, I looked up at my new desired destination--the bathroom.

I took three or four more steps until an arm was thrown around me, and I immediately recognized the feeling. It was Braden.

"Jay...? *JAY*...."

"Bathroom..." I slurred.

"What's-... You alright??"

"BATHROOM!" I shouted, now looking at him face to face while he helped me walk straight. "I need to throw up."

My head gradually got heavier, and I felt butterflies in my chest and gut.

"H-he... I think he roofied me..." I said softly.

"I've got you," Braden said as he shoved the bathroom door open. "Get out! Get the fuck out!"

I may not have been able to see Braden's face, but judging from the frightened faces of the guys in the bathroom, I could tell Braden appeared to be a threat. Bodies hurried out of the bathroom, and I used my full body weight to shove myself over a toilet.

Within seconds of me sliding my index finger to the back of my throat, a flood of clear liquid projected itself into the toilet. My eyes watered, and I shivered as I dry-heaved between sudden spurts of salty clear liquid. I could feel my heavy head become lighter and lighter as the fluid continued spewing out with little effort now.

"Water to the men's restroom," Braden said, most likely into his earpiece. "Now, please. Just bring a pitcher."

With my knees pressed against the floor and both hands placed on the rim of the toilet seat, my tunnel vision and unsteady breathing stabilized. My heaves slowly transitioned into a calm breathing pattern. I could hear the muffled music coming from the other side of the bathroom wall. The door swung open.

"Thanks," I heard Braden say.

The door swung open and shut again. There was silence. I slid my finger to the back of my mouth, slower this time.

"HOOOAAAGGGHHH-...."

Nothing but air came out. It was out of my system. I leaned back, slipping into a seated position as my back slammed against the stall door. I inhaled, then exhaled, looking up at the dimmed light directly above me.

"You get it out?" Braden asked.

I let out a sigh of both relief and exhaustion.

"I think so," I replied with the little strength I had left.

With a firm grip on the toilet seat, I flushed, pulled myself up to my feet and opened the stall door.

"The last shot I took…" I said while grabbing the pitcher of water. "He drugged it. He put it in the shot."

I pressed the chilled pitcher to my lips and took a few big gulps. Braden watched.

"Why would he roofie you?" he asked. "I feel like he wouldn't want you making an ass of yourself in front of his guests."

"I don't know… Maybe because he feels threatened? Because I overstepped again by being up there? Maybe to get me out of the way? I mean, it almost worked, didn't it? I'm here and not up *there*."

Braden crossed his arms and shook his head.

"He was really tryna shake you… Damn. Santi has lost his mind."

"It's fine," I uttered while setting the pitcher down. "They asked for Val and some of her friends. Let's get 'em up there, quick."

I turned on the sink and began splashing water in my face.

"You wanna keep *going*?? Jay, he's out to *get* you!! He knows…."

"Well, he hasn't gotten me yet," I snapped back while fixing my hair in the mirror. "We're almost there."

"Jay, man… Come on. He's too-…."

"We're. Almost. THERE," I retorted, causing him to bite his tongue.

Braden was still leaning against the sink, with his arms crossed and his head now lowered. I couldn't tell whether I simply startled him or completely broke him down… Or *both*. I placed my hand on his shoulder.

"We're almost out, Braden. I told you I'd get you--us… Out of this."

He slowly lifted his chin so that he was now looking at the ceiling, then at the ground in front of us. My back was pressed against the wall, hands shoved into my pockets as I awaited his response.

"What's next?" he asked.

"We get Val and some of her friends up there like he wants. Once we order the drinks, all you need to do is swap the marker on them before they get back up to us. Stick to the plan."

"Okay," he nodded before turning to me.

"Vamo."

He turned, opened the bathroom door, and the two of us walked right back into the madness. We walked side by side through the dimmed walkway that opened up into the ground level.

"Tables 9 and 10," I said as I pointed left toward the V.I.P. section lining the eastern wall of The Willow. "It's a conjoined party. We should be fine getting one or two girls to come up with Val."

"Perfect," Braden uttered as he led the way.

Val now sat on top of the booth, in deep conversation with another girl who matched her intensity. As we approached the stairs in front of the elevated section, the bouncer undid the stanchion for us, and we were greeted by the large group with open arms.

Braden was embraced by a man in a collared shirt and slacks. His gold-plated Rolex glimmered in contrast with his unamused aura, which showed in the way he greeted us. He seemed to be about 50 and an overall good-looking guy with the help of some facial injections. Come to think of it, I've also seen him on several billboards in Beverly Hills promoting his practice as a plastic surgeon.

"This is my brother, Jay," Braden said loud enough for the girls on the booth to hear. "He hosts here with me, as well."

The man gave a subtle smile, not exposing a single wrinkle on his face.

"Pleasure's mine!" he shouted while shaking my hand. "I'm Dr. Amir."

"Ah, you're all over Beverly Hills!" I shouted, well-knowing this wasn't the first time he's probably heard that.

He let out a laugh as he rolled his eyes.

"Guess we aren't strangers, after all," he chuckled. "Please, come drink. We were *just* about to order another bottle."

"I appreciate that, really..." Braden replied warmly. "We've actually got some friends here that Santi wants to introduce some of his guests to. Next bottle is on us for the minor inconvenience--a bottle of 1942 alright?"

"Right on. That would be amazing," Dr. Amir said as he respectfully raised his drink.

He turned back to the group he was previously talking to.

"Two bottles of 42 to Tables 9 and 10. Put it on my tab," Braden spoke into his earpiece as we approached Val and her friend.

Braden leaned toward the girl sitting to Val's left. "Hi, I'm Bra-... Holy shit... Tiffany?!"

Tiffany had chopped her hair so that it was just above her shoulders and dyed it a dark brown. She looked like a *completely* different person, but either way, she looked great. She knew it, too.

"You didn't recognize me?!" Tiffany shouted back, competing with the music. She gave him a playful slap on the arm.

"Your hair," Braden blurted out. "I mean, you're hot... But wow, it's so... You look *different*."

"Mmm, you have such a way with words, B!" Tiffany snarled sarcastically before giggling.

I smiled at Val. She smiled back.

"Santi's friends wanna meet you two," Braden said with a half-smirk.

"You had me at *Santi*," Tiffany blushed before turning to Val. "It's up to you if you wanna go up!"

Val turned to face me with a skeptical look complemented by a subtle smile. She raised her eyebrows, looking up at the villa over my shoulder, then back at me. I nodded. She knew what was happening and what she needed to do, but neither of us knew if any of this was actually gonna work.

Regardless, I offered her my hand. She took it.

SEVENTEEN | TO THE BEGINNING OF THE END

THE WILLOW
NORTH HOLLYWOOD, CALIFORNIA
SATURDAY, 11:59P.M. - JULY 20TH, 2019

With one hand on Val's lower back, I gently guided her down the steps from the V.I.P. section. To my left, Braden did the same for Tiffany, and the four of us made our way through the crowd toward Santi's villa.

I took a deep breath, looking up at the overwhelming setup that made up the front of The Willow. Directly ahead of us, lifted 10 feet off the ground, was Niall with his hands raised, orchestrating the crowd's energy with the music he played. An intricately crafted floral design made up the 10-foot wall below him. Above him to his right and left were the two villas, each made up of their own private gazebos and balconies serving as the overlooks which were now swarming with people.

My eyes panned left of Niall, and I could see women now inside and around the gazebo that Santi, Rodrigo, and Mateo occupied. The four of us stepped up to the bouncer manning the staircase to the left of the floral wall. Val and Tiffany led the way up the stairs as Braden and I paused before taking the first step.

"I know what to do," Braden assured me one last time. "I'll make sure the markers on the drinks are switched."

"You got this," I replied. "Make sure to meet us on the way to the sprinter van."

He nodded, and I turned to head up the stairs but was stopped by Braden's grasp.

"What's up??" I asked.

"Don't let them touch her," he demanded. "The second we lose control of the situation, get Val and Tiffany out of there. It's not worth it at that point."

"I know."

He let go of my arm and disappeared back into the crowd. I jogged up the stairs to meet Val and Tiffany, and we continued into the gazebo between the white drapes. Women swarmed the inside of the gazebo and the overlook, and amidst the swarm were Santi, Mateo, and Rodrigo, smoking cigars while having an animated conversation.

Fresh food was being placed on the table in exchange for empty plates, almost in a single motion. Smoke trailed up through the vents built into the floral ceiling, and the smoke was intertwined with the usual fragrance Santi trademarked for his venues. They caught sight of us, and Mateo jumped to his feet with a massive smile on his face.

"There they are!!!" Mateo shouted with arms wide open, causing heads to turn toward us.

Val stepped forward without hesitation, leaning over the table to hug Mateo and introduce herself. As if in slow motion, I watched Santi undress her with his eyes as he remained sitting with a cigar in hand. He puffed, and even as Rodrigo stood and introduced himself to Val and Tiffany, Santi remained seated.

Mateo immediately dove into conversation, using a hand gesture with almost every word spoken. Rodrigo was now standing with his back to the table, talking to a few girls sitting on an adjacent booth, while Santi just continued staring at Val, straight-faced yet infatuated, puffing his cigar with one leg crossed over the other.

In an instant, his eyes darted from Val to me. My heart dropped, well-knowing that he had caught me in the act of catching him lust over Val. He smiled, stood, grabbed an appetizer from the table, tossed it in his mouth, and made his way over to me. I chose not to move as he stood beside me, looking back into the bustling villa.

"Where have you been hiding her?" Santi asked between puffs of his cigar.

"Tiffany?" I asked. "She's here all the time."

"I know *Tiffany* is here all the time. Valentina is the one you've been hiding," he accused smoothly.

"I met her tonight...."

"You met her in Miami," Santi said, leaning closer to me.

He reeked of cigars and gin, practically pressing his mouth against my ear as he asked the one question I wish never left his lips.

"Are you playing me, hero?" he whispered. "All you had to do was lie once, and now I have no choice but to question all your truths."

Santi and I watched Tiffany and Val sit on the booth between Mateo and Rodrigo as the other girls danced and talked among themselves. Here I was, next to the don of it all--all the deception, the manipulation, and the game itself--and he was next to *me*. Was I a fool to cross the man who crosses for a living? I was about to find out.

"Are you *threatened* by me?" I turned to him, hoping to catch him off guard. "Did you try to drug me tonight because you feel *threatened* by me?"

He took another puff of his cigar without taking his eyes off of Val.

"I did it to save you," he replied calmly. "... From making a big mistake, should your intent be to get involved in *my* business tonight. I don't know what you did to make Mateo and Rodrigo like you so much--for them to ask for you to be here… But I'm gonna allow you to slip out right now because of a 'pressing family matter' outside of work."

"*Don't let them touch her*," Braden told me before I came up to the villa.

I thought about the way Santi had looked at Val.

I thought about what Santi had been proclaiming since we met--the reason I'm still here--for my *family*.

"There's no family matter outside of work. My family's all *here*," I declared as I stared into the gray. "You *are* my family."

Santi stared back, studying the authenticity behind what I had just said. He stared into my eyes, at me, and through me. I almost thought for a second that he wanted me to say more, but I knew that if I did, it would diminish what I had just said. He gently used his left hand to pull the cigar from his mouth as he placed his right hand on my shoulder.

"You were made for this business," he said while gently patting me. "You're gonna do more than I *ever* did."

He slowly removed his hand and went back to puffing his cigar as he approached Mateo and Val. His words echoed over and over again in the forefront of my mind.

Made for this business.
More than I ever did.
Made for this business.
More than I ever did.

I stood with my hands in my pockets, watching Santi move from Mateo and Val to Rodrigo and Tiffany. He leaned over and they nodded their heads, and that's when it hit me. They were ordering their drinks. Val held up two fingers as I read her lips.

"I'll do the same," she mouthed.

I stepped back behind the drapes and looked down over the stairs, scanning the crowd for Braden.

Please be ready, I thought. *Please be ready*.

I let out a sigh of relief as I spotted him by the bar, having a conversation with a small group. He's ready… Or at least I *hope* he is.

"Excuse me!" said a high-pitched voice to my right.

I stepped back to let the waitress pass me from inside the

gazebo. She held what I pray is the drink order, checking it once again before she stepped down the stairs. I kept my eyes on her as she maneuvered her way through the crowd, then I lost her. I needed a better view.

As inconspicuous as possible, I slipped between the drapes toward the overlook on the other side of the gazebo. Flashing lights of red and blue seeped through the openings between the hanging drapes and floral decor. I caught a glimpse from behind the girls dancing on the booths of Santi entertaining Val and the others. Keeping a low profile with ease, I squeezed between a number of dancers that were nothing but just a physical presence for Santi and his guests at this point.

I slipped into the corner of the overlook against one of the floral pillars that held up the entire villa. There was hardly a foot of open space in The Willow, but my eyes went straight to the bar where I found our waitress waiting for the drink order to be fulfilled by Kai. Hands beginning to nervously shake, I pulled out the transmitter to double-check that I was on the right channel. I held down the button and spoke into the earpiece.

"Braden, you got eyes on the bar? Small blonde waiting on drinks in all black has Santi's drinks."

I prayed that Skylar wouldn't question the statement. I also prayed that Braden would be able to pick up on the crucial statement I just made. Braden, who was mid-conversation with the group he was tending to, made a polite gesture as a way of dismissing himself, then turned toward the bar. My hands tightened on the railing and my legs stiffened, watching--waiting--it was all I could do.

Braden discreetly made room for himself on the staff's end of the bar next to the blonde, leaning over the counter to say something to Kai. Kai turned to Braden, quickly nodded his head, poured a shot of what looked like Grey Goose, then went back to putting together the original drink order. Braden looked left, then right. The waitress was still patiently waiting for Kai to finish the order as Braden started talking to her.

My stomach tightened at the thought of what was unraveling before my eyes. What is he saying? What is she hearing? Did Santi even order a drink? Was it the same drink as Val's? Will Braden be able to pull this off?

At this point, it's do or die.
And I pray to God that it be done.

Kai applied what seemed to be the finishing touches to the tray of drinks. He lifted the tray and walked it to the staff's section of the bar, where Braden was making the waitress laugh and engage in conversation with him. Kai reached for a sliced lime and placed it on the rim of one of the drinks--the one intended for Val--the lime was officially the *marker*.

Please, God, I prayed, tightening my grip on the railing while watching Braden.

I watched as Kai said something to Braden and the waitress, then turned right back toward the herd of people surrounding the bar to fulfill their orders. Braden raised his shot glass with a flirtatious shrug and tilted his head. He was getting her to take the shot... *Genius*. She shook her head, but with a big smile on her face. She seemed playfully indifferent about it. He lowered the shot glass, then raised it again, and I could see from over his shoulder that she was biting her lip, contemplating taking him up on the offer.

She took the glass, then lifted it up toward her mouth. Braden pressed his elbow on the countertop as she lifted her chin to take the shot, and in one swift motion, Braden took the lime from one glass and placed it on the other.

The waitress lowered her head, cringing at the taste, then laughed. He laughed, too. After all these years, it was evident that you could take the kid out of the hood, but you couldn't take the hood out of the kid. Years had passed, but Braden was still able to finesse the same way he did back when we were kids.

She gestured toward the tray, and Braden respectfully made room for her to take it from the bar top. Security now created a path for her to walk with the tray through the crowd, and I saw Braden lean his back against the countertop as he put a hand in his pocket.

"*Drinks are on the way up to the villa*," his voice warned.

"I see 'em," I responded with a big smile on my face.

All of the wrong Braden had committed as a teenager--the shoplifting, fights, and other juvenile stunts--now had some sort of morally good trade-off.

Security flashed their lights, and the people made way for the drinks as the waitress approached the stairs leading up to the villa. She walked up, one step at a time, until I lost sight of her behind the floral pillar separating the overlook from Niall's platform. I peeked through the drapes, and between dancing silhouettes, I watched the drinks being handed to Santi and the group inside the gazebo.

Rum for Mateo.
Rum for Rodrigo.
Margarita for Tiffany.
Gin and tonic with the lime for Val.
Gin and tonic *without* the lime for Santi.

I let out a sigh of relief. The deed was done, and now it was just a matter of waiting. They clinked their glasses together, took their sips, and continued their conversation. I watched for the next ten minutes as they laughed, shouted, danced, and continued sipping.

A "cheers" here. A "cheers" there.

A few girls stumbled onto the overlook beside me, taking pictures.

"Ugh this balcony is sooo cute. Okay, OKAY, *okay*...!" the girl behind the phone shouted in a drunken slur. "Smile onnn threee!!! Ready... Thrrreeee, tttwwwooo, one... Sssmmmiiiillleee!"

"Take a bunch!" one of the girls insisted as they faked smiles and laughter. "Make sure my titties look big--never mind I'll-... I'll edit them later... Fuck it, just-... Did you get it?"

Girls funneled out of the gazebo onto the balcony, taking pictures and videos, only to once again disappear back behind the drapes. Each time the drapes were pulled open, I managed to catch a glimpse of Santi and the others, waiting for some sort of sign that suggested the roofie was kicking in.

About 20 minutes had passed, and there was no sign of it, until...

CRASH!

The sound of something shattering came from inside the gazebo. I pushed aside the drapes to see a broken plate in front of Santi as he laughed it off in front of the others. Using this as an opportunity to get back in the mix, I stepped in and leaned over to pick up pieces of the plate.

"You good??" I asked, hoping he wouldn't give me a sane or sober answer.

"Let the staff get it, Jay... Get off the floor!" Santi insisted with a lighthearted giggle. "Come sit with us here next to me--come here, for the example-... I wanna use you for an example."

His words were gradually beginning to slur as he stood and placed a hand on my shoulder.

"*THIS* is my little prodigy... Right here! This is him..." Santi shouted for everyone in the villa to hear.

I was shocked and also a bit flattered. The girls around us continued dancing as unfiltered words continued spilling out of Santi's mouth. He shouted, competing with the music. In his defense, he was winning.

"I TOOK HIM IN," Santi shouted, raising his roofied drink with one hand while the other hand gripped my shoulder. He pulled me in. "JAY, HIS BROTHER, AND ALL MY BOYS. I LOVE ALL MY BOYS. THEY ARE ALL I HAVE AND ALL I NEED… MY FAMILY."

Val, Mateo, Rodrigo, Tiffany, and the other women scattered around gave looks of admiration, but they quickly became looks of discomfort as he continued.

"I HAD NOTHING--NO… I *HAVE* NOTHING… Without my boys… He… Jay… He's going to do *amazing* things here--far more amazing than me--more amazing than *anybody*. Mark my words… Mark 'em... Go on…."

Santi wobbled a bit, accidentally bumping Tiffany's glass, causing it to spill on the booth beside her.

"He's going--amazing--to do *amazing* things…!" Santi shouted again as he stumbled down toward the booth, bringing me down with him.

Mateo smiled at the sight of Santi's gradual deviation from sobriety. At this point, he knew the drinks had been successfully swapped. We *all* did.

"Come here, hero…" Santi said softly, pulling me in.

I could smell the gin on his breath as his forehead pressed against mine. His diamond chains hung between us as he tried with everything in him to look me in the eyes. He began to doze off until he was practically fighting to keep his eyes open--to speak the last bit of sense he had left before intoxication ran its course and took over.

"You won't beat me, hero," Santi whispered. "We're too... Alike--too… *Alike*. If anything… And I know this for a *fact*… You'll *become* me… Not beat me…."

He spoke softly--his breaths getting deeper as he struggled to keep his composure.

"There's no hero without the villain… Listen-... If I'm *your* villain in *your* story, Jay, and you *beat* me… You--like I already have--will become what you *can't forgive*… And slowly... You will bring yourself-... To your own demise. *You* will. And if you, yourself, don't… Your brother *will*. Just a thought."

"*Just a thought….*"

Santi's words pierced through my mind like a dagger through the heart. He smiled, and I saw it in him--not Santi--but the monster living within… The chaos behind the order. Santi was no longer with us. He was no longer Santi. I stared into his eyes--the eternal gray--and they stared *back*, but with sudden realization. He smiled.

"You beat me… Didn't you?" he asked, slowly lifting his drink to his chin, almost missing his own mouth. "I knew when we met… That you would take me down at some point…."

He tilted his head back, downing the rest of his glass, then dropped it to the floor. It shattered.

CRASH!

He laid back in his seat, looking at the floral decor that lined the ceiling above him. It was almost as if he knew what I had done without actually knowing.

"*You--like I already have--will become what you can't forgive.*"

The words cemented themselves into my very soul. Crossing Santi would free Braden and me from his grasp, but it was the fear of the unknown that crept into my mind without welcome.

Without Santi, what battle would I have to fight next? Focusing myself on saving my brother kept *me* from becoming someone in need of saving. Without Santi, who would fulfill the role of the villain in my story…? And what if it's me? What if *I'm* the villain?

I watched as Santi leaned forward, grabbing shot glasses and handing them to everyone sitting around him with a hollow smirk on his face. Everyone accepted and down went the shots... Then another and another… Until he was face-up, eyes closed on the booth, slurring under his breath with another cigar in hand.

Mateo now gave me a look from across the table to validate if what he was seeing was real. Santi was out for the count. I placed my hand in my pocket and held down on the transmitter.

"Braden, prep the sprinter van. Santi and his guests are heading out."

"*Got it*," Braden replied.

I turned toward the group, and to my surprise, Val was already standing just inches away, waiting for direction.

"Is it time?" she asked, keeping her voice down in front of a now-sedated Santi. "He's mumbling about random things. I don't even think he's speaking English anymore."

"Yeah, Braden's prepping the van," I replied, taking another look at Santi. "Mateo, tell him you're ready to head back… And Val… You still need to sell your interest in Mateo in case there's any bit of suspicion in Santi."

She agreed, and Mateo briefed Rodrigo in Spanish before confronting Santi.

"MY *HOUSE*," Santi blurted aloud enthusiastically. "The party goes on… Come, come… My house!!!"

Santi stumbled to his feet, putting half of his weight on Mateo and the other half into tossing his cigar onto the table into one of the bowls of tagliolini pasta. Rodrigo and Mateo helped him down the stairs as Val and I watched from behind.

"Jay Love, be honest," Val said. "Did you expect this to work out the way it's worked out so far?"

I raised my eyebrows and shook my head slowly, watching Santi rely on the Ramos brothers to get him down the stairs.

"Honestly, no," I replied. "But I also didn't really have a choice but to make it work… Right?"

She nodded, then lifted her drink.

"To the beginning of the end," Val slurred with a smile.

I smiled back. She downed her drink, and upon stepping toward the stairs, she stumbled into my arms.

"You alright??" I asked.

She let out a laugh.

"I'm fine!! Let's go let's go I'm fine-...."

Val's slur was becoming more prominent, but I casually dismissed it.

We followed the group, now led by security toward the backdoor. As we walked through the crowd, I removed my earpiece and tossed it onto the floor behind me, relieved to leave it behind once and for all. I didn't bother looking back at Niall or at the bar for Kai. They were behind us now as we stepped out into the alley.

Santi climbed into the black van and threw his own limp body back against the plush leather booth that wrapped around the back. He continued laughing and shouting random phrases in both English and Greek. I watched as Val used Mateo's hand to help herself up but tripped over the step.

"Whoops!" she giggled. "Sorry…."

"Coño, Valentina!" Mateo uttered with a laugh. "You partied a little too hard, huh??"

Val sat on the booth a few feet from Santi, continuing to laugh as Mateo, Rodrigo, and Tiffany piled in beside them. Braden grabbed me by the arm just before I stepped up into the van.

"Let's get Val and Tiffany a ride home. They don't need to be here anymore," he said.

Braden was right. Santi was the primary concern, and it was evident that *he* was the one not in his right mind… Which is exactly what we needed--it's *all* we needed.

"She's fine," I assured him. "We need them here to make sure he doesn't get suspicious, Braden. We have a plan… Just see it through."

"Alright," he sighed, letting go of my arm.

We stepped into the van, and the door closed behind us. The driver was off, and within minutes, we were on our way up to the hills.

The group continued to drink and jab at one another while singing songs and mixing in variations of Latin music the Ramos brothers listen to.

"When we get to the house…" Mateo whispered. "You know what to do?"

"I do," I replied sternly, watching Santi struggle to stand and dance on the booth. "We'll be fine. He's *done*."

Mateo nodded and sat back, making himself comfortable next to me. With the back of his left hand, he tapped my chest twice and said... "You're good, mang. Got a good head on you. Your brother, too."

Braden and I smiled, though we both knew deep down that the job wasn't finished yet. The sprinter van arrived in front of Santi's home, and after briefly stopping at the gate, the van was able to continue through as it opened. The colorful lights within the back of the van continued flashing until the door slid open to Santi's modern estate.

"The festivities continue…!" Santi shouted as he stumbled toward the open van door.

"Woah!" Rodrigo practically caught Santi, then helped him down from the vehicle.

"Cigarette…" Santi murmured under his breath, patting his pockets for his pack.

He pulled one out, lifted it to his mouth, and called for Braden to light it. Braden lit the cig as the rest of us stepped out of the van. Tiffany and Val stumbled out. They laughed and twirled along the massive open driveway that curved across the front yard toward a second gate the van now made its way out of. I couldn't help but notice Val was in rare form, but maybe it's because she usually doesn't drink this much… From what I remember.

"Mateo... Rodrigo… WELCOME!" Santi shouted as he gestured for them to follow. "Everyone, inside. My home is *your* home tonight... Please…."

With the cigarette pinned between his lips, he escorted Val and Tiffany up the stairs, then Rodrigo and Mateo, and finally Braden and myself. Once we gathered in front of the overwhelmingly large glass door, he pulled out a matte black card from his wallet and scanned it against a camouflaged pad on the stone.

BEEP! BEEP!

The door made an unlocking sound as Santi made his way through the group to the glass door, now pulling out his keys. He struggled to fit the right one into the keyhole. Suddenly, the keys slipped out of his hands onto the floor. I leaned forward to pick them up for him and rose so that we were standing less than a foot apart from each other.

"Which one is it?" I asked, looking down at about five keys bound to a chain.

Santi shrugged and laughed before taking a long drag of his cigarette. He exhaled. After trying two different keys, the third was a perfect fit, and the door slowly opened. Santi stumbled in and headed directly for the bar across the living room. Mateo and Rodrigo joined him, requesting another cigar.

"Braden!!!" Tiffany's voice echoed throughout the spacious living room. "I waaannnttt cccoookkkeee… You *promised*!!!"

I subtly nudged Braden, ignoring Tiffany's request.

"You know where it is??" I whispered.

He reluctantly nodded, staring at Santi across the room.

"The laptop, Braden…" I spoke a bit louder this time. "Do you know where it is??"

He snapped out of his trance and faced me.

"Jay, we should *really* get Val and Tiffany out of here…."

I looked back at the bar where the entire group now gathered. Music began to play from speakers built into the walls, and the girls started dancing barefoot on the couch across from the men at the bar.

"Braden, what's the *matter* with you?? Get the fucking laptop," I demanded once again in a whisper.

I could feel the vein throbbing on the side of my head, triggered by frustration. There's so much that could go wrong. Now?? Braden wants to throw us for a loop *now*? The mess *he* got us into… The same mess I've worked to get us out of… He wants to g-… He wants to m-....

"Braden," I whispered one last time before losing my composure. "Please… Get… The laptop… And bring it to the kitchen."

I opened my phone and pulled up the picture I took of the humidor password. I shoved it in Braden's hand. Taking one last look across the living room, he slowly stepped back and ran quietly up the stairs. Santi continued pouring shots for the group, spilling across the bar top and making jokes about it. Seeing that he was preoccupied, I snuck behind a modern art sculpture and into the kitchen, anxiously waiting for Braden's return.

Sounds of music and laughter from the living room filled the entirety of the home. I listened, praying that there wouldn't be a break in laughter or a situation where they realized Braden and I had disappeared. Within moments, Braden swiftly entered the kitchen with my phone and the laptop in hand.

"YES," I whispered.

I placed the laptop on the marble countertop, and I nervously opened it to a blank screen requiring a password. My hands shook.

"Keep watch," I whispered as I reached for my phone.

Laughter echoed throughout the front of the house. I tried to keep calm. Braden's fingers anxiously tapped against the countertop next to the laptop. He continuously looked left and then down at the laptop as I laid my phone beside the keyboard and pulled up the photo of Kai's passwords.

"Did you find it??" Braden asked.

"Keep watch," I snapped back as I zoomed in on the humidor password.

"1401 Bryer Summit," I read aloud. "His home address is the password to the humidor at The Willow?"

He leaned over my shoulder to get a better look at the phone.

"That sounds about right. I know his passwords are usually addresses to his venues."

I slowly typed in the address, making sure I got it right the first time. My palms were sweaty--fingers practically slipping over each letter.

"*INCORRECT PASSWORD. TRY AGAIN OR USE TOUCH I.D. TO SIGN IN*," the text on the screen read.

CRASH!

A loud crashing sound came from the living room, sending chills down my spine as my heart dropped into my stomach. Braden quickly turned his head at the sound of the crash. I did the same.

"What was that??" I asked, keeping my fingers on the keys. "You gotta stall them, man. Make sure they don't come over here."

Braden quickly ran across the kitchen toward the living room, then slowly turned the corner. I began typing out the address again--slower this time…

It was now or never.

Do or die.

When I finished, I gently pressed *enter*.

"*INCORRECT PASSWORD. TRY AGAIN OR USE TOUCH I.D. TO SIGN IN*," the text on the screen read again.

"No," I whispered under my breath. "No, no, no, no…."

"JAY!" Braden shouted from the other room.

"HANG ON!" I shouted back.

I erased the password and typed in the address to The Willow this time, carefully watching each letter I pressed. I pressed *enter*.

"*INCORRECT PASSWORD. TRY AGAIN OR USE TOUCH I.D. TO SIGN IN*," the text on the screen read.

I opened up the picture on my phone once again to double-check... Then triple-check. I had it right. It *had* to be the right password. They said... Braden confirmed... Braden said Santi usually uses addresses for the passwords. This *should* work. I immediately felt sick, leaning back in my seat. It was our best bet, and we had lost it all.

"JAY..." Mateo called from the other room.

I slid the chair back and quickly made my way through the kitchen with the laptop. The music was no longer playing, and nothing but the sound of my footsteps echoed throughout the downstairs of the house. I turned the corner, and to my demise... An unconscious Val lay on the couch next to Tiffany while Rodrigo and Mateo silently stood against the bar top. Sitting on the bar top was a fully coherent and completely sober *Santi*.

He was leaning forward, with his elbows resting on his knees--feet on top of a barstool. He had a peaceful, calm, cool, and collected composure accompanied by a subtle smile as he watched me step out into the open. In his hand was a Glock--in mine, the laptop.

Santi squinted his eyes as he looked directly at me, then down at the laptop, and back up at me again. I stared back in utter shock, unable to process how he managed to sober up so fast. It didn't make sense. *Nothing* in this moment made sense. My eyes panned from Braden, who sat on a stool just behind Santi, to Val, who was sound asleep on the couch.

"How...?" I asked, frozen in place.

Santi smiled and let out a sigh, then tapped the gun against his knee a few times. He looked across the room at Val in a way that served as a signal for me to do the same--as if she was part of the answer to my question.

I looked, and all at once, it hit me. Val's rapid decline on the way here... And then there was Braden's concern for her.

"*Let's get Val and Tiffany a ride home. They don't need to be here anymore*," Braden had said before we left The Willow.

Why would he have said that if he knew Santi was pretty much blacked out for the night? He had mentioned not going through with the plan back in the bathroom. Santi knew. He knew everything that was gonna happen and changed the password last-minute.

Braden was radiating *reluctance* all night, and it was for a reason. I now knew Santi was the reason. Santi knew our plan all along, and only because Braden had told him. Kai must've poured the drinks, knowing Braden was gonna switch the markers.

"You told him," I declared, staring directly at Braden, who sat sheepishly behind Santi on the stool. He avoided eye contact. "After everything I did and set out to do for you… You told him."

Braden looked everywhere but back at me while leaning against the countertop.

"I'm sorry," he said.

I lowered my head in disappointment.

"I figured," I said softly. "But I trusted you. That's *my* mistake, so I can't blame anybody but myself for that."

Braden looked at the ground, arms now crossed.

"Switching the markers on the drinks??" Santi laughed as he hopped down from the bar top. "I gave you money. I gave you a job. I gave you a family… A *purpose*! And you *still* went behind my back to my *partners* to cross me, Jay."

Santi slowly walked from the bar to the couch Val and Tiffany were on, waving the gun around as he continued to speak. Tiffany stared into her own lap, hands and arms quivering in fear. Santi's tone gradually became more and more aggressive as he went on.

"Do you know how *insulting* it is… How *embarrassed* I feel... How *torn* I am…?? To know that the one I expected the most out of considered the life I gave him as so *little*. And then your own *brother* turns on you...? Do you have *any* respect for family?? Either of you??"

He stopped, standing just behind Val, now turning his head left and right as he addressed both Braden and me. Braden stared at Santi, listening attentively. Santi pointed the gun at Braden.

"What kind of *coward* crosses his own brother???" Santi laughed, then pointed the gun at me. "And what kind of *idiot* threatens his own mentor's life's work?? I promised you the world, Jay. And you, Braden… You snitch on your brother. What makes you think that I don't think you'll do the same to me at some point??"

He took a deep breath, then tapped the gun against his hip, while looking up at the ceiling. He looked straight at the Ramos brothers who remained silent, now standing against the wall. They were straight-faced, taking in the entirety of the situation.

"Do you see what I'm dealing with?" Santi asked them, holding back a smile.

He continued tapping the gun against his hip, then he stared at the laptop in my hand.

"The way I choose to do business is the way I choose to do business. *My* business," he continued. "*My* fucking business, and you couldn't mind your own, Jay."

Santi looked at the ground, deep in thought.

The Ramos brothers stared at Santi, awaiting his next move.

Braden did the same.

Tiffany didn't look up.

Val slept.

And I didn't know *what* to do.

Santi let out a laugh behind a cunning, devilish smirk. He pointed the gun at Braden.

"Braden, reach into the top drawer behind the bar. Grab what you see on the far right."

Braden obediently did so, silently stepping around the bar and pulling out the top drawer.

"You two obviously can't work together… Given the hassle you've been the past few weeks. Now... I'd rather have one of you *fully* focused rather than the two of you distracting each other. Grab what you see, Braden… It's shiny."

I could see the cold sweat come over Braden as he nervously reached into the drawer and pulled out a switchblade. Now holding up the blade, Braden finally looked at me.

"Woah, woah," I cautioned Santi as I placed the laptop on the floor next to me. "We can work something out... Santi, you got us… We're done. Leave everyone else out of this. It was all me… I put everyone up to it. All me--*my* doing…."

"Shhh, you think *now* I'm gonna let you be the hero… To take the fall for your friends?" Santi shushed. "This is gonna be incredibly simple…."

I closed my eyes and lowered my head, fearing I might know where Santi is going with this.

"*One* out of the two of you leaves tonight, or *nobody* leaves tonight," Santi said as he pressed the gun to the side of Val's head.

Tiffany's breathing became heavy as she continued to shake, and tears trickled down the sides of her face. I held back tears of my own. I didn't know what to do. I didn't bother thinking about an alternative or any other potential outcome--all were out of my control.

"*You--like I already have--will become what you can't forgive,*" Santi had told me tonight at The Willow. He knew it would come to this… And if I'm going to walk out of this alive, it was going to be at the cost of Braden's life. I reluctantly let a tear fall, then another. Braden stared at me, emotionally vacant, as he stepped toward the middle of the living room with the knife held firmly in his grasp. Mateo looked at the ground and Rodrigo in another direction. They had no desire to witness the barbaric display Santi was actively orchestrating.

Santi's grin turned into a sick smile from ear to ear as Braden slowly stepped toward me, wielding the blade. Seeing this gave Santi a sick pleasure I couldn't fathom feeling in an abundance of lifetimes.

I eyed the blade as it got closer and closer--slowly. Never in my life did I expect to be here… To be murdered by my own brother, who's been manipulated into believing his only family is a sick and twisted nightclub owner.

"Braden… Don't…" I urged as I stuck both hands out, bracing myself.

He was almost halfway across the living room when he suddenly stopped and tossed the switchblade so that it landed halfway between us.

"Okay, interesting…" Santi blurted out as he awaited my move.

"Pick it up," Braden insisted.

I looked at the knife on the floor, then back up at Braden.

"I'm not gonna-...."

"Pick… It up," Braden insisted again, but louder.

"You should probably pick it up, Jay," Santi teased.

I walked forward and picked up the switchblade--my hand shaking as I prepared myself to reject his next idea if it meant using it on him.

"I'm not gonna use it," I said while keeping the blade at my side.

"You don't have to," Braden replied softly.

He reached behind his back and slowly pulled out a revolver, pointing it directly at Santi. My jaw dropped as my eyes darted between both Braden and Santi--Braden with his gun pointed at Santi and Santi with his gun still pressed against Val's unconscious head. Mateo and Rodrigo's eyes were now wide open, equally as shocked at the showdown unraveling before our very own eyes.

"Coño," Rodrigo whispered.

Santi laughed under his breath, locking eyes with Braden. Then he pointed his gun at me. I slowly raised my hands.

"My right-hand man," Santi chuckled with a smirk. "Did you not think this through?"

"Shoot him," Braden replied without moving a muscle.

"WHAT??" I shouted. "Braden…."

Santi laughed with his gun still pointed at me. I stared directly into the barrel of the gun that stared directly back, ready to take my life any second.

"It's a damn shame, Jay," Santi said. "I was rooting for *you*."

"No, no, no, no… Don't…."

With my hands now raised, my muscles tightened, and I braced myself with my eyes closed.

"Don't shoot, Santi… Don't shoot, don't… SHOOT!"

CLICK!

After pulling the trigger, Santi stared at the gun, appalled at the result.

No shot.
No bullet.
Just a... *Click*.

I looked down and patted my chest, looking for a bullet. Am I already dead? Is this *really* happening? Santi cocked the gun back and pulled the trigger again.

CLICK!

Braden remained calm--gun still pointed at Santi, who cocked the gun back again.

CLICK!
CLICK!
CLICK!

Santi laughed aloud, rubbing the top of his head with his free hand and holding up the gun with the other. Pressing his thumb to the side of the gun, the empty magazine fell into his hand, and he observed it closely--no bullets inside of it.

"You messed with my gun..." Santi accused. "And how do I know yours is loaded?"

Braden shot a bullet into the ground next to the couch, sending Tiffany into a panic as she screamed. Val remained motionless, completely passed out. Braden cocked back the revolver and raised it up to Santi's face once again.

"Brilliant… The most loyal one of all," Santi said with a grin. "You were the last one I expected to do this, but well-deserved. I only wanted the best for you."

Santi didn't move. He maintained his cheeky half-smirk, assuming Braden would never pull the trigger. If it were a couple of hours ago, I would have agreed with Santi, but after the way the night has panned out, I wouldn't be too sure of Braden's next move. Usually, I have a decent understanding of the situation, but at this point… I have no idea what might happen next.

"I'm not gonna shoot you," Braden said calmly, with the gun still pointed at Santi. "Tiffany, you can go… Quietly. Jay, give him the laptop."

I obeyed, immediately picking up and giving the laptop to Santi, who didn't take his eyes off of Braden. Tiffany, still quivering in fear and holding back tears, quickly tiptoed out the front door. I stepped back as we all awaited Braden's next command. He pulled out the barstool and calmly gestured for Santi to sit on it. Santi did so without question and with the same half-smirk on his face.

"Stop smiling..." Braden demanded with his jaw clenched. "Put your password in."

The revolver was now pointed at the side of Santi's head. Braden's grip tightened. Santi silently used the fingerprint I.D. to unlock the laptop.

"It's ironic..." Santi said with a grin.

"Shut up," Braden demanded. "Find my video... *Now*."

Braden's voice was shaking out of frustration. Mateo and Rodrigo patiently observed from a distance while I stood just over Braden's shoulder. After a few clicks and scrolls, Santi came across a file with a plethora of video files, each labeled with names belonging to various different men. He clicked on a file simply named "Braden" and began playing the video.

"*DON'T*," Braden demanded as he looked away from the screen.

"You can erase the video, but you can't erase what you *did*," Santi stated as he watched the screen.

On the screen, I saw Braden, recorded from a surveillance camera placed in Santi's guest house. In the video, Braden drunkenly stumbled into the room just after the girl laid on the bed, now motionless.

"Delete... It," Braden demanded once more, his finger now wrapped around the trigger--the vein on his forehead throbbing.

"Braden, don't..." I spoke softly, afraid he would actually pull the trigger.

"Should I fast-forward?" Santi giggled as he clicked.

The video played, and now Braden was on top of the unconscious girl.

"Delete the *FUCKING* video, Santi!" Braden shouted with tears in his eyes--hands shaking.

"Okay, okay... Only because you asked nicely," Santi said.

He deleted the video, opened the "recently deleted" folder, and confirmed the permanent deletion.

"Alright, it's done," Santi said, lifting his hands. "I only want the best for you, Braden. Eventually, you'll see why I kept that video for you. Unfortunately, you'll see once it's already too late."

"Wipe the laptop," Braden said sternly.

Santi paused, and his jaw dropped.

"All of it??" Santi asked. "Like delete it *all*?"

"Get rid of everything," Braden uttered. "All the files."

"I deleted what I have on you, Braden. I have important files on here... You won't have a job if I get rid of some of this intel... *None* of us will."

Braden lightly shoved the barrel of the revolver against Santi's head.

"Alright, *alright*," Santi sighed.

He wiped the laptop, and after a matter of a minute, it was rid of every file, as if brand new--absolved... Simply just... Made *new* again. We *all* were. Santi clapped his hands as I let out a sigh of relief. Braden had done it. We both took a step back... To finally breathe.

"So I was saying it's *ironic*," Santi continued, turning toward us in his seat. "That you almost took my life with a revolver the *same* way you took your brother's...."

Braden suddenly clenched his jaw and tightened his grip on the revolver.

"BRADEN!" I shouted. "DON'T...."

BANG!

I looked away and dropped to my knees in utter shock--my ears ringing from the sound of the gunshot. Santi's lifeless body instantly fell back between the barstools and onto the floor. A puddle of blood formed underneath his lifeless head.

The room was dead silent, and I turned back to the Ramos brothers, who were now standing just behind us. My head became hot, and my breath, unsteady.

"WHAT'D YOU JUST DO...?" I asked in a panic. "We weren't supposed to *kill* him, Braden...."

Braden lowered the gun with his eyes now closed. He took a few deep breaths, and squatted down to the floor where he set down the gun, then stood up again. He wiped his hands against his pants as if he were ridding himself of what he had just done.

"A guy like that doesn't deserve to fucking live, Jay," Braden declared before facing the Ramos brothers. "And they would've done the same."

Mateo shrugged as Rodrigo observed Santi's body from where he stood.

"It was going to be you or one of us that did it..." Mateo stated as he lifted his shirt, revealing the gun tucked into his waistband.

Braden nodded as he took a deep breath and let out a long exhale, remaining completely calm. He pointed at the Ramos brothers.

"You wanted in on his distribution channels, right?" Braden asked. "What I did just got you them. Maybe you wouldn't have handled this exactly the way I did... Maybe you would've... But I know that what I did will be good for your sake."

Braden's face was both pale and expressionless. His words, just words... But as I replayed the words back in my mind, I realized he was telling the truth, and the Ramos brothers did, too. Without looking back, Braden quietly walked over to the bar and poured himself a shot. Mateo sat back down on the couch, staring at what was left of Santi.

I stood to my feet, unable to take my eyes off of Santi's body lying at the foot of the bar in a puddle of his own blood. I wondered what *wise* quote or reference he would use in a situation like this--what he would say to justify Braden's actions if he hadn't been the one catching the bullet with his head.

"You're not wrong…" Mateo said softly. "He was your hell, and to us, he was bad business, but we'll still see this through--we will *finish* it--as a matter of business."

"What do you mean...?" I asked. "You'll finish it?"

Braden poured himself another shot as Mateo stood and walked over to Santi's body.

"We'll get rid of… Him--of all of this," Mateo said. "We'll make it look like... Like he left or something… Rodrigo?"

Mateo and I turned back to Rodrigo, who silently nodded his head.

"Jay…" Mateo placed one hand along the side of my face and the other toward Braden. "Your heart was always in the right place. What you did for us--for your brother… Good will come of this. You are free of Santi--done. Ya está… It's done. I am a man of my word. You've done my brothers and I a great service. We'll finish this here."

He smiled and released me, calling to Rodrigo in Spanish as they made their way to what was left of Santi. Val was still peacefully asleep on the couch, oblivious to the madness undergone. In a way, I envied her and her innocence. I felt Braden now standing by my side as we both watched Val sleep.

"Let's take her home," I said. "When she wakes up, none of this ever happened. She can't know."

"Understood," Braden replied as he pulled out his phone. "Let's walk down the hill, and I'll get us a ride."

I gently hoisted Val onto my shoulder, and we made our way to the front door.

"Jay! Braden! One last thing!" Mateo shouted from the bar. "L.A.X. Tomorrow morning. Meet us at the jet terminal. We will finalize our business with *you* since Santi is no longer able to… 6:30a.m."

Before we could even respond, Mateo and Rodrigo turned back to Santi and the bar. Completely numb to everything we had just witnessed and orchestrated, Braden and I continued out the door into the warm summer night, and I couldn't help but reflect….

I didn't really feel free of Santi.
I wasn't really traumatized by what I had just witnessed.
I wasn't really proud of Braden.
I didn't really know what to think or how to feel.
With Val over my shoulder, Braden and I just… Walked.

"What do you think he means by finalizing business?" Braden asked as we walked down the street in silence.

"I don't know," I replied honestly.

EIGHTEEN | NO STONE LEFT UNTURNED

INTERSTATE 405
WESTCHESTER, LOS ANGELES
SUNDAY, 6:12A.M. - JULY 21ST, 2019

I rested my head back against the passenger seat, staring at the nearly vacant freeway stretching on before us. Music played silently in the background as Braden and I looked directly ahead without saying a word. We hadn't spoken in the four hours we've shared since leaving Santi's house--silence--only *silence*. Maybe a word here and there, but there was ultimately no conversation.

Maybe there was just *nothing* to be said. Maybe there was *too much* to be said. I don't know what Braden's reasoning behind his silence was, but in my case, I was simply too tired--too tired to even sleep.

Around five hours ago, we belonged to Santi.
Around four hours ago, Braden murdered the man.
Around three hours ago, we tucked Val safely into her bed.
Since then, there was nothing but silence--until now....

"Why didn't you tell me you emptied out his gun?" I asked.

After a long pause, Braden answered.

"I didn't wanna overcomplicate your plan," he explained. "If you and I were completely on the same page with everything, Santi would've somehow caught on and found a way to be one step ahead like he usually is-... *Was*...."

I remembered Braden's reluctance and hesitation when I reminded him to stick to the plan. I was so *frustrated*, but now I couldn't help but admire that Braden was juggling *two* agendas, both mine and his own.

"Do you think Tiffany will go to the police?" I asked.

"She knew the risk," Braden replied. "Her group being at The Willow wasn't a coincidence. I made sure they were gonna be there and tipped her off about an after-party and how things could get ugly. She was fine with it, though... She got her coke fix, and now I owe her a shit ton more. I'll still follow-up today to make sure she keeps quiet. Don't worry."

I nodded my head, running through how much depth there was to what Braden had planned all along, and I respected him for it. Since I could remember, Braden always found ways to make ends meet, constantly finessing his way through life.

"I didn't doubt your plan would work," he added. "I just thought we needed a fallback in case the password wasn't the right one."

"Which it wasn't," I replied. "If you didn't do what you did *and* the password we had wasn't the right one… I'd hate to picture where we'd be now."

"We'd be the ones dead."

Braden was silent after his statement, and I figured it was for good reason. He had taken a man's life in an instant. Braden isn't a murderer. He's not a bad guy at all, though there was no doubt in my mind that Santi painted him that way. For Braden to live with the guilt of thinking he caused Josh's death, then move on to be framed for taking advantage of an innocent girl, then to later on learn that there's a video of it being held over his head by a man he considered family and would eventually *KILL*… It's more than I could ever bear.

I understood why Braden pulled the trigger, and a part of me didn't blame him for doing it. A part of me wanted to believe that Santi *knew* Braden would pull the trigger… That Santi *knew* blaming Braden for Josh's death would trigger Braden into *literally* pulling the trigger. When the laptop was cleared of its substance, so was Santi--there was nothing left--all he ever had to his name was *dirt*… Dirt on the people he worked with and dirt on the ones he claimed to love… Dirt on his *family*.

Deep down, I genuinely hoped that last night served as some sort of redemption for Braden. For years and years of having been manipulated and engulfed by toxicity and deception... This was no way for my brother to live--no way for *anybody* to live.

"Do you think we can trust them?" Braden asked as we pulled up in front of the private jet terminal. "Do you think they *really* dealt with Santi's body and that we're off the hook?"

I took a deep breath.

"We don't have a choice," I replied. "It's not like we know what to do with a dead body, let alone the body of one of the biggest names in nightlife…."

"You're right," Braden said as he unbuckled his seat belt.

We stepped out to a modern one-story building lined with a blue glass that popped in contrast to the sunrise just behind it. The sound of airplanes departing and arriving was in the distance, soon to be muffled as we entered through the front glass doors that read "The Private Suite."

Upon entering, a man in a perfectly-tailored suit smiled from behind a wide desk.

"Good morning, gentlemen," he greeted as a woman stepped up to his right. "Departing or awaiting an arrival?"

It was a simple question, but come to think of it, I honestly didn't know the answer. Mateo had just asked for us to meet them here.

"We're actually here to... Um-... We're here to say goodbye to a departure, I guess?"

The suited man and woman let out a laugh, sizing up both Braden and myself.

"You must be the Amor brothers. We just escorted the Ramos group out to their aircraft. Ms. Herndon here will take you to say bye to your friends."

The lady smiled and gestured for us to follow her down the hall. After no more than 30 seconds of going through T.S.A., we were in the back of a black S.U.V., making our way along the runway. We rolled down the windows, feeling the cool morning breeze as we approached a jet positioned just next to a small airplane hangar.

Mateo and Rodrigo stood at the foot of the staircase that extended from the entrance of the jet. They were speaking to each other as the flight attendant patiently waited for them at the top of the stairs.

As our S.U.V. pulled up less than 20 yards away from the jet, Mateo and Rodrigo stepped forward. We slowly stumbled out of the car, and I ran my fingers through my hair to look somewhat presentable, but at this point, I genuinely don't care how I look or even know how to approach the situation.

"¡Buenos días!" greeted Mateo with open arms. "You two look... *Like shit*!"

He and Rodrigo laughed. I turned to see Braden standing next to me. He was right. We were still in the same clothes--no shower or sleep since we had seen them last. I let out a subtle laugh, lifting my hand to shield me from the rising sun. Rodrigo turned back, looking up at the flight attendant.

"Can you get them two coffees, please? Thank you."

She smiled and turned back into the jet.

"I know it's early..." Mateo continued. "I just want to make sure there is... How you say... No stone left unturned? That's what you say, no?"

Braden and I nodded.

"Santi is gone--so if you're still thinking on that, don't. You report to nobody but yourselves. Now I don't assume that either one of those girls will be an issue...."

"They won't be," Braden replied.

"Bueno. It should be known that we've made it look like Santi has left... On his own. If anybody comes to look for him or asks about him, you don't know what happened. So, now you stay... *Under the radar*. Don't be loud, for your own sake. Very simple."

Braden and I nodded once again.

"You think someone will come looking for him?" Braden asked.

"The police won't," Rodrigo interjected as he handed us each a cup of coffee. "Santi is on top, so if anyone is going to ask about him, it's going to be one of his employees or a business partner outside of the nightlife business around here."

"What we're saying here is... You have no answers... *Nada*," Mateo added. "Are we good with that? Do we understand? Or no?"

Braden and I nodded... Again.

"Do we understand? Or no?" Mateo repeated with open palms.

"Yes," we replied aloud.

"Perfecto. Last stone..." Mateo tilted his head, observing the two of us. "We want you to come work for *us*."

My jaw nearly dropped. I turned to Braden, who was already looking at me for an answer--his eyebrows raised.

"You want *us*... To work for *you*...? Out there? In the Caribbean?"

Mateo and Rodrigo smiled at our reactions.

"I told you," Mateo turned to Rodrigo before mumbling something in Spanish.

"You've got that dream..." Rodrigo said. "You won't find it out here in this mess. And there's a lot we can teach you on the *resort* side of hospitality."

Mateo took a few steps forward and firmly grabbed our shoulders while smiling cheek to cheek.

"We could use two more hermanos. There are already five of us brothers. What harm will two more be? Plus, we have a lot to teach you and even more to learn from you."

Braden and I both stood, speechless. Mateo dug into his breast pocket and pulled out a thin card holder made of gold. He unclipped it and pulled out one of his cards.

"I know *you* have one," he said to me with a wink before turning to Braden. "This is for you. Let us know before the end of summer if you're interested. And Jay... Feel free to bring your girlfriend, mang."

Mateo winked once more, and with a laugh, he and Rodrigo made their way up the staircase.

"Hasta luego, mangs! See you soon!" Mateo shouted as the stairs folded up, sealing the entrance closed.

Not knowing what to think or say, Braden and I watched the jet slowly move up the runway. The morning sunrise reflected off of the aluminum and steel as the aircraft drove further away under the pink clouds hovering above L.A.

And for the first time in a *long* time, it was *quiet*.

I felt a vibration in my pocket and pulled out my phone to see a text from Val.

VAL: Goood morning Jay Love. What happened last night?

ACKNOWLEDGMENTS

I'm going to go ahead and thank Jay Amor for being my outlet. The love, the hate, the in-between… Everything I've taken on up to this point in my life has been poured into Jay Amor, and I am forever grateful.

Now for the real people. My family. I thank you for the endless support and love in every instance of my life. Whether it be a call, text, or shout, you have always been responsive and it is you I dedicate my work to.

Mom, I owe you a whole lot for being my rock when it came to starting and finishing this book. It was our constant conversations about decisions made by characters and how the story played out that made it easy for me to write. Jay Amor's ability to choose family over anything and everything is an ability entirely influenced by you.

Patrick and Paris, I thank you for the genuine support and constructive feedback. It means the world to have had you two checking in on the progress of the book as it took shape.

Above all and most importantly, I thank God for this book and this journey. I've prayed and prayed for answers, and Lord knows that during the past two years, this manuscript has seen both the best and the worst of me. It has recently become known to me, that He has given me the answers to my prayers through my writing that I will continuously apply for the rest of my life.

I wrote *Night After Night* in an attempt to find myself, and I think I did exactly that. Just before I wrote this novel, I found myself seeking purpose and inspiration. I looked just about everywhere until I dug up some old journals on the bottom shelf of my closet. In these journals, I was reminded of my passion for writing and putting myself inside the minds of characters who intrigue me.

If you know me, you know I love to tell stories…
And I plan to do exactly that for as long as I live.

Thank you.

Made in the USA
Middletown, DE
08 May 2022

65478227R00163